THEY STAYED A SOLDIER

THEY STAYED
A SOLDIER

Don MacNaughton

Galago Publishing Ltd

First published in Great Britain in 1986 by Galago Publishing Ltd.,
16–20 Widmore Road, Bromley, Kent BR1 1RY.

Copyright © 1986 Don Mac Naughton

ISBN 0–946995–86–9 HB
        0–946995–81–8 PB

Cover design by A.P. Tyson
Typeset by Suripace Ltd., Milton Keynes.
Printed in Great Britain by The Garden City Press Limited

This book is dedicated to all
members of:
The 5th Airbone Brigade

A formation which has been formed to replace the
previously disbanded
16th Independent Parachute Brigade

And in memory of:
all Army personnel and members of the
Royal Ulster Constabulary
who have given their lives while
trying to maintain law and order
in the Provence of
Northern Ireland

And especially:
for those civilians, both Catholic and Protestant
who have been murdered for daring to have
the courage to stand up and say no
to terrorism

Although a factual and descriptive story in its own right this book is but a follow on of the author's first novel 'They Stood in the Door'. In so writing he has retained many of the original characters, bringing them away from the brushfire wars of the 1960s into the turbulent confusion of Northern Ireland in the early '70s. A difficult and challenging time for the British soldier, for he now found himself killing and being killed by his fellow countrymen. However, his reaction and response to this, as accounted here, may surprise and shock many unfamiliar with the British 'squaddies' temperament.

> For when the One Great Scorer comes
> To write against your name,
> He marks — not that you won or lost —
> But how you played the game,
> Grantland Rice

CHAPTER ONE

Hard pounding this, gentlemen;
Let's see who will pound longest.

Duke of Wellington

Weaving his way through a maze of boxes, crates and loose stores, Regimental Quarter Master Sergeant Ron Allander hopped up onto the concrete veranda that ran the length of the building at the rear of the Batalion's new Company stores. Across a twenty yard asphalt gap were more stores, equipment and heavy weapons belonging mainly to the Signals and Support Platoons. Allander stood, hands on hips, observing the organized chaos that filled this space to his front. A hundred men from a dozen different sub-units milled about in tangled groups, moving boxes, shifting kit and unloading vehicles, producing a magnified din of banging, shouting and engine-revving that rebounded off the enclosing overhead awning.

The 5th Battalion, the Parachute Regiment, returning from leave after their Aden withdrawal, were moving barracks. All day a steady round-circuit of four-ton lorries had been moving the Battalion's mountain of bits and pieces up Queens Avenue from Victorian billets, to this recently completed barracks. The RQMS studied the volume of kit being unloaded, trying to mentally allocate it all to a room or shelf within the new barracks. He knew it was going to be a problem before the work began, for as prehistoric as the last lines were, they at least proved to have plenty of space. These new ones, although modern, had been built to house lightly-equipped Parachute Battalions, who like to boast 'anything that can't be squeezed into a bergan isn't of any use'. This was fine for the troops but Allander, responsible for bulky stores and training equipment for the day-to-day running of the Battalion, knew differently.

Lifting his beret, he gave a resigned scratch through his neatly trimmed, blond hair. Then, taking a deep breath, he replaced his head-dress. More storage space was going to have to be found, he told himself, but that was up to his immediate superior, the Quarter Master, to sort out. Allander stepped off the veranda towards the QM's office, hoping to catch him before he left for the golf course.

Across in the Rifle Company's three storey accommodation blocks the men were busy trying to turn them into homes. Corporal Bobby MacIntyre had charge of 8 Platoon's fatigue party, furnishing their floor of C Company's block. Although outside it was a cool February day, the men, because of the central heating and the effort of heaving heavy, six foot steel lockers about, were flushed and sweating. Private Stanley 'No Way' Ottoway, a tall, dark haired, gangly youth, who had just joined the Battalion after completing his recruit training, whilst rummaging around in a locker drawer found an abandoned thunderflash. Ottoway, who was rapidly proving to be the Platoon balloon, began playing chicken with the striker and fuse. Phil Haydon, his mate and also a recent recruit, warned him to stop playing silly bastards before he did himself an injury, but 'No Way' had begun to carry himself away on a wave of inspirational baffoonery.

'How would you like this stuck up your nose', he warned Haydon, advancing towards him in mock drama, striker poised over the fuse.

At that moment Bobby entered the room to check on his work detail. Seeing the thunderflash in Ottoway's hand, he instantly became the responsible junior NCO.

'Ottoway', he barked at the top of his voice, but this triggered the wrong reaction, startling 'No Way' into dragging the striker across the fuse igniter. As this began to smoke, the mood of those in the room suddenly turned to low key panic.

'Get ride of it, Ottoway, get rid of it, you cunt. Out the window! Out the window!' shouted MacIntyre, backing against an open locker.

Ottoway, a changed man, stared transfixed with fear, his hand locked in a death grip around the explosive. Hearing his corporal as if a voice from another planet, he rushed the short distance to the window and pawed frantically with one hand at the latch. Being a modern building, the window was of an unfamiliar design, frustrating the desperate soldier's efforts to open it. In a blind panic, Ottoway,now holding the thunderflash in both hands, began hopping up and down, attempting to blow out a fuse that had been designed to burn under water, with quick puffs of breath.

This fuse had a seven second time limit; four had now been used up. For the rest of the fatigue party in the room, this was no longer a joke. With smiles disappearing from faces, bodies quickly moved towards exits. MacIntyre, with eyes transfixed on the thunderflash, found himself backing deeper into the locker.

On the five second mark 'No Way', realising that this lethal charge had to be disposed of, settled in desperation for the nearest container, the Platoon dustbin resting in the centre of the room. On six seconds he lifted the metal lid, threw in the thunderflash, replaced the lid and collapsed over it in relief. Seeing this, the rest of those left in the room dived for cover. MacIntyre, with his own escape blocked by beds and boxes, fell backwards into the locker, pulling the door shut as he did so. enclosing himself within the steel frame.

The Army thunderflash, a heavy duty firework with a low powered explosive charge was used mainly in training to simulate hand grenades and was not considered dangerous out of doors, but on detonating in a confined space it tended to take on the characteristics of TNT.

The explosion, vibrating around the room like an anti-tank mine, fired the dustbin lid straight for the ceiling, Ottoway draped across it, a fledgling astronaut. However, his trajectory for orbit was halted by a solid roof and the fluorescent lighting system on which he struck his head, knocking himself unconcious.

Instantly the explosing occurred, MacIntyre burst from his locker as if a lunatic superman from a phone kiosk, to dive with an hysterical cry for 'No Way's' throat. Gripping him in a two-handed strangle while still in mid-air, the corporal flooded the misfortunate youth with disjointed and unintelligible verbal rebuke.

10

'Cunt! Kill ya! Kill ya! Fifty-eight jumps, bastard! Bastard! Borneo! Jungle! Not a scratch, prick! Aden, nothing! Blow me up, kill ya! Ya bastard, kill ya!'

The fatigue party carried the still unconscious Ottoway up to the newly-staffed Brigade Medical Centre, struggling and laughing all the way.

*   *   *

For some years now the Fifth Battalion had been in perpetual motion, hardly resting in one place long enough to have a decent NAAFI break. This, many of the married members of the Battalion hoped, would now change, giving them a chance to enjoy a spell of family life. This tranquil state had been brought about by an unusual occasion. Britain was experiencing a rare world-wide lull where, for the moment, no one was trying to kill its servicemen. It wasn't to last.

Taking advantage of this, 5 Para swung into a full programme of training, polishing basic skills, practicing new ones and generally rewelding the Battalion back into a complete operational unit after its Company-size deployments during the Aden with-drawel. The C.O. gave his Company Commanders eight weeks and a free hand before he would take the reins for a series of Battalion group exercises in the U.K. and Denmark. The Company Commanders in their turn released the Platoon Commanders with orders to work their men up with a series of local schemes putting the emphasis on minor tactics, field craft and physical fitness.

*   *   *

'Company Commander's orders, orders atten...shun.' The deep, authoritative voice of Colour Sergeant 'Taff' Lewis, who had the job of acting Company Sergeant Major, brought the three men of Patrol Company's orders smartly to attention. After confirming their number, rank and name and reading each's charge, the reason for their presence on O.C.'s orders, he stood them at ease. Paddy Kieron was one of these; he had drunk too much in the NAAFI one night a few days earlier and had refused to leave the building when the Battalion Orderly Sergeant ordered him to do so. Also being dealt with, and the first in to see the Company Commander, were men on interview. Major Coe believed in conducting this in an informal manner with the intention of putting the interviewee at ease. After entering the office and acknowledging his Officer Commanding with a salute, Corporal David Urwin, a sandy-blond haired Belfast Irishman, was waved into a chair.

'Corporal Urwin', began the Major, studying an official form which he held in both hands as they rested at arms'length on his desk, 'it seems in the eight years you have been with 5 Para, the opportunity of a posting has not been offered to you.'

'No Sir, never wanted one, been quite happy with the Battalion', answered Urwin defensively, beginning to twig the reason for this interview.

'Well, I intend to give you a break; this summer you will be going to the Depot for a two year posting.'

The corporal, sitting up more erect in the chair, squirming slightly, began attempting an escape from this, for a posting to the Depot was generally looked upon as an unnecessary tour in purgatory.

'I would prefer to remain with the Company, Sir.'

'Yes, but this period of time will be thoroughly beneficial for your future career prospects', replied Coe, pushing an invisible stick with dangling carrot across his desk.

'I'm not all that interested in promotion at the moment, Sir! I'm too busy running my Patrol', countered Urwin.

'Yes, but we must all move outwards and up, and the experience of two years in the Depot will put you in good stead on your return to us', pointed out the O.C.

'But the Depot, Sir, that involves teaching drill and weapon training. I've never done that sort of thing', pleaded Dave, now thinking hard for new excuses.

'Nonsense, Corporal Urwin, I've seen you take lessons with adequate knowledge and bags of confidence. As for drill, you will be give a short cadre on this before you are allowed anywhere near a squad of recruits', assured Coe, returning the ball to Urwin's court.

'Well, why me, Sir? I'm sure someone in the Company would jump at the chance', proposed the corporal now reduced to bubbling his mates.

'It's not just one, Corporal Urwin, the Battalion must supply twelve J/NCOs, three from this Company alone', blocked the Major with a half smile to himself, for he knew Urwin was passionately attached to Patrol Company and had armed himself before the interview against every counter-argument that Urwin could put forward.

'Besides,' he added as the final nail in Dave's posting coffin, 'your wife will nodoubt be thrilled to know that for the next two years there will be no chance of you being wrenched away to some far-flung corner of the Queen's Empire.'

Beaten and knowing it, Urwin voiced one last weak attempt.

'The patrol is pretty rusty, and with a new man to train, I was looking forward to using our months training in Iceland to get it up to scratch.'

The Major, sitting back in his chair to draw a hand through his blond hair, began to speak in a more serious tone, unable to hold Urwin's eyes for the first sentence.

'You won't have a patrol now — it's going to have to go. I don't have a replacement for you; Pridmore I'm posting to C Company and Kieron I may be letting go as well, and until you depart for the Depot I'm bringing you into Company HQ where your signals experience is sorely needed.'

'Why, Sir? What's the reason? It's a good Patrol', enquired the corporal painfully, his Ulster accent softening, no longer concerned for his own future.

'Haven't the skilled men, must trim down', came the straight but frustrated reply.

'You can't let Kieron go Sir, he's too good a soldier to lose.'

'I know that, Corporal Urwin, and if he could adjust to accepting his answerability to authority he would be an even better one. This is the reason he's stood outside that door right now', came Coe's reply, as he pointed in annoyance at his office entrance.

'He's from the South, Sir! Has these rushes of blood to the head. Saved my life once', defended Urwin, holding his O.C.'s eyes, speaking as he felt which sounded more like a plea than a statement of fact.

'Yes' replied Coe, looking down at his desk. 'Well, I haven't come to a final decision on this, we will have to see.'

That was good enough for Dave, he knew Kieron now had a better than even chance of staying in the Company.

'Did Pridmore ask to go to Charlie Company, Sir?' asked Urwin, shifting his concern to the other members of his Patrol.

'No, my idea but only for promotional reasons. I haven't the establishment within the Patrols so it has to be a move for the big man.'

'He's not going to want to go, Sir' warned Urwin with a smile, but seeing the sense of the proposal.

'Well, he damn well will, it's for his own good', smiled back the O.C.

The corporal, feeling the interview had reached a conclusion, stood up to salute before leaving but then, remembering someone else, asked one final question.

'Corporal Sinclair, is he coming to the Depot as well, Sir?'

'I can't afford to lose all my junior NCOs, Corporal Urwin; He will be remaining at present, but I haven't neglected his promotion prospect. I'm sending him to Brecon on the senior tactics course.'

'Charming, Sir, does he know?' grinned Urwin.

'Not yet, I'll be seeing him later this morning', replied Coe, a trace of a smile appearing as he stiffened in his chair in response to the corporal's salute.

On the ground floor Dave found his mate, Jim Sinclair, standing outside the Company stores.

Sinclair, a square-shouldered Scotsman with loose dark hair, spoke first.

'The O.C. slap your wrist for being naughty?' he asked, curious as to his friend's interview.

'No, I talked the Major out of sending you for tour in the Depot', joked Urwin.

'You what?' queried Sinclair, not too sure he heard right.

'Ya,' replied Dave, 'but you got to do senior Brecon instead.'

'What! What!' exclaimed the Scot loudly going cold at the thought of the pressure and pain of a two month course at the mid Wales Regimental Battle School.

'Come on, son, I'll tell you all about it over a cup of tea', assured Urwin, laying a hand on his friend's shoulder to guide him out of the narrow main entrance.

'A Rifle Company! A Rifle Company, Sir....' Private Mick Pridmore bolted out of the square, foam-rubbered, army easy chair in which Major Coe had informed him of his move from the Battalion's Patrol Company.

'Sit down, Pridmore', Coe ordered of the broad shouldered, six foot three paratrooper towering over his desk, beginning to question his informal manner of holding interviews.

'I'm doing this for a very good reason; now sit down and let me explain.'

Pridmore, recovering himself, did as he was asked backing up to reach behind with one hand and guiding himself down into the chair. His concentration focussed on the O.C., willing his explanation to be a satisfactory one.

With the angry-faced giant backing off, Coe collecting his slightly shaky composure, began to explain his motives.

'Because of the shortage of skilled patrol men, I am having to reduce the number of patrols within the Company. I have already told Corporal Urwin he will no longer have a command. Now my plan for you is promotion, but at the moment, because of the cutback, it's not possible in this Company, so I'm sending you to a Rifle Company with a Lance Corporal's stripe for a one year period, after which I will then fetch you back.'

'Don't like the idea, Sir. Charlie Company O.C. might put the blocks on that and keep me', replied the big man voicing his fears, for in the past he had found most of the Army's promises worth neither piss nor prune juice.

'Not to worry on that score, the plan is air tight. Captain Aldrich is to be promoted and will be handing over as our 2 I/C to take command of Charlie Company. I have already spoken to him about this and he is prepared to retain you for the one year only'.

'Is there no other way, Sir? I don't really want to leave the Company.' Pridmore accepting his O.C.'s word on the proposal, for both Coe and Aldrich were men he had learned to trust.

'Not really; this is long term planning, I want you back to command a Patrol when we begin again building our numbers up. Besides in today's army thirty year old professional privates are going out of fashion.'

The Major's good natured comment about Pridmore's age washed over the big man, who was lost in thoughts of his future.

'When do I go, Sir?'

'Next week', came the O.C.'s answer.

'Bloody hell, Sir, that's a bit quick. I was looking forward to going to Iceland, never been before', was Pridmore's surprised and disappointed reply.

'Yes, well that's how it goes in the army. I feel the same about Botswanaland', teased Coe, an incurable micky-taker, hiding his smile behind his cupped hands.

*   *   *

8 Platoon, sweating under full battle order, pushed themselves in sharp determined paces, fighting to maintain the momentum at which their Platoon Commander was driving them along. As the speed of the march stabled at a point that most of the men found unacceptable, the weaker ones began to slacken, then drop back. Lieutenant Dean Davidson, who was setting the pace at the front, turned to see this happening and immediately began to shout his disapproval.

'You men, what the hell are you dropping back for? Get up here with the Platoon. Open your legs, come on. Corporal MacIntyre, drop back and chase those men up here. I want to see them at the front with me.'

Bobby MacIntyre, whose short legs were finding the pace painful, welcomed the brief reprieve as he halted to wait for the stragglers to make their way to him. The next several minutes were spend pushing, pulling and swearing, doubling back and forth amongst the tail-enders, but it was wasted effort. For with the march continuing at its blistering speed the number of stragglers only increased, flooding MacIntyre with their numbers. The Platoon, like the rest of the Battalion, had done little on their six weeks leave but drink, collapse in front of the family television or indulge in the weakness of the flesh, the sins for which they were now being punished. Lance Corporal Pridmore, new to the Platoon, also dropped down the extending line of men, but not from fatigue. He wished to ask some questions.

'Does Davidson always gallop away like this?' he queried, falling into step with Bobby MacIntyre, who was beasting 'No Way' Ottoway along with threats and little nudges.

'Never!' barked Bobby angrily, his face awash in little streamlets of sweat 'and it's stupid, He's burning the lads up. No one will finish this ten miler at this rate.'

'You know the route then', continued Pridmore.

'Not a fucking clue, never been here before. He knows where he's going but we don't' nodded MacIntyre towards his Platoon Commander at the head of the broken column.

This only confirmed the big man's curiousity, for he was puzzled as to why they had travelled in four-tonlorries for almost two hours just to run around the picture-book country lanes of East Sussex. This could so easily have been duplicated somewhere around Aldershot.

MacIntyre, losing patience with the situation, shouldered his responsibility as acting Platoon Sergeant and made a quick decision.

'Mick, I'm going to have to stay back here and sweep up. Can you go up to the front and try to keep Davidson sensible.'

'Ya, sure', replied the lance corporal, breaking into a jog.

On arriving back with the leaders he found the main body now whittled down to a half dozen, fighting to match their Platoon Commander stride for stride. This, however, was proving difficult; will and determination could not make up for six weeks of relaxed leave, the fire in the forge had been allowed to cool. One by one as weakened muscles, burning lungs and multiplying blisters took their toll they first slowed, then fell back.

Mick, seeing this, moved up beside Davidson to bring it to his notice. 'Sir, we're losing everyone, might be a good idea to ease up a bit.'

The officer, pouncing on this as a cry for pity, turned his head to give Pridmore a wrathful reply.

'It's just laziness on their part. They're supposed to be paratroopers. If they can't keep up with me they shouldn't be in the Regiment in the first place.

Pridmore made no reply, drifting rearward a few yards instead, for those words to him had shown the lance corporal the root of the Platoon's dilemma. Exchanging his rifle for a machine gun with one of the remaining soldiers, he stepped in beside the Platoon's other Section Commander, a tall, blond haired lance corporal.

'Jonesy, don't try to stay with Davidson. You and Bobby bring the lads on at your best pace. I'll stick with him. If he turns off I'll scratch a sign beside the road.'

'Good idea, Mick! Cheers!' replied Jones, continuing in frustration 'he's a cunt, ya know, all he's doing is crippling everyone.'

Pridmore didn't reply, doubling forward to slot in behind his Platoon Commander.

'How far we got to go now, Sir?' he asked, not concerned with the reply, for his question was only intended to make his presence known.

'We're nowhere near half-way, Corporal Pridmore', came Davidson's tart reply, not bothering to look around.

'OK Sir, you lead, we'll be with you all the way', promised the big man loyally,turning to transmit his and the Platoon Commander's enthusiasm to the rest of their happy band.

'Come on lads, keep it going, only another six or seven miles to go.'

The nearest man, fifty yards or so down the road, did not even bother to look up from his boot caps.

For the next mile Pridmore locked into Davidson, forcing him to maintain the pace of the march, stopping only at junctions and turning to scratch a broad arrow with his boot on the dirt verge. Finally, he noticed a faint slackening as the Platoon Commander, deciding he had shown his men the meaning of a battle march, slowed. But the big Lancastrian lance corporal was having none of that, and picking the step up, he moved to Davidson's shoulder.

'It's up to you and me, Sir, the rest have dropped out.'

The Lieutenant, now faced with a not too subtle challenge, increased his stride to put himself in front. There he remained over the next mile but only through increased effort, feeling himself weakening, having to keep himself ahead of his lance corporal.

Pridmore positioned behind and just to one side, separated by no more than the thickness of their two camouflage smocks, constantly watched the tall officer monitoring his physical state. Although young, only just turned twenty, and obviously fit,he lacked the grit which men like Pridmore thrived on, who, nodding his head forward in a quick glance, could see the extra exertion was beginning to tell. Davidson's face was losing its colour, his eyes no longer active but staring downward. Mick, deciding it was time to apply some barrack room psychology, began innocently:

'Nice country around here, eh Sir?'

The younger man, caught off guard with this conversational query, could only reply 'What?'

'The scenery, Sir, pretty good for this time of year. What do you think?'

Davidson, finding breath at a premium, gave a brisk answer 'Yes, lovely.'

Which the drab, end of winter surroundings were not.

'I know this road,' lied the lance corporal, 'it leads into Lewes, doesn't it Sir?' A name he had seen on a junction sign.

'Yes, two or three miles', responded Davidson reluctantly.

'Thought so', continued Pridmore. 'I used to go with a nurse from there,' another lie, 'Shagged her in that lay-by we just passed back there.'

'Really', was his Platoon Commander's only comment.

'Ya, did it in her mini. You ever done it in a mini, Sir?'

'No.'

'Don't blame you, Sir, had to do it in the back, her legs stuck over the front, bloody tight. Not her, the mini', he quickly clarified, 'she had a cunt like the Black Wall tunnel.'

Mick allowed himself a short pause before disturbing the officer's concentration further.

'You got a girl, Sir?'

'Not just now', replied Davidson, annoyed that the lance corporal should ask about his private life.

'But you have been out with girls, haven't ya, Sir?'

'Yes, of course' responded the officer sharply.

'You just fuck them and leave them, eh Sir' assumed Pridmore cheerfully.

'Something like that' was the guarded reply.

'Ya, me too, best way. Ever had one fellatio ya, Sir?'

'Eh, well I...' began Davidson haltingly, but Mick's rambling on cut him short.

'That nurse was really good at it, took all of me, drove me crazy.

Pridmore paused for a brief moment to get the pronounciation right, before continuing 'how about cunnilingus, Sir, you done that haven't you?'

Not that he was going to get one, Pridmore gave no chance for a reply; 'that nurse liked it, said I had a tongue like an alsation. How do you suppose she could tell that? What about sodomy, Sir, ever tried that?'

The young officer looked up to find his lance corporal, shifting his machine gun to another shoulder, had moved up beside him.

'What about it, Sir, ever pushed it up hill?'

For the next three miles Pridmore forced the pace, propelling the two men forward. Davidson, with gasping short breaths, his legs becoming painful;

16

Pridmore apparently unaffected continuing to relate a stream of sexual adventures he had experienced from Hong Kong to Hamburg, some true, most imaginary, all devised to shock his younger companion. Mid-way through relating the Benghazie donkey and women act, Davidson lurched at right angles into a driveway. Just as Mick was about to scratch another arrow in the dirt with the toe of his boot, he noticed this was a stone gatewayed entrance, on the other side of which he joined his officer.

'This it then, Sir, this the finish?'

Davidson, who had stumbled over a low pebble, was clutching the trunk of a cherry tree for support.

'Yes! Yes!' he stammered, out of breath, his face ashen grey.

Then, pushing himself up straight, he laid his rifle down on the grass verge, and dropped his equipment beside it. Facing the lance corporal he gave a series of orders before limping up the driveway.

'You stay here, keep an eye on my weapon and kit, catch the others as they come in; I'll be up at the house.'

Pridmore, using his beret to wipe his sweaty, salt-encrusted face, sat down to wait.

Some minutes later he turned on hearing a rhythmical tapping, this being the shoe heels of a woman carrying a tray ladened with glasses and a pitcher of fruit juice.

'Dean said some of his men were here at the gate, so I thought perhaps you would like something to drink.'

'That's kind of you, love', replied Pridmore, having risen to his feet.

'Where are the others?' she asked, her face showing mild puzzlement.

'They'll be along shortly. I'm just the first', assured the lance corporal.

'Oh well, that's fine. Would you like some of this? I'm afraid it's only pineapple juice', she said, placing the tray on the driveway.

'Yes ma'am, thank you. That's very kind', responded Pridmore, a pillar of politeness, eyeing the pitcher, his parched throat prepared to accept sugared yaks urine.

'You needn't call me ma'am. Lynda will do', she corrected, squatting to pour a glass of juice. 'What shall I call you?'

'Lance Corporal Pridmore' replied the paratrooper formally.

'Oh, I can't do that, it's too much of a mouthful. What's your first name?'

'Mick' came the short reply.

'Michael, yes that would be better' she smiled, rising to offer the paratrooper his glass; a woman of forty with a trim, attractive figure, apparent even though she wore a thick skirt and a fluffy wool sweater. Her blond hair, with only light traces of silver, hung in natural waves to her shoulders. Taking the drink, Mick silently admired her blue eyes and pale smooth skin, and her perfume which he sucked deeply into his lungs.

'What is this place?' he asked, attempting to find out who she was and where he was.

'Oh, we live here, I'm Dean's mother. It was a farm but now we have a small dairy and factory farm chickens' she explained, pointing to several long buildings visible beyond a newly modernised seventeenth century house.

'It must keep your husband busy', said the big man, impressed by what she was showing him.

'I'm afraid I do most things myself, Dean's father died five years ago.'

Before Mick could reply to this she changed the subject.

'I'm so glad Dean has had others for company on this march. It must have

17

been so boring for him while on leave'.

At this Pridmore's chin rose sharply. 'Has he been out a lot then?'

'Oh yes,' she replied; 'every day while on leave. I've never seen him so tired though; he's having a little lie down on the couch just now.'

Mick made no reply to this. His only reaction was to grip with one hand the muzzle of his machine gun, lifting it to thump the butt several times on the driveway's surface.

Shortly 'Jonesy' Jones steered the lead group of the Platoon through the gate to collapse on the grass verge. This had Lynda hurrying back and forth to the the house refilling her pitcher.

Bobby MacIntyre arrived some time later to report two men were missing. With this news Lieutenant Davidson climbed into the family Rover and set out to find them. He returned an hour later having found Phil Haydon and 'No Way' Ottoway window shopping in Lewes. As they spilled out of the car Bobby waded into them.

'Where have you two cunts been? Yah fuck'n blind, we left signs on the side of the road. Think we got fuck all else to do but hang around here waiting for you two pricks. Get over there on the grass and sit down.'

The two fugitives slunk away, Haydon snapping off his beret to slap his bigger mate's shoulder. 'I told you we should have followed the arrows. Twat! Twat!

Davidson, entering the kitchen, found his mother and Pridmore washing glasses, both laughing.

'Oh Michael, I don't believe that at all', his mother was giggling.

'Corporal Pridmore, the vehicles have arrived. Get everyone aboard, we're leaving' he ordered, his face a scowl.

'Right Sir' obeyed Pridmore, laying down a tea towel, 'we've just finished. I'll say goodbye Mrs. Davidson; thanks for the pineapple juice, the lads appreciated that.'

'Not at all Michael, I've enjoyed meeting so many of Dean's friends' was the attractive woman's smiling farewell.

'You shouldn't call these men by their first names, Mother, they're members of my Platoon' reprimanded the officer after his lance corporal had left.

'But that's silly. Michael is such a gentleman and very courteous' she replied, defending her actions.

'Gentleman! Courteous!' Davidson flamed, the veins in his neck standing out. 'The man's a sexual degenerate.'

'Oh-h-h', replied his mother, 'he didn't strike me that sort at all.'

As Pridmore finished directing the last four-tonner out of the gates, he turned to throw his Regimental signet ring into a rhododendron bush.

In future months Davidson, smarting because of Pridmore's familiarity with his mother, ensured he was given the worst of the Platoon's fatigues and duties. But in the end these infantile acts proved pointless for in nine months time Lance Corporal Michael Pridmore would marry his Platoon Commander's mother.

CHAPTER TWO

The Camel's hump is an ugly lump
Which well you may see at the zoo;
But uglier yet is the Hump we get
From having too little to do.

Rudyard Kipling

Returning from their final N.A.T.O. exercise in Denmark, 5 Para took over as the U.K. Spearhead Battalion. This entailed being on standby to deal with any emergency anywhere in the world. Although it sounded exciting, the men looked on it only as an inconvenience.

For a month the Companies took it in weekly turns to be on twenty-four hours notice to move. A simple task one would think but not so. From Battalion H.Q. a stream of orders, memos and kit lists arrived which had everyone working into the wee hours.

As C Company came on standby they were inspected individually and systematically by the C.O. With every article of kit spread out before them, they waited while weapons, webbing and helmets were checked for serviceability, socks unfolded and searched for holes, housewives opened to see the correct number of buttons, pins, needles, cotton and wool was present. The junior N.C.O.s, having to follow instructions as to where all items were to be found, had a top left hand smock pocket that bulged like a woman's purse. With the smock's other three empty, this had to contain note book, pencil, chinagraph, compass, whistle, ear defenders, five fish hooks (?), fifty feet of string, camouflage cream, an orders aidememoir, and one shell dressing for the personal use of.

It took two hours, in which the C.O. discovered a multitude of discrepancies, all potentially crippling the soldiers' ability to kill the Queen's enemies. Sea kit bags without labels, puttees cut in half, shirts without wings sewn on, pencils unsharpened. The C.O., a fair man, berated everyone from the Company Commander down. The members of Charlie returned to their billetts, officers fuming, sergeants shouting and the men threatening to go diffy.

A few days before the Company had come on to its week's shift of standby the National newspapers began reporting a dispute between neighbouring islands in the Caribbean. When Independence was being cast about the West Indies in the late Fifties and early Sixties a number of these smaller, scattered islands were lumped together in order to have the respectability of size. Now some of these shotgun marriages were proving unwise. The East Corals, guarding the Caribbean's Atlantic frontier, were a Confederacy of seven islands. A group of five and two others, each north and south by forty or fifty miles from the other five.

On a clear day the cluster of five were visible to one another. The largest, Lagos, thirty by twenty miles, held the seat of Government. This Confederation, on its release from British administration was given two million pounds a year for ten years with the proviso that it be used to build roads, air-fields and improvements in harbour and port facilities throughout the seven islands. As for other means of Governmental income, there was non, having to rely solely on taxes taken from the islanders themselves.

The upheaval reported in the Press told of rebellion from the northern island, Saint Verde, which was refusing to send its taxes to the East Corals Treasury, accompanied by rumblings of cessation from the Association altogether. The Islands' Prime Minister, with the diplomacy of Attila the Hun, asked Britain for a gun boat to shell the rebels. Westminster refused, sending instead a representative from the Foreign Office. He, on arrival was confronted with allegations and eye witness reports of out and out rebellion, burning of the national flag, seizure of public administration buildings and the expulsion of a judge, the police and all Civil Servants loyal to the Lagos Government. On this Her Britannic Majesty's lot acted.

Twenty Metropolitan policemen arrived in their barracks to join C Company on standby.

Three days later, unhappy about the priority listing his problem had been allocated, the East Corals' Prime Minister produced evidence that the Saint Verdes were about to hand their island over to the Mafia, who in turn, were intending to build hotels and casinos which would become the H.Q. for their Caribbean gambling, prostitution and drugs trade. One day before they were due to hand over the duties of standby to 'A' Company, 'C' Company were fired out of the camp gate, accompanied by the Police detachment, for RAF Brize Norton. There they boarded Airforce VC 10s and flew first to Bermuda and then on to Lagos.

Britain being between wars, the Press decided to invent one. The headlines began modestly enough with phrases such as 'Red Devils fly out' — 'Crack airborne force to deal with rebels' — 'Sky men to assault island'.

The Company missed all these ego-inflating black headlines; they were being cast away to the remoteness of blue skies, white sandy beaches and pale green seas. At the Lagos airport the man from the Foreign Office, with a delegation of East Coral Ministers, met the first plane-load of Paratroopers. One member of this group who proved to be the Prime Minster, Joseph Vincent, kept bursting into little tantrums of arm-waving and finger-gesturing, impatient for the Company to fly on and parachute into Saint Verde from the VC 10s. Major Hanley and the Foreign Office representative explained with restraint that the jet air-crafts were not suitable and arrival on Saint Verde would have to be by sea. This was to be preceded by all the intelligence and recent information being gathered, the geography of the island studied for suitable landing points, briefings and an assault plan devised; one which all Services involved must agree upon. In short, the Prime Minister was being politely told that this was now a military operation and that he should leave it to the experts.

The Company, shaking off the effects of jet lag and travel fatigue, got settled into their temporary billet, a newly constructed aircraft hanger. Stripped to the waist, fatigue parties and ammunition details were set to work, and an evening guard mounted throughout the night. In the morning, before breakfast, each Platoon did a five mile run around the perimeter of the airfield, giving everyone a chance to view the nearby town and surrounding farms that stretched away on a fertile plain towards lush green tropically forested hills. Throughout the day the Company remained in constant motion with bursts of action and periods of waiting.

Sam Kyle, 8 Platoon's Platoon Sergeant, having recovered from a balindicide wound received in Aden and now back from sick leave, found himself in the middle of a fit of organized confusion that only the Army could produce. The time for the Company's briefing having been brought forward, he gathered his Platoon in from the numberous work details only to find it had been cancelled. Then on returning the men to their jobs, was told it was back on again. Teams were despatched to the harbour for training with the recently arrived, eight-man assault boats to discover that the out-board engines had been left back in Blighty. The right people were issued with the wrong maps. Lance Corporal Jones drew 7 Platoon's rations, 9 Platoon collected 8 Platoon's ammunition. Sam received a rollicking from the Company Sergeant Major for not submitting to him a Platoon nominal roll and orbat. Pleading ignorance, he was told that the O.C. had instructed all Platoon Commanders to inform Platoon Sergeants. It turned out the message had been passed down from Davidson to Corporal MacIntyre, who told Private Wier, who told Private Tomlinson, who forgot because he was just going down to the harbour for boat training. All this continued well into the night with inspections and briefing to ensure the Company was prepared for war and to give the men as little sleep as possible. They took all this with the minimum amount of effort and maximum amount of chuntering, while waiting for the next move. This occurred early in the morning when London granted permission for the operation to go ahead.

At dawn, the Company paraded in battle order to leave, with a few slight amendments to the kit list. Out went all the chinagraph pencil and fish hook rubbish, in went rations, water and ammunition.

The Press, who had been keeping a high profile around the perimeter of the airfield, took telescopic photographs of the paratroopers boarding trucks and driving out of the gate. Then, weaving amongst the convoy in assorted cars and pick-up trucks, snapped them as if they were film stars, even pursuing them in small boats as they were carried by launches to board a Royal Navy frigate anchored in the bay.

On sailing that evening there should have been a reprieve from the persistent media, but they were not to be put off by the mere obstacle of thousands of square miles of Caribbean Sea. By mid-morning the first light aircraft was circling low overhead, with a succession of others to follow throughout the day.

Meanwhile, aboard the frigate tension began to rear its jittery head, for an H-hour had been decided upon for storming the beaches. With the ship steering a north-westerly course, well away from Saint Verde, Major Hanley gathered his Command onto a cramped stern deck to give a final attack briefing. For over an hour, with the aid of a large sketch map, he meticulously talked the Company through, stage by stage, confirming timings, adjectives and alternative actions to be taken. Because the 'enemy' was an unknown factor, he could only repeat what had already been stated by earlier unconfirmed reports, that the island's four thousand inhabitants had formed a militia force armed with rifles and machine guns supplied by the mafia. His end of briefing summing up, referring to their ace card of total surprise that was being brought about by security moves and the Navy's present deception plan, was drowned out by Fleet Street's latest low-level photo reconnaisance and had to be repeated.

With twilight diminishing, the ship's Captain brought his Command to action stations. Extinguishing all lights and increasing his speed to maximum knots, he turned onto a new course putting the frigate, two hours later, off a stretch of sandy shore. Eleven o'clock that evening, with the operation running to schedule, the war ship dropped anchor five miles out to sea off Red Beach. The Navy had done their bit; now it was up to the Army.

Although it had not been rehearsed, the time allocated for the assault boats to be lowered into the water, the men clambering down into them and the journey to the shore, was an hour. However, considering the Normandy invasion had taken four years in the planning, with rehearsals at Dieppe, North Africa and Sicily, the lessons learned on those occasions proved to be grossly ignored.

Getting the ten boats into the water took over an hour, and three of the crafts' outboard engines could not be started so they kept drifting away on the tide. These were being manned by the Support Company Detachment, for unable to operate their 81 millimetre mortars and heavy anti-tank guns, their redundancy had freed them for this other, semi-skilled employment.

Faced with a reduced number of boats, the O.C. had to do some fast reshuffling. This caused immense confusion for the disembarking troops, with one third being told to draw back and await a second wave. In the dark, with heavily equipped bodies pushing and shoving about the crowded deck, Sam Kyle struggled desperately to maintain control of his Platoon. With orders rumours and and fairy tales being freely passed about by everyone, the troops began to lose interest. Every man was told at least once that he was not going, then that he was. As the muddle increased, soldiers began to sit down or lean on handy things, with whispered, four-lettered odjectives flying around the deck. Some took this opportunity to skive off and hide, for a five mile canoe ride across the open sea did not appeal to all the paratroopers. Sam found two of these, Ottoway and Haydon, hiding below a companionway stairs, and chased them back on deck with threats of being charged or drowned or both.

What had originally been planned as an orderly disembarkation now degenerated into a shambles. All of 9 Platoon should have remained behind but in the dark and confusion of the re-shuffle it didn't work out that simple. 7 Platoon, descending the scramble nets, found themselves asking the Support Company crews which was their boat. As negative replies were exchanged the situation became comical. Wrong boats, finding themselves out of the loading order, sped off to rejoin the queue, leaving the Cpmpany's Senior Platoon verging on panic as they clung, camouflage-creamed and battle laden, to bits of hemp rope, as the ship gently rocked up and down over eighteen fathoms of shark-infested ocean. After two hours of uncontrolled poncing about, the boats were eventually filled with men and pointed towards the shore. This to the relief of the Navy, who all the time, closed up to action stations, had patiently remained silent and professional while the Army blundered about in their normal manner.

To an on-looker the Company's approach to the beach would have appeared a skilled well-practiced manoeuvre, with six boats abreast bearing down on the shore and the O.C.'s a short tactical distance to the rear. In truth, only Major Hanley's boat had the correct men, the others were a mixed hodge podge with one craft being jointly commanded by eight privates. Bobby MacIntyre and Mick Pridmore, who should have been in different boats found the machine gun team in the prow was from 7 Platoon while one of the rifle men was from 9 Platoon.

A mile from the assault beach the engine of the O.C.'s craft conked out, which left them, unnoticed by the other, drifting gently on the sedate swell. As the Support Company helmsman struggled to restart his machine Major Hanley silently went bonkers.

Meanwhile, three and a half hours late, the rest of the flotilla, ignorant of the loss of their Commander, accelerated in a final spring to the island. Crouching low as possible below the aluminium sides of the shallow crafts, everyone's eyes were now glued to the white line of surf as it bubbled in even, tender strokes on the beach.

Suddenly a quarter of a mile out, Red Beach began to erupt in flashes of light. Corporal MacIntyre, the first to realise what this was, shouted a warning above the noise of the out-board motors.

'Don't shoot, don't shoot, it's not guns, it's not guns, don't shoot.'

Mick Pridmore threw himself forward to stop the 7 Platoon gun team, who had cocked their machine gun, from firing. While from the shore several dozen Press cameramen, who had arrived by sea and air earlier the previous day, gaily snapped away on their flash cameras, blissfully unaware of the eternal oblivion they had almost brought upon themselves. As each boat skidded to a halt on the smooth wet sand, the battle-ready paratroopers leaped into the surf and stormed Red Beach, weaving like rugby forwards, their bodies swerved the scrum-thick newsmen to rush their high tide line objectives. Several found themselves stumbling wide-eyed and blind for some seconds, having been caught full-faced by a flash bulb triggered by photographers eager to snap the action close-ups.

After consolidating his Platoon's initial defence Mr. Rudick the 7 Platoon Commander decided to put out two scouts to give him an indication of the ground further inland.

Crouching beside a figure he believed to be one of his Section Commanders, he whispered short but clear instructions.

'Take one man and carry out a recce to our front. Don't go beyond three hundred metres. Be no longer than twenty minutes. Every man on the perimeter will be warned to expect you back but when challenged, use the pass word. Now off you go.'

Without replying 'No Way' Ottoway rose to his feet and moved across to fetch his mate.

'Come on, you and me are doing lead scout. I'm in charge, follow me.'

Phil Haydon, not believing what he heard, scrambled up from the sand to chase after him. 'Hey, hey cunt,' he demanded, bringing the other man to a halt with a tug on his shirt, 'who told you we got to go lead scouting?'

'Rudick picked me personally, he did', replied 'No Way', flushed with command.

'Well, what the fuck did you accept for? We're supposed to be playing lost and keeping out of Kyle's way.'

'Never mind that, we got important work to do, now follow me' ordered Ottoway shrugging off his subordinate's question with a Montgomerian air, leading the way into no man's land.

Once over the brow of the beach, the ground, a thin layer of sandy soil on volcanic rock, stretched away more or less flat into the warm, Caribbean, star-lit darkness.

Haydon, uneasy about his new assignment, gave a hard rearward stare, then doubled forward to once again tug at his mate's shirt.

'Hold up a sec, we've lost the rest. There's no one following', anxious that they remain in contact with what he believed would be 7 Platoon's advancing point section.

'What, what,' replied 'No Way' indignantly, whose mind was concentrated on a higher plane of strategy. 'No, course not, why should they? It's you and me that's having a look see.'

'Look see! Look see! fumed Haydon, his whisper gaining a higher pitch. 'It's a recce, that's what this is. You got us out here all on our own on a fucking recce.'

Ottoway, impervious to the doubt being cast upon his leadership, put a finger to his lips and blew a low 'Shhhh', then turning, he continued deeper inland.

At a junction of the pathway they had been following where it forked out in two separate but parallel directions, 'No Way' paused to revise his tactics. Having made his plan he turned to his companion to give operational instructions.

'You go left, I'll go right, see you back here in five minutes.'

Then in the style of the Old West, with eyes narrowed, rifle at the ready, he stalked off like a Buffalo Bill Indian scout.

Phil Haydon, caught off guard by this, one of the dumbest acts in all of Creation, could only stand and stare at the dark shape disappearing up the path.

'Ottoway, you fucker, come back', screeched Haydon in a shrill whisper, but his response was too late; his leader was gone, leaving him to ponder the situation for half a minute, whilst kicking frustratedly at little sand bumps.

'I'm going to shoot that prick the first chance I get', he swore to himself, grasping his rifle in both hands before picking his way up the left-hand path.

On the other route 'No Way's' hawk-eyed alertness paid off. Spotting a silhouette against the starry horizon, he flattened himself behind a small shrub. Gradually, as it approached, this outline became a man pedalling a bicycle. Ottoway, watching him over his rifle sights, instantly assumed this to be the advance guard of an enemy column. When the rider stopped ten yards or so from him, 'No Way's' finger tightened on his trigger. As the lid of a bin, which was carried over the bicycle's front wheel, was raised, Ottoway, whose imagination conjured up a mafia-type, Chicago drum-magazined machine gun about to be pointed at him, got ready to blast the bicycle rider to Kingdom Come.

'Hy Mon' came a lilting, West Indian voice from the stranger, who held up a soft drinks bottle. 'Want to buy a coke?'

Throwing devotion, duty and loyalty for hearth and home to the wind, 'No Way' rushed across to demand: 'How much?'

'Special price for soldiers today', replied the smiling black man. 'One shilling.'

Leaning his rifle against the bicycle, our Commander of forward reconnaissance began digging through pockets to finally come up with a pound note.

'Got change for a quid, chief?' he asked.

'Sure mon, got plenty of change. How do you want it? Sterling, French Francs or Yankee Dollars?'

'Give us two then', Ottoway requested eagerly.

'What took you folks so long?' continued the pop pedlar, snapping the cap off with a hand opener to offer the first bottle. 'I've been waiting since ten o'clock last night. Just come back from the store, had to fill up with some fresh ice.'

Ottoway, whose craving for liquid, brought on by the night's events and the exertion of moving about fully equipped in the warm, humid Caribbean climate,gulped the sweet fluid while, in the true tradition of Burgess, MacLean and Philby, he explained between swallows the reason for their lateness.

'Ya well, some of the boats wouldn't work --- pigs bastard trying to get into them. ---We never practised this, ya know --- fucking near came unstuck --- sodden shambles the whole show.'

'Where can I find the rest?' asked the enemy drinks vendor, exchanging the second bottle for 'No Way's' empty. 'I bet they would like a nice cold drink too, eh?'

'Too bloody true; they're back on the beach.'

'OK mon, I'll just ride down and relieve the rest of the gentlemen's thirst.'

'Ya well, cheers for the cokes mate' thanked Ottoway. 'If you get stopped by the lads just give the password 'Butter Dish'; say 'Butter' to them — that will get you through. See ya!' Then watching the man peddle away,he sat down to enjoy his second drink between longish pauses.

This was how he was found by Phil Haydon who, exasperated at waiting, suddenly appeared,glaring down at his recce Commander.

'What the fuck you doing sat here, Ottoway? You said five minutes back there.' Half turning to point behind him, then pausing for a brief second on spotting the bottle, stopped whispering to demand in a clear voice.

'What's that?'

'No Way's' reply was an innocent 'eh?'

'That! That! Bollock features, the coke' Haydon's voice was getting louder.

'Oh ya,' began 'No Way' as if he had been sitting on a bench in Hyde Park. 'A bloke came past flogging them.'

'Where's mine then?'

'Didn't get you one' answered Ottoway feeling an ever so slight twinge of conscience.

'Didn't get me one! Didn't get me one!' Phil was shouting now as he pulled off his beret to pelt his leader with maroon slaps.

'Someone turns up out of nowhere flogging cokes and you didn't get me one! Twat! Twat!'

Ottoway and Haydon had not cornered the pantomime market. Back on the beach, with the first slivers of dawn appearing, the troops were being pestered by the Press to pose and even re-enact a more photogenic daylight assault. Faced with blunt refusals most thought they would have to make do with the O.C.'s boat which arrived an hour late, paddling in with the aid of hands and rifle butts. However, God, smiling kindly on Fleet Street, sent them 9 Platoon in the full light of day, battle laden and ready for war. By this time those already on the shore had long since given up believing they were really at war with anyone. This had begun to take effect at just about the time a fella on a bike, selling soft drinks, appeared on the scene, shouting the operational password to everyone he met.

Faced with the alarming reports that had initially been conveyed to them by the Governing Officials of the East Corals, Britain had set this operation in motion to prevent what they had been lead to believe was a rebellion. Over the following days of consolidating this non-violent, and as it proved, friendly objective, Charlie Company and London learned the truth.

Yes, the islanders had refused to pay their taxes. Yes, some Government Officials had left Saint Verde, but through their own choice. No, there was no mafia. These original claims were found to be lies put out by Prime Minister Vincent, in order that the weight of British military power would intervene to teach St. Verde a lesson and force it back under East Coralian control. What was eventually discsovered was that Vincent was a rogue, creaming off a percentage of the grant provided by Britain and allowing his cronies to charge exorbitant prices for building work contracted out by him.

Here again, Vincent did the dirty, for this construction work should have been evenly spread throughout all the islands but was infact confined solely to Lagos, Vincent's capital and home island. These acts of selfishness should have been detected by Britain monitoring the building programme, but Britain was happy instead to accept photos sent from East Coral. Each was supposedly a different facility built on a different island. However, they were photographs of harbours, airfield or road installations taken from different angles and bogusly captioned.

With the true facts coming to light, Whitehall and the Foreign Office now turned their attentions to implementing a hurriedly-constituted Cabinet directive.

On the political side, a Governor took up residence on St. Verde, which effectively removed them from Prime Minister Vincent's contro. Then, to make amends, a Squadron of Royal Engineers was sent in to build a much-needed concrete air-strip, several miles of roadway to replace gravel tracks and to supervise improvements to the island's only fuelling jetty.

In order to justify the invasion it was decided C Company would remain on Saint Verde. The London police detachment was also deployed as a temporary measure until a local force could be recruited and trained. Britain, as can be expected was still rather hot under the collar over the whole affair, and, believing it unwise for Vincent to remain unbridled, also had a further two Companies and a large H.Q. element of the Battalion flow out to be stationed on Lagos under the pretext of providing backup assistance to the troops on St. Verde. Her Majesty's Government was now hopefully in a position to point Vincent along the straight and narrow.

C Company, who had expected nothing more than a brisk little action to be followed by a speedy return to Aldershot, now found themselves taking up residence on St. Verde's sunny shores. A Company tented base camp was erected near a beach on the outskirts of the island's main settlement, while one Platoon-size Detachment occupied a small cove several miles to the north. The sold military task allotted to them was that of providing two-man foot Patrols to wander around swatting flies and chasing pale green sand crabs about the surf.

They were also expected to carry out a census of the local population by calling at all homes in the area and logging the names of who lived where. This should have taken only a few days, but because each family ran their own backyard still producing white rum, it was never completed. Not many got further than three stops, and more than one was brought back paralytic in a wheel-barrow. Inevitably not everyone would have the opportunity to sample this good life to the full. Mick Pridmore left the Company having been schedule beforehand to attend a junior N.C.O. carde back in the U.K., which gave him the opportunity to retrieve his signet ring from the rhododendrons and in so doing woo and wed the widow Davidson.

Major Hanley also left, to take up a new posting in the Far East. His replacement, who should have been as promised Captain Carrol, the Patrol Company 2 I/C, turned out instead to be a stranger. Major Bates, who before transferring to the Parachute Regiment from the Kings Regiment where, as a Lieutenant, he became an Army middle-weight boxing champion, was preceded from the 3rd Battalion by his reputation. A large man, with a broken nose from his earlier sport, he was known to be fair but of an impatient nature, which exploded in erratic ways when he found himself dealing with incompetence or indiscipline.

Shortly after he arrived, the Company Sergeant Major also changed. Deposited on the landing jetty, from a launch the Army had chartered for ferrying personnel and stores back and forth to Lagos, pissed out of his mind, was CSM Jerry Kettler. Sam Kyle and the Company driver, who had been sent to collect him, wedged him with the aid of his luggage into a sort of sitting position in the back of C Company's only landsrover. Kettler, who on the short journey along the dusty road kept advertising his arrival with drunken shouts and floppy hand-waves at the locals by the roadside, was already known to Sam and some others of the Company. As a corporal, Kettler was attached to Sam's Platoon when he had been a recruit in the Depot eight years earlier. In those days his personal make-up was, among other things, a habitual liar, a vindictive coward and totally unable to organise, the latter of these causing him during his recent years of service to add another, that of alcoholic. To escape from his responsibilities he had turned to drink, which only compounded his problems, causing his superiors to post or promote him in order to get shot of him.

With the weeks extending into months a monotony-inspiring routine began to envelop C Company. The endless white beaches, unlimited swimming and exotic, tropical, starry nights were becoming ordinary. Paradise was losing its sheen. As can be expected, anything happening outside of the regular programme was eagerly welcomed. One of these was Ottoway's discovery of a machine gun.

Before the invasion two brothers were said to be in possession of one of these, but with the arrival of Britain's Forces they and their fishing boat had disappeared. Ottoway, running back to the Company camp, reported his find with breathless exuberance to Mr. Davidson, who then followed the jubilant soldier, accompanied by a crowd of half naked, off duty men. Several hundred yards down the shore-line they found Phil Haydon, the second member of Ottoway's two-man afternoon Patrol. He sat on a bump of sand, his rifle across his lap and his beret pushed back on his head. Nearby was a shack with a corrugated iron roof, which was the home of the alleged machine gun owners. 'No Way' lead his Platoon Commander to the edge of a clump of scrub bushes to proudly point down, sure enough, there, partly uncovered, was the butt and body of an American .30 calibre BAR light machine gun.

'Bloody well done' contratulated Davidson. 'How the hell did you come to find it?'

'Well, it's like this, Sir', began Ottoway, slipping into his Sherlock Holmes role. 'Ever since you told us about those two Compton brothers I've been coming down here searching, because I had a good idea they wouldn't take the thing with them.

On hearing this Phil Haydon closed his eyes and gritted his teeth.

'But how did you find it here?' quizzed the officer, dropping to his knees to quickly scoop the unusually damp sand away from the weapon with his hands.

'Well, I knew they wouldn't be stupid enough to hide it in their pad, so bit by bit I've systematically been working my way around the whole area.'

At this point 'No Way' paused to sweep an arm in a dramatic half-circle. However, before he could continue, Haydon, who could stand his mate's glorified explanation no longer, jumped to his feet and advanced on Ottoway.

'Bollocks, bollocks, tell the truth yah cunt.' Then addressing his Platoon Commander, 'he stopped to piss over this cactus and ended up washing the sand away from the fucking thing.'

Mr. Davidson suddenly ceased his digging to stare at the damp sand clinging to his fingers, then glared a burning stare up at his story-telling soldier. Ottoway, saying nothing, smiled back a sheepish grin, accompanied by a shrug of the shoulders. Then he cringed away as Haydon swung the first blow with his beret.

'Cunt.'

*   *   *

This boredom, and the men's attempts to escape from it reached a peak one morning when 7 Platoon, overcome by the historical and geographical atmosphere of this, the old Spanish Main, got carried away and committed piracy. So that the Company would not become rusty on its military skills, a small deserted island five miles off St. Verde's southern tip was used alternately by each Platoon for field training. At first light Mr. Redick, his Platoon Sergeant and his Section Commanders left by launch to recce the ground and plan the day's exercises, leaving a lance corporal to bring along the rest of the Platoon in a hired pleasure boat a coupld of hours later. The men, with nothing to look forward to during the day except hard work and a lot a sweaty running about in the hot Caribbean sun, put a rifle to the boat captain's head,and hijacked his craft. The lance corporal, being threatened with the black spot, reluctantly joined the brotherhood. But after a morning's punting about the shore line playing chicken with assorted reefs and sand bars, he was able to convince everyone the best thing to do was give themselves up. This was agreed, more because the novelty of acting the role of Captain Kidd was wearing thin, then any sense of guilt.

On finding the Police H.Q. close at hand, they decided to surrender there. After coming alongside a small jetty where command of the vessel was returned to the boat's captain, everyone rushed across the sand, screeching like a herd of chimpanzees, to turn themselves in. The Met. Constables, not unsympathetic to what they had done, placed them under close arrest in the Detachment's bar where the afternoon was spent getting unconscious with alcoholic anaesthetics.

The next morning twenty-three privates and one lance corporal, all in the working dress of the day — beret, blue PT shorts, maroon Regimental belts and boots with socks rolled down — were paraded in one straight line outside the Company HQ office tent on O.C.'s orders. The first to face the music was the lance corporal; stripped of his belt and beret, CSM Kettler marched him in, in quick time, across the tent's sand floor to mark time in front of a six-foot folding table which was the O.C.'s desk. On being halted to attention, Major Bates began to read out his list of offences from an Army buff-coloured charge sheet, at the end of which he looked up to glare at the lance corporal.

'Corporal Fowler, are you aware of the seriousness of these charges?' His voice was icy.

Fowler admitted he was, but over the next five minutes staunchly refused to say whose idea the hijacking was or give names of ring leaders. In so doing, being the senior rank involved, Bates had no choice, and with the powers of detached command he stripped the lance corporal of his rank, posting him to another Company. Bates knew Fowler had no hand in the incident, and was only carrying the can for the rest of the Platoon which made him angry, for this had forced him to sacrifice a first-class junior N.C.O.

Determined to nail the real culprits, the O.C. had the remaining rogues of the bounding main marched before him individually. The first did not play it very tactfully, causing unexpected terror and pain for himself and his mates. Bates controlled his temper during his initial questioning of the man, for his answers were given in a bland, who-cares manner, a cheeky smirk seldom leaving his face. But his reply to the Major's query as to why the act of hijacking was done in the first place proved to be the spark that lit the powder keg.

'Ya, well it was just a lark, Sir' — broad smile.

'A lark!' roared Bates, clenching his fists.

'Ya! Ya! It was only a joke, Sir,' broad smile fading.

'A joke! A joke!' repeated the O.C., rising to his feet.

'That's right, Sir, just a bit of fun', smile gone, replaced by very worried look.

'A bit of fun! A bit of fun! I'll give you a bit of fun', screamed the Major.

The blow not only knocked the soldier down, but his falling backwards also sent CSM Kettler sprawling.

'Get this thing out of here, Sergeant Major, and march the next bastard in', bellowed Bates.

Kettler, scrambling to his feet, ushered the dazed soldier out with shouts and a few kicks, then ordering the next to take off his belt and beret, marched him in.

Bates, now re-seated behind his desk, dispensed with reading out the charge, and came straight to the point with a bark.

'Well, what have you to say about yesterday?'

He, deciding his best defence would be attack, began to voice what the men had only discreetly mumbled to each other.

'You can't really blame us, Sir, everything's so boring here, the food, the fatigues, the training, and there's no place to go in the eve......'

'Boring', interrupted Bates, jumping up to rush around the table. 'Well, I'll give you something to take your mind off that.'

Kettler dragged him outside the tent to lie unconscious in the sand. The next he marched in without bothering to disrobe him of his belt and beret, meeting the O.C. just inside the tent.

'And I suppose you're bored as well, eh?'

'No! No! Not me, Sir. I like it here', he pleaded, his legs flashing up and down still at the mark time.

'Liar', responded the Major before flattening him into the doorway.

The rest of the men in the queue, who had heard every word and blow, were now suffering varying degrees of panic, depending on how close they stood to the tent. This was shown by the next man who Kettler, taking his O.C.'s lead, grabbed and pushed through into the tent. Even before he had come to a halt his mouth was working in top gear.

'It wasn't my idea, Sir. I only went along with the others. It was Three Section, Sir, Dobson, Morgan, McGinnis, O'Keefe.'

Bates put a stop to this frantic ramble through the Platoon's nominal roll with a right hook. Then casting Queen's rules and regulations to the four winds, he stepped over the heap of bodies in the doorway to take his unique form of instant justice to the rest of the waiting boat pinchers. Standing before each he would ask just one question.

'Do you accept my punishment?'

Then, not waiting for a reply, laid them out, working his way down the line with sledge hammer blows to either head or solar plexus. There was a brief pause in his journey as he confronted the Platoon's resident, public school-accented potential offier. Unable to comprehend why he should be judged guilty along with the rest of this rabble, he astutely fixed his O.C. with a detached stare, naively stating:

'I do not accept your punishment Major Bates, Sir, and I wish to request an interview with the Commanding Officer.'

'Commanding Officer! Commanding Officer!' roared Bates, reaching back to dip the knuckles of his right fist in the Caribbean surf a quarter of a mile away.

'Why bother with him when I'm about to give you the opportunity to take any complaints you got to your fucking Creator.'

Considering the numbers involved, orders that morning was an unusually speedy affair with an uncharacteristic ending. Normally CSM Kettler would have held a formal dismissal with everyone turning smartly to their right then doubling away. Instead, as Major Bates stormed off to the officers' bar tent for a whisky to take away the pain of his bruised knuckles, he left 7 Platoon behind sprawled about in a general state of massacre.

Some were staggering off, holding heads and stomachs; others crawled around on hands and knees or rolled in the sand groaning, while two remained motionless, still unconscious. Needless to say, for the remainder of Charlie Company's stay on St. Verde the men were as good as gold.

*   *   *

Sam Kyle halted momentarily at the open entrance of his Platoon Commander's tent to peer in before stepping through. Standing still to allow his eyes a few seconds to adjust to the evening gloom that was several shades denser within the tent, he spied his officer, apparently asleep, on a canvas camp bed in one corner.

With several points and questions that needed to be dealt with, Sam cleared his throat before speaking.

8 Platoon, the last to occupy the detached beach camp, were in the process of dismantling it prior to moving back to the main Company location in preparation for their return to the U.K. Sam had found himself organising this on his todd, for on receiving the latest weekly mail delivery Mr. Davidson had jumped into the Platoon's duty pick-up truck and disappeared for the better part of three days. He returned that afternoon and without a word had vanished into the seclusion of his tent.

'Are you awake, Sir?' began the sergeant.

'Sorry to bother you', he continued, raising his voice while stepping nearer to the camp bed. 'It's about the move tomorrow. I need to confirm timing and the vehicle arrival time from the Company.'

The officer, still wearing the khaki dress uniform he had returned in, rolled onto his back to stare with a groggy expression at his sergeant.

'The move, Sir, I've got to have the transportation timing to post on Platoon orders tonight', he repeated.

'Oh yes, Sergeant Kyle, of course', he slowly replied, swinging his legs onto the sand to sit with his face momentarily buried in his hands.

'Nine, they'll be here at nine', now looking up and blinking several times.

'I've sorted a programme for tomorrow. Would you like to check through it before I put it out to the Platoon?' enquired Kyle, holding out a sheet of paper.

'Yes, of course', responded Davidson, rising to accept the paper before sitting at a nearby table. Putting the sheet down, he lit a kerosene lamp to see by. As he read, Sam noticed a half-empty bottle of white rum also on the table.

'Yes, you seem to have covered everything. What have you arranged for meals?' his manner professional but voice tired.

'The cook's all geared to lay on a hot breakfast but once we pull his tent down and pack up the rations, lunch will have to be sandwiches and a dixie of tea', replied Kyle.

'Fine, that's fine' was the lieutenant's only comment, handing back his sergeant's programme, his eyes fixed on a dark corner of the tent.

'Thanks very much, Sir, I'll let you get back to kip now. Sorry about having to wake yah', apologised Sam, taking the paper and saluting before turning to the tent entrance.

'Sergeant Kyle, how well do you know Corporal Pridmore?'

Kyle, half out of the tent, turned, holding a handful of canvas to steady himself as he answered his Platoon Commander's surprise question.

'Quite well, Sir. We were privates together in Cyprus. Why do you ask?'

'He and my mother are planning to be married next week.' Davidson reached for the rum bottle as he spoke.

Sam stepped back into the tent, laughing at his Platoon Commander's joke.

'I'm serious, Sergeant Kyle. It was all in a letter I received the other day.'

The officer's tone checked Sam's laughter, but his smile remained for several seconds, half expecting the younger man to also begin to laugh.

Instead, fingering a glass of rum while staring at the table, Davidson began to explain his turmoil.

'I'm afraid that's why I've left you on your own for the last few days. Been across to Lagos, seen the Adjutant and C.O., phoned my mother twice. No good. Kept saying things like 'kind', 'gentle', 'compassionate.''

Davidson looked up at his sergeant. 'Can you imagine that she thinks Pridmore's compassionate?'

His eyes returned to the table. 'The C.O. said I can have a transfer to the Depot, or anywhere else, if I wish.'

Those few sentences of his Platoon Commander's high-lighted for Sam just what an emotionally desperate state he was in. Career, family, future, all devastated.

'I wouldn't refuse a drink if you offered, Sir', said Kyle, realising his officer, needing to talk the situation out, had turned to the only person available who would understand his plight.1

'Oh yes, of course', replied Davidson offering a chair while pouring some of the rum into a plastic cup and asking, 'Would you rather see the men first?'

'Fuck them! They're happy enough drinking up what's left of the canteen stock. I'll see them in the morning', he replied, placing his beret and millboard on the table before sitting down.

Until well after midnight Kyle, in a firm but soft voice, his pale brown eyes never once showing insincerity, unfolded Pridmore's true nature to the young officer. On returning to his bed, Davidson, although still not happy about his mother's choice, was at least aware she was not marrying quite the animal he had at first thought.

*   *   *

'Okay, here it comes! Up you get; let's have this lot loaded so we can get the fuck out of here.

Bobby MacIntyre rose to his feet, beating his beret against a pant-leg, as he warned the men of his Platoon of the arrival of the civilian lorry. This had been hired several times by C Company during their stay on the island, but was now probably doing its last assignment for them, as the paras were leaving. With an infantry contingent now considered not necessary they were pulling back to Blighty. The only troops remaining would be an RAF Detachment for the running of the new concrete air strip, and a Squadron of Royal Engineers still involved in a lengthy building programme.

As the Chevrolet truck halted on the dirt track, MacIntyre tried to direct its reversal up to the pile of canvas tents and stores that was the last to be moved down to the embarkation jetty, but found it unco-operative.

'Come on Tommy, stop stalling about, we want to get out of here', he said, striding up to the cab.

'Money first, mon', answerd the small, grey haired, mahogany black driver, staring down at the corporal with a firm gaze.

'Money! Money! What fucking money?' quizzed MacIntyre impatiently, wishing to get the job done quickly.

'My money, mon, my money', elaborated the indignant driver, jerking a thumb at his chest. 'You people still owe me for the last two times I work for you. Now money first, then work.

'Oh, for fuck's sake Tommy, the Army will see you right; it's a big firm, it's not about to go bust' assured the corporal.

'Money' the black man stubbornly demanded, pushing one hand out of his window rubbing a thumb and two fingers together.

MacIntyre turned away in frustration. He could see the driver was digging his heels in and would not be shifting the remainder of the Company's stores until paid, or convinced of forthcoming payment by someone with more authority than he. Against his better judgement, but with the bulk of the Company including all officers and senior N.C.O.s having moved to the embarkation jetty earlier that morning, Bobby turned to the only person present with higher rank than himself. With the members of his Platoon's fatigue party philosophically accepting this delay to again crash out in the prone position, he slowly made his way across the sand to the recently vacated Company Stores. This was an empty, wooden-framed, open-sided, skeleton structure, fifteen feet high with a corrugated iron, lean-to roof, which had been a combined Company stores and cookhouse. In one corner was a small room recently used as the cook's ration store. On reaching the half-closed door, Bobby gave a tap before pulling it open. Sitting at a table was C.S.M. Kettler, shirtless, his head resting back against the wall, eyes closed. On the table was an empty whisky bottle.

'Got a problem, Sir' began the corporal, raising his voice to ensure that he penetrated Kettler's alcohol-clouded nap.

The warrant officer's eyes opened, staring to his front.

'The driver, Sir! Won't load the kit, says he's got to be paid first.'

Kettler's eyes slowly arched the room to rest on MacIntyre, standing just inside the door.

'What?' came a sluggish reply.

'The driver, Sir, he won't do the detail. Not until he's given the cash he says is owed to him', repeated Bobby.

As if triggered by an electric jolt, Kettler sprang from his chair, red-eyed and raving.

'Won't what? Won't what? Where is this cunt?' demanded the C.S.M., pushing past his corporal to storm out into the bright sunlight.

'What's this about you not prepared to do your fucking job?' shouted Kettler, storming up to the lorry cab.

'I'll drive when you people pay me my money', shouted back the driver, unimpressed by the C.S.M.'s loud voice.

'Listen, you black bastard', warned Kettler, 'I'm giving you a direct order. Move your vehicle over to that pile of kit so my men can start loading. Do you understand what I'm saying to you?'

The driver, with a frozen stare, replied by winding his windowshut. Kettler had called him a black bastard. Nothing would induce him to move C Company's tents and stores now.

'He's disobeying an order! He's disobeying a direct fucking order!' raved the C.S.M. towards the Heavens, while turning red in the face.

'Nothing you can do, Sir; he's a civvy', informed MacIntyre, who had followed him to the lorry, beginning to regret involving the drunken idiot.

Kettler, without acknowledging his corporal, began to magnify the driver's crime.

'Mutiny! That's what it is. Mutiny!' As he said this, the black man started the engine of his truck, deciding he had had enough abuse for one day.

'Desertion! Desertion! Now it's desertion!' screamed the C.S.M., leaping for the door handle to wrench it open. With both hands he pulled the driver out of his cab, whereupon the two men ended up sprawled in the sand. Kettler recovered first to sit on the older man's chest, his hands around his throat.

'Mutiny! Desertion! I'll show you what we do to people like you', Kettler threatened. Then raising his voice to a shout. 'Somebody get a rope, we'll hang the bastard.'

The men of the fatigue party, who had been watching their C.S.M. making a fool of himself, now sat up; all, that is, except Ottoway and Haydon. They, like the mad professor's two willing asistants, Hugo and Egor, rushed forward in answer to his call.

'This one do, Sir?' asked Ottoway,holding out a tent rope while attempting to noose a free end.

Bobby MacIntyre, shocked at the way the situation was escalating, lept forward.

'You can't do that, Sir, he's not in the Army.' Then, continuing out of the corner of his mouth, directed at Ottoway and Haydon, 'and you two cunts piss off.'

They grudgingly sulked back a few steps, but then eagerly lept forward in response to Kettler's order, as he released his hold on the driver's throat to climb to his feet.

'You two — tie this undisciplined individual's hands behind his back and parade him over at the stores building.'

Then, snatching the noosed rope from Ottoway, he began weaving towards the empty structure, while beckoning his corporal with a bold sweep of his arm.

'Corporal MacIntyre, come with me.'

Bobby, making little hops first towards the sandy tussle involving Ottoway, Haydon and the driver, and then towards Kettler, now began to flap.

Turning in the direction of a parked pick-up truck, he broke into a run towards its driver, who was seated on a low pile of canvas.

'Vince, for Christ's sake, take your wagon and get down to the pier and fetch the O.C. back here quick.'

'Fuck off, Bobby. I've never seen a lynching', replied the driver, leaning back to rest on one elbow.

With a swift kick at the soldier's feet, MacIntyre reached forward to pull him upright.

'I haven't time to play silly cunts with you. Now go get Bates and bring him back here at the double.'

'Alright! Alright!' He obeyed, strolling towards his vehicle with one hand fishing in a hip pocket for the ignition keys.

'But we would be better off letting the twat get on with it; then we would be rid of that useless wanker for good.'

Bobby was not able to ponder the logic of this, for Kettler again began to demand his assistance.

'Corporal MacIntyre, back that black cunt's lorry under here', he drunkenly called, staring up at a wooden cross beam supporting the building's roof.

'Can't' countered MacIntyre, thinking fast. 'It's a Yank job: I don't know how to work the gears.

'Well, I'll drive the fucking thing', responded the C.S.M., pausing briefly to give Haydon and Ottoway orders before stumbling towards the lorry.

'You two get him over here, and one of you get that rope over this beam.'

Bobby MacIntyre watched all these preliminaries being carried out in a fog of helplessness. He turned to view the smiling faces of his fatigue party, who were now on their feet eagerly awaiting the outcome of Kettler's lynching party, and realised that to put a stop to this homicidal nonsense drastic action would have to be taken by him alone.

Rushing across to the laid out tent stores, he opened a canvas bag, and pulled out a broad-headed wooden mallet used for driving tent pegs into the ground. With a quick determined pace he walked around to the passenger side of the vehicle cab; then, out of Kettler's sight, he climbed up onto the lorry's flat deck.

Spurred on by the excitement of this novel event, Ottoway and Haydon had complied with all instructions. Tied to a corner support post, the noosed rope hung down from the beam, below which Kettler had reversed into position the tail portion of the lorry's cargo-carrying platform. The two executioners, having dragged the driver up onto the back of his truck, held him between them as he stood defiant, with cool dignity, while Ottoway clamped the noose around his neck. His actions, in refusing to struggle or plead, were of a man who, knowing he is right, was prepared to die rather than beg for his life or comply with the wishes of this insulting, drunken British swine of a sergeant major.

'Ask that bastard if he's ready to drive this fucking truck' screamed Kettler, who, with the cab door flung open, stood revving the throttle with one foot, his body half twisted around looking backwards at the three men on the tail board.

'How about it chief?' relayed Haydon, reaching up to test the slack in the rope.

'Tell that man I have nothing to say to him', replied the white-haired driver in a calm, measured tone.

'He says you can get fucked, Sir', interpreted Ottoway, fearful that his C.S.M. might be having second thoughts.

'Right! We'll swing the bastard' howled the red-eyed warrant officer, turning to struggle back into the driver's seat. But he did not make it. For this was the move Bobby MacIntyre had been waiting for. As Kettler turned his head, MacIntyre leaned forward and, with a downward stroke, he knocked his sergeant major unconscious with the wooden mallet. Then, with Kettler tumbling into the sand, and the released clutch causing the engine to stall, he turned to glare with a Boris Karloff scowl at his sergeant major's two willing henchmen. They, glancing first at where Kettler had fallen, then seeing Bobby advancing towards them, gripping and re-gripping the handle of his wooden weapon, suddenly remembered they had not said their goodbyes to the sand crabs down on the beach, and quickly scrambled off the lorry to disappear among the dunes.

Half an hour later, with the lorry piled with men and tents, Bobby driving and Kettler sprawled groggily in the passenger seat, they came across Vince and his pick-up truck, conveniently stuck in roadside sand, having not completed his initial journey. Luckily on arrival at the embarkation jetty, the black driver merely accepted his cash payment from the Battalion Pay Master, who had just arrived for that sole purpose, and surprisingly said nothing of his ordeal. Major Bates, on smelling his sergeant major's breath, accepted the reason for his cut head as an accident on climbing into the lorry cab. The only punishment that was meted out because of this gallows comedy was by Kettler, who charged Ottoway and Haydon for being absent.

CHAPTER 3

For the great Gaels of Ireland
Are the men that God made mad.

Gilbert Keith Chesterton.

These many months of 5 Para's tropical island confinement, although in most cases pleasant, was considered by many of the Battalion's senior officers as wasted time. Prior to their departure, the Companies had been brought to a high standard of training and should have progressed on to an even more advanced state, with the men being sent on courses and given specialised cardes. Now the whole unit was once again back at square one, with the soldiers on ranges doing simple small arms firing, and out among the woods and bracken of nearby training areas, practising basic section and platoon attacks.

However, fate was again about to end these latest attempts by the Battalion to raise its standard of conventional warfare dead in their tracks.

In the summer of 1969, street rioting broke out between extremists of the Protestant and Catholic communities of Northern Ireland. In seeking the reason for this, it was found by those from the mainland of Britain that a deep investigation into Irish history had to be undertaken. But the simple answer was religious bigotry.

For several decades, tolerance had prevailed with only minor flashes of violence, that were quickly quelled by a Police Force that stood no nonsense. This tranquility could possibly have been the foundation from which those of the two religious communities of Ulster could at last push aside the veils of mistrust and hatred, and accept each other as neighbours; but it was not to be. During the mid-Sixties, a fanatical Protestant preacher set out on a campaign warning of doom and damnation which was to be brought upon them by the Catholics. This he did, not only from his own pulpit but also through a series of mass meetings and marches. Considered by most to be nothing more than a misguided evangelistic fool, he nonetheless gained support. The simple-minded members of the Protestant ghetto areas flocked to his rallies and marches, which consequently increased in size and frequency. in turn causing worry within the Catholic communities. They, in retaliation, began their own meetings and marches, using as their theme the unfairness in housing and job allocation, which was heavily biased against them. As these spread and grew, alarm and fear of each other sparked violence.

The Royal Ulster Constabulary, placing themselves between the two hostile groups, did their best to break up the confrontations by the traditional method of driving the Catholic faction away with the maximum force. This obtained limited success, until the Provence literally erupted. Centred mainly around the two major cities of Londonderry and Belfast, Loyalist and Republican mobs stormed into each others districts, burning and looting. For several days the R.U.C. battled to contain the numerous areas of violence, but as injuries and fatigue took their toll, the government was forced to deploy troops onto the streets to assist them. The Republican element of the Catholic community, recognising this as a major political coup, began to make demands: The withdrawal of all R.U.C. presence from the more volatile ghetto area, and the disbandment of a Police Auxiliary Force known as the 'B' Specials. The Westminster Government of the day, believing the first to be only a temporary concession, and the second an acceptable loss of a supernumerary organisation, ordered Stormont, Ulster's Provincial Government to comply.

However, both were disastrous, laying the foundation for all future disorder and terrorism: one giving an unpoliced base for radicals, criminals and political extremist groups, while the other, in a single stroke, deprived the forces of law and order of an extremely dedicated and professional organisation that had been the community's eyes and ears, identifying and reporting on crime and criminals with constant accuracy. Their absense was to cause a catastrophic void.

*   *   *

With the room falling silent as the education Officer entered, Sam Kyle opened his stationery folder in preparation for the morning's first lesson. He, along with the other twenty or so N.C.O.s in the room, was sitting the Army's Advance Education Certificate Course which was compulsory for those who wished to gain further promotion. As the Officer approached his desk, he turned to face the class, pushing his hands into his pockets.

'Gentlemen, I'm afraid we have to say 'fond adieu' to some of you. I've just received a message that all members of 5 Para must return to duties.' Then with a smile he continued, 'of course, I know nothing of what it's about or where you may be going, but if I was you I'd go easy on the Irish jokes.'

Rejoining the Battalion, Kyle found an over-excited but familiar scene, vehicles and men hurrying about everywhere, while the barrack dustbin area began to overflow with spare treasures as the soldiers, responding to the urgency of the move, discarded their buckshee kit.

On his way up the stairs to report in to the Company Office, Sam first paused on the ground floor to look into C Company's stores. It was turmoil. The Colour Sergeant and his two storemen were stripped to the waist, desperately clearing their shelves of all stores and equipment, forcing everything into large plywood boxes.

'What's the panic, Danny, you off somewhere?' grinned Kyle.

Company Quarter Master Sergeant Danny Simpkin straightened up to cut the air with a stiff, flat-handed chop, the expression on his face that of a man under pressure.

'No jokes Sam, I'm not in the fucking mood!'

'Come on, it can't be that bad. When do we leave?' humoured the sergeant, not yet a participant of this controlled hysteria gripping the Battalion.

'You leave tomorrow,' answered Simpkin, 'but I'm going tonight with the advance party.' Then spreading his arms, and looking at the upheaval around him he muttered to no one in general 'Tonight! Tonight!'

Upstairs, Sam found the Company office in the same chaotic state as the stores but here it was under the direction of a calming influence. This was the Company Clerk, who was supervising two membersof the Company, on light duties through parachuting injuries, in the packing of files, documents and stationary.

'Going somewhere, Corporal Pearson?' asked the sergeant nonchalantly, announcing his presence to the slim, dark-haired lance corporal.

'You can't laugh, Sergeant' smiled back Pearson, lifting a sheet of pale green paper off his desk with a thumb and fore-finger. 'I've just put your name back on the Company orbat.'

This exchange of words was interrupted by the frenzied voice of C.S.M. Kettler calling through the open door of his office.

'Sam! Sam! Is that you? In here quick.'

With the rest of the Battalion in mild turmoil, Jerry Kettler was terror-stricken.

On entering his office, Kyle found him clutching his telephone with one palm covering the voice piece, the expression on his face mirroring the panic within his mind.

'Sam, get your Platoon up to the Armoury, bundle all the weapons for the move, then see the Q.M. about where he wants them.'

'Fine' responded Sam with a false business-like tone, aware that Kettler was pushing a detail onto him that he himself should be supervising. 'Have we timings, chalk lists, movement orders? are they out yet?'

'Don't know, I haven't time; the R.S.M. wants to see all Company Sergeant Majors in half an hour. See the Clerk', dismissed Kettler, waving a limp wrist at Pearson.

Sam could see by the state his sergeant major was in that more drama from him was yet to come.

Returning through the Clerk's office, Pearson, with his usual foresight, handed him a hand-written note on which was scribbled events and timings. The sergeant acknowledge his appreciation with a wink and a thumbs-up, before turning out of the door.

Bobby MacIntyre welcomed his Platoon Sergeant's return with a beaming smile, the heavy weight of command fluttering from his shoulders. With Lieutenant Davidson accepting a posting to the 3rd Battalion, who were at present on a two year tour in Malta, and Sam committed to an Education Course, he, as senior corporal, had been 8 Platoon's leader.

'Thank fuck you're back, Sergeant', was his greeting as they stood together in the Platoon's billett accommodation. 'I've been trying to get some sense out of the Company Office all morning, but all I'm get'n' from the Sergeant Major is 'don't bother me! don't bother me!' so I've set the lads to clearing their lockers and packing everything up.'

'Yah, good move', replied Kyle, surveying the room's untidiness of half empty lockers, scattered kit bags, suitcases and the floor's ankle deep rubbish. 'I've got some timings here, so let's have everyone into this room. I'll give them a quick briefing. Then after that I want you to take your Section up to the Armoury. We've been lumbered with packing the Company's weapons. I'll see the other Platoon Sergeants to make sure their men draw theirs and give them to you. Once I've talked to the Q.M. about how these bundles are to travel, I'll come around just in case there are any hiccoughs.'

Compared to the rest of 5 Para, the Quarter Master's department was a calm laggon. This, of course, should not have been the case, for presented with a snap move pandemonium should have flowed rampant. This was due to just one man, Regimental Quarter Master Sergeant Ron Allander.

'Morning, Sir, is the Q.M. in?' asked Kyle, entering the R.Q.M.S.'s office, next to that of the Quarter Master's.

'You should know better than that, Sam', replied Ron Allander, leaning forward on his desk to shout through an open door leading into the Q.M.'s office.

'Corporal Styles, Radiator!'

'It's there, Sir', came back the coded reply, confirming that the Quarter Master was not at the golf course, for his bag and clubs were still leaning in their usual place.

'Well, he must be in camp somewhere', commented Allander, relaxing back in his chair to tap a pencil on the desk.

'Can I help?'

'Weapon bundles, Sir. I'm sorting them for the Company, but I've got no gen on the where, when or how, for the move.'

'Right' responded Allander, with the assurance of a man who had mastered his appointment.

'Five weapons to a bundle, each weapon labelled with the man's name. Machine guns to be conveyed in their boxes. All bundles and boxes to be clearly marked as to Unit and Company, with a 1033 sheet containing butt and registration numbers. Once packing is completed, all the bundles and boxes are to be stacked in separate Company piles outside the Guardroom. I told your sergeant major this already', he ended.

Kyle shrugged. 'He's got a lot on his plate at the moment', offered the sergeant.

'That's what he gets paid for, Sam. If the man can't cut it, he can be replaced just like the rest of us', was Allander's uncompromising reply.

*   *   *

Beth Kyle, returning from her part-time, morning job at a chemists to the Waterloo Park married quarter, found her husband busy packing a suitcase and bergen.

'Oh Sam, you're not off again are you?' her voice a mixture of despair and disappointment.

Sam, standing in a sea of scattered military clothes and kit, flung his arms outward in apology.

'I'm sorry, pet, we've only just been told this morning ourselves.'

Beth sat down on the edge of an easy chair to confess a wish she now knew would not happen.

'I was hoping you would be settled for a year or so. You haven't really been home any great length for years. When do you leave?'

Sam looked at his wife for a moment before replying.

'Now! I'm on the advance party. We leave this evening. So when I walk out the door shortly, you won't see me again until the Battalion gets back.'

Beth sagged. 'Oh Sam, what will I tell Suzanne and the twins? You'll be going before they return from school.'

Kyle crossed the living room to pull his wife up into his arms, pecking little kisses on her cheeks and eyes.

'I know, love; you'll have to tell them what we always say. The Army needs me, so I had to go.' Then, suppressing his compassion because of time, broke away to ask: 'Have you seen my respirator? I thought I left it in my sea kit bag, but it's not there.'

'What does it look like?' enquired Beth, her tone unhappy, but resigned to the fact she was once again to lose her husband for an indefinite length of time.

'Oh, squarish, green canvas thing about the size of a loaf of bread', answered Kyle, pushing a fistful of olive green clothing into his bergen.

'It's in the airing cupboard', she replied, turning towards the kitchen. 'I'll bring it through.'

Beth Kyle's annoyance on being left again, a grass widow, was wholly justifiable. She and her husband, both in their mid-thirties, could account for only half their time as a Service family together. The rest of the time, the Army had found it necessary for Sam to go off on unaccompanied postings or for operational service in the Middle or Far East.

They were, however, not unique; most couples serving with 16 Parachute Brigade, and for that matter the Army as a whole, could match a similar record.

*   *   *

'Jesus Christ.'

Jim Sinclair's two-word exclamation expressed the disbelief suddenly felt by everyone on the coach transporting part of C Company from Aldergrove Airport into the heart of Belfast. The members of 5 Para, like the rest of the world, had watched television film reports of the fires and violent rioting for the last few weeks. But no one had imagined that the damage to property was extensive as they now found. During the thirty minute drive through countryside and villages, no hint of the disorder for which they had been rushed from Aldershot could be detected. Even the view as they dropped down off the high ridge above Belfast into the outskirts of the City revealed little. Then as houses with gardens and trees gave way to cramped, brick terraced streets, the bus suddenly entered an area that looked as if it had suffered a bombing blitz.

Rows of streets were but burnt out shells, the pavements heaped with rubble, household goods and furniture. What had been only days before a community of homes, shops and small businesses was now destroyed.

On the fringe of this distruction, the bus halted beside a small, disused, grimy gray warehouse. The entrance to this building was straight off the street through a set of large double doors. Here a small knot of the advance party greeted them.

With Colour Sergeant Simpkin directing everyone off the bus into the warehouse, Bobby MacIntyre and Jim Sinclair approached Sam Kyle for a quick low-down on the situation.

Both were greeted unsmilingly by the sergeant.

'What are you doing here with the common people, Jim.?' he asked of Sinclair.

'You got about ten of us from Partol Company. Back up for your Int's Cell', replied Sinclair.

'Int's. Don't need fucking Int's here', mocked Kyle drily. 'There's no intelligence to be sorted. What's wanted is bodies on the ground to get between this lot and stop them from burning the whole bloody place down.

'What's the billett like?' asked MacIntyre, turning to watch the men file through the two large doors.

'Rough' replied his sergeant. 'Nothing but four walls and a dirty floor; no lights, the roof's suspect and the whole place is damp as hell. When the lads have settled, we'll get the Platoon together for a quick briefing.'

Their conversation was interrupted by C.S.M. Kettler, shouting orders as he approached.

'Corporal MacIntyre, get your baggage party together and off-load the weapon bundles into the warehouse. The O.C. wants men out on the streets right away.'

'Right Sir. Which wagon are they on?' replied the corporal, stepping off towards the two baggage lorries parked behind the coaches.

'I don't know' replied the Sergeant Major sharply, flicking one arm in the air. 'You loaded the damn things — you tell me.'

MacIntyre stopped short. 'Not my lads, Sir; we were baggage only. I haven't seen the weapon bundles the whole trip.'

'Don't talk bloody nonsense, I detailed you off for baggage and weapons' corrected Kettler, rubbing his hands together, about to address a set of commands to Sam Kyle.

'Not me, Sir; baggage you said and that's what I've been looking after' was Bobby's indignant but respectful reply.

Kettler froze, his expression rapidly altering from puzzlement to panic. With his eyes darting around their sockets, he turned at a run. Halting briefly at the tail-board of the first lorry and finding it already empty, he sprinted to the second. Brushing those unloading aside, he began to burrow about the bags and suitcases.

MacIntyre unhurriedly, for he knew the cupboard to be bare, ambled to the rear of the truck, watching his frantic sergeant major. He, after several moments of fruitless pawing about, stormed off the vehicle red-faced and screaming threats.

'I told you to bring those weapons Corporal MacIntyre, and they're not here. I'm charging you for disobeying a direct order.'

Kettler knew he was to blame, but he also knew he had to cover his back.

'Sir,' pleaded the corporal, spreading his arms in innocence, 'you never mentioned weapons to me.'

'Don't argue with me, Corporal MacIntyre, 'checked Kettler; 'you're in serious trouble as it is. Now where have you left those bundles?'

'I haven't left them anywhere, Sir', replied the dark, stocky corporal, with cold, controlled fury. 'The last time I seen them was when they were stacked outside the Guardroom.'

The sergeant major, being reminded where he had left them, but keeping the truth to himself, sprung into action.

'Sam,' he only used Kyle's first name when he was desperate or in a flap, ''phone, where can I get one quick?'

'Well, there's nothing in the warehouse here', began the sergeant after a moment's thought. 'Our only comms is the radio link. Probably the nearest is at the Police Station where Battalion HQ have set themselves up.'

'Where's that? Which way?' demanded Kettler, turning in several directions at once.

'Down there and across a couple of streets. About a half mile' replied Kyle, lifting an arm to point.

The sergeant major took two steps then stopped, suddenly aware that on that phone the call, and its reason, could well become public to many senior members of the Battalion.

'Too far, Sam, got to be something closer.'

'Well, there's a call box just up around the corner, Sir', offered the sergeant as a second thought, not responding with quite the urgency that his C.S.M. was showing.

'Where? Where? Show me!' ordered Kettler, hurrying off in the direction Sam had nodded.

Considering the local damage done in the recent rioting, the C.S.M. was lucky to get the dial tone he did; the Devil looks after his own.

'Sam, give us your two bob bits', demanded Kettler, half out of the kiosk, the telephone receiver in one hand, his voice a pathetic whinge.

Kyle produced two from his pocket.

'Fuck! This won't do' Kettler stormed with annoyed frustration. Then, seeing MacIntyre and Sinclair approaching, demanded in his lovable way:

'Here you two cunts, empty your pockets. I want all your change.'

Four hundred miles away, Ron Allander reached for his ringing office phone.

'R.Q.M.S.'

'Sir, Sir,' came a desperate, unintroduced voice. 'My baggage party have dropped the Company right in the shit.'

'Oh hello, Jerry' interrupted Allander, leaning back in his chair with a half smile, scratching a hand through his hair. 'I thought I'd be hearing from you fairly rapid.'

'It's our weapon bundles' continued Kettler, not listening to a word Allander said. 'the brainless gits left the fucking lot back there somewhere.'

'No kidding, Private Kettler' broke in Allander with a firm tone, but still smiling.

The joke washed unnoticed over the sergeant major's head.

'Yes! Yes! Sir. Do you think you could track them down? These bastards really dropped me in the cart this time.'

The R.Q.M.S., deciding not to string Kettler along as far as he would have liked, put him out of his misery.

'Calm down, Jerry, you can stop flapping. I've given them to Support Company to bring out to you. Your weapons should be arriving at Aldergrove on one of their flights in about an hour's time. I suggest you get a vehicle up that way sharpish.'

At the other end of the telphone, Charlie Company's sergeant major sagged with relief.

'Oh thank Christ! Thank Christ, Sir! I owe you a drink for that one.' Then returning to his old self, continued 'but that bunch of wankers who were supposed to be looking after the bundle will be getting it in the neck; I'm going to charge the whole pissing lot.'

'Bollocks, Kettler' responded Allander, coming forward onto his desk. 'No fatigue party would have forgotten weapons. You just didn't remember to detail them off as per my instructions.' Silence from the other end.

'Come on! Come on! Admit it.'

Kettler, struggling for an acceptable answer to a man who knew him far too well, was reprieved by the intervention of bleeps indicating the call was about to be terminated, and seized his change to escape.

'Have to go, Sir, got no more change', shooting the receiver onto its cradle.

'Right, Corporal MacIntyre', began Kettler, pushing out of the kiosk to admonish himself of all blame. I've found your weapons. They're to be collected at Aldergrove, but don't think this gets you off the hook. I'm charging you and your fatigue party for failing to comply with a direct order.'

Then leaving the other three standing, he strode off towards the warehouse.

Bobby MacIntyre watched him go for a second, then snapped. For a brief moment he was on the verge of rushing after the man to assault him, but was halted after just a few steps by Sam Kyle, who blocked his path, waving one hand palm downwards as a gesture to calm down.

'I'm going to do that cunt' threatened MacIntyre, in anger.

'Leave it' warned Sam coldly. 'I'll see the O.C., explain the case to him.'

Major Bates did listen to Sam and, once the facts of the charge had been put to him, he also suspected a cover up on his sergeant major's part, but his hands were tied. It was a warrant officer's word against a corporal's, leaving the O.C. no choice but to back Kettler. Bobby MacIntyre was placed on six months formal warning, which meant all promotional prospects were held in limbo and was generally viewed as an uncomfortable situation to be in.

Although the Company knew their C.S.M. to be a prize balloon, any damage done was normally self-inflicted; but now he had gone too far, saving his own skin by possibly jeopardising someone else's career. This was an act that could not pass unavenged, and so it was to be. For awaiting on the horizon was a crusader of justice, a saintly defender of the weak and oppressed, a righter of wrongs and one who would nail Kettler's coffin lid firmly down. It was the Phantom Postman!

*   *   *

5 Para's deployment, like the rest of the several thousand troops rushed into Ulster, was a simple one; that of getting between the two warring communities. Like a khaki garden fence, the soldiers were lined along streets and roadways that were designated boundaries separating defined Roman Catholic and Protestant districts.

Charlie Company's link in the fence ran from a main shopping street, extending out from the commercial heart of Belfast, to finish among rows of burnt out shells that bordered opposing, brick-terraced ghetto areas. In the past, during the days of the Empire, the Army operated a simple procedure in situations like this. Rioters were either dispersed, arrested or shot, and not necessarily in that order; but here on British soil, involving Britons, it was deemed that a more tolerant policy would be adopted.

Although the past rioting had been bloody, resulting in a number of deaths, the two factions now stopped their sectarian attacks on each other: Mainly because the Catholic community saw the Army as a neutral protector, while the Protestants view confrontation with the Queen's soldiers, whom they believed to be on their side, as unacceptable. This is not to say that it ended completely, for events were far too fresh in everyone's minds. There were scores still to be settled, deaths to be avenged.

For the troops, they had entered a phase of their career that one could rightly term as character building. Although their intervention had brought a halt to the inter-community attacks, the Army at the time was not to know this, resulting in an initial policy of blanket occupation of the streets. The men were allocated a section of street which became their home for a number of weeks; that is the pavement, not the bordering houses or shops, just the pavement. There they stood guard, watching and waiting, trying to fathom what all the flapping had been about in rushing them into the Provence just to stand around the street. This proved to be a short limbo period of peace, with a false normality settling over areas that only days before had had crazed rioters burning and looting through them.

*   *   *

Jim Sinclair pushed himself off the door frame he had been leaning against, to step onto the pavement, disturbed by the lock being freed and the door opening.

'Morning, Jim', smiled a brown haired, ten year old girl, holding a small try on which there were four cups. 'Did you get very wet?'

'Morning, Alice, yes some', replied the corporal, cradling his rifle under one arm to accept the tray.

From inside the hallway another voice greeted him, that of a woman who was crouched down, tying the shoe laces of a small boy.

'Hello, Jim, goodness you must have had a terrible night.'

'Not at all, Mrs. McKellen ' grinned back the soldier. 'A doorway to sleep in, a terrific view that stimulates the senses and tea in bed served by a gorgeous little chamber maid. It's better than Butlins.'

'Ah, away with you,' replied the woman, accepting the humorous rejection of her sympathy with a smile. 'Leave the cups by the door when you're finished. I'll make you another before I take the wee'uns to school.'

Placing the tray on a window sill, Jim did not feel as cheeerful as his reply had sounded. Like the rest of the Company, he and his Patrol had been sitting on this street for three days now, with the weather a constant alternation between drizzle and downpour. Pushing the hood of his waterproof anorak back onto his shoulders, he called to the other three members of his Patrol.

'Tea up.'

Reg Berrill, a brown haired, Wiltshireman of medium height, having just finished shaving with cold water from a mess tin, pulled his shirt on to follow his dark haired, Irish mate, Paddy Kieran. The last to arrive did so with a beaming smile that was seldom suppressed. With a shrug to shake the rain from the poncho he wore, 'Yorky' Rush, a tall, heavy-set youth from Hull, took the last of the cups.

'Hot char! Champion, better than bloody roast chicken on Sunday,' then continuing between gulps, 'good kip last night, got a bit of cardboard under me, slept like a good'n. How did you all get on?'

'Smashing', replied Reg Berrill drily, zipping the front of his smock with a shiver. The young Yorkshireman's warm cheeriness was not shared by his three mates. After three days and nights in the damp they were beginning to long for a few basics of life, like four walls, a roof and a bed, whereas, in the short time he had been with Patrol Company, 'Yorky' had shown he could find comfort and slumber in an Alaskan swamp.

Later that morning, shortly after C Company's Colour Sergeant had been around serving a breakfast of cold beans and scrambled eggs from a heavy, insulated hay box, Jim Sinclair became aware of Reg and Paddy speaking to a man in a blue, windproof, quilted jacket. Seeing both his men addressing the stranger in a happy mood, he walked towards their end of the street to investigate but quickly broke into a trot on recognising who it was.

'Fucking hell, Davy' he began his greeting, 'can't you stay away from this poxy Battalion. What are you doing here?'

With hands pushed into his jacket side-pockets, David Urwin turned towards him, returning the greeting in a friendly tone but with a sober expression.

'Hi, Jim. No, I sure as hell didn't come across here to pay a social call. It's the family; with all this trouble about, I'm just settling my mind that everyone's safe.

'Christ! Your folks don't live around here, do they?' replied the Scotsman, concerned that one of the burnt out shells a few streets away may have belonged to his friend's parents.

'No, they're safe enough, over the other side of the Shankill Road, but with all this nonsense about I thought it best to get across and check. It's the sister, Penny; she and her husband are just up the way about half a mile'; Urwin finished with a nod of his head, indicating the direction of his sister's house.

'It's fucking big of Depot letting you have the time off', commented Reg Berrill.

'They don't know', began Dave in a flat tone. 'There's a clamp on all Army personnel travelling across here. Roger Thomson, Recruit Company C.S.M. okayed the leave. I think he knew what I wanted off for, but you know Roger, he didn't say anything, just got my leave pass signed and told me to be back on time.'

'Well, you don't want to hang about here', warned Sinclair. 'If the wrong people see you, you're liable to be bubbled.'

'Ya, I know', agreed the Ulsterman. 'Don't intend staying long. I'm booked back on the ferry tonight. Just thought I'd see how you're getting on before I left. Where's Mick? Got to take the piss out of that big animal before I go.'

'Pridmore', replied Paddy Kieran, raising an arm to point, 'dats him up in the other street, leaning against the lamp post. But be careful, Company HQ is around the next corner.'

'Yah, right, well I'll just have a quick chat with him before I'm off.' Then, with a smile, he turned up the street, leaving his comrades to resume staring at the surrounding, drab brick work. 'You know, tomorrow evening I'll be in Aldershot supping a pint in the Trafalgar.'

The only comment in response to that unappreciated jest came from Jim Sinclair.

'Fuck off, Urwin.'

*   *   *

Late in the afternoon, with the skies opening up in a downpour of rain, Sinclair and the three men of his Patrol were relieved for a rest and a night's sleep in the Company HQ warehouse. Although it was also meant for administration and accommodation, it was plain to see there had been neither time nor manpower to improve its facilities. The yard to the rear of the building was the Company MT park. In one corner of this a small, open-sided shed, aided by hastily erected tarpaulins, was being utilised by Colour Sergeant Simpkin as a cooking area. Here the Company's two cooks struggled from meal time to meal time over metal dixies and petrol-fired No. 1 burners, boiling, frying, washing, peeling, producing food for men who had little else to look forward to. As for the interior of the warehouse, conditions were even less welcoming. The rain streamed in through missing or broken roof slates to spread in puddles, seeking out the floor cracks. leaving all three of its levels sodden and water-logged.

As Sinclair's party entered the building's ground floor through a doorless archway, they were met by Sam Kyle. A Stirling sub-machine gun in one hand, aluminium mug and mess tin in the other, he was on his way to collect his tea meal.

'Just been relieved?' he asked in a matter-of-fact tone.

The corporal's answer was a silent puckering of the lips with a nod of the head.

'Here, I'll show you where you doss down', volunteered Kyle, turning back the way he had come. 'We're only using the upstairs floors; down here it's like a fucking bog.'

This was plain enough for the newcomers to see, for the building's floor was only visible through the odd island of concrete not yet submerged by a shallow sea of rainwater.

Threading a course through the low water areas, Sam lead the way towards a staircase.

'The billet for the Rifle Platoons is the top floor', continued Sam as they arrived on the first landing. Here we got the HQ Command Post, Officers and Senior/N.C.O.s accommodation and stores.' As he talked his head jerked towards cubicles that had been partitioned off from each other with canvas, blankets and odd bits of timber.

'The driest place we could find for you Patrol people to kip down on is around the back of those pillars, past the TV area. Mick and his crew are already there. When you've picked a spot to get your head down on come back, collect your sea kit bags from the Colour Sergeant, then go get some scoff.'

With that Kyle left them for his own meal.

Jim's party followed him past a television set mounted at head height on two large crates. To shield it from the constant dripping from the floor above a teepee of ponchos and polythene sheeting had been rigged around it. Half a dozen men, sitting on boxes and planks, also draped in ponchos, solemnly ate their tea meal from mess tins whilst watching a children's puppet show.

'Presidential suite, eh', commented Reg Berrill on arriving in their area.

Mick Pridmore, lying on a sleeping bag, his head propped on a bergen, looked up from reading a two day old paper.

'Stay away from the windows, when the wind blows the rain pisses through', warned the big man.

'Christ, I just left a drier doorway than this', stated Paddy Kieran, wearily surveying the dripping roof and puddled floor in the unlit gloom.

'Yorky' Rush, undaunted by the damp, could only see the potential of this dank palace.

'No bother here; get the ponchos out, rig a basher between these posts, punch a couple of holes in the floor with a pick to drain off the water and we'll be as comfy as kittens.'

'Aye', agreed Sinclair, seeing no alternative as he cast his bergen to the floor.

'Let's have scoff first, then we'll get stuck in.'

*　　　　　*　　　　　*

For the next fortnight a shift routine was introduced, by which the men found themselves spending two days on the perimeter line, then one off duty in the warehouse. Higher authorities were hoping that gradually the Army's presence could be withdrawn, the Police taking over, and then hopefully things reverting to normal. However, this proved to be nothing more than cuckoo land dreams. The future 'normal' was soon to be unleashed violence.

A foretaste of this was given to C Company as they entered their second month in the Provence. Given the good news that 5 Para were to remain in their Belfast location for a further four months, extending then into January of 1970, the Battalion began to thin out on the ground and concentrate on turning the Company's warehouses, factories and mills into habitable accommodation.

Over the weeks, soldiers at all levels had been lulled by the absence of unrest. Except for the odd drunken bar fight or domestic squabble, the troops had little to occupy them. Because of this their presence was reduced to two-man unarmed foot patrols roaming the area with a radio and one pick handle, plus guard duties on Company location entrances and key street junctions. For some days an autumn hot spell had basked Belfast in warm, humid days and sultry, sticky evenings. This not only brought people onto the streets but kept them there until late at night. Whilst most were content just to enjoy the warmth, others found it an opportunity to start aggro.

The warning to C Company that an incident was brewing in their area came from one of the standing junction pickets.

'Hello Three, this is Three Zulu, over.'

The Duty Signaller, sitting at a table with two C42 radio sets on it, looked up from the paperback western to answer the call.

'Three! Send, over.'

'Three four Zulu, have we been told about a street party or some sort of gathering that's going on up the street from me? Over.'

'Wait one', replied the Signaller, turning his head to give Sam Kyle an inquisitive look.

Sam was the Duty Watch Keeper, but before he could answer the O.C. stepped in.

The Command post room was small and should have been out of bounds to everyone not on duty, but because it had an electric point where water could be boiled it had become a rest area for Officers and S.N.C.O.s while drinking coffee.

'Tell him no, and ask him why he asks', directed Major Bates, interrupting his conversation with Jerry Kettler.

'Hello, three four Zulu referemce street party. No! Why? Over', replied the Signaller, clearly but simply.

'Three four Zulu, for the last ten minutes we've had loud shouting coming from the top end of Symore Street, over.'

The Signaller did not reply, but instead looked at his O.C.

'Ask them... No, here let me speak', decided the Major, standing up to take the Signaller's microphone and press the transmission button.

'Hello three four Zulu, this is three niner, can you see who or what is causing this noise? Over.'

'Three four Zulu, no, it seems to be off one of the side streets. Over.'

'That could either be Billow or Sackwall Street, Sir', offered Kyle, standing up to track his finger over a large scale street map pinned to the wall above the radios.

'Roger three four Zulu', continued the O.C., acknowledging the sergeant's words with a raised hand. 'Keep us informed if anything develops. Meanwhile we'll try to find out more at our end, over.'

'Three four Zulu. Roger out.'

'Sergeant Kyle, get on to Battalion by phone. See if they know anything', ordered the major, then to the Signaller: 'Calder, give the Foot Patrol a buzz and have them get around to the top end of Symore Street to find out what's up.'

Having set enquiries in motion, he sat down to finish his coffee.

After some minutes Sam replaced the telephone receiver, telling his O.C. that Battalion could only give him a negative reply.

Calder was also having no success; repeatedly calling the Foot Patrol call sign over the net to be answered only by the odd electrical crackle and a constant, low mush.

Mildly frustrated, Sam Kyle picked up the radio's hand set.

'Here Calder, I'll have a try. Maybe their radio is U.S.'

'Hello, all stations three, has anyone recently seen call sign three five Romeo? Over.'

There was a pause before replies began coming in, in alphabetical order.

'Three four Whiskey, no, over.'

'Three four Yankee. They left us about figures one five minutes ago, moving to the north of Symore Street on their way to three four Zulu's location, over.'

'Three four Zulu, no! Over.'

'It could be a domestic barney and the Foot Patrol is caught up in trying to sort the buggers out', offered Kettler, more as a joke than a theory.

'No' replied Major Bates abruptly. 'My standing orders are that the men will not get involved in any street incidents', clarifying a point that, as Company Sergeant Major, Kettler should have known.

Then turning to Sam he asked, 'who is the Foot Patrol?'

Calder, reaching for the day's duty roster sheet, had a quick glance, them began to laugh as he handed it to the sergeant.

'Oh Jesus, it's Haydon and Ottoway' exclaimed Sam, bolting upright in his chair.

'What! Who put those two clowns out together?' demanded Kettler loudly to the room's four walls.

The O.C., also showing concern, began to take the situation seriously.

'Sergeant Major, take over as Duty Watch Keeper. Sergeant Kyly, collect the standby Section and meet me at the main entrance in five minutes.'

For the last three streets there was no need to seek the Foot Patrol out. Major Bates lead the way at a run towards the sound of loud shouting. On turning a final corner they found the two soldiers fifty yards further on in the centre of the street, defiantly standing their ground. A stones throw to their front stood a mob of jeering youths, and it was a measured stone throw for lumps of bricks were being exchanged between the two. Although out numbered, any advance by the yobs was quickly checked by Haydon, who would simply take a pace forward while raising his pick handle – an invitation to come and get a caved in skull.

'What the bloody hell are you two playing at?' demanded the officer, arriving breathlessly at the two men's side.

'Its these cunts, Sir, they started to have a go at us', answered Ottoway, surprised to see the O.C. at his elbow.

'Well, what's the idea of trying to take them on on your own? Why didn't you call for assistance; is your radio working?'

'Ya, it's alright, Sir. We've just been too busy with this lot', replied Haydon, pointing his pick handle at the mob.

'Look' began Bates, with visible anger. 'It's not your job to get invoved in street fights. You should have pulled back and informed the Company of the

48

situation.'

'Well fuck me, Sir, that would have looked as if we were running away', protested Ottoway.

'No matter' continued the Major. 'Because of your incompetence the rest of us have been completely in the dark. I've a good mind to have the both of you charged.'

'But Sarg. . .'

'Shut up.'

The crowd of youths. who on seeing the arrival of reinforcements had initially shrunk back, now thought, with no action from the Paras, that they could continue the game, and began gathering bits of brick.

Bates, sensing the mob was not being intimidated by he and his men's presence, decided to disperse them.

'Sargeant Kyle, take your men forward and chase that rabble away.'

This was just what the soldiers wanted to hear; a chance to take their built up frustration out on something with flesh and blood.

Sam, holding his arms outwards, arranged his duty Section across the street in an extended line, and then with a sharp command ordered them forward. To begin with it was at walking pace, but as the mob turned away they began to run. The chase was short and fruitless for their prey, running around corners and up alleys, literally disappeared into brick walls.

Unknown to C Company, this little incident was but the beginning of street violence which, over the following week of hot weather, was to increase building up and spilling out to crash about like uncontrolled flood waters.

This occurred solely in the Protestant areas, possibly due to the anger of the criminally inclined and hot-tempered people who resented the Police, and their authority being maintained over them, while the Catholic ghetto areas had none. The show would start about mid-evening, with the sun dropping behind the Black Mountains, drawing those who wished for mischief out into the shadowed streets.

*　　　　*　　　　*

'Okay now, listen; we're going to swing left at the next junction into Sutcliffe Street.'

None of Bobby MacIntyre's Section bothered to respond to his warning instructions, for they were in a sullen, unhappy mood. Being on standby, they had all been watching 'Top of the Pops' on the location television, but then, just as Pans People came on to raise everyone's temperature by gyrating like crazy in skimpy dresses, they had been called out.

'Willie, tell Control we're in Sutcliffe moving north', directed the corporal to his Aberdonian Signaller, walking a few paces to his rear . The reply was a simple confirmation, giving him no clue or guidance as to where they could expect to find the source of the disturbance they were supposed to be investigating.

Wheeling his seven men in a loose formation into a side street, they found most of the occupants standing at their front doors. Each household advertised the fact that they were staunchly British: For every curb stone was painted alternately red, white and blue, while Union Jacks and Saint George's crosses fluttered above doorways.

On seeing the soldiers, everyone began to cheer and applaud. With shouts of 'Well done. lads' and 'Up the Paras', Bobby's Patrol passed through, smiling and nodding, some receiving pats on the back.

With everyone walking a few inches taller, the Patrol again swung around a corner into an adjoining street.

Here the mood took a sudden reversal. Because of more flags and bright paint work the men kept the smile on their faces, expecting a repeat of the reception from the last street, but had MacIntyre and his Section studied the slogans painted on walls, 'No Pope here' and 'Up King Billy', they might have realised they were walking into a hard, militant, Loyalist street. No friendly cheers or kind comments greeted them, instead it was hostile stares and cold silence. As they passed, those watching began following up behind, a steady murmur building as the crowd swelled.

'Why don't you cunts get down the Lover Falls and sort those bastards out?'

'We don't fucking wan'ch here, get out and stay out.'

With the verbal abuse increasing, the Paras began to quicken their footsteps until their speed was just less that that of running. The crowd, pressing close behind, also increased its pace. When stones began to land amongst them, the Paratroopers broke into a run. The mob, men, women and children, with a primitive tribal chant that chilled the blood, took up pursuit.

The Patrol, that only a minute earlier had been cheered and applauded, were now fleeing before a ghoulish mass.

The Section's Signaller, Willie Durrant, came the closest to falling into their howling clutches. For with the extra weight of the heavy A41 Radio he was soon overtaken, and out-strethed hands pulled at his equipment and smock, whilst a woman's fingnails raked one cheek. Bobby MacIntyre, glancing over his shoulder, rescued him by halting and bringing his rifle up into the aim, pointing it from one blood-crazed face to another. Threatened with the rifle, the front of the mob baulked for a second but that was just long enough for MacIntyre's Section to gain a safe lead. Turning at the run, Bobby sprinted after his men, who suddenly ran into the protective arms of a Platoon from B Company. Having again taken up the chase, on seeing the appearance of reinforcements, the savages pulled up and then sullenly melted back to a safe distance.

The C Company Patrol, ignoring the jokes and snipes directed at them by their rescuers, silently thanked the Saints for their escape, while trying to justify the terror that had overcome them all. Willie Durrant sank, panting, his legs unable to hold his weight, into a hunched sitting position on the pavement. Bobby MacIntyre had had also found the situation unnerving, never remembering in all his years of past service, ever being so frightened, even under fire.

With a screech of brakes, the Battalion Commanding Officer arrived in his tactical, stripped-down Landrover. Leaping out, he first spoke to the B Company Platoon Commander and then called MacIntyre over to him.

'What the hell's been going on here, Corporal MacIntyre?' demanded to C.O..

Bobby, explaining what had happened, brought the colonel to a boil.

'You mean they chased you out of the street?'

'Like animals, Sir. I came very close to squeezing a round into them. If I hadn't made them think I meant business, they would have ripped my Signaller to pieces', explained the corporal.

'I'm not having this', was the officer's response, speaking through clenched teeth as he turned back to his Landrover.

After several minutes, giving directions over his Command radio, he returned to give MacIntyre and his Section the outline plan he was shortly to put into operation.

'Right Corporal MacIntyre, this is what's going to happen. The bulk of your Company will be here shortly. I will be positioning them in the side streets here. What I want you and your men to do is make your way back into that street, and then lure that crowd of goons back down here, where I and the rest of your Company can pounce on them and arrest some of the ringleaders. Understood?'

He then stopped only long enough to hear Bobby's weak, disbelieving reply of 'right, Sir', before moving off to put the B Company Platoon Commander in the picture.

As the corporal glanced up the street to find the crowd had now withdrawn out of sight, his Section began to voice their feelings.

'I'm not going back up there, C.O. or no C.O.. He can get stuffed.'

'No fear, me neither.'

'For fuck's sake, Bobby, he can't be serious.'

'You heard the man. If he says we go, we go!' shot back MacIntyre, knowing the order would have to be obeyed.

It was Durrant who put the whole thing in its correct prospective.

'Bobby, if we go back up that street, I'm going to splatter one of those bastards all over the pavement. Am I fuck going to be chased like that again!'

Half an hour later they did go, but this time all streets were empty. The reason for this was because the mob had moved up onto the Shankhill Road, where a large gathering was building up. Here, for a few hours, they blocked streets, hindered traffic, obstructed and assaulted the Police and generally acted in a riotous manner.

The next evening there was a repeat performance but with greater numbers. The Army was wisely kept away from all this, fearing their presence could inflame the mobs even more. It was left to the Police to cool and disperse the hot-headed trouble seekers. This they were unable to do, thanks to a policy which did not allow them to use excessive force.

The following evening the Police played an even lesser part, keeping well back from the fringes of the crowd. This was on the request of leading members of the Orange Order. They, seeing the escalating violence each evening, had asked that they be allowed to go in and talk with the crowd in an attempt to reason with them. As members of an honored and respected organisation it was hoped the rioters would comply with their pleas and return to their homes. A noble act, but an unwise one.

For the rioters were members of an even older organisation, the Ulster branch of the 'international body of mindless louts'. For over an hour, with the sincerest of intentions, singly or in small groups, they talked, joked, cajoled, remonstrated and argued, cooly doing their utmost to persuade the crowd to disperse. With abuse and threats steadily mounting from ringleaders and fringe-station agitators, these samaritans of the Orange Lodge were forced to give up, but refused to run. As the mob's restlessness increased, the more fanatical began shouting for a march to be made down the Shankhill Road to burn the Catholics out of the Unity Flats, a complex in the heart of a Protestant area. Realising that the Police would not be able to stop this mass of several thousand should it suddenly decide to surge forward, the members of the Orange Lodge blocked their route be linking arms in ranks across the Shankhill.

Their line was formed just in time, for the mob had begun to move. At first they pushed and cursed. but when this failed to gain them a passage punches and kicks were used. With arms linked in order to hold the line, the Orangemen took the blows without flinching. From a nearby timber yard lengths of wood were brought forward with which to club and ram the front ranks. These brave bowler-hatted men, proudly wearing their orange sashed badges of office angled across their chests, stood firm. A number went down unconscious, bleeding and in pain, but their places were quickly taken by others pushing through from the rear.

The attackers were finally chased away by an assault out of a side street by a small but determined knot of baton wielding Policeman.

The crowd simmered at a distance for a time but gradually, in groups and pairs, thy began to melt away.

Jim Sinclair, with his three man Patrol and a driver, mounted in an open Landrover, had been monitoring the disturbance from a side street since early evening. Although not deploying the Army for fear of escalating the situation, the authorilties were allowing them to discreetly observe but but not become involved. With a splinter group of noisy youths breaking away from the area of the disturbance to make their way down his street, Jim ordered the driver to reverse back to the next junction. The driver complied until he got one wheel too close to the curb, stalling the engine. Sinclair, looking over to watch the driver fumbling with the ignition, did not notice the lead youths running forward to hurl stones and bits of brick in their direction. With the windscreen folded down, the missile that struck the corporal, knocking him senseless, had a clear path to its target. Jim only fleetingly heard Reg Berrill's shouted warning before he went out.

Swearing loudly the three Patrol Company soldiers leapt from the vehicle, Paddy Kieran grabbing Sinclair as he began to tumble out of the front passenger's seat into the street. Berrill and Rush ran several steps forward of the Landrover, the Yorkshireman picking up one of the thrown stones return it back to its owner, while Reg, bringing his rifle into the aim, threw a challenge at the yobs.

'You bastards, want'a play, then come a little closer and I'll give you something to play with.'

Looking down the business end of two rifles, the stone throwers pulled up, some retreating several steps.

Paddy Kieran, propping up Jim Sinclair in the front seat of the Landrover, pulled a field dressing from his smock pocket, quickly applying it to a wide cut Jim had received to his forehead.

Jim's eyes were closed and as he worked with the bandage, Kieran fired questions at his corporal hoping for a verbal response. Completing his medical task the Irishman took command, first giving orders to the driver.

Stevie, get dis wagon turned around. Jims out cold, we got'a get him back to the location fast.'

Then, holding Sinclair in his arms as the driver spun the vehicle around, he called in his protection party.

'Reg! Yorky! Get aboard we're taking Jim back.'

As the two men leapt into the Landrover, Kieran reached out with a free hand towards the radio.

'Hello four Foxtrot, over.'

'Send, over' came back the Company operator.

'Four Foxtrot, am returning to location with a casualty, head wound and unconscious, will require Starlight assistance, over.'

With the Landrover speeding away the stone throwers celebrated with cheers and jeers. Berrill and Rush just stared back defiantly, each silently vowing revenge.

*   *   *

The following evening the mobsters found the Police had sealed off the Shankhill Road, depriving them of their main assembly area. This effectively neutralised any mass disturbances there but caused frustrated minor mobs to look elsewhere for a quarrel.

Charlie Company, who along with the rest of 5 Para, had been on standby since late afternoon, were now deployed to key junctions which could give access for the trouble makers into Catholic areas. At one of these points, a street crossroads, a steady build up yobs, youths and young children began. At first they did little, shouting threats and making faces but as agitators appeared the crowd became braver, pushing forward. The Commander on the spot, a sergeant with two Sections fron 7 Platoon, lined his men across the street entrance in an attempt to block it. But as the atmosphere became ugly, with the odd stone being thrown at them, he pulled his men back to the centre of the road junction, while radioing for assestance.

This, at first, was Major Bates with his Rover group who arrived to assess the situation, followed shortly by Sam Kyle and his 8 Platoon. The O.C., once he was satisfied with the deployment of his men, stepped into the centre of the junction in the hope of starting a dialogue with some of the ringleaders. He knew that if he could ger them talking there was a good chance things would calm down and perhaps the crowd would drift away. A fair assumption in most cases, but Bates, like the rest of the Army, was as yet unfamiliar with the fact that the Ulster mob was immune to reason, communicating only in abusive insults and demands.

The Paras, despite what their O.C. was trying to do, wished for only one thing: That they be let loose to flatten this bunch of goons. Although out-numbered ten to one, they did not care; numbers meant nothing to them, all they wanted to do was get some of their own back for all the hassle they had gone through over the last few weeks. Standing quietly on their side of the junction they watched. Gone was the bulky webbed equipment; instead they were stripped for freedom of movement to a single ammunition pouch on their belt. Because of possible injuries from stones each wore a helmet, their weapons were rifles, a number of baton guns and for each soldier a wooden riot truncheon tucked under their belts. The rifles, being held in the low ready position, was secured to one wrist with the looped end of their rifle sling so that it could not be snatched away in a close crowd situation.

Major Bates, predictably, was not having much success. With patience and controlled anger he presented sensible, non-violent suggestions and alternatives, whilst pointing out that they were breaking the law because under the Emergency Powers Act this large gathering was illegal. The reward for this brave endeavour was abuse, vile threats and bigotted, anti-Catholic statements.

When the O.C. came out to speak to the crowd he initially stood alone, but as a red-faced, drunken brute, with a nose like a King Edward potato, pushed forward to make demands while poking his finger into the Major's chest, Pearson, the Company Clark, took up a position one pace from his O.C., a hand on the wooden baton in his belt.

Thus occupied, Bates was unaware that the mob, as well as increasing, was also beginning to filter its way up one of the streets. Mick Pridmore, having arrived with his Patrol and the three members of Jim Sinclair's, spotted this and moved his men out to that flank. As they stationed themselves, one of the low life youths brazenly came forward to sit in the street just to Reg Berrill's front. There he sat for some minutes, mouthing curses and spitting in Reg's direction. Pridmore, seeing this, gave a cautionary command.

'Ignore the cunt, Reg.'

Berrill did.

The lance corporal now looked around the area, assessing the situation that was steadily mushrooming, At all points the mob was pressing in and moving down side streets in an attempt to get around the soldiers. With the O.C. tied down in arguments, unaware of what was happening outside his immidiate field of vision, Pridmore decided to bring things to a head.

Stepping into the street, he crouched on his haunches to address the re-headed low life still sitting in front of Berrill.

'Okay chum, its time you went back across the street and joined your mates.'

'Fuck ya' was his reply, followed by an attempt to spit on the soldier.

'You got two choices' continued Pridmore, 'Either go back to your buddies or I'll plug ya with this,' He held up his riot baton gun in both hands.

'Go screw yourself', came back the foul reply.

Mick, cocking the hammer with his thumb and pushing the safety catch to fire, raised the weapon into the aim. The red-headed yob four feet away just smirked back, knowing full well the Army would never fire on members of the Protestant community. The baton gun was a short, single-barrelled weapon designed to fire tear gas canisters, but it was also capable of firing hard rubber bullets in order to disperse rioters. Fired at a distance the rubber projectile gave a painful blow, but to date few people in C Company had witnessed the damage inflicted at close quarters, not that is until Mick squeezed the trigger.

Blinking through the smoke, Pridmore now found Red-head lying on his back, his limbs cocked in the posture of a dead beetle, unconscious and bleedinbg from ruptured skin on his forehead where the rubber bullet had sledge-hammered him backwards, The rest of the Company, who at that moment were desperate for any excuse to have a go, interpreted that single shot as a priority War Office directive to attack. With a line of airborne smocks charging forward, Pearson stepped up to his O.C.'s elbow and in the same movement drew his wooden baton. He shouted: 'Look out, Sir',then crashed it down on Potato Nose's skull, like a Samurai sword, decking him onto the street.

'Sorry, Sir', apologised the Company Clerk, trying to cover his unprovoked action. 'I thought he was going to hit you.'

This was hardly needed for war had broken out all around them, the Paras wading in gleefully with rifle butts, batons, boots and bare fists. The mischievous mob of trouble seekers reacted in much the same way as all rabble reacts when faced with determined force; they ran. With shocked surprise showing on the faces of those in front, they turned to get away. However, the ones in the rear, unaware of what was coming at them, hesitated, causing a minor log jam of bodies. Into this the soldiers flung themselves, bludgeoning flesh and bone in all directions. With casualties scattered all over the street. Many were caught in alleys and doorways, receiving painful blows and broken limbs from men lacking sympathy. For most the only escape was to run, but some sought sanctuary in their homes or those of friends. This proved fateful for the red veil had come down; the Paras were respecting neither boundaries nor shrines. The hunt was continued into hallways, kitchens and backyards.'York' Rush followed his chosen prey up a flight of stairs and into a bedroom. When he dived under the bed, this was quickly upended into a corner. When York returned to the street he left his victim sprawled, battered, bleeding and moaning amongst a number of used French letters and the spillings from a bed pan.

'No Way' Ottoway and Phil Haydon chased two youths up a side street to see them dash into one of the houses. Without checking his gallop, Ottoway crashed through the unlocked door into the hall. In the livingroom was a normal domestic family scene. The father sat in an easy chair reading a paper, the mother likewise knitting, and a young daughter lying on her stomach watching television. Sitting on a couch with their backs to the door, chests heaving, taking in sharp breaths of air, eyes glued to the television screen, were the two youths. Because of the noise at the front door, the family looked up to see the two Paratroopers, wooden batons raised, springing into the room like Batman and Robin, to begin pulverising the two young men into the family settee.

Unable to restrain or control his men's rush, Major Bates became little more than a spectator. Dragging Kettler away from one of the more foul-mouthed women, whom he had knocked to the ground and was now beating senseless, the Major ordered him to round up the Rover group. The rest of the Company he left to the Senior N.C.O.s and corporals, hoping they would do their duty and herd everyone back.

As they returned, giggling and smiling, Major Bates reprimanded each one for losing control and charging away like mad fools. But secretly he was extremely proud of them. His attempt at talking the crowd down had failed, leaving himself exposed and with no options. The men, God bless them, had dealt with the situation in the only way that remained possible. Relieved to see that no one had returned with scalps tucked into thier belts, the O.C. stood the bulk of the Company down, returning to normal patrolling.

Over the next two evenings the soldiers of Charlie Company eagerly awaited a return match, but the other team would not come out and play. Then the weather broke, Autumn squalls raced in on high winds from the Atlantic to be followed daily by banks of heavy black clouds that spilled sheets of icy rain onto Belfast's cheerless streets.

Violence-wise this was just the job, clearing the streets like a tear gas shell; winter was now approaching and the campaigning season was over.

*   *   *

On the visitor's bell ringing to allow visitors into the ward, Jim Sinclair covered his naked lower limbs with a sheet. The wound he had received from the stone, although having to be closed with a dozen stitches, was not serious. However, on detecting a hair-line crack in the bone above his right eye, the civilian doctors of the Royal Victorian Hospital made the cautionary decision to keep him under observation for a week or so.

Glancing towards the doorway and seeing no one from Battalion who might be visiting, he resumed reading his paperback. The only person making her way to the top beds was an attractive woman in the advanced stages of pregnancy. She was in her early twenties, with light brown, shoulder length hair.

'Hello Jim, how are you feeling?'

Looking up, Sinclair found the woman at his bedside. 'Ahh' he replied, unable to register identification.

'I bet you're surprised to see me here', she continued.

'Yes ye....' stuttered Sinclair.

'After all we did only have that one night together, but it was fantastic', the woman confirmed this by wiggling her shoulders. 'Luckily I found out you were in here from your HQ people.'

Puzzled, Jim just stared blankly.

'You know I had a devil of a time trying to find you. At one stage I thought I wouldn't be able to locate you until after the happy event'. signalling her meaning by placing a hand on the large bulge pushing out from under her pleated maternity dress.

Suddenly realising what was being implied, Jim's body went rigid. The book slipping from his fingers, he rose to 10,000 feet, flapping like a budgie, whilst shifting names and faces like a computer. 'That girl at the party in Frimley last March ... took her home ... had it away in the car ... No! No! She had black hair, and this girl has an Irish accent ... That Q.A. Army nurse then ... picked her up in the Queens ... took me back to the billet ... spent all night in her bunk ... no can't be, she was shorter ...'

Within the corporal's head, in frustrated desperation, his mind began to scream. 'Who the hell is she then? Who the fucking hell is she?'

As if in answer to his silent, pathetic cry, the young women stopped relating the details of how she had tracked him down to give a slowly unfolding, peaches and cream smile.

'You don't really know who I am, do you, Jim Sinclair?'

'Oh, Aye! Aye!...' he began, playing for time whilst hoping for a clue.

'Penny Roberts', came the answer.

Sinclair gave a blank look.

'David's sister', she prompted.

Still nothing registered.

'David Urwin, your mate; you were his best man at his wedding, before you all went off to Borneo. You danced with me.' The peaches and cream smile returned but this time the eyes had a wicked twinkle.

Hearing this, Sinclair melted into his pillow and sheets, a hiss of air escaping his lips. But only for an instant. Bolting upright, his eyes flashed sparks.

'Who put you up to this little stunt?' demanded the Scot angrily, answering his own question: 'It was Davy wasn't it? That brother of yours.'

'Oh calm down, James. I thought Paras were supposed to be able to take a joke', replied the young woman, easing her unaccustomed bulk into a bedside chair. 'Besides, you have nothing to feel guilty about , have you?' The wicked twinkle re-appeared in her eyes.

Gradually Sinclair began to cool down, unable to remain mad at someone with a smile as lovely as hers.

'I'm going to banjo that brother of yours', warned Jim, lying back to stare at the ceiling.

Penny reached into the shopping bag she had carried into the ward to produce a banana, placing it in his hand.

'Here, shut up and get this down you.'

Sinclair looked at the fruit and then at the woman with her disarming smile.

'You enjoyed that little act, didn't you?' unable to supress the beginning of his own smile.

'You should have seen the look on your face', she teased. 'Eat your banana.'

Holding it up, he began to peel back the thick yellow skin, returning her unsympathetic banter.

'Mrs. Roberts, you're a bitch.'

*   *   *

With the onset of cold days and long nights and the total lack of facilities both for training and otherwise, the Army in Nothern Ireland settled into a state of stagnation. Committed to remaining at full strength at all times because of possible renewed flare-ups, a trip home on a spell of local leave of any length was forbidden.

In order to get to grips with the accommodation short-commings, the Commanding Officer told the Q.M. who had taken over an exhibition hall bordering a golf course for his HQ, to get around the locations and submit to him an assessment of repairs and maintenance that would have to me done.

C Company's warehouse was typical of what the Army was expected to live in, and required a lot of work and expense. To offset the cost, and because the men had to be kept occupied, a programme of self help was implemented with a list of priorities drawn up. The repair of leaking floors and roofs, a proper dining hall, lighting everywhere, showers and wash basins, billets with beds, all vital to the needs of the men, and of course in time an all ranks bar. The men, quickly assessing this list, built the bar first!

With little to do and boredom taking a strangle hold, this bar soon became the major social point of the location. Although unable to see female company during their off duty periods, the men did have the opportunity while on foot patrols or occupying a check point. This resulted in invitations being given to come around to the Company bar. As word spread, the girls flooded in and every night became a disco night. The men no longer complained of Belfast and this operational confinement, for each evening their bar would be packed, with wall to wall fanny.

The only ones who dipped out on all the frolicing was the handful of soldiers who each evening were detailed off as the night's gate guard.

Christopher Braithwaite, 7 Platoon's resident potential officer, stepped out of his small shelter to prod the coals of the metal brazier which was his only means of keeping warm. His duty, although accepted as a necassary function, was becoming but a token gesture.

As soon as the bar/disco opened a stream of girls flooded through the gate. A list of guide rules had been laid down by the O.C. governing the control of all this buckshee talent, like each one having to be signed in by a member of the company. But this was hard to enforce and was soon kicked into touch by men too randy to comply.

Braithwaite was happy enough to be on guard for he had no wish to be involved in the nightly programme of drinking, dancing and screwing, that continued non-stop until the compusory closing time of 23.00 hours. Not one to drink much, preferring to listen to music rather than dance to it, and finding the Irish girls abominably uncouth, he would occupy his evenings reading or writing.

Placing the metal rod that was his poker to one side, the young soldier clapped his hands and then held them out to absorb the warmth from the glowing coals he had just stirred. Looking up, he watched as a man and a young child came towards him, moving from one pool of street lamp light to another.

The street, being a main thoroughfare used by both Catholics and Protestants moving between the main Belfast shopping centre and their respective areas, was always well travelled.

Seeing Braithwaite as he passed on the opposite pavement, the man pulled the child to a halt and changed his route towards the guard.

Braithwaite watched this thing of humble ghetto stock wobble in his direction, dragging the child by one hand, all the time staring straight at the Para's face in drunken determination. Dressed in an old, worn suit, heavy with urban grime, his unshaven, bar-room pale and lined face concealed his age somewhere between thirty-five and sixty-five. The child, a girl of four or five, matched the man's appearance; greasy matted hair and dirty light green coat.

The man hailed Braithwaite in a drunken voice with the traditional greeting of someone with entrenched Republican feelings.

'English bastard.'

The young man, deciding it unnecessary to dispute that he was neither, for his parent's wedding licence clearly stated a satisfactory date and both to be Welsh, instead took a more passive approach to the remark.

'Time the youngster was in bed, don't you think, sir?'

'Why don't you's fuck off back to your own country and leave us alone?' demanded the man, ignoring Braithwaite's suggestion.

He, unable to reason the sense of this remark, responded with the logical reply.

'As long as there is civil unrest, sir, we will have to remain.'

'Unrest', the other scoffed. 'It's you's bastards dat cause unrest. Ireland was a happy and peaceful place until that murder'on, Protestant swine, Cromwell, started his killin'.'

'Well, yes, there is no question of that', agreed Braithwaite, bringing his public school history knowledge into play. 'But I must point out that he also executed a large number of Englishmen as well. Besides the Vikings and Normans inflicted for more slaughter on...'

'Then that other murder'on orange bastard, King fucking Billy', interrupted the Irishman, deaf to any argument. 'He comes across here with his army of butchers.'

'Yes, of course, but he reacted in response to local pressures and because of Continental influence out...' persisted Braithwaite, believing truthful fact would win his argument, but he was again cut off.

'Then when Napoleon sent an army across ta free us from your English slavery, what do ya do?' was the next atrocity thrown up. The man paused and then answered his own question. 'Hang and butcher the poor lads who tried to help. Dat's bloody what.'

'Yes, a black page of Irish history', agreed Braithwaite, 'but then how else would you deal with rebels? We did have our hands full with France at the time, you know', continued the young soldier, still trying to make the man see broader historical implications.

The drunk, sick of always being given a reply, decided to kill the younger man off with a question the Paratrooper would never give a believable answer to.

'What about da potato famine den? When da bastard English landlords poisoned da crops to kill us all off. Ya can't deny dem facts.'

Braithwaite did not reply. In fact he could not speak. Something within him had suddenly and uncontrollably begun to come apart. Releasing his rifle, the veins in his neck bulging, both hands began to form claws.

Reg Berrill, locked in mutual grope in the shadows of the gate wall with the tart he had been knocking off for the last few evenings, found himself being interrupted by a tug on his pant leg. Extricating his tongue from the back of his partner's throat, he looked down to see a dirty faced young girl in a dirty pale green coat pleading at him.

'Soja! Soja!

'Fuck off' was Reg's initial response, nudging his knee away from her hand. But she persisted, again grabbing a tiny handful of olive drab material.

' Ma dada! He's killin' ma Dada.!

'What?' was Berrill's annoyed reply.

'Ma Dada! Ma Dada!' continued the child desperately, one hand attempting to pull him along, the other pointing out the gate.

Reg, his sexual intentions disturbed, now became aware of someone shouting in a hysterical manner from just outside the location.

Knowing only one man to be on guard, he thought it best to investigate. With the little girl half dragging him, he broke from his bird's embrace, waving away her protest with a promise to shortly return.

On passing through the gateway, Berrill's steps first slowed and then stopped, as he tried to comprehend the scene. Two men were sprawled on the ground. Braithwaite, his beret missing, was sitting on someones chest, his hands around his throat. The young girl, no longer waiting for Reg, ran forward to plant feeble kicks in the Paratrooper's ribs whilst tugging at his smock in an attempt to drag him off. Braithwaite, impervious to this, had the Irishman on the verge of death, his hands clamped around the man's neck while screaming vile suggestions.

'Fuck King Billy, fuck the Pope, fuck Cromwell, and fuck you, ya stinking Irish dirt box.'

Poor Christopher, he had just become the latest Ulster casualty. Gone forever was his naive public school assumptions that everyone on planet Earth is basically good and that all differences can be solved by understanding and reason. From now on Braithwaite would no longer attempt to talk a situation out; in future Ulster tours anyone who would not do as he said first time, he would hit.

Of course this unprovoked assault was reported to the Police by the Irishman, resulting in Braithwaite being marched in front of the Commanding Officer for disciplining. The C.O. listened to his explanation of why he went beserk through trying to reason with a moronic imbecile, but although he understood, the C.O. had no choice. He punished him with a twenty pound stoppage of pay and, because the act cast doubt on his character, his application for Commission was postponed for re-submittal at a latter date.

The only consolation Chris Braithwaite gained from this was that at last he had become one of the lads.

CHAPTER 4

Ere yet we loose the legions . . .
Ere yet we draw the blade,
Jehovah of the Thunders,
Lord God of Battle, aid.

Rudyard Kipling

The members of the sergeants' mess who had been laughing over jokes or in conversation, politely fell silent and stood up to pay their respects to the Regimental Sergeant Major as he entered the mess dining room. This had been cleared of its tables, which were replaced instead with rows of chairs. For this was the monthly sergeants' mess meeting. Before taking his seat at a table in front of the mess members, the R.S.M. first put everyone at their ease.

'Sit down, gentlemen. You may smoke.'

The R.S.M., whose height of six feet two inches complemented his position as the Senior Warrant Officer of the Battalion, pulled a slip of paper from his breast pocket and sat down.

'Before the Chief Clerk reads the minutes of the last meeting,' he began, 'I have a few bits of gen from the Regimental postings conference you may be interested in. First the R.Q. is moving on.'

He extended a hand towards Ron Allander.

'He's been promoted to W.O. 1, and will shortly be posted to 4 Para. Congratulations, Ron.'

A short ripple of applause sounded around the room.

Allander responded by raising an arm, smiling.

The R.S.M. continued for some minutes, explaining any changes taking place among the top ranks within the other regular Battalions' sergeants' messes. At the end he paused for a moment to look up at the men filling the room. Then with a sober expression he continued.

'It's also been decided that I too will move on. Taking over that soft number Bill Stainworth has had for the last two years, as R.S.M. of the Depot.'

A smile now spread across his face.

'The man who will be arriving to take over this chair is Mat Norris.'

A vacuum of silence descended on the room for a second, then the mess members erupted in dismay.

'Fucking hell.'

'No! Anybody but that cunt.'

'Jesus Christ, what did we do to deserve him?'

The R.S.M., still smiling, let it wash about the room for a moment before passing a simple, up-the-sleeve comment.

'Oh, so some of you know him then?'

This was answered by a chorus of replies.

'Sir! Unfortunately everyone knows that twit.'

'Thank God I got a posting to the T.A..'

'Oh, I couldn't stick two years with him. I'm buying out.'

Sergeant 'Tutty' McBride, the Battalion's Glaswegian Anti-Tank Platoon sergeant, stood up to formally state the feelings of the mess on this individual's pending arrival.

'Sir, they can't send 'Nuts' Norris to 5 Para. The man's a complete idiot. He's stark raving bonkers.'

McBride's face was a picture of desperation.

'Thank you, Sergeant McBride,' replied the R.S.M., 'but the decision has been made and I'm afraid you're stuck with him. Now sit down.'

The sergeant did not comply but held his arms out to his front to attempt one more forlorn plea.

'But, Sir, he's not in control of his faculties. He's totally around the twist. He should be in a padded cell in Netley.'

The R.S.M. inwardly agreed with every word, but because of his position was not free to say so. Still smiling he sat the sergeant down with one simple suggestion.

'Sergeant McBride, how would you like ten extras?'

*　　　　*　　　　*

Bobby MacIntyre's head snapped forward, his eyes flashing open to stare tiredly about him. Like almost everyone of the Battalion group waiting in the large R.A.F. hangar, he had been sitting, parachute clad, trying to catch a few minutes sleep before they were called forward to emplane. Seeing the reason he was woken—movement at the head of the two lines of men, which was his aircraft stick—the corporal reached behind to pull out the helmet on which he had been propping his parachute and then slowly climbed to his feet.

The fatigue Bobby felt was general throughout the hangar, for mounting an airborne exercise of this size was always preceded by many busy, sleepless hours. Having spent the previous day drawing stores, rations, blank ammunition and weapons, being briefed, rehearsed, and then packing weapon containers, the Battalion had paraded on the square in their allotted chalk order at 23:00 hours. Now, four hours later, after making the long journey from Aldershot to R.A.F. Lyneham, they were just taking the first steps to getting aboard their aircraft.

The bus, not the best of conveyances for men wearing parachutes, which were cramped amongst the seats, was then driven off to pull up opposite an American-built C130 Hercules aircraft. There were twenty or so of these, in two rows on the airfield's parking area. This was a large four engine plane, the wings of which sat above the body, allowing easy entrance and exit either through the side doors or from the tail ramp.

Once they had filtered off the bus the men collected their bulky weapon containers from the 4-ton lorry that had followed the bus, and fell in at the rear of the aircraft in two straight lines of port and starboard stick. In avenues of clear, artificial light this could be seen happening at each of the Hercules that sat silently waiting for its crew to arrive and bring it to roaring, fume-smelling life. Up and down the sticks two blue overalled R.A.F. despatchers moved, checking the men's containers were safely packed and rigged. Satisfied, they supervised the stacking of these within the aircraft and on the surface of the tail board ramp so they would be out of the jumper's way during flight. As an eastern brightness began to dim the power of the tall, evenly spaced perimeter lights, the Paratroopers were at last called forward to take their places on the four rows of fold-up seats, the frames of which were clamped to the plane's floor and roof. With everyone settling down, seat belts pulled tight, the two centre rows sitting back to back, the pilot and crew began their pre-take off checks.

At this stage, during the early days of MacIntyre's parachuting career, he used to be quite nervous. The long sequence of events in building up to that final step out of the door tended to bring on the frighteners. For a number of years Bobby had been unable to combat this, causing him much anxiety whenever he found himself on a parachuting roll. He was finally able to disperse his imaginary fears of impending doom, such as the plane crashing or his parachute not opening, and cure the constant anxiety pain in his stomach and the gagging of his throat by reaching a simple conclusion.

Whilst trying to keep his imagination in check prior to one parachute descent, he found himself looking around the aircraft at the others waiting to jump. Most of them he knew as friends, they had seen good times together, suffered under some pretty grim conditions and fought together in a number of distant parts of the world.

'Bollocks,' he thought to himself, 'if I'm going to go, then I'm going in fucking good company.'

From that moment MacIntyre no longer worried about parachuting; whenever he felt anticipation or fear building up he would just swallow it down.

Half an hour later those disturbed from their dozing felt the plane begin to taxi. Ten minutes of continual movement was followed by a pause as the powerful propeller engines were wound up to full throttle. Then, with a lurch that tilted everyone sideways, the Hercules catapulted down the runway, building up to the acceptable rate of knots that would propel it into the air. Once the plane had levelled off at five thousand feet, the dispatchers indicated over the din of the engines with hand signals for everyone to remove their seat belts and helmets and relax. Most did this, for the men knew they had a long way to go.

The North Atlantic Treaty Organisation had been formed shortly after the Second World War in response to Russia's large military presence in the Eastern European countries which she occupied. Although repeatedly asked to scale down this force by western governments, their requests were ignored. With the lack of preparation prior to 1939 still fresh in many people's minds, and the awareness that a militarily weak Europe would be vulnerable to Russian intimidation, the Alliance of N.A.T.O. was brought into being.

In order to counter any attacks by Russia or her Communist Bloc allies, the N.A.T.O. countries constantly carried out combined exercises to test readiness and formulate contingency plans which would forestall any such move.

One of the areas that worried the N.A.T.O. Commanders in particular was the northern flank where Norway and Russia faced each other. Here, in the sparsely populated mountains and forests, a large force could very easily brush aside the light border defence troops and strike southwards. Because of this the Western Alliance was almost annually revising plans and practicing with realistic manoeuvres, the troops that would be reacting to this threat.

This was the reason 5 Para were mounting this drop. In a few hours the Paratroopers would be stepping into the slip-stream over a valley somewhere in Norway.

Not all of 5 Para were aboard the twenty odd Hercules aircraft which, flying in stream formation, were now down skimming the wave tops of the North Sea. The previous night one lone plane had preceded them, keeping below radar detection, weaving low through fjords and mountains to the Battalion's pre-arranged drop zone. This was Patrol Company, going in twelve hours early under cover of darkness to secure the D.Z. for the rest of the Battalion group following them.

In this exercise 5 Para had been given the role of enemy; that is to say the pretend Russian forces, and were consequently jumping into enemy-held territory. On the face of it D Company's sixty man advance party looked pathetically weak but this was deceiving. For these men were trained by the Special Air Service and geared to operate along similar lines. As four man Patrols, each cross-trained as medics, explosives and radio specialists or linguists, they made a highly professional team.

Once they had concealed their parachutes and container equipment, the Patrols moved independently to begin allotted tasks. For some it was a short move, that of D.Z. security, going to ground in the local area to ensure the drop zone was free of enemy when the main force of the Battalion arrived. Others scattered further afield to pre-selected observation points to act as eyes and ears, giving long distance warning of the movements of unfriendly troops. The remaining Patrols of the Company had been ordered into a nearby valley to conceal themselves in hides. Through this valley ran a major road system, which would have to be used by any force sent to counter 5 Para's sudden arrival. So it was only good tactics that troops be placed where they could watch, report, and if necessary attack.

Jim Sinclair's Patrol was part of this operation, one of five. They had all made their way separately, through the chilly early spring night, to previously agreed points where each would disappear. Jim had selected the wood he thought would be suitable from his map back in Aldershot, but he could not confirm his choice as the right one until he had actually examined it in some detail. This he was just about to do.

Stopping his men at the edge of the wood, he positioned them in a small defensive circle to cover all approaches. Then, leaving his bergen, he set off to recce a hide site. Fifty metres further along the wood's edge he found what he was looking for, a large patch of bracken with gaps that could be crawled into. Mentally ticking off the first point on his tactical shopping list, the corporal began his search for the next. Turning into the wood he began to crawl, his rifle in one hand, feeling the earth with the other. The wood was not dense, but because of thick, overhead cloud, the night blackness under the limbs was like that of a cave. Being high on a hillside the trees were mostly pine, the large of which Sinclair steered away from. After half an hour of painstaking searching on his hands and knees he discovered a position that seemed suitable. It was a small, level area of ground, flanked on three sides by young pines and far enough away from larger ones to escape their roots. Shifting little patches of the top layer of needles and soil with his hand, he drew a knife from his belt and began to prod for large boulders and roots. Satisfied, he returned to collect the rest of his Patrol, bringing them back with him to await the visibility of a grey Norwegian dawn.

As the sky brightened Jim told his men to get a brew on, their last until they had finished the job in hand, while he went to the edge of the wood where he confirmed their position by taking compass bearings. Twenty minutes later, with all cooking gear stowed away in their equipment, he gave everyone a orders brief.

'Right, this is the way we'll play it', he began. 'The sentry position will be on the far edge of the bracken where we will be hiding the spoil. Reg, you'll be on first. The change round will be every hour.'

Berrill raised a hand.

'Take the radio with you. The sentry will be radio watch as well. We are due for a net radio check from Company H.Q. in forty minutes. If they ask for our location this is it here', handing Berrill a slip of paper. 'If they want a sitrep tell them we are on normal procedure with nothing to report but send all this in gridel, not clear. Okay?'

'Now, if we're rumbled we pack up and fuck off quick, but if it's a case of having to bug out in a hurry then we'll leave our bergens and run for it with belt order. If we have to split up we rejoin at the second R.V. across the valley at midnight.'

Stripping off his shirt, which showed a stark contrast between his camouflage cream-stained face and hands and the rest of his white body, he ended the briefing with one final order.

'Right, let's get digging.'

Marking out a cross on the ground with each arm eight feet long by two wide, they first raked the top soil off and placed it to one side. Then, spreading ponchos out, Jim and Paddy Kieran began to shovel the earth onto them. As each was filled 'Yorky' Rush would drag it to the patch of bracken where, crawling inside, he spread the soil so it could not be seen. Throughout the morning they dug down to six feet, cutting roots and struggling with rocks. On the surface of each arm, eighteen inches down, a shelf was cut on which a waterproof sheet was placed, then the top soil was returned over it to give concealment and overhead cover.

The mid-afternoon found them ready to take up residence in their newly dug hole, each occupying one arm of the cross to sleep and just wait. Cooking was done at the junction of the cross, which had a camouflaged entrance with a door propped up to allow air and light in and fumes out. When danger was near the door was dropped, sealing them in with little chance of discovery by anyone without the aid of trained search dogs.

With one man on radio watch, the others slept or rested throughout the remainder of the day, for they knew that both sleep and rest would be at a premium: Before noon they had heard the prolonged crescendo of aircraft noise from the next valley as the rest of the Battalion arrived.

*   *   *

'Prepare for action.'

Bobby MacIntyre looked up to see the two R.A.F. dispatchers gesturing for everyone to get themselves ready to jump. This was the beginning of well practiced drills that no one enjoyed, in most cases causing annoyance and much suffering. On each side of the aeroplane the men of both sticks stood up to fold the lightweight aluminium and canvas bench seating out of their way. This was necessary for sixty men were now expected to assemble themselves in bulky helmets, parachutes and weapon containers. Given the expanse of a telephone kiosk this could be completed relatively quickly with the minimum of fuss, but parachuting-wise the C130 was not built for roominess.

Locked in a crush as cramped as a January department store they struggled to get themselves ready to jump.

Sweating and swearing they fought with straps and hooks to dress their bodies with the bulky weapon containers. Reaching up, they then connected the staticline to the thick overhead wire cable which was the strong point within the aircraft that would anchor the strap, pulling their parachute canopies free. Once everyone had replaced their reserve parachute, the men stood in two cramped, ragged lines while a series of checks were carried out both by themselves and by the swift but methodical R.A.F. dispatchers. Normally this should take a period of no more than ten minutes, but for those like MacIntyre who had been through all this before that rule seldom held true. As the pressure of straps began digging into flesh, restricting circulation and numbing limbs, the men, racked with discomfort and soaked in perspiration, gritted their teeth and waited.

For most, this was the beginning of the end of an unhappy flight. For tactical and navigational purposes, the Royal Air Force had flown in stream formation, one behind the other and only a hundred feet or so above the grey-green waters of the North Sea. Because of this, extreme buffeting was caused to the following aircraft by the air wash from the propellers of the Hercules in front. This constant, sharp rocking and dropping in turn caused a plague of air sickness among the parachutists. A number of sick bags had been distributed at the beginning of the flight, but these were of limited quantity and quickly filled. The reminder of the journey was spent with the floor becoming layered with greasy, repugnant vomit.

*   *   *

High above the dropping zone, on the slope of one of the dominating mountains, Mick Pridmore raised his binoculars to once again scan the far entrance of the valley. He and his Patrol had been watching from this observation post since their arrival just after dawn. Throughout the night they had struggled in a sweaty climb up the mountain side to this rocky crag between the tree line below and the unthawed winter snows above. Lowering the binos to let them hang by the strap around his neck, he rubbed his hands to chase out the cold that had persisted all morning. This uncomfortable cold that Mick and his Patrol were experiencing was a localised one, for they had been placed on the shadowed side of the valley. Below them the sun's rays had long since reached the fields and woods, while on the opposite mountains two other Patrols positioned there had stripped to shirt sleeve order.

Noticing some activity on the cultivated fields that were to be 5 Para's D.Z., the corporal again raised his binoculars. Someone had lit a stationary sodium flare giving out a white string of smoke that gently drifted upwards and away. Knowing this was being done to give the R.A.F. aircrews an indication of the ground wind and would only be set off when their arrival was near at hand, Mick once again focused his glasses on the head of the valley.

Thousands of years ago this had been a sea-filled fjord. Now, due to changing geographic and climatic conditions, it had become an agricultural basin which twisted and turned its way for thirty miles to the jagged, hilly coast, where it spread open to the sea. There, at that moment, the aircraft of R.A.F. Transport Command were climbing up from the wave tops to staggered jump heights of between eight and twelve hundred feet.

Pridmore, resting his arms on a surface of granite rock to steady the binos, braced his wrists even more, for gliding around the far corner of the valley, ten miles away, the lead planes came into sight. This was the first pair, one behind and to one side of the other. As more came into view, similarly positioned, their formation made two even, multiplying straight lines. With engines throttled back, slowing each aircraft to an acceptable jump speed, the Hercules of 38 Group, their noise drowning all conversation in the hamlets and farms they flew over, roared up the valley towards the drop zone, coming in like the Liverpoole Kop.

*   *   *

'Stand in the door.'

Bobby MacIntyre, as number twenty-six of the thirty men in the starboard stick, faintly heard this new command, but because of the crush he detected no movement that should have been the number ones obeying the order to take their final pace into the door. And at this stage neither did he care, for like most of the men in the aircraft, he was hanging with both hands gripping the static line, his body slouched. They had been standing for over half an hour now, their parachutes and weapon containers draining leg muscles and bending knees as the combined weights pulled them towards the floor. Some, still air sick, had given up the fight to remain upright, and collapsed on their knees, overcome by pain and periodical vomiting. Through a gap in the line of men to his front MacIntyre watched two lights, one red, the other green, positioned above the starboard door. When these came on it would be the signal for the men to start leaving the aircraft, the red a warning, the green a visual order to jump.

Finally, the red came on followed quickly by the green. This was greeted by a chorus of cheers, curses and foul suggestions that the men in front get a move on. Stepping through the door into space held no fear for anyone now, with longed for relief they knew the agony and suffering of the last half hour was about to end. Approaching the door, Bobby could now hear other sounds above the roar of the engines. The scream of the despatchers ushering each jumper through the exit with one single high pitched word 'Go! Go! Go!'; the howl of air as it rushed past the door, and the sharp slap of the static lines as they completed their job of pulling the parachute into inflation, cracking along the outside of the fuselage.

With relief, hardly feeling the despatcher's slap on his shoulder, MacIntyre heaved himself and his crippling attached weight through the door, to be snatched sideways by a hurricane of solid air.

The increasing silence as he glided down the coolness of the slipstream went unnoticed for every tissue of his body was giving thanks that all weight was now being suspended by the inflated parachute above his head.

Pridmore no longer used his binoculars, for the full naked eye was now needed to take in the action-filled splendour of this airborne assault. As the first two aircraft finished unloading their long lines of khaki canopies and climbed out of the valley to turn southwards across Norway, another two began to discharge their parachutists. For the next twelve minutes continual layers of parachutes were being spread above the D.Z. to gently rock or float their way towards the deck. On the whole it was an uneventful descent, but for some there was reason for worry. Here and there the odd entanglement could be seen, one man through another's rigging line. Reserve parachutes could also be seen, flying either by accident or because of an emergency.

At one point Pridmore watched as a tiny speck dropped away from one of the jumpers to thud with a small circular puff of dust on striking the ground. This was a weapon container that had somehow broken free of the suspension rope that, when lowered, should have hung below its owner prior to landing. This was a highly dangerous incident, for it could very easily have struck someone who had already landed.

Fields, that only minutes before had been a picture of tranquility, now began to boil with military activity. Medics hurried among the Paras checking for injuries, and the men, freeing themselves from their harnesses quickly, opened their containers to slip on equipment and sling weapons. Gathering up their parachutes, they carried these with them to a central point and then on to Company R.V.s scattered around the perimeter of the drop zone.

Shortly after the last chalk had landed another wave of Hercules began their jump run over a D.Z. to one side of the first; this was the heavy drop coming in, vehicles, guns and stores belonging to the support elements of the Battalion Group.

As the last of these large platforms, suspended under three monstrous parachutes, thumped into the young spring green corn fields, soldiers raced to de-rig the loads. These were the men of Support Company and those attached arms of 16 Independent Parachute Brigade, 7 Royal Horse Artillery, 9 Squadron Engineers, 23 PFA Surgical Teams, Signals, Drivers, Ordnance Corps, all units knitting together to form a formidable strike force. Sweating and cursing, they struggled among the platforms, dismantling chucks and chains, in a desperate effort to free their guns and vehicles in order to get off the D.Z. and into cover.

An hour later all that remained below Pridmore's O.P. was the debris and non-tactical D.Z. party clearing and collecting this discarded but expensive equipment. The Battalion Group had moved to a defensive position in some foot-hills further up the valley to await enemy reaction.

Seeing them away, the big man had his own Patrol packed up to leave. They were about to enter the second phase of this exercise. As soon as the code word was given to them, Pridmore and his men would set off over the mountains to the coast where they would again establish another observation post. This time it was to watch for and report on the movements of any enemy reinforcements which might be building up to be sent against the Battalion.

                    *   *   *

Crouched in the bracken at the edge of the wood in which they had dug their hide, Jim Sinclair's Patrol silently waited. In the fading dusk light he was on his stomach, sighting a bearing with his compass. Having done so he spun the glass face, setting the instrument for a night march. Since completing their hide, Jim and his men had spent the better part of three days and two nights concealing themselves within it. Now, on the eve of the third night, they had received a signal giving them the opportunity to raise havoc.

The day following the Battalion's arrival, enemy advance troops began to answer the challenge. Firstly, light Norwegian armour and scout cars were observed passing through the valley below, on reconnaissance over the connecting pass into the valley which 5 Para occupied. They were soon followed by a British Infantry Battalion who halted only long enough to organise a rear echlon base. Close behind them came a Norwegian Artillary

Battery to bring their six American 155 millimetre guns into action across one edge of a farmer's pasture. Throughout the night, more transport could be heard and seen arriving, which in the light of morning turned out to be a Brigade Headquarters. For the rest of the day Sinclair's Patrol worked two man shifts; four hours recording movements and plotting locations, and then four hours resting or sleeping in the hide. Now with stars beginning to appear in the navy blue of the darkening eastern sky, they followed their compass bearing to an arranged Patrol rendezvous.

'Halt.'

Paddy Kieran had been expecting this challenge and instantly froze.

'Hands up' was the next whispered command from out of the wall of darkness, a wood edge a few feet to his front.

Paddy, holding his rifle in one hand, raised his arms.

'Punch' came the first half of the password. Without pausing, Kieran whispered back the reply.

'Bowl.'

'Advance one and be recognised.'

Leaving the other three remaining motionless in single file, he stepped forward several slow steps to again be stopped by the same voice coming from ground level.

'Who are you?'

Knowing the voice to be that of a sergeant, Paddy lowered his arms to reply.

'Kieran, Sarg, Corporal Sinclair's number six Patrol.'

'Right, bring your lads in. You and the other two put yourselves down here as a defensive perimeter. Corporal Sinclair will come with me for a briefing by Lieutenant Holding.'

A half hour wait ensued before the Lieutenant could give his briefing, while they waited for the last of the five Patrols to arrive.

The briefing took place with everyone flat on their stomachs under the cover of a spread-out poncho. Each Patrol Commander, a shaded torch in one hand, notebook and pencil in the other, the lower half of their bodies protruding from under the poncho, listened as Lieutenant Holding began his introduction to the night's operation.

'Just to bring everyone up to date it seems that 5 Para has caught the enemy on the hop. They did expect an airborne attack, but not here. This is the reason for their slow reaction. However, according to our Patrol O.P.s spread out towards the coast, one of our Marine Commandos and a Brigade of U.S. Marines have been landed and should arrive sometime tomorrow. Because of this, the C.O. wants us to work this H.Q. area over and cause them as much inconvenience as possible.'

The Lieutenant paused briefly before continuing.

'Right, this is the way it's to be done. My Patrol and Corporal Sinclair's will dust up the main Headquarters. Sergeant Gill with his and 7 Patrol will get amongst the Gunners and play merry hell.'

Then, looking at a young fair-haired corporal, he completed his brief outline of events before commencing his orders in full.

'9 Patrol, Corporal Morris, I want you to set up an ambush on the road about half a mile west of us. You may spring it on anything you think you can handle, but only after you hear us getting stuck in. Right, any quick questions?'

The Lieutenant paused again before continuing his orders briefing, giving a full detailed plan.

Two hours later, having brought their Patrols up to the perimeter of the enemy H.Q. area, Holding crouched side by side watching the movements within. Being a Headquarters complex they suffered many faults. Normally being well back from the front line, they seldom found themselves being interfered with, which bred complacency and slackness on basic concealment points. Tent flaps were being pulled open without first extinguishing the lights within, vehicle engines were loudly revved up and headlights used to move about. Torches were used indiscriminately, whilst talking was rarely done in a whisper.

The Command Post, Holding's intended target, was easily located by the amount of people toing and froing about it and from the nearby bank of noisy generators, feeding power to the batteries that run the vital radios of the Brigade communications net.

Security was a token affair, for being the organisation that it was, officers and senior N.C.O.s far out-numbered the private soldiers, which resulted in very few men who could be called upon for guard duties. This handicap of too many chiefs and not enough Indians Mr. Holding was now about to exploit.

Stepping softly, the young lieutenant led his seven men in single file into the heart of the larger area. Their ease of entry was made possible by the hour of patient observation they had just spent on the nearby cold ground. The men, apprehensive but glad to be on the move, were vigilant to every sound and object. It was now past two o'clock in the morning and all was quiet. Except for those on duty and the sentry, smoking a cigarette beside a tree at the road entrance to the wood, everyone had taken to their sleeping bags.

Free of their heavy bergens, wearing belt order and carrying only weapons these intruders moved with silent confidence among the vehicles and camouflage net-covered tents.

Halting just short of a large dark mass, Holding with whispers and hand signals stationed the three members of his Patrol outside it. Then, ducking under the outer netting, brought Jim Sinclair's men up to a canvas entrance. With one hand he gently pushed this aside to peer into the crack of light.

The tent, the size of a large room, contained several chairs, tables, plotting boards, wall maps and two banks of radios. Operating this Command Post were four men, two officers, a major and a captain, one sergeant and a lance corporal.

The officers were both sitting at the same table facing one of the banks of radios. The lance corporal was hunched in front of the second bank, a set of headphones over his ears. The sergeant, sitting with his feet up on a spare table, was apparently napping.

Replacing the flap to whisper to each of his men in turn, Holding tasked them off and then turned again to the tent.

Pushing the canvas doorway to one side he bounded across to the two officers, grabbing the major by the shoulder and pushing him onto his knees whilst pointing his rifle one-handedly at the captain.

'On the floor both of you', he ordered.

Following quickly behind, Reg Berrill assisted the captain with a gentle shove.

'Here steady on,' protested the major. 'I'm an officer.'

'That's alright then', replied Holding. 'So am I.'

Rush, with true Yorkshire grace, dumped the sergeant flat on his face by giving his upright legs a twist spilling him out of his chair.

'What the fuck's this' he angrily exclaimed, trying to rise to his feet.

'Shut your moosh and stay down', Rush cautioned, pushing his rifle barrel into the small of the sergeant's back. 'You're lucky, if we had been playing for real I'd a stuck a knife in yah.'

The lance corporal, his eyes as wide as they could get, looking six different ways at once, was grabbed by his shirt front to be dragged from his chair by Paddy Kieran and forced down beside the sergeant.

Jim Sinclair, stationing himself at the tent entrance, softly shouted a warning to the others.

'Paddy, over in the corner; the sleeping bag.'

Kieran and Berrill rushed across to pull the bag and it's sleepy-eyed occupant over to join the two officers.

'There, there, now squire, you just lie still, all cozy like and don't make a sound', warned Reg Berrill, bending down to imprison him by pulling the zipper of the sleeping bag up under the man's chin.

Meanwhile, Holder had begun ripping maps off display boards, gathering up code sheets and signals documents, and stuffing them all into an empty bergen that Jim Sinclair had passed to him. Speed was essential. The occupants of the tent were at that moment overwhelmed and confused. Now in order to take advantage of this they had to work fast. With Kieran handing him the last of the documents from in front of the second bank of radios, Holder signalled to Sinclair. The corporal, who had been waiting for this, pulled the pins on two smoke grenades, dropping them a short distance either side of himself. With the smoke beginning to billow up within the tent, the young lieutenant motioned his men outside, dropping a third smoke grenade in the doorway as he left.

From entering the tent to exiting, it took just over two minutes.

As Holding's men hurried through the Brigade H.Q. area to make their escape, loud frantic voices could be heard coming from the Command Post as they fought to escape from the blinding smoke which filled the tent. Pausing briefly at an agreed R.V. before splitting up to return to their respective hides, the two Patrols listened as the night air erupted in distant thunderflash explosions and blank rifle fire. This was the sergeant's party taking out the Artillery gun line.

*   *   *

Two Section, who had been talking in low whispers, fell silent as three men approached down the trench line. This was Major Bates, Lieutenant Taplow, 8 Platoon's new Commander, and Corporal MacIntyre, the acting Platoon Sergeant. The Company was at stand to, something always done first thing before dawn and again before last light at night. This was when a unit had to be at full alert in case they were attacked, as these were the two most crucial times of the day. The O.C. always took this opportunity to do his rounds, checking the men, their trench defenses and camouflage and to point out to the Platoon Commanders any changes or redeployments necessary.

'Have your men been cleaning their weapons regularly, Peter?' asked the major of the Platoon Commander, halting beside the Section gun trench.

The lieutenant's sleep-robbed mind stumbled his reply.

'Yes . . . the last time was . . .'

'The Section Commanders have got this in hand, Sir', interrupted MacIntyre, seeing Taplow was not thinking clearly. 'It's done in rotation never more than two weapons being stripped at any one time.'

Satisfied, the O.C. knelt to speak to Haydon and Ottoway, the gun team, leaning on the forward lip of their trench.

Normally Peter Taplow would not have needed prompting from anyone. For, in his short period of time with the Company, he was proving to be a good officer. The reason for his inability to answer his O.C.'s question was that of chronic fatigue.

It was the morning of the Battalion's fifth day in Norway, the past four of which had been filled with little more than hard work and sleeplessness. On occupying the C.O.'s selected defensive position, the Battalion Group spent the first day and night digging in. The second day, with the arrival of the enemy British Battalion, found them playing cat and mouse with each other. This hostile force had positioned themselves in Company groups securing the roadway from the neighbouring valley over a saddle entrance down to the floor of their valley. From these two locations the opposing Battalions sent out reconnaissance, ambush and fighting Patrols against each other, keeping both constantly on the alert.

Early into the third night, as Lieutenant Holding was gathering his Patrols in to dust up the Brigade H.Q. in the valley next door, C Company left their trenches. The C.O., not prepared to sit back and let the enemy build up sufficient forces from within a safe area with which to attack and overrun him, was about to put a kink in their plans.

The enemy Battalion Commander, thinking 5 Para would sit tight and let the main battle come to them, had spread his Companies thinly, occupying maximum ground.

The Para Colonel, assessing the intelligence brought to him by his Patrols, spotted a vulnerable, undefended section of the road leading down from the crestline of the saddle.

As well as his own Company, Major Bates also had under command a troop of 9 Squadron Engineers and a forward observation officer from 7 R.H.A. who could call on supporting artillery fire. This force he guided through the night in a looped course arriving at their destination an hour or two before dawn.

In the foot-hills between the mountain range and the valley floor was a small river gorge that sloped upwards to wooded hill tops. The road negotiated this gorge by snaking sharply down and then crossing a small stone and concrete bridge.

With the sun just beginning to show on the horizon, Bates's defending disposition was completed. On the crown of the hill facing the mountains 8 and 9 Platoons dug in, straddling the road, while the hilltop on the valley side was secured by 7 Platoon and two Sections of the 9 Squadron troop. The remaining section of Engineers took control of the bridge, mining it with simulated demolition charges. Although Company H.Q. was tucked away in a nook half-way up the valley hill. Major Bates and the Artillery F.O.O. spent the day floating from one position to the other, this being dictated by which side was under attack at the time.

Theoretically, the Company Group was trapped between two enemy companies and a Battalion H.Q. in the valley at the fringe of the foot-hills and two further companies back up the mountains. However, being trapped and being caught were two different things.

The first of the enemy to find that the road was now unsafe was a colour sergeant's Landrover on a journey from their base area in the next valley to re-supply one of the forward Companies with rations and water. They were captured, the O.C. commandeering the vehicle for his own transportation. The next was the dawn Patrol road check, two Norwegian armoured cars.

They were ambushed by 7 Platoon and the two Engineer Sections, destroyed in a hail of blank rounds and thunderflashes. Reversing out of the killing ground to make their escape they were nonetheless dead. For the white arm banded umpire, a captain from the Fusilier Brigade attached to C Company, observing the incident reported over his radio net that Major Bates's men had drawn first blood.

Throughout the rest of the day, cowboy and Indian games were played in among the trees and rocks above the gorge bridge. C Company had to be dislodged, for they were astride N.A.T.O.'s only route into the valley. At first this was attempted by probing Patrols and Platoons, then full Company attacks. The last of these from the valley side was broken up by the Engineers. Running out of thunderflashes, they threw little balls of plastic explosive with short fuses. This was dangerous, but 9 Squadron, being 9 Squadron and seeming never to be without a pocket full of the stuff and with nothing else to throw, merrily pitched away.

Not one inch of ground was lost during all this but the exercise umpires, with a time table to keep to, judged the last attack to be a success, so waving their magic wand, killed every Para within a mile of the bridge stone dead.

Rigour mortis, however, was short lived. Resurrecting his 123 corpses, Major Bates once again marched them through the night, back to their old position.

Soon after the O.C. left Lieutenant Taplow and his 8 Platoon, word was given for the men to stand down from the morning alert. On hearing this, Lance Corporal Jones pulled himself up out of his trench. Moving around his men, he directed them to wash, shave, clean their weapons and eat something before crashing out into a much needed sleep.

Dropping to his knees at the gun trench, he tiredly gave out a set of orders to the two men leaning in each corner.

'Stan, you're on sentry go first', directing his words to Ottoway. Then, turning to Haydon, 'Roy, you take over from him, make it an hour each stag, after you, hand . . .'

'For fuck's sake, Jonesy, I'm wacked; can't you give it to some other cunt', protested Ottoway.

The tall, blond corporal, reaching forward with one hand, pinched the soldier's unshaven, camouflage cream stained cheek.

'Poor didums, are we feeling fragile? Did we have a bad night? What's the matter, has mummy-kins taken away your teddy bear again?'

Then, with a cuff to the top of Ottoway's beret and a final order, stood up to move to the next weapon pit.

'Just do it, ya tosser.'

'No Way', sulking, spat into the bottom of his trench.

'For fuck's sake, Jonesy, I'm wacked', mimicked Haydon with a smirk.

'Well I am', defended Ottoway, turning to lay his head and arms on his machine gun resting on the lip of the trench.

'Well, so's every bloke on this fucking hillside, so what makes you so special?' retorted Haydon.

'Ah, fuck ya', replied 'No Way', still collapsed across his gun, making no effort to keep his eyes open. 'Put a brew on for us, I'm on guard.'

As Haydon struggled out of his equipment to get at his water and rations, he caught sight of Chris Braithwaite in the next trench, stripped to the waist shaving.

'Hi, Chrissy! Alright?' he called.

Braithwaite acknowledged by nodding his lathered face and wiggling his razor.

After throwing a wobbler outside the Company location and attacking the drunken Paddy he had been posted from 7 Platoon to 8. Ever since his arrival Haydon and Ottoway had gone out of their way to gain his friendship, for they were hatching a scheme. If somehow they could get Braithwaite, a handsome, blond wavy haired youth with a smooth golden unblemished skin, up to London and drunk, they would try to sell him to a Soho white slaver. The fact that he would probably end his days as a depraved Middle Eastern potentate's sex toy weighed upon them not.

'Here, Sir, get this down ya.'

Lieutenant Taplow, sitting with his back against a tree, opened his eyes to find Durrant, the Platoon's Signaller, offering him a mug of tea.

'Cheers' thanked the officer sluggishly, his arms woodenly reaching out to accept it.

A few yards away, eating breakfast in his trench, a small tin of chopped ham and a packet of hardtack biscuits, Bobby MacIntyre watched the lieutenant slowly sip his tea.

'That's it, Sir,' thought the corporal to himself. 'Drink it up, then get your head down.'

During the entire battle for the bridge he had more than done his part. Commanding from his Section's forward trenches during assaults, leading local counter-attacks, and never resting between actions. Whereas the bulk of 8 Platoon grabbed snatches of sleep during lulls, he remained awake and alert, always in command. Now he was paying the price for his dedication.

'Jock', the corporal hissed in warning to his Platoon Signaller, while pointing with his spoon towards Lieutenant Taplow. The Scotsman reached forward to take the half empty mug of tea from his Platoon Commander before it slipped completely from his hands. The lieutenant, his head drooped, had been overcome by well-earned and much overdue sleep.

Less than an hour later he was reluctantly shaken awake by his acting Platoon sergeant.

'Sir! Sir! O Group, Sir!'

'What! What!' Taplow's reply was an instinctive one, his mind not yet aware he had spoken.

'O Group, Sir. They want you at Company H.Q. in ten minutes.' MacIntyre, squatting beside his officer, waited several moments for a reply. Finally it came.

Without opening his eyes, Taplow asked: 'What time is it now?'

'Seven twenty, Sir.'

His tired mind unable to assess this, the lieutenant asked another question, this time opening his eyes.

'How long have I been asleep?'

'About an hour, Sir! Little less, don't worry, you didn't miss anything. Here, Sir, have a sip.'

MacIntyre was holding another mug of tea.

'God, that's good', commented Taplow after taking a swallow. 'Have the Section Commanders been warned?'

'Not yet, Sir', replied the corporal.

'Let them know! Call them in while I'm away. I'll hold my orders here when I get back', directed the young officer, his words coming lazily before taking another swallow of hot sweet tea.

Some minutes later Taplow dropped down within the cluster of trenches that was Company H.Q., to rest his back against a small rock. The staff of this tight little nerve cell looked as if someone had called time out.

Two occupying sleeping bags were tucked away in a nearby bush. Sergeant Major Kettler, on radio watch with a set of headphones clamped over his ears, his mouth wide open, was asleep against a tree. Lance Corporal Pearson, also manning a radio, the only one awake in sight, leaned on the lip of his trench wall.

'What's happening, Corporal Pearson?' asked the lieutenant, pulling a map from a side trouser pocket.

'The Company Commander's not back from C.O's orders yet, Sir', came the dry reply.

'That's not the question I asked', smiled the officer. 'Now, what's going on?'

'We're moving, Sir! Corporal Elliot got the word from his base plate position a few minutes ago', smiled back Pearson, pointing to the big mortar fire controller dozing in the next trench.

On hearing this, Taplow turned his head away to curse.

'Oh, piss.'

There would be no sleep for anyone today and precious little tonight.

5 Para had proved to be too much of a hindrance to N.A.T.O.'s battle plans. The exercise was scheduled to end in two day's time, but, because the C.O. had chosen his ground with too clever a tactical eye, the Alliance forces were finding it difficult to throw in a punch that could dislodge them. D Company's surveillance, their attacks on rear elements and the Battalion's awkward defensive positioning all cost N.A.T.O. much in time and manpower. Because of this, the exercise umpires had no choice but to hurry things along with Gulliver-like moves.

By mid-morning 5 Para battle group had vacated their hill position. With rear recce parties racing in Landrovers to a location two valleys away, where the final exercise battle was to be fought and lost, the rest of the Battalion marched out.

As 7 R.H.A., Support Company and all other units with vehicles to spare dropped their weapons and crews, they were immediately turned around and sent back to ferry the marching troops forward. For many this journey was made in over-crowded Landrovers, clinging painfully in whatever cramped position they could fit into. But few complained, being Infantry, everyone accepted that a third class ride beat a first class walk every time.

CHAPTER 5

There is a dreadful Hell,
And everlasting pains;
There sinners must with devils dwell
In darkness, fire, and chains.

Isaac Watts

Pushing aside a half open door marked Weapon Training Wing, Classroom One, Sam Kyle walked in. The room was bare, except for twenty or so chairs and a six foot folding table placed below a large blackboard which took up one complete wall. Standing at the blackboard, stripped of his number two dress jacket and beret, was a stocky, dark-haired man, just completing a diagram of a range card in white chalk.

'Sorry! You couldn't tell me where I can find the Training Wing Office?' interrupted Sam.

'Sure! Sure!' he happily assured Kyle as he put the chalk down to wipe his fingers on a cloth. 'I'm just off around there now. We got a General coming around for a look-see shortly, but I got a lesson here as soon he's gone. I wish these brass hats would leave us alone so we can get on with the job', he concluded, springing forward to extend a hand. 'Ben Gardin.'

Kyle took the hand also stating his name.

'You wouldn't be the replacement for Larry Fiddler, would you?' asked Gardin, picking up his jacket with sergeant's stripes on the sleeves from a chair to slip it on.

'Ya, that's right. The Chief Clerk sent me down to report to the Wing Sergeant Major. He's supposed to be arranging interviews with the R.S.M. and the C.O. later on this morning.'

Chuckling, the sergeant placed a dark green Light Infantry beret on his head.

'Well, welcome aboard but Sam, son, I wouldn't be in your shoes for the Crown Jewels.' With this deflatory statement he lead the way out of the door.

Sam did not ask what he meant for he already knew. A week before 5 Para were due to take part in their Norwegian exercise he had been rushed in front of the Commanding Officer to be told he was being promoted and posted, filling a vacancy that had suddenly come up. A few hours later he learned the true reason for his hasty promotion and move. Colour Sergeant Larry Fiddler had been attached to the weapon training staff at a local Army Junior Leaders college. With just under a year of his two year tour to do, he left his wife and young son and ran off with the Adjutant's wife. Sam, by accepting this posting, realised he was putting his head on the block. For following in the footsteps of his predecessor, in order to survive, he would have to be as pure as the driven snow throughout.

On a veranda outside the Wing Office, Sam was introduced to half a dozen Senior N.C.O.s of different Regiments who were the other staff instructors. The sergeant major was not in his office; he had been called to the H.Q. building as one of those making up the reception party meeting the District Commander. Sam, with no other choice, joined the rest to make small talk and wait. This was not for long, for soon a gaggle of officers and warrant officers, surrounding a major general, were seen coming towards them down a narrow road.

'We better fall in', suggested a colour sergeant from the Irish Rangers, stepping down from the veranda.

Kyle hesitated, not sure what the right thing for him was, but followed everyone down when Ben Gardin pointed out: 'Come on Sam, you're one of us now.'

The general, wishing to meet everyone, began working his way down the line of instructors. After being introduced by the lieutenant colonel commanding the college he would chat for a short period before moving to the next man.

The colonel, unaware of the new arrival in the line, gagged while laughing at one of the general's jokes as he found this stranger in front of him waiting to be introduced to the District Commander. His eyes shot sideways, looking to the adjutant to provide a name; the adjutant looked in turn to the R.S.M.. The R.S.M., ram-rod straight, rotated his head to stare into the face of the wing sergeant major. The wing sergeant major, baffled, stood staring back at them all.

Presented with a situation too good to pass up, the slightly hunched general stepped forward with a smile to grasp the colour sergeant's right hand in both of his, pumping it up and down.

'Hello, Colour Sergeant Kyle. How's Beth and the children?'

'Just fine, Sir! Thank you', replied Sam, grinning up into the face of Robert Alistair Scott, who ten years earlier had been 5 Paras Commanding Officer.

*   *   *

With four months of Ulster and the Norwegian exercise behind them, the members of 5 Para were hoping for a period of slack in which they could take things easy for a bit. This was denied because Royalty had decided to pay them a visit. The men, on their part, could have quite cheerfully overcome all the niggling inconveniences that this involved, but unfortunately for them from the moment the signal arrived warning of the visit, Battalion H.Q. zoomed up to 40,000 feet and stayed there for the entire three weeks proceding the visit.

Of course there had to be a parade, which meant rehearsals, which in turn meant polished boots, pressed uniforms, clean brasses, and men being rushed off the square into jail for being lazy, slow or caught.

On the final rehearsals the band appeared to give musical accompaniment. This they did from the centre of the square while the Battalion, in Company formations, marched around them at either slow or quick time.

At one point in the morning rehearsal on the second day, R.S.M. Norris, who had been scouting about the ranks, brought the parade to an unscheduled stop. With his pace stick in one hand, his arms aloft, standing like Moses trying to part the seas, he shouted 'Halt! Halt!'

As if the communications cord had been pulled on this khaki train the men stumbled to ragged, uneven stillness. The officers, swords in hands looked about them, puzzled. The men, just as puzzled but knowing better than to move, investigated only as far as their eyes could rotate.

The R.S.M., striding up to a section of B Company, revealed to everyone the reason for the halt.

'Alright, gentlemen, which one of you was whistling?'

Someone, wishing to escape the boredom of all this plodding about, had been whistling along with the band.

'Come on! Come on! Who was it?' demanded Norris of the motionless ranks before him.

'Well, stand there then gentlemen. I've got all morning', warned the R.S.M., losing patience.

After a longish pause, a soldier in the near rank turned to his right and took a pace forward.

'It was me, Sir', he confessed in a loud clear voice.

Norris, placing his pace stick under one arm, approached the man to ask: 'You were the one doing the whistling?'

'Yes, Sir', shouted the man, rigidly at attention.

'Good! Good!' replied the big, hook-nosed warrant officer, taking his pace stick from under his arm to tap the point on the soldier's chest.

'I do like to see a man enjoy himself in his work. When the parade is finished I want you to report to your sergeant major and tell him that I said you are to have three days leave, starting tomorrow morning. Now be a good lad and fall back in the ranks.'

Then, leaving the soldier rooted to the asphalt in dumb-founded bewilderment, he stepped back to raise his pace stick in the air as a signal to the adjutant, who, leading the parade, had himself been waiting just as mystified about the delay as everyone else.

'Alright, Sir, carry on.'

The adjutant, giving the appropriate commands, again stepped the Battalion off, the band playing and the men, each and everyone, whistling.

They called the R.S.M. 'Nuts' Norris and, by the Lord God Jehova, did he live up to his nickname.

                    *   *   *

As well as the parade, a number of other activities were laid on to occupy the Royal visitors during their stay. But above all the camp area had to be of a high standard of tidiness. This, by directives and instructions from the officers and S/N.C.O.s, meant unwanted work for the men.

Bobby MacIntyre had been given by C.S.M. Kettler the task of taking his Platoon and sweeping up all the leaves around Montgomery Square where the parade was to be held. This his Platoon was able to complete by working through one full morning. Just as the corporal was about to fall his men out for lunch a distraught Sergeant Major Kettler appeared at the run.

'Corporal MacIntyre, what have you done with all the leaves?'

'We carried them across the Farnborough Road in dustbins and dumped them in the woods, Sir.'

'Well, get them back! Get them back now!' ordered Kettler frantically.

'What!' exclaimed Bobby.

'Don't argue; just get them back', repeated the C.S.M. in desperation. 'The C.O. has just had a conference, and it's been decided that everything must look natural.'

And so it went from silliness to silliness, each act of preparational blunder exceeding the last. The annoyance of all this was eased somewhat for Charlie Company by someone removing the Company weekly programme and replacing it with a forgery which read:

C Company
WEEKLY TRAINING PROGRAMME

Officer of the week	Private Ottoway
Telephone orderly	Major Bates
Duty runner	7 Platoon
Duty pilot	C.S.M. Kettler

Monday 08.00 hrs — Red indian chief is being buried at Westminster Abbey. Company to collect coffin at Southampton, line route and act as bearer party to London.

Tuesday 10.00 hrs — Chinese Admiral will be coming to use the bath.

Wednesday 08.30 hrs — Battalion M.O. to test the theory of source of recent diphtheria epidemic by having everyone in 8 Platoon drink a cup of N.A.A.F.I tea.

Thursday 07.45 hrs — Cossack Corporal will watch 9 Platoon area cleaning the north wall of the Education Centre.

Friday 08.15 hrs — Japanese Samurai Colonel to lead Company in suicide Banzai attack on machine gun bunkers firing live ammunition. Survivors are to commit hari kari before N.A.A.F.I break.

The culprit responsible was never discovered, which is surprising for whoever did it was not only able to use a typewriter, but could spell as well. Discounting the officers, this left a very narrow field for anyone wishing to point an accusing finger. In future days whenever the subject was raised or joked about, Lance Corporal Pearson kept unusually quiet.

*   *   *

On the morning of the final rehearsal for the Royal visit, the Battalion Medical Inspection Room was packed out. A small number of these soldiers were present because of genuine ailments but most were not. They were just fed up with marching around the square for hours on end in the hot sun.

The first to see the Medical Officer was Roy Haydon. He was ushered into a large office containing a couch, a wall sink, and a medical cabinet in one corner. The M.O., Tom Ravenscroft, a tall, red-headed, boyish-faced captain in his late twenties, sat writing at a desk.

'Come in, come in', he called. 'Sit down.'

Haydon sat in a chair opposite the desk.

'Right then,' began the officer, 'what's the trouble?'

'Oh, it's my head, Sir. Just lately I've been coming on a bit funny.' The young soldier emphasised this by placing a hand to his head and giving a pained expression.

'Oh yes, and how long have you had this funniness?' asked the doctor, his voice giving Haydon the impression of professional concern.

'About a week now, Sir. I get it every time I go on the square, but I've tried not to let it affect me.'

The young soldier sat back to raise his head just that little bit higher.

'Yes! Yes!' pondered the captain. 'I think I know what's caused it.'

'Yes?' prompted Roy, looking brighter.

'Yup. They call it skivensitis', and then, without giving Haydon the chance to think on what he had just said, the captain put forward a proposal.

'Haydon, how would you like a weeks's light duties?' he asked, looking down at the sick report to check the name.

'You think it's that bad, Sir?' beamed the soldier with delight.

'I'm going to make a bargain with you. I'll give you a test. If you pass, you get a week's light duties but if you fail you'll have to return to the square, okay?'

'Sure, sure, Sir', Haydon readily agreed, believing he could fake his way through any test the doctor could give him.

'Right, go put that belt and holster on.'

The M.O. pointed to a cowboy belt and holster, with a real sixgun in it, hanging on a coat rack by the door.

'What this, Sir?' replied the puzzled patient, moving across to lift it off the hock.

'Yes, yes, put it on' confirmed the tall doctor, standing up to come around his desk, a similar belt and holster already hanging from his own waist. Taking the pistol out and twirling it several times as Haydon fumbled with the buckle, he asked 'How's your quick draw?'

'Quick, draw, Sir?' replied Roy, even more puzzled.

'Ya, that's the test. If you outdraw me, you get your light duties; if I outdraw you, you'll have to get out of my office and walk around that square some more. Now, have a couple of tries with the pistol. Go on have a feel of it.'

Haydon, unsure of himself, pulled the weapon out of its holster a few times, feeling the weight.

'Okay, that's enough. Get yourself ready', ordered the officer, taking up a classical Wyatt Earp ready-to-draw stance.

Roy, adopting what he thought was a similar pose, could not believe what was happening.

'When you're ready, go for your gun partner', coaxed the tall, red-headed officer.

Haydon, as fast as he could, dropped his right hand to the pistol butt, only to find as he touched it, he was looking into the barrel of Ravencroft's.

'Bang', said the distinguished graduate of medicine.

'Oh, for fuck's sake', groaned the instantly cured patient, turning away to unbuckle his gun belt. 'You win, Sir, you win.'

'Be a good chap, Haydon', requested the doctor, returning to his seat. 'On your way out send the next man in.'

'What'ja get?' asked Ottoway hopefully as he re-entered the waiting room.

'Screwed 'No Way'. I got good and screwed', replied his shorter friend, jerking a thumb over his shoulder. 'Go on in, you're next.'

Haydon paused on the front steps for a few minutes before deciding to go back to the Company Office and give himself up.

Passing the M.O.'s office window he heard his mate questioning the doctor's first diagnosis.

'Hang about, Sir, I wasn't ready that time. How about the best of two out of three?'

*   *   *

Murmuring softly and rocking his arms, Jim Sinclair walked up and down the livingroom to still the bursts of crying that the baby he held periodically gave. This was Neil and Penny Robert's baby son, Steven. They had come across from Belfast to spend a week with Dave Urwin's family. Jim, arriving earlier that evening to see if Dave would like to go out for a drink, found he and his guests in a state of disappointment.

The two couples had made arrangements to go out for dinner together, but the baby-sitter had just phoned to say she could not make it. The only drink Jim saw that night was one of milk which he tried to make the baby take when he first began to cry. His rejection of it was understandable, for Jim, knowing no better, had taken the bottle straight from the refrigerator to push the ice cold rubber nipple into the baby's mouth. An hour later, every attempt to silence the child's crying frustrated, here he was walking up and down and surprisingly enjoying this unaccustomed parental act.

With the time not far off midnight, a key sounding in the front door lock brought Sinclair to a halt. The Urwins and Roberts, talking softly so as not to wake the children, entered the livingroom to find Jim with a finger to his lips.

'What are you playing at?' asked Dave Urwin, a smile spreading across his face.

'Little beggar wouldn't stop crying', explained Sinclair in defence.

'Oh, so he's at that game again, is he?' said Neil Roberts, stripping off his coat.

'Jim Sinclair, you big soft bunny, you should have left him; he only wanted someone to pick him up', scolded Penny Roberts, reaching to take the sleepy-eyed infant from Jim's arms.

'Well, I di'na know that', protested the Scotsman. 'I was just trying to stop his crying from waking the other wee 'uns.'

'Don't worry, Jim, you did the right thing, and probably more than some people would have', defended Mary Urwin, giving her husband a sideways glance.

'How long's young Stevie had you ponsing around the room then?' asked Urwin, ignoring his wife.

'About an hour', confessed the Scot.

'About an hour' repeated Urwin. Both husbands looked at each other and chuckled.

'Wait till I tell Paddy Kieron about this' threatened Urwin.

'David stop teasing', interrupted Mary. 'Jim, sit down and have a cup of tea with us. I'm just putting the kettle on.'

As the men made themselves comfortable, the women took the baby up to bed.

'How was the dinner, Neil?' asked Jim, offering a cigarette.

'Quiet! Like everything over here, quiet.'

'How do you mean?' Jim asked, extending a cigarette lighter.

'No bullets, no bombs.'

'It's still bad then?' asked the Scot.

'Grim, and getting grimmer', replied Roberts, his face stern.

'Police and Army must be doing something though, Neil' suggested Dave Urwin.

'Not much; the R.U.C. are pretty demoralised. Westminster has taken much of their authority away from them, and put them under a lot of restrictions. Some areas are totally unpoliced, either because they have been ordered to stay out or in most cases because it's too dangerous to go in. The Army are committed almost everywhere, but because they aren't trained for the job, sometimes their reactions are ham-fisted.'

'There are moments when we're given good reason, ya know Neil', smiled Jim fingering the thin pink scar on his forehead.

'Oh, aye! I'm not blaming them. It's the way everything's are being handled. No one seems to be interested in getting a grip of the place.'

'Well, surely the people are pissed off with it. They are bound to see sense soon', offered Urwin.

'You're out of touch over here, Davy. You don't know what's going on. The people of the Protestant areas and for that matter most of the Provence are getting on living their lives normally. But that isn't the case in the Catholic no go areas', explained Roberts to his brother-in-law, then turning to the Scotsman continued, 'I'm a telephone engineer, Jim, and the gang I work with is mixed. We're both Protestants and Catholics, so we are kept up to date on what's happening around Belfast and I'll tell ya the gunmen are taking over. At first calling themselves I.R.A., they were welcomed by most people as saviours; the only men they could count on to fight back against the R.U.C. and the Protestant mobs. But they soon showed everyone that they were nothing but bully boys and gangsters, out to get money by running protection rackets or stealing.'

'I still say the people won't sit still for it. Sooner or later they got to start bubbling these bastards', cut in Urwin.

'Hell, Davy, bubble them to who?' retorted Roberts, now speaking with an angry tone. 'The Police? The Army? Around the Springfield and Lower Falls they are still the enemy, and besides that would make them informers. Anyone brave enough to do that would be lucky to get into a court room. More than likely he would be knee-capped or done in.'

'Well, we're due out in a couple of months so we'll see it all for ourselves', reminded Sinclair, leaning forward to the coffee table to tap the end of his cigarette into an ashtray.

'Sounds a bloody mess', commented Urwin in mild anger.

'Well, it wouldn't be that way if the politicians would stop giving in to all these jumped up men of the minute who keep screaming to have their way.'

Robert's emotional out-burst was interrupted by his wife entering the room, carrying a tray of tea cups.

'What are you getting so red in the face for, Neil?' she asked.

'None of your business, woman' cut in her brother jokingly 'just give us our char.'

*   *   *

With elbows propped on the desk, mouth buried in the knuckles of his clasped hand, Sergeant Major Jerry Kettler stared at the small, brown paper package resting a few feet in front of him. He had been in this pose for half an hour now and looked to be set to remain so for the duration of the morning. This package, addressed to Kettler, was but the most recent of many.

For the last few months an anonymous campaign had been going on against Charlie Company's sergeant major. To begin with it was treated by Kettler as childish. Order forms for women's underwear, butcher's cutlery, wig firms and travel brochures to South America, the Far East, Russia and so on. But then gradually it became serious. Undertaker's advertisements, offers of grave plots, packages containing small wooden crosses, garlic and little sergeant major dolls with pins in. People also began to turn up.

Two men in a hearse, detailed to collect Kettler's last remains, arrived at the guard room. A ready mix cement lorry also turned up at the sergeant's mess to lay, as their written directions stated, two yards of wet concrete on the R.S.M.'s parking space. The invoice showed the order to have been indented for by a C.S.M. Kettler.

One morning, two representatives from an old, well-established Scottish insurance company, travelling overnight from Edinburgh, appeared at Charlie Company's office door. On placing the £100,000 life insurance policy before Kettler, they were at first politely surprised that he did not spring forward, pen poised, to sign; then none too pleased as the C.S.M. strongly denied any knowledge of this 'damn' policy. As they persisted, waving a typed and signed letter requesting them to bring the policy to him for signing. Kettler lost control and jumped up, swearing and screaming, to throw them out of his office. Unable to see the funny side of this little jest, both men stormed around to the adjutant's office, where, some minutes later, an abrupt telephone call brought Kettler around to join them.

For the next twenty minutes the adjutant strived to act the role of adjudicator while about him voices were being raised, arms waved and fingers pointed. This was finally ended by the adjutant losing patience, ordering C Company's sergeant major to reimburse the men from Scotland for any inconvenience caused by taking out a nominal £10,000 life insurance policy.

Whatever Kettler thought was in the little package on his desk, it had a mesmerising effect. No work was done that morning, except to answer the telephone, which rang from time to time. From the Company office next door, Corporal Pearson monitored his lack of activity by occasionally rocking his chair to one side so he could see the undisturbed package through the C.S.M.'s open door. At noon Kettler, being divorced and living in the mess, got up from his desk to take his lunch break there. He did not eat but went straight to the bar where he stayed drinking throughout the day. At midnight he returned to his office with a fire axe where, in a demented drunken rage, he began to chop the package and his desk into oblivion.

The Camp's two prowler guards, on hearing the noise, rushed up the Company office stairs to investigate, but rushed back down again as soon as they spotted the axe swinging lunatic. The Duty Officer, on being informed of the incident, collected the Medical Officer from his room and hurried down to C Company's office. There, between them, they spent some minutes trying to convince Kettler that the best thing was for him to put aside the axe and come with them. He agreed to come but refused to give up the axe. The M.O., not happy with this, smiling broadly stepped towards the C.S.M. and sedated his patient with a right upper cut to the jaw.

Kettler was taken first to the Cambridge Hospital for observation, where the local Army shrinks, diagnosing the sergeant major as having gone dually, sent him to Netley, outside Southampton, the Army's funny farm.

Of course the men of Charlie Company took his departure with feelings of relief, looking on it as if they had all suddenly found themselves cured of a long, lingering dose of the clap.

The Phantom Postman in his subtle little way didn't half get the job done right.

With one of his sergeant majors doing time in a padded cell and having to be replaced, the Commanding Officer compiled a short list of those colour sergeants he thought would be suitable for promotion, then submitted it to records for approval and selection.

*   *   *

Beth Kyle, pleased about her husband's sudden promotion to the rank of Warrant Officer, Second Class and looking forward to the extra money that it would provide, was also saddened. Over the past year that Sam had been posted to the Junior Leaders College, she had had, for the first time in a decade, a husband that worked regular hours. Home in the evenings, most weekends off and a fortnight's holiday that was actually proposed, planned and taken without one whisper of Sam being snatched away to some remote corner of the globe. Now with his unexpected return to 5 Para she knew that it was once more back to unhappy surprises and unwanted separations.

'Sam, where did you want this?' asked Beth, holding up a khaki embroidered cloth crown and the sleeve of his camouflaged airborne smock. Her husband, without replying, set his writing aside to rise from an easy chair. Moving around behind the livingroom couch, he leant over his wife's shoulder, brushing his face against her blond hair.

'Just here, love, about six inches from the cuff', he pointed, pausing to nibble her ear.

'Sam' she protested, pulling her head to one side. 'Now, what about your Number Two dress uniforms?'

'No, don't; I'll put them and my mess dress into the tailors', replied Kyle, moving around to sit beside his wife. Careful not to interfere with her sewing as he circled an arm over her shoulders. 'you'll have to put crowns on the pullovers though; I'll need them next week for Northern Ireland.'

'How long will you be away, Dad?' asked one of his seven year old twin sons, turning his attention from the television programme he and his brother were watching.

'About four months, Dave', replied Kyle.

'Hey, Dad, can you bring us back one of those rubber bullets like Bobby Collins's dad got for him,' asked the other son.

'Don't be stupid, Bobby. Dad will be far too busy with other things than to run around picking up souvenirs for you', cut in his fifteen year old sister, looking up from her school homework.

'I wasn't talking to you, big ear', retorted the boy.

'Don't call me names, you little devil', warned the slim, blond girl, standing, a ruler in her hand.

'Alright, alright' leaped in their father. 'Suzanna, the kettle's just boiled. Go rustle up a tea for your mother and me.'

'Bobby, your sister's right', explained Beth to her young son. 'Your father will have far too much to do with his new job than to run around the streets picking up bits of rubber for you.'

'Oh, okay', accepted the boy, disappointedly rolling back onto his stomach.

'Your mother worries too much, Bob. No promises but I'll see what I can do', contradicted Kyle.

'Great, Dad. Thanks', beamed the youngster.

'Yes, of course I worry', defended his wife, pushing an elbow into her husband's ribs. 'I worry every time you go away to these dangerous places.'

'Ulster's different, honey', assured Sam. 'The Paddys know better than to really start anything with the Army.'

'But they are killing soldiers', pointed out his wife.

'Oh, aye, unarmed ones or from ambush', replied her husband, playing it down. 'I'm not about to go anywhere unarmed or be ambushed.'

'Well, I still worry.'

'No need; paratroopers are too tough to die', joked Kyle, reaching up to accept one of the cups of tea his daughter had carried in from the kitchen.

*   *   *

'Coffee, Sir?'

Captain Dean Davidson lowered his arms and opened his eyes, recovering from the stretching yawn he had just allowed himself.

'Yes, thank you, Dick', he replied, looking at his watch. 'Two sugars please.'

'Right! It will be a minute or two. I'll just let them know in the back.'

The captain watched as the tall, dark R.U.C. constable left his desk. Then standing up, he walked to the doorway of Belfast's Summerhill Police Station to watch the Sunday morning traffic through the half-opened compound gateway.

Since his departure from 5 Para he had been with the Third Battalion, where, promoted, he was now serving as the 2 I/C of a Rifle Company. His role at the moment was that of community relations. The Commanding Officer, hoping to defuse tension between the Army and the local population, directed that an officer should be present at the Police desk during most of the day, listening to and sorting out any complaints that might come in about the Army. Now approaching the end of the tour, Davidson was looking forward to returning to his mother's farm in Sussex for a few weeks leave. For the first year of her marriage to Mick Pridmore, Davidson had spent very few days at the farm he once considered his home. But gradually, as he became aware that both were truly in love with each other, he began to return more often. There was still some embarrassment for him because of his mother re-marrying a man who was a corporal in his Regiment but this was never so great that he could not brush it aside, especially since accepting Mick for the soldier that he was.

'Here we are, Sir.'

'Ah, cheers, Dick', thanked the officer, taking the plain mug to raise it to his lips.

A woman of about thirty, scruffily dressed and accompanied by three small children, entered the station to approach the desk.

'Yes, dear?' asked the constable, placing his coffee behind him.

'It's my John. He's been hit by a sol'jer', she stated in a loud, rasping voice.

'You're saying a soldier has hit your son, is that right?' clarified the constable.

'You bet I am' she confirmed.

'Just where and when?' questioned the policeman further.

'About an hour ago, that's right, about an hour ago, wasn't it?' she asked of a dirty six year old boy at her side.

'Here, Constable MacKay, I'll deal with this. If it's a valid complaint I'll come back to you', offered the captain.

The constable, nodding his head, moved down the counter to deal with a young couple, the man, with a short beard and sunglasses, carried a plastic shopping bag.

'Here you are, love', began the Para captain, offering the woman a chair at his small desk. 'If I could just first have your name and address.'

For several minutes Davidson tried unsuccessfully to deduce from the youngster's story as to why a soldier out on foot patrol should, for some unexplained reason, just walk up and cuff the side of his head.

'Alright, Mrs. Delanney, we will have to take a statement from you and your son', he decided looking up for assistance. 'Constable McKay, could you . . .'

The officer's request was cut short by an object catching his eye.

'What's that?' he asked.

'What's what?' responded McKay, unable to see what Davidson was looking at because of the broad overhang of the counter.

'That' said the captain, standing up to walk across to a plastic shopping bag propped against the front of the counter, just below the young constable.

Standing above it to look directly inside, Davidson could see something wrapped in brown paper with two thin electrical wires protruding.

'Christ, Dick, it's a bomb. Clear the room', he shouted, rushing across to grab the two smaller children.

'This way, Sir, through the blast doors' shouted back the constable, pointing behind him.

The captain pulled the two children through the counter's swinging door.

'I'll take them, Sir', directed McKay, holding open a large door which lead to the back of the building while reaching forward for the two children. 'You grab that stupid bitch and the other kid; she doesn't know what time of fucking day it is.'

Turning back, Davidson took hold of the oldest child and the mother, who had stood up gripping her purse across her chest.

'God Almighty', she howled. 'What's the bloody fuss?'

The officer had to drag her and the boy to the other side of the counter, where the woman lost hold of her purse.

'My purse, you've taken my purse', she screamed as Davidson threw her and her son through the blast door.

Before taking shelter himself the officer reached back to retrieve the purse. As his right hand closed over it, the bomb exploded blowing the purse and arm away to the far wall.

Five pounds of gelignite set off in a confined space can do a powerful lot of damage. Instantaneously following the blast there is tremendous suction as the vacuum of the blast is refilled. Dean Davidson, already dead, would not have felt his eyes being wrenched from his head.

*   *   *

Stepping out of the kitchen door, Mick Pridmore pulled on an old army combat jacket in preparation for an afternoon's work around his wife's farm. Pausing after several steps, he turned to watch a car coming up the drive. As it halted, Pridmore remained still, overcome with puzzlement on seeing who it was. Major Bates, dressed in civilian clothes, climbed from the car to walk stern-faced towards him.

'Hello, Sir' greeted the big men simply, still too baffled to say more.

'Hello, Corporal Pridmore. I'd like you to meet my wife', replied Bates without a change of expression, turning to introduce the slim, attractive woman in her late twenties coming around from the passenger side of the car to join them.

'Hello, Mick' said the woman informally, extending her hand to briefly smile as she shook his. 'Is your wife in?'

'Yes, in the kitchen? we've just had a late lunch and she's washing the dishes', was the mystified reply.

'It's your wife we've come to see. Mick' began the major. 'Dean, her son, he was killed this morning in Belfast.'

Pridmore, stunned, stared for some seconds at the officer and then uttered just one word.

'How?'

'Bomb! It was placed in the Summerhill Police Station.'

Again there was a pause, this time broken by Mrs. Bates stepping forward to rest a hand on the corporal's arm.

'Mick, take us into the livingroom. Then bring your wife in. The major and I will break this terrible news to her. Don't you say anything about the reason for our visit to her, just be close when we tell her.'

Lynda Pridmore turned from the kitchen sink as her husband entered.

'Mick, I wish you wouldn't walk about the house with those dirty boots on', she scolded.

'We have some visitors, Lynda', stated Pridmore in a flat tone.

'Oh, I didn't hear them arrive. Who is it?' enquired his wife, wiping her damp hands on an apron as she walked towards the hallway door.

'It's Major Bates and his wife. Dean's old Company Commander', replied her sad husband turning to follow but being stopped by the house-proud woman pointing a finger.

'Mick, boots! Boots!'

Pridmore, kicking off the rubber boots, slipped into a pair of sandals to hurry after his wife.

'Hello', was her cheerful greeting to both. 'I'm sorry, Major, if you're looking for Dean he's not here. He's in Northern Ireland with the Third Battalion. I thought you would have known.'

'No, it's not Dean, Mrs. Pridmore. We came to see you but the reason we are here is because of your son. Can we sit down?' replied the solemn officer.

'Of course, forgive me', apologised the older woman, offering everyone seats with a quick, one-handed gesture before tucking her skirt against her legs and sitting down on a coffee coloured couch.

Sitting opposite on the edge of a large soft chair, John Bates, in a calm sympathetic voice, began to explain why he and his wife had made the long drive from Aldershot.

'Mrs. Pridmore, I'm sorry for having to tell you this, but I'm afraid your son is dead. He was killed this morning in Belfast by a terrorist bomb.'

Lynda Pridmore stared for a second.

'No! No! Not Dean. Are you sure?'

The major, looking directly at her, gently nodded his head.

'But! But! He phoned Friday night, he was well and happy', she desperately explained, unaware of the action as her hand shot across to grasp the one Mick had placed on her shoulder as he positioned himself behind her.

'I'm sorry', was all the major could think to say.

'But a bomb. That must mean a lot of disfigurement. Are they sure it's

Dean?' pleaded the mother in desperation, glancing quickly up at her husband for support.

'There is no doubt. I spoke to 3 Para's adjutant by telephone before leaving Aldershot', Bates reluctantly confirmed. 'I'm sorry.'

'Oh Dean, oh Dean', repeated Lynda Pridmore in a distraught voice, now clutching her husband's hand wth both of hers.

Mrs. Bates, standing up, asked softly, 'Mick, do you have any spirits in the house?'

'There's brandy in the cabinet', answered the big man, looking up fleetingly to indicate towards a corner of the room.

'Here Mrs. Pridmore', said the younger woman some moments later, sitting beside her to offer a small but full glass. 'Drink this.'

'Was anyone else injured?' asked the grief-stricken woman, releasing her husband to take the glass in both hands.

'No one seriously. A police constable with slight facial wounds, but other than that Dean was the only casualty.'

Major Bates paused to allow the woman to ask any other questions. But with none forthcoming, he began to explain in more detail the circumstances of the captain's death.

'He didn't die needlessly, Mrs. Pridmore. He was killed saving the lives of a mother and her children. It seems that if it hadn't been for the actions of your son, the family would more than likely have died.'

The major looked nervously at his hands before continuing.

'He gave his life to save others.'

'He would. Yes, Dean would. He was like that', replied the woman, fingering the glass between her hands.

Then, giving a nervous start, placed the drink to one side.

'Oh here, you'll have to excuse me, I've forgotten the dishes. The water will be getting cold.'

'Don't bother love, they'll keep', protested her husband, reaching out to stop her from standing, but was halted in doing so by Mrs. Bates coming to the older woman's aid.

'Quite right. Of course you do, and I'll give you a hand with the drying.'

Then, taking her arm, the two women made their way to the kitchen, where Lynda Pridmore collapsed sobbing over the sink.

In the early light of the following morning Mick watched his sleeping wife from a chair in which he had spent the entire night. Sleep had not come easily for her, kept at bay by anguish. The big paratrooper had found this sad situation one very hard to cope with. It was not death, for over the years he had experienced much of that, suffering the sorrow of dead mates as well as having killed himself. The pain he now felt was not for himself but for his wife, who he so wished to comfort but was unable to. Mick Pridmore had spent most of his Army service living in a world of boisterous exuberance punctuated by excitement and violence. Now, although since his marriage he had curtailed his hot impulsive nature, he was still unable to put into words the soothing phrases with which he so wished to console his wife. The previous evening she had begged him to leave the Army. With tears streaming down her face he could only sit and watch as he added to her tormented sorrow by simply shaking his head. He had no firm plans of completing a career with the Colours, nor was his refusal due to a lack of compassion towards his wife. On the contrary he loved her deeply. No, his reason was that of revenge, for Lynda

Pridmore had been savagely scarred and for that some bastard was going to pay.

*   *   *

'Look hang on a minute.' Dave Urwin's voice, full of apprehension, brought his two companions to a halt several yards from his Salamanca Park quarter.

'This isn't going to work; we'll never carry it off. Mary's no mug, she'll see through this straight away.'

'Sure we will, Davy. All I got to do is mumble a bit of French now and again and we've cracked it. Piece of piss', assured 'Yorky' Rush confidently.

'I don't know. I don't like having to lie to Mary', continued Urwin, not convinced.

'Dave, you got to come. Even though you've been down the Depot for two years you're still part of the Company', assured Reg Berrill.

'But Reg, it's our wedding anniversary. How do you think Mary's going to take this?'

'We'll just have to convince her that taking Yorky out is more important than that. Besides anniversaries come around every year anyway', pressed Berrill.

'Okay. But that's not the way women look at it', gave in Urwin, letting them know what the consequences of this hair-brained scheme could be.

'You two are going to land me in the divorce courts.'

Urwin had just cause for concern, for what his two mates were proposing was the sort of idea that is normally only conjured out of the bottom of a beer mug.

On finishing the day's training of the recruit Platoon to which he was attached, Dave had found the two privates waiting for him as he left the Depot. They had come to take him to a Patrol Company going away smoker that was being held in the Battalion N.A.F.F.I.. Urwin, although posted to the Depot for the last two years, had continued to keep close contact with his old firm, confident that at the end of his tour he would be returning to Delta Company.

He did very much wish to take the opportunity of having a last drink with these men before they departed on the Battalion's latest four month tour of Northern Ireland. So it was with some reluctance, explaining about his anniversary, that he had to refuse. However, Berrill and Rush, finding this totally unacceptable, walked their mate home, throwing up a number of sneaky deception plans as they did so.

Finally, Reg Berrill suggested a ruse that was so scatter-brained it was bound to work.

'Davy, remember the other year when the Company did that French parachute course at Pau?'

'Yah, what about it?' answered the Irishman.

'Well, Mary's never met 'Yorky'; suppose we say he's a French Para we met over there and he came across special to see you. So you got to take him to the Company party.'

As Urwin took in a deep breath, Reg turned to the Yorkshireman.

'How about it 'Yorky', ya think you can be a Frog for an hour or so?'

'Oui' replied Rush, not batting an eyelid.

'I don't think so . . .' began Urwin, but his doubts were unvoiced as Berrill impatiently interrupted.

'No problem, don't worry Davy, don't worry.'

'Hello, Dad', greeted Urwin's two children, as he lead the way into his combined livingroom-diningroom. The children, a boy of six and a girl of five, were sitting at the dining table eating their tea.

'Hi kids, where's your mother?' he asked.

'In here, Dave', came his wife's voice through the kitchen hatchway.

'Can you come into the front room, love? We got visitors', said Urwin.

'Hello, Reg', smiled Mary Urwin as she entered the room, her hair covered by a head scarf.

'Hi, Mary. Mary, I'd like you to meet Francois, he's French Airborne. He's across just for the day visiting', announced Berrill, not trusting Urwin to get it right.

'Oh yes', responded Mary. 'How do you do?'

'Enchanté, Mademoiselle, enchanté', replied Rush, in a Yorkshire-dressed Maurice Chevalier accent, stepping forward to kiss the young housewife's hand.

'Oh charmed', she joked, trying to suppress a blush, while turning to slap her husband's chest. 'Why don't you do that now and again?'

Urwin could only grin weakly. 'They're going to blow it, these two cunts are going to blow it', he thought to himself.

'Francois doesn't speak any English, Mary', he warned.

'"C'est bien rendez vous', thanked the woman, venturing into half forgotten school French.

Rush stared back blankly as Reg leaped in with a far-fetched cover.

'He probably can't understand you, Mary; he comes from the south, he's a Basque. They got a funny dialect there.'

Not allowing her to think on this, Dave quickly broke in with his trumped up tale of woe.

'Honey, bad news. I won't be able to take you out tonight. Francois is only in the Shot for the one night, and I feel obliged to take him out for a drink.'

'But Dave, it's our anniversary', replied his wife, shocked.

'I know, love, I know, but Francois took good care of me and some of the others when we were at Pau a couple of years ago, and I can't just ignore him now', he lied, feeling big enough to walk under the front door.

'But Dave, I've had my hair done. The babysitter's coming. . . .'

'I'm sorry, honey. Look we'll go out tomorrow,' he comforted, taking her in his arms to glare over her shoulder at his two accomplices.

'Alright, Dave' gave in his wife. 'I suppose if he only has the one night you'll have to entertain him.'

'Cheers honey, thanks. I'll make it up to you tomorrow. We'll go out for dinner to that pub you like in Hartley Wintney.' Then, kissing her temple, he pulled away. 'I'll just nip upstairs for a wash and change into civvies.'

'Because we were going out I didn't cook anything; are you hungry?' she asked.

'A little, but don't go out of your way. We'll have anything you can whip up', he replied, disappearing into the hallway.

'Well', she said, exhaling a breath of air, absent-mindedly making her proposal to the Frenchman, 'I suppose I could do a fry up, bacon, eggs, sausages; how does that sound?'

'Oh, a'oop lass, that sounds champion', replied the Yorkshireman. Then his beaming smile slowly receded to an expression of shocked horror as he realised what he had just said.

Mary, frozen speechless, her puzzled expression gradually turning to one of anger, stared first at Rush and then, slowly turning her head, she watched Reg

Berrill as he rolled back and forth on the family sofa, roaring with laughter.

Mary Urwin, her gaze striking sparks off the walls, rotated her head to shout just one slow deliberate word that was more than loud enough to carry into the hall and up the stairs.

'D–A–V–I–D.'

CHAPTER 6

There is no mistake; there has been no mistake;
and there shall be no mistake.

Duke of Wellington

Depending on the time of year, the sea approach to Belfast Lough can be as picturesque as any post card. 5 Para, or at least those who cared to step out onto the deck of the British Rail ferry in which they were being taken across the Irish Sea, found this morning one of those times. The sun, traffic light red from climbing through industrial haze of the English north west, stained the new day's landscape an artificial pink. To the south a purple skyline of rounded edges marked the location of the Mourne Mountains, while on either side of the water bright green early summer fields and woods rippled away towards townships and foot-hills. At the head of the Lough the first sight of Belfast was the huge shipyard cranes, standing testimony to the city's historic reputation of being one of Britain's main shipbuilders.

On approaching the dock area, the shore line beauty gave way to port necessities. Ships, tugs, small boats of all types, drab piers, ugly warehouses, rusty shipyard scrap and dirty water. A mirror image of any of a hundred ports throughout the world.

On the quay-side a knot of paratroopers stood watching as the ferry was secured to the dock. These were a mixture of 5 Para's advance party and escorts from the Third Battalion, each distinguishable by the square green patch on the upper smock arm of those from 3 and the tartan triangle sewn behind the beret's cap badge of the 5 Para men.

Leaving the ship was neither quick nor smooth, for the Army always worked to a standard drill in movement situations like this. While the main body cleaned the vessel, work parties and fatigue details busied themselves with baggage, vehicles and weapon bundles. Then, within the dock area, each Company held parades and roll calls to check for lost kit and account for numbers. An hour or so after the Battalion had completed disembarkation, amid much shouting and arm waving, the Companies climbed aboard waiting lorries to be dispatched to their respective locations.

Charlie Company, with its Patrol Company attachments, were first driven through the city centre, then cut along the Summerhill Road for a mile and a half, their destination a Police Station in the heart of a predominantly Republican council housing area.

Prior to the summer riots of '69, the Colinglen had been a small efficient post with a staff of perhaps a dozen, dealing with not much more than traffic problems and domestic squabbles. However, since the flare up it had become an island in a troubled sea. Despite this, the location's perimeter defences were, to say the least, low key. The station, a flat roofed brick building just off the Summerhill Road, stood open to view. At its vehicle entrance a sentry box was the only visable military presence at ground level, while on the roof there was a squat, sandbagged observation bunker. Above the police post on the hill slope that ran down from the Black Mountains was a children's primary school. This had recently been incorporated within the location, with part of the building being taken over to be used as the Company Command Post, sleeping accommodation and for cooking facilities. On top of the school were another two observation bunkers. Access for the children was a single gateway whose width was restricted by the token presence of the location's second sentry box.

Enclosing these two buildings, securing them, the school yard and the grassy slope behind the Police Station, were strung side by side two low rolls of concertina wire. Its use was little more than that of boundary marking for as a barrier it did little, allowing stray cats and dogs to roam through at will.

No one had to be a Sandhurst graduate to see that the position was not only a bad inheritance but also extremely vulnerable. To the north, on the slope above the location, were blocks of flats that literally hung above the wire enclosure. To the west, where the school gate was, houses only a few yards from the perimeter also looked in. The eastern side, although half dominated by flats, did give a degree of space. Waste ground dropped away for a hundred yards to a small stream that trickled down a re-entrance angling off the Black Mountains. On the far high lip of this re-entrance could be seen house tops, the fringe of a large Protestant estate spreading eastwards above Belfast. South, facing the Police Station from across the Summerhill Road was the Broughshane housing estate, a sprawling council complex that had become one of the more militant Republican ghetto.

It took some time for C Company to acclimatize themselves to patrolling in the 'Shane', for most of the occupants there seemed to lack the basic rudiments in the use of soap, water and rubbish removal. From this corner of Belfast, both night and day, a foul stench constantly oozed.

It was through the Police Station entrance that C Company's four tonners came, parking themselves tightly in the small yard. Behind, standing in groups or lying on the grassy slope leading up to the school, was the bulk of the 3 Para Company they were relieving. All smiles and jokes, they waited with their baggage and weapons for the newcomers to vacate the vehicles so that they might climb aboard and get out of the place.

On jumping from the tailboard of his lorry, Bobby MacIntyre found Lieutenant Taplow coming towards him, a holstered 9 millimetre automatic pistol on his hip.

'Good trip, Corporal MacIntyre?' he asked, with a half grin.

'I'm not the best of sailors, Sir, but it was smooth enough', replied the corporal, believing the night's voyage to be a one off, little knowing that 5 Para had just been given an unwished for season ticket to Ulster, guaranteeing MacIntyre many more ferry rides to come.

'How's our numbers?' asked Taplow, pushing both hands into the lower pockets of his smock.

'Down to twenty three now, Sir', answered the corporal, pulling his webbing equipment onto one shoulder while clutching his rifle in the other hand.

92

'Tyler's knee trouble came back when we did a run the other day. He was whipped into the Cambridge yesterday by the M.O.'

'Damn', cursed the young officer. 'We can't afford to lose men like that. We'll be working like slaves here, need every bloke we got.'

'What's the score then, Sir?' enquired MacIntyre, getting down to the business at hand.

'Basically we'll be working in Platoons, rotating jobs every three days. Once you have all settled into the accommodation and had an early lunch I'll brief everyone. But it will have to be quick; Corporal Jones will be taking his Section out on vehicle patrol at noon.'

On collecting their baggage, Taplow led his Platoon up to the school where the three Section Commanders who had accompanied him as the advance party a week earlier were waiting. They took charge of the men, allocating beds, room jobs and explaining the layout of the location. Those on early duty like Corporal Jones' Section were hurried into the school's small assembly room which had been turned into a dining room.

There to greet everyone, giving loud, almost non-stop directions and orders in his Cockney accent, was Corporal Len Hatton of the Army Catering Corps. Five foot six with sandy brown hair and a rosy face, clad in whites, he commanded the Battalion cooks attached to Charlie Company. From the back of the hot plate he organised the movement and food distribution of both those eating and his own men cooking and serving.

'Move chips, come on you're running out. If you want bread lads it's on the corner table—'ere, cunt, you just give them one chop. If they want more they come back—tea in the urn, no cups, you got to use your own mugs—Keith go get clean ladles from the wash up for this veg.'

'All cooks are queer', slagged a voice out of the queue of men waiting to be served.

'That's not what your wife thought the other night', responded Hatton as he slapped a spoon of mash potatoes onto an outstretched plate.

*   *   *

From minute one the Company found itself on a war footing. Since they had last been in the Provence events had escalated alarmingly. The two men unarmed foot Patrol they had last operated with over a year ago was gone forever. Instead sections of six to eight men, wearing flack jackets and fully armed, patrolling either on foot or in vehicles, toured the cities and countryside policing as best they could. The situation was bad and getting worse. There were sectarian murders and attacks on the security forces almost daily.

Up to now the Army had been relatively lucky; the number of deaths caused to them by terrorist acts was still in single figures. This was not due to any lack of attempts for they were numerous. The saving factor was military inexperience and mis-use of weaponry. The enemy was from the Roman Catholic section of the community, but split into two opposing camps. Both were known as the Irish Republican Army, a name taken from the rebelling forces that had caused the British Government to grant independence to Southern Ireland in the early 1920s. However, when the recent trouble began the I.R.A., previously a small impotant body, emerged from the chaos of the no go areas to take control. They did this initially in order to police and administrate but gradually, as their ranks were filled by opportunist, hot-headed patriots and criminals, internal feuding broke out in the organisation, renting it apart.

The moderates wished to operate the I.R.A. as a political force which would eventually win union with the South, whilst the extremists wanted out and out revolution, shooting and bombing their way to the same objective. Their inevitable parting was not amicable, but one of bloody assassinations and reprisals, fighting gangland style for territorial control. When the carve-up had settled, the extremists, known as the Provisional I.R.A., had secured the lion's share of the Republican ghetto areas, while the moderates, the Official I.R.A., were left with a number of isolated islands.

To combat all this lawlessness, C Company settled in to a well-practised routine, one to which they would be operating for the duration of their four month tour. 8 Platoon kicked off doing the location's patrol duties. For three days they would provide continual round the clock patrols throughout their Company area. 7 Platoon took over the guard programme, their men doing stags throughout the three days in the entrance sentry boxes and the roof top observation sangars. 9 Platoon were given what was supposed to have been the rest phase, that of standby Platoon. They were in theory only to have been used when an emergency arose, but found themselves the busiest of the three. As well as providing six men, dressed and fully armed, as the quick reaction, ready at all times in the standby room, they were also expected to supply the location's fatigue parties, men for escort duties and any impromptu patrols that might be laid on.

It did not take long for the novelty of this new situation to wear off. For boredom and drudgery generated by the operational routine to which they were working soon had most lulled into a false sense of apathy. This was understandable, for although 3 Para had one man blown up at the Summerhill Police Station and a number of shooting and bombing attacks on them, 5 Para had as yet no incidents to report. Perhaps this was acceptably comfortable to some but it was also dangerous. Heads, that during the first week had been erect and constantly turning, now spent long periods with the chin down. Eyes which had searched all buildings, people, patches of darkness and blind spots with suspicion, now began to glaze or stare. And why not—despite the sullen ignorance of most of the local population, this was still a major British city. The school children laughed and played, mothers came to the gate to collect them like anywhere else. Traffic flowed normally through the area, buses took people to work, day to day shopping was done by the housewives and everyone spoke English. Because of this the average soldier could not help but have the odd doubt as to why he was here.

This was dispersed for some one morning at the end of their second week. Bobby MacIntyre, whose Section had been driving around the area in a Humber four wheeled armoured personnel carrier, designated with the name Pig, probably because as a troop carrier it was one, decided to de-bus his men. They had been dozing in the back so the corporal to shake out cobwebs and keep them alert, lead them off on foot in two files, one either side of the street, the Humber following in a low gear close behind. As most street lights were not working due to vandalism or had possibly been shot out at some time, the only light was that given by the stars, the moon having long since set. At a street junction Bobby was signalled to come over by the lead man of his opposite file.

'Look at this cunt, Bobby', he pointed out, standing over a male figure, whose head lay unseen under a garden hedge. 'I've given him a kick but he ain't budged; must be paralytic.'

94

MacIntyre, also prodding with the toe of his boot and not liking what he felt, took a torch off his belt to shine it over the man's body. The light revealed the shirt he was wearing to be blood stained.

'Grab his arm, Wally, pull him out of the hedge', ordered the corporal.

The man's dark shoulder length haired head flopped sideways onto the pavement, a bullet hole in one temple.

Wally Forbes, eighteen years old and fresh from the Depot turned away to vomit into the gutter.

MacIntyre, placing his Patrol at nearby key points to cordon off the junction, radioed his Command Post to report their find. Shortly, Battalion vehicles began to arrive, the first being the M.O. with his Army ambulance.

'What have you got?' he asked of the corporal.

'Body, Sir, over here', MacIntyre replied, leading the way.

Pulling a handkerchief out, the officer blew his nose as he knelt down to examine the body.

'Yes, quite dead, gun shot wound to the head', was his instant autopsy.

'Fuck me, Sir, I could have told you that', replied MacIntyre with a dry, comical grimace.

'Ah, but one must make these things official', explained Ravencroft with subtle humour, placing his handkerchief back in his pocket.

'Now, what do we have here?' he asked, pulling back the bloody shirt to expose a gaping wound in the abdomen.

'Oh, very nice. I think I'll have that', he commented, opening his medical bag. From it he took out a pair of surgical scissors and a small jar. With the scissors he severed the thin tubes that held one of the man's kidneys as it hung from the wound.

'Souvenir for the M.I. room', he explained, popping it into the jar.

Wally Forbes, who was standing nearby, fetched what was left of yesterday's tea into the gutter.

It required little investigation to discover the reason for the murder. Sean Duggan, a known member of the local Official I.R.A., had been taken from his house in the Dunmarray Estate, an Official stronghold, the previous evening by several armed men. As he was lead away, his wife and three young children could only sit and watch.

*   *   *

With the Battalion settling in, visitors began to arrive. One of the first of these was their Brigade Commander, assessing operational practices adopted by 5 Para. The Commanding Officer, wishing to show the brigadier in some detail the ground his companies were occupying, took him up the gravel surfaced Gresham Road to the high ground above Charlie Company. The field into which the three Landrovers pulled had already been secured by a Section from 8 Platoon, a wise step on Major Bates's part for the party was a tempting target.

Accompanying the brigadier were three officers from his staff, whilst 5 Para's C.O. had brought along the adjutant, the Intelligence Officer and the R.S.M.. Major Bates had also invited his newly arrived Second-in-Command, a short, ginger haired man in his late twenties. He had already served once with C Company as 8 Platoon Commander, when the Battalion was on active service in Borneo. His name was Captain Simon 'Shush' Austen.

While the C.O. and Major Bates pointed out locations, boundaries and key points among the streets and houses below, Austen drifted off to one flank. There Roy Haydon, one of the picket sentries, watched as he drew his automatic pistol from its holster. With the eagle-eyed stare of an Indian scout, he took aim on selected I.R.A. pubs and houses and systematically began to blow them away with little 'krr's' and 'koo's'. While Roy Haydon collapsed into a bush giggling, the C.O., spotting what was happening, tried to edge his body around to block the brigadier's view of Austen. C Company's C.S.M., Sam Kyle, having experienced the captain's idiot actions in the past, closed his eyes and dropped his shaking head forward, saying to himself 'is that man never going to grow up?'

Grown up or not, Austen, in a schizophrenic way, had matured somewhat since his earlier days of no confidence. He had overcome this through hatred of everyone taller than himself, which was 95 per cent of the population of Britain, also acquiring a hairtrigger temper. That at times was not a bad thing.

One of these times occurred a few days later when a foot patrol from 7 Platoon spotted a wanted youth, suspected of carrying out a bomb attack on a 3 Para Saracen. The Patrol, playing it cagey, made as if to walk past, and then sprang on him. With both arms bent behind his back, he was run the quarter of a mile back to the location. Once word of this had spread, the hard core housewives, trouble-making youths and aggro stirrers from the Broughshane gathered at the Police Station entrance. This small but noisy mob was at first kept at bay by six or seven off-duty men of the Guard Platoon, but as they began to close in more tightly around the entrance, raising the decibel level by banging metal pots, pans and dustbin lids, 8 Platoon's standby section was ordered down from the school.

Captain Austen, sent by the O.C. to take command, also arrived, with instructions to disperse the crowd by talking them around to leaving peaceably. Passing to the front of the dozen soldiers who formed a half circle blocking the gateway, Austen began a dialogue with the crowd.

'Ladies, gentlemen', he began. This was Austen's first tour in Ulster and he had just made his first mistake by thinking that they were.

'This is an illegal assembly and you are acting in a riotous manner.'

'English fuckers!'

'Give us back Michael Foyle, ya Para bastards', howled the crowd in response.

'Michael Foyle is a wanted man and is now being held for questioning', defended the captain.

This was answered by more curses and repeated demands from the crowd.

'This behaviour will get you nowhere; return to your homes', he shouted.

The reply to this was jeering and an increase in metal banging noise. The men on the perimeter line behind 'Shush' were a picture of patient discipline. Dressed in their multi coloured camouflage airborne smoke and steel helmets, armed with either riot guns or long wooden batons, they stood holding their riot shields before them and waited. In the yard behind more men had gathered as an unofficial reserve. These were off duty drivers, cooks and Company Headquarters staff. Len Hatton, unable to acquire a baton, appeared with the cook house rolling pin pushed into his belt. Opportunities of inflicting pain on those who were responsible for imprisoning them in this little compound were rare and at all costs not to be missed.

Austen, speaking with the full force of his authority, gave the unruly gathering before him a final warning.

'Disperse! All of you disperse. I command you to disperse', he cried, his arms raised above his head.

This was ignored, producing instead more jeers and laughter.

The captain, about to repeat his order, caught from the corner of his eye one of the flank soldiers raising his baton to strike a woman. She, after edging up close to the perimeter guard, had just spat in his face.

'Stop! That man stop!' shouted Austen, pointing with one finger. 'Lower your baton. You must not lose control. Tolerance, you all must show tolerance'.

However, to the glee of Charlie Company, 'Shush' did not practice what he preached.

From the back of the crowd a stone was thrown, striking the side of the captain's face and spilling him backwards in a sprawl at Phil Haydon's feet.

Leaping up in a furious rage, with a downward swing of his arm he gave his command, a brief but unrestricted mandate.

'Kill them.'

As his men rushed forward he snatched Haydon's riot gun to take aim and began squeezing the trigger. Phil watched for a second as this demented creature tried to make the weapon fire, then reaching forward pushed a small metal lever.

'Safety catch, Sir', he recommended.

'Shush' never heard him. He merely shoved the gun back at Haydon as the rubber bullet from his first shot pitched a running woman forward on her face in the middle of the Summerhill Road.

'Load it, hurry up and load it again', he screamed.

From that moment on C Company, out of curiosity as to what he would do next, were prepared to follow 'Shush' Austen anywhere.

*   *   *

Over the next week a number of minor protests and demonstrations were organised by supporters of the I.R.A. to highlight, as propaganda, the unprovoked brutality exercised on the innocent women and children who had gathered that day outside the location. Normally these would be instigated about mid-morning, after the mothers had delivered their children to school. The standby Platoon was obliged to react to this for containment purposes, restricting the demonstration to as small an area as possible.

One of the first to be dealt with was in the 'Shane'. Corporal 'Jonesy' Jones was dispatched to block one of the streets and thus ensure that the mob did not spill out, obstructing traffic on the busy Summerhill Road.

With riot shields raised they waited as a large party of women chanting and banging pans together swarmed towards them. As they pushed up to the line of soldiers, the Paras gripped their weapons ready, if necessary and without compulsion, to start cracking skulls. One of the women, a few feet to the front of Chris Braithwaite, banging and chanting 'British troops out' like the rest, leaned towards him. Braithwaite braced himself, expecting to receive a mouthful of fluid, instead, what she did shocked him much more than any act of violence.

In a voice just loud enough to be heard above the din she pleaded, 'don't go, lads, don't leave us to these murdering bastards', then straightening up, rejoined the chanting 'British troops out, British troops out'.

*   *   *

Some days later the I.R.A., satisfied that Charlie Company had been lulled into a sense of routine, decided to escalate things.

Lieutenant Taplow, holding a street junction with two sections of his Platoon, watched as a thin man in his forties, controlling two mongrel dogs on leads, approached from his rear. With mute hand signs he asked to go through the cordon. Taplow granted permission by waving him on with an arm. Ducking under a soldier's riot shield, dragging the two dogs behind him, he pushed through the crowd of chanting, swearing, pot-banging women and youths. On reaching their far side he turned around, produced a whistle from his pocket and began to blow it in long drawn out shrills. On hearing that signal the mob melted away through front doors and pathways leading to the rear of houses. It only took ten to fifteen seconds for the street to empty, leaving the line of Paratroopers alone and exposed.

Lieutenant Taplow, like the rest of his men, stood for a moment, mystified by this action, before realising the danger and then began to shout.

'Take cover! Take cover!'

Before the men could react to this urgent warning, an American Thompson sub-machine gun began to fire from somewhere down the street. With riot shields being discarded the cordon broke apart, some driving behind garden hedges and low walls others into doorways, kicking the door in if more cover was needed.

Crouching in a gateway, Taplow began to shout orders.

'Can anyone see him? If you can for Christ's sake shoot back.'

For most this was not possible. They had been dealing with a riot situation and had armed themselves accordingly. Only a few carried rifles; the rest had left theirs in the Humber a street length to the rear.

As another burst of enemy fire skipped down the street, a soldier sheltering in a doorway shouted, 'there he is.'

'Where? Where? For fuck's sake', demanded 'No Way' Ottoway, one of those armed with a rifle.

'On the right side of the street, in the hedge just below that pink rose bush', came a high pitched, rushed reply.

Ottoway, quickly raising his rifle above the low wall he had chosen for cover, took aim and fired several times.

'Can you see him Ottoway?' cried his Platoon Commander.

'No, Sir, but I bet I scared the shit out of him', came the reply.

'Right, well watch out for him. I want you to keep the bastard's head down', ordered Taplow before looking around for his Signaller.

Seeing him in the opposite garden, the officer, crouching low, sprinted across the street.

'Durrant, have you sent Zero a contact report?'

'Yes, Sir, but they keep asking for you', he replied, holding out the hand set of the radio he carried on his back.

'No time' was the lieutenant's sharp answer before giving the soldier a set of brief orders.

'Tell them we have at least one gunman here and that I'm about to deal with him. But the Company has got to get cut offs out on the ground quick in case he gets away. Understood?'

'Understood, Sir', replied the young Scotsman, raising the radio's mouth piece to his lips.

'Okay. Now whatever happens you stay here. If I want you I'll send for you. Just keep Zero off my back for ten minutes', was his last command before standing up to wave one of the armoured cars forward. Then, turning to shout at his nearest Section Commander, he began motivating his men for a counter-attack.

'Corporal Jones, get your men into the Pig. We're going after the gunman. Ottoway, can you see him yet?'

'No, Sir', came the loud negative reply.

'Well, keep watching and when we start to move I want you to open up and pin him down.'

As the heavily armoured Humber crashed to a halt, Jones and his Section rushed from cover, throwing themselves into the back compartment, snatching up the first rifle that came to hand.

Taplow, pulling open the passenger door, shouted to the driver.

'Straight down the street, Buckley, and hammer it. Don't stop till I say so but when I do I want the anchors on. Now let's go. Come on, go!'

As Buckley threw the vehicle into gear, to stand on the accelerator, Ottoway opened up. The armoured car, racing for a hundred and fifty yards, was still building up speed when Taplow shouted to stop. The Humber screeched to a halt in a sideways skid just where the lieutenant wished it, two houses the far side of where the gunmen was thought to be. As everyone de-bused into cover he ordered his Section Commander to take two men into the back gardens to cut off any retreat, but it was too late. On skirmishing forward with the rest of his men they found the fire position to be abandoned. All that was discovered in the area of the rose bush was a scattered number of empty 45 calibre cases.

*   *   *

5 Para, although on an active posting combating urban terrorism, was not considered to be that fully committed operationally, resulting in the Battalion's normal peacetime routine hardly being interrupted. This involved sending men home on leave, whether it be entitled or compassionate and releasing those due for courses and duties. There was also a steady turn around of personnel being posted out and in.

A month into the tour the latest of these posting ins, a newly promoted sergeant, arrived at the Colinglen. Climbing from the back of the Humber, he slung his bergen over one shoulder, while reaching back inside it to pull out his Army issue suitcase.

'H.Q.'s up in the school, Sarg, I'll send one of my lads with ya to show ya where to report', offered the lance corporal who had collected him from the Summerhill Police Station which was 5 Para's H.Q..

'No, that's alright, I'll find it', declined the tall, sandy blond haired sergeant setting off up the pathway.

The time being just after midday he found himself crossing a school yard of laughing, shouting children at play. One corner of the yard, just outside a side entrance to the school building, had been set aside as a dining area. There, seated at several six-foot tables eating lunch, were twenty or so of the Company. Making his way down a hall he entered the assembly room where a small queue of men were being served their meal by the Company cooks. Standing with them, behind the hot plate, as the Duty Officer of the day, was Sam Kyle. When the two men's eyes met both broke into broad grins. Kyle, hurrying out from behind the hot plate, said nothing until he was close enough to reach out and shake the newcomer's hand.

'Congratulations, Davy. I heard we were getting a new sergeant but I didn't know it was to be you.'

'Thanks, Sir. I didn't expect to be coming here either', replied David Urwin, who had received his promotion while attached to the Depot and was now 5 Para's newest senior non-commissioned officer.

'Well, like it or not, we need you. You'll be going to 8 Platooon. Corporal MacIntyre has been holding the fort as Platoon Sergeant, but he's off to Brecon shortly on his S/N.C.O. tactics course. You got a good Platoon Commander there so it'll be alright', explained the Company Sergeant Major.

'Oh aye, but still, Sir! Fucking hell, I'm Patrol Company. I thought I was coming back to them', replied the sergeant, showing his disappointment.

'Well, perhaps you can talk the C.O. around when you go on your joining interview', offered Kyle.

'Already had it', explained Urwin sickly. 'The adjutant whipped me in front of him when I arrived at Battalion H.Q. from the airport. I tried to explain I was Patrol Company trained and wanted to go back to them, but he wasn't buying it. Kept telling me about how stagnant promotion could be in D Company and how I should be broadening my base within the framework of the Battalion.'

'Ya, good that', smiled Kyle. 'We've all heard it before but you can't argue against it.'

'I did go and see the R.S.M., thought he might help', continued Urwin.

'You went to 'Nuts'', interrupted the C.S.M., no longer smiling. 'Any Joy?'

'Not a sausage', snickered Urwin. 'When I walked into his office to see him, he set me down in a chair. When I told him I wanted him to ask the C.O. to change his mind, he kicked me out and threatened to put me in close arrest.'

On hearing this, Sam Kyle folded up with laughter before giving the sergeant a few words of wisdom.

'Dave, never! But never, go to 'Nuts' Norris for anything', then laying a hand on his shoulder lead him across the room. 'Come on, leave your kit behind the hot plate for now. Let's grab something to eat. I'll take you in to meet the O.C.; he's having lunch in our lounge room.'

'Hello, Sergeant Urwin', came a cheery Cockney voice as they approached the cook's serving counter.

'Hello, Corporal Hatton', replied Dave in a similar false cheery voice, each man smiled broadly at the other. Both, very good friends, were normally on first name terms, but because of Urwin's promotion a barrier of rank now existed which they acknowledged with mimical greetings.

'Are you going to eat now, Sir?' the corporal asked the C.S.M..

'Ya, I suppose so. What is it, that cardboard liver you've been giving everyone?' said Kyle sarcastically.

'You know better than that, Sir. Have I ever seen yuh wrong?' defended Hatton, opening one of the hot plate compartment doors to produce a steak covered plate.

The officers and S/N.C.O.s lounge used to be a small classroom, but it had been taken over by them as a mess and off-duty relaxation room. One half was taken up with dining chairs and tables, the other half with easy chairs and a few coffee tables. A television set sat on a sideboard in one corner. The room was lit by fluorescent lighting. For like every other part of the building occupied by the army, the windows were blacked out and boarded to frustrate snipers.

As Kyle and Urwin entered, Major Bates, putting his tea cup down, stood up from one of the easy chairs to greet them.

'Sergeant Urwin, Sir. It seems he's just been posted in', introduced the sergeant major.

'Yes, I know' welcomed the O.C., stepping forward to shake the sergeant's hand. 'The adjutant rang earlier on the blower to say you would be arriving; said you didn't seem too happy about coming to a Rifle Company.'

'Nothing personal, Sir. It's just that I've been with Patrol Company for a long time, and after the Depot I was looking forward to coming back', replied Urwin sheepishly.

'Yes, I know, I was 2 I/C of 3 Para's Patrol Company for a year and a half so I know what it's like having to return to basic infantry work', offered Bates, sympathetically extending an arm towards one of the dining tables. 'However, we'll talk about it in a moment over a cup of tea. But first, please have your lunch.'

Later Sam Kyle took him on a tour of the location finishing in the Company C.P.. This Command Post room, constantly manned by a Signaller and a Duty Watch Keeper, who was either an officer or senior N.C.O., was the Company nerve centre. From it all communications were transmitted; informing and being kept informed by Patrols and those involved in operations throughout the Company's very large area of responsibility.

Two radio nets were in use, one for the Company and the other for the Battalion of which they were a sub-station. Above and around the table where the radios were mounted, fixed on the walls, were maps, photos of key locations, lists of names, places, telephone numbers, patrol details and operational code words. On one wall was a large aerial photograph of the housing estates around the Colinglen Station. Pinned beside this, marked in multicoloured chinagraph, was a detailed map of Belfast.

'Got you a new Platoon Sergeant here, Sir', introduced Sam Kyle to Lieutenant Taplow, who, as Duty Watch Keeper, was standing, coffee cup in one hand, tracing his finger over a street map.

'Well, it's about time. I'm sick of doing double shifts in this C.P.', joked the officer, stepping forward to shake Urwin's hand.

Over the next twenty minutes, Taplow and the C.S.M. took Urwin through a casual briefing of the command post's set up and operating procedure and of the area they were looking after. This was interrupted by a head appearing through the small window hatch that looked into the intelligence cell next door.

'Looks like they let anyone in the sergeant's mess nowadays, eh Sir?' said Reg Berrill, addressing the Company Sergeant Major.

On hearing the voice, Urwin spun around with a smile, moving quickly across to the window to grab Berrill's ears.

'Don't give me your lip, Private Berrill, or I'll put you in the fucking slammer.'

Then, looking beyond him into the room and seeing more familiar faces, continued the private humour.

'Christ, who let you bunch of wankers loose in an Int's room?' Without waiting for replies he asked of Reg, 'How do I get around?'

'Out into the hall, then first left', was his reply.

Still smiling he turned to his new Platoon Officer with an apology.

'Excuse me a minute, Sir, they look a bit slack next door.'

As he left Taplow turned to the C.S.M. with a satisfied look. 'He seems alright.'

Sam, with a sideways glance at the Duty Signaller who was reading a paper, confirmed his approval with a pucker of his lips.

For half an hour Dave remained in the Intelligence room chatting to old friends as they drank coffee or busied themselves with paperwork, showing surprise when he revealed his lack of knowledge of the local area.

'Sorry', he confessed. 'Around here it's mainly Catholic. As far as I'm concerned it may just as well be the Gobi Desert.'

'Fucking hell, you were born in this town and you mean you've never been here before?' asked Yorky Rush, finding this hard to believe.

'Sure and I bet not many of them have been down your street either. Eh Dave?' stepped in Paddy Kieron, answering the question for him.

'Shouldn't think so', replied Urwin, lifting his eyebrows.

'They really opened a can of worms when they nailed that cunt to the cross, didn't they?' commented Berrill drily.

'You wouldn't know this character then, would you?' asked Jim Sinclair, tapping a large display board above where he was sitting.

Standing up the sergeant studied one of several head and shoulder photographs, of a man in his late thirties, for some moments before shaking his head.

'Nope.'

'This is public enemy number one, Patrick Noyan', explained the dark Scotsman with distaste. 'Picks his nose and eats the black bits. He's the Company Commander of the local Provisional I.R.A..'

'Yuk' winced Urwin. 'Any chance of picking him up?'

'Uh'ah' replied Sinclair, shaking his head. 'This gungy creep has knocked people off. Just last week we're pretty sure he did an official in, but we got no proof.'

'It's the same with all of them', he continued, passing his hand over the board. '3 Para fingered a lot of active people and we've added more names but we can't touch them without evidence.'

'What about the R.U.C.? Can't they help?' asked Urwin.

'Not here. They can't operate; it's too dangerous. Down in the station you'll only find one copper on duty and he goes home at five o'clock', answered Sinclair.

Inwardly Urwin cursed, for he remembered the Royal Ulster Constabulary in the past to be men highly respected throughout the Province.

At the end of Lieutenant Taplow's C.P. duty he took his new sergeant to meet the men of the Platoon. Being the Guard Platoon this was done as a tour around the billets, observation posts and sentry boxes, meeting them individually or in small groups. Some, like Wally Forbes, Urwin already knew having been one of his Recruit Platoon Corporals during the youngster's Depot training.

After the better part of half a day in which to settle in, Dave Urwin began the duties of his new appointment. At midnight he took over as Watch Keeper in the C.P., on the dog watch from twelve to four in the morning.

CHAPTER 7

A single death is a tragedy,
a million deaths is a statistic.

Joseph Stalin

Despite the number of troops now involved in internal security throughout the Provence, day to day policing in many parts was almost non-existent. Without the constant presence of an authoritative body responsible for dealing with minor and major crimes, the law-abiding members of the community had become frustrated and frightened. When wrongs were committed, whether it be a window smashed or a murder, they did not dare go to the Police or Army. This would very likely only bring reprisals by the local I.R.A. thuggery against them. The only option left by which to seek justice was this very same thuggery.

The I.R.A. were supposed to be the protectors of the community maintaining law and order within an anarchist situation which they had helped to engineer. If they did respond to a citizen's request for justice this probably meant he was either paying protection money or had strong Republican ties. And even then the only judicial punishment they could provide was that administered from the barrel of a gun. For the I.R.A., regardless of their claims of being the protectors of the Catholic community, operated nothing more than godfather style gangsterism.

Many Catholics were appalled by all this but there was little they could do about it, for they were in the grip of a 1984 situation. To voice disapproval of the I.R.A. and their methods would only result in being informed on by work colleagues or neighbours, which would soon follow with a visit from the I.R.A.'s gestapo who would either cripple or kill.

Outwardly the Army's armed patrols looked to be a deterrent but their effectiveness was limited. The presence of soldiers in a street was momentarily reassuring, but when they moved on their authority and ability to protect moved with them. These were unhappy circumstances for everyone except the I.R.A. who, through terror, could now rule and persecute at will.

Becoming more aware of this the Provisional I.R.A. stepped up the number of bombing and shooting attacks. By doing this they could show that they had the freedom and capability of implementing their intended policy of blasting Britain out of Ulster. There was also a secondary intention, one which some Provisionals considered more important than the first. That of showing the

Republican ghetto population that they were now the dominating force and not the Officials.

*   *   *

With a yawn Bobby MacIntyre slid into the front passenger seat of the stripped down Landrover, that would be his patrol vehicle for the next four hours. Giving an involuntary shiver from the coldness of the seat covers as it penetrated his olive green trousers, he glanced over his shoulder to check that the men in the second Landrover behind were ready to move.

'Okay Danny. Let's go', he ordered his driver, laying the baton gun he held in both hands across his lap.

'Out the gate, turn left down the Summerhill Road, then right down Lisnacarrol. We'll take a spin through Hopefield Street, then swing back up into the 'Shane'.'

While pausing at the barrier to wait for the sentry to pull the wooden pole to one side, Bobby gave another yawn. It was midnight and the corporal, unable to find sleep between patrols during the day, was showing his tiredness.

Turning into the Summerhill Road in the direction of the city centre he reached for the radio hand set.

'Hello Three, this is Three Two Alfa. On patrol over.'

'Hello Three Two Alfa Roger, out', came back the C.P. Signaller's sterile reply.

Although unenthusiastic about driving around for the next four hours in the bleakness of a Belfast night, MacIntyre had been looking forward to this patrol for several weeks. Hopefully this was to be his last, of the Battalion's present tour. For he was due to start his Senior/N.C.O. tactics course at Brecon in Wales in a few days time, and was booked on a flight out of Aldergrove Airport at nine o'clock that morning, a move he was looking forward to immensely.

Following the corporal's instructions the driver turned off the Summerhill Road into a dark deserted street. On their left high concrete fencing with barbwire on the top hid a large timber yard. To the right were buildings that had housed small businesses but many were now vacant, either frightened away because of the trouble or not prepared to pay the I.R.A. protection money.

Here the vehicles slowed to give the soldiers more of an opportunity to spy out the shadows and alley ways, a drill that had not gone unnoticed by the local hoods.

On passing abreast of a parking recess enclosed by two buildings either side and a high wall, behind which was a shrub covered bank, the Patrol ceased to be ordinary. Ahead of the first Landrover a line of sparks arced into the roadway, followed closely by a second.

'Take cover', shouted MacIntyre, recovering himself from the sudden jolt to tumble out into the street.

Behind the second Landrover, which had also braked sharply to a halt, another two fuse spluttering home-made blast bombs clattered into the road.

From the banking above the car park a low velocity shot was fired, striking the concrete wall beyond the first Landrover.

MacIntyre, scrambling to his feet, peered over the Rover's protective framework. With the driver and the other two men who had been riding in the back diving for cover, he was the only one to see a figure stand up and then turn to run up the bank. Taking a snap shot with his baton gun, he watched in frustration as the rubber slug struck the shoulder of his target causing the man to stumble but not stop.

'Shoot! Shoot for fuck's sake, somebody shoot those bastards', hollered the corporal as two more figures rose to follow the first.

Wally Forbes, crouched at the tailboard of the vehicle, came up to aim his rifle in the direction MacIntyre was pointing, but was stopped by one of the front blast bombs exploding sending him, like the rest of the Patrol, down onto the surface of the roadway.

'Stay down! Stay down!' shouted the corporal again, expecting the other bombs to detonate as well.

For fifteen long seconds the Paras remained pinned down awaiting the explosions. When none came Bobby took a gamble.

'Chris, get your lads mounted, then get back up onto Summerhill and turn down the Ballyclare. They're heading back into the 'Shane'. Try and cut the bastards off.'

'Right you heard, Bobby', screamed Chris Braithwaite, the senior soldier in charge of the rear vehicle. 'Get on board, come on, mount! Mount!'

With Braithwaite and his men scrambling back into their Landrover, MacIntrye struggled physically and mentally to get half a dozen things done at once. Reaching for the radio hand set, he shouted to the two men who had been riding in the back.

'Wally, Joe, get over that wall on to the bank. Don't go far, but if anything moves, shoot it.'

Pressing the send button on the hand set, he gave his headquarters the beginning of his incident report.

'Hello Three, this is Three Two Alfa, contact! I say again contact! Wait out.'

Then releasing the button he shouted more directions, this time at his driver.

'Danny, get this wagon off the road, over there by that building', he pointed.

Then again he began speaking over the radio.

'Three Two Alfa. Reference contact, ambush, gunmen, Lisna Carrol Road opposite Franklin's woodyard. I think they've run off towards the Broughshane. Have sent my sub-unit around to Ballyclare Street to try and cut them off.'

In the C.P. the first indication that something was up was a report over the field telephone from the observation post above the Police Station that shots and an explosion had been heard. This was shortly followed by Three Two Alfa's contact report. With that the location's midnight calm evaporated.

While the Duty Officer took control of the Company radio net, the Signaller informed Battalion H.Q. that C Company had a contact. In the same instant the C.P. runner was shaken out of his dozing to be hurried off to warn the standby Sections to get ready to move, and inform Major Bates that some of his men had been shot at.

Dave Urwin, having been on patrol with Corporal Jones' Section, was having a cup of tea with the O.C. in the lounge room. On the runner's news he sped off to collect his Patrol, also waking Lieutenant Taplow, who bolted bleary-eyed from his bed to bring his Platoon's Third Section onto the alert.

Meanwhile back at the ambush, Corporal MacIntyre was coming under more pressure.

'Bobby', shouted Wally Forbes, 'we're fucked, there's not a chance of getting over this wall, it's too high.'

'Hello Three Two Alfa', crackled his radio. 'Send sitrep, send sitrep, over.'

'Hello Three, this is Three Two Alfa, wait out. Wally, try through one of the buildings. I don't care how—if you got to kick doors and windows in, then do it —but get up onto that bank.'

'Bobby,' broke in the driver, 'we can't stay here with those bombs. The pissing things could be on a slow fuse.'

'For fuck's sake I know that, just keep your head down. If they go off we'll let the Rover catch the shit.'

'Hello Three Two Alfa! Three Two Alfa, over!' interrupted an annoyed Duty Watch Keeper's voice over the radio.

'Three Two Alfa send, over', responded the corporal.

'Three Two Alfa, you must remain on this net. I repeat you must remain on this net, we must be kept informed as to what is happening. Now send sitrep.'

MacIntyre, battling with the heat and confusion of an ambush situation, held his temper to comply.

'Roger! Do you require starlight?' he was asked after describing what had been done and what he was doing.

'Three Two Alfa, reference Starlight. No. However will require Alfa Tango Oscar rep to deal with unexploded blast bombs, over', replied the corporal, declining the offer of medical assistance but requesting that of the Royal Army Ordnance Corps Bomb Disposal Squad.

The corporal, having survived a well planned but badly executed ambush with no injury to either himself or his men, had no one but lady luck to thank. On A.T.O.'s examination of the bombs it was found that the reason only one exploded was due to botched manufacturing; the home-made detonators falling out of two, whilst the other had no detonator at all. In future months it was learnt that on the firearms side they had been equally fortunate. The main fire power was to have been a Thomson machine gun and two pistols. But on the machine gun jamming after firing only one round, the three gunmen fled, leaving behind the two pistols which were found during a search of the area at dawn.

Bobby, whose priorities had been first the safety of his men and then instigating some sort of anti-ambush move, soon learnt how bad his appreciation of what should have been done was.

First Major Bates rifted him for splitting his Command, sending the second Landrover off with no radio of their own to remain in communication with. He also demanded to know why Bobby had stayed within the ambush area, in close proximity to three known unexploded devices.

The C.O.'s arrival only continued the movement, pointing out that the ambush area should have been closed off to minimise any risk to civilian life and demanding to know what justification MacIntyre had in ordering his men to damage private property of the nearby buildings in gaining access to the banking.

Approval of his actions came from limited quarters. After the dressing down, Sam Kyle and Dave Urwin, who between them over the last ten years with 5 Para, had probably been shot at more times than the rest of the Battalion put together, with guarded winks and a slap on the back gave him confirmation that everything he had done had not been totally wrong.

Lieutenant Taplow was even more frank, congratulating his corporal for the positive action he took in trying to cut off the ambushers' escape.

For the remainder of Three Two Alfa's Patrol, all of 8 Platoon, plus the standby Section, odds and sods from Company H.Q. and outside support elements were kept on an active footing. Most were on the move in ever broadening sweeps, patrolling the western half of the Broughshane hoping to flush out one or more of the ambushers, while the rest provided security pickets at the attack site guarding search teams and A.T.O. personnel.

Bobby MacIntyre, reflecting on the events of his final Patrol and irritated that his reaction to the ambush had been considered by his Commanders as questionable, made to check off duty. Tired, with stiff, aching limbs, he entered the C.P. to give a brief verbal report on the incident to the Watch Officer. He, a young Second Lieutenant commanding Nine Platoon, scolded the older corporal for further negligences, like not informing him of all actions as they happened and his gross laxness in updating situation reports. What he meant and did not mention was that Battalion, in the early stages of the ambush had been continuously putting him on embarrassing spots by asking by radio and telephone for information which he did not have.

Bobby, aware that those who sit over radios in warm cosy rooms were galaxies away from understanding the priorities of men under fire, was too numb to put up a defence. With what he hoped was a passable expression of guilt, he stood, eyes downcast, murmuring little submissions of 'Yes, Sir! No, Sir!'

MacIntyre, his future for the next two months to be rain, cold, sweat and lack of sleep at a Welsh mountain battle school, paused in the hallway to kick the wall twice and scream at the top of his voice.

'Roll on bloody Brecon!'

It was a childish thing to do but it made him feel a hell of a lot better.

*   *   *

'Okay, hold it here Buckley, pull into the side of the road and switch off.'

The Humber driver, obeying Dave Urwin's request, eased his heavy vehicle half onto a grassy verge and stopped the engine.

With the aid of moonlight and lighting from the odd street lamp, the sergeant tried to study the ground to his front. They were parked on the brow of a slight rise, looking down the slope of a road that crossed a culvert allowing a small stream to pass under the roadway. On either side of this, as it climbed gradually away from the stream bed, was overgrown waste ground. This ended after two hundred yards as the road, bending around to the right, disappeared behind the first perimeter houses of the Broughshane. Further on but unseen, the road junctioned with the Summerhill. On the south west corner of this junction was a notorious Republican pub, Murphy's Bar. Over the last year this waste ground below Muphy's had become a favourite ambush site for the I.R.A.. Once they had fired their weapon or thrown a bomb, escape was a simple matter of either slipping into the Broughshane or running west across the waste ground into another Republican estate, Connaught Park.

For some minutes Urwin studied the road and ground each side, trying to pick out anything of suspicion hidden in the varying shades of darkness. There was ample justification for the Patrol Commander's caution.

Earlier, a person not giving his name had telephoned the location to say there was a body lying in the road below Murphy's Bar. The call could be a genuine one made by someone with good intentions, but more likely it was a hoax or worse. For this was a common method of the I.R.A. of luring the Security Forces into traps, resulting recently in the death of a number of policemen and soldiers.

On being dispatched to investigate this, Urwin, heedful of the risk, set off with understandable prudence. Instead of driving the short distance from the location up the Summerhill Road to Murphy's Bar he took the long way round. Turning down Lisnacarrol they swung south of the Broughshane estate to join the road they were now halted on, driving the last quarter of a mile without lights.

'See anything Buckley?' asked Urwin, not taking his eyes off the road beyond the stream.

'Nope! Not a thing', replied the driver. 'But I'll tell you what, Sergeant, for 11.30 at night I've never seen this road so empty. Normally there's at least half a dozen Paddy's staggering back from Murphy's along here.'

Not answering, Urwin twisted in his seat to speak through a small hatch window which was the only way of communicating with his Patrol in the back.

'Corporal Jones', he softly called.

'Yup', came back a voice from the depths of the darkened personnel compartment.

'Between here and Murphy's it's like a graveyard, so we're not going to take any chances. In a couple of minutes we'll coast down to the stream and stop on the other side. When we do, you get your lads out either side of the road, then sweep up it to the Summerhill. I'll stay on the road with the pig following us up. Okay?'

'Right, Sergeant', confirmed the corporal, before giving out his own brief orders. 'Right, you all heard that. When the vehicle stops bail out quick. Haydon, Ottoway, Forbes, go to the left. The rest of you come with me on the right.'

Dave Urwin spent the next few minutes on the radio informing the Duty Officer of where he was and what he planned to do. Then, clamping the headphones over the driver's ears, Urwin put him in control of both vehicle and radio net.

'If 3 comes up for me just whistle. I'll be on the road in front. Now release the hand brake and let this beast roll forward.'

On crossing the culvert, Dave put his hand on the driver's arm as a signal to stop. Up to this point their arrival had been a silent one but as both he and his men struggled to de-bus, it was done so with the metal din of heavy iron doors crashing against the body of the armoured personnel carrier.

Shaking out in a loose extended line, Wally Forbes found himself the extreme left hand man from the road, with Haydon and Ottoway on his right. Cautiously he began to pick his way through the low bush parallel to the road onto a small bank. At the crest, he adopted a low crouch to minimise his skyline silhouette. Taking but a few paces in this position his ears caught a low metallic click. Instinctively he threw himself to the ground while shouting a warning to the others.

'Get down! Get down!'

His words had not died when a large blast erupted from the side of the bank several yards to his front. The explosion was an improvised Claymore-type device, which hurled nuts, bolts, nails and other bits of metal debris across the front of the advancing Patrol. Fortunately, prematurely ignited, it caused no casualties, scattering its deadly ironmongery over the vacant ground opposite.

Recovering himself, Forbes looked up to see a dark blur rise from the ground a short distance in front of him. Wally, from his sprawled position, awkwardly pushed his rifle forward. Half pointing, half aiming, his right thumb snapped the safety catch down as his trigger finger squeezed off two shots. The blur, with a cry, dropped to one side.

Dave Urwin, who had dived onto the road as the mine went off, scrambled for the protection of the verge. The Humber, a short distance behind, joined him there. Buckley, crashing the nose of his vehicle into some leafy undergrowth, boiled out to take cover.

'Buckley, get back on that radio and report contact', screamed Urwin at his driver. Then to the whole Patrol, recognising the two shots as British 7.62mm, 'Who fired? Who fired? Can anyone see anything?'

'I did, up here, I think I hit him', came back Forbes's not too confident reply.

Calling to Corporal Jones to remain with his men on their side of the road, Urwin set off to find Forbes.

'Who's that?' he whispered at a crouched figure in an airborne smock.

'It's me, Sarg', was the vague reply.

'Me who yah cunt?' demanded the sergeant in a low impatient bark.

'Ottoway, Sarg.'

'Who's that with you?' he then asked, spying another figure.

'Haydon', replied Ottoway.

'Who fired the shots?'

'Forbes, he's up there', answered Haydon pointing.

'Right! We'll go up to him. Both of you stay on my left.'

They found Forbes still lying in his original position.

As they approached, the young soldier put his fingers to his lips.

'I got one, Sergeant; he's just out in front there. Can't be dead though, he's still moaning', he informed his sergeant, as Urwin got down beside him.

'Let's have a look then', he suggested. Then turning to the other two he said 'Haydon, Ottoway, you two stay here and cover us, we're going for a look see.'

Then standing up, he gave Forbes a brief battle plan.

'Stay behind me and to the left. I'll watch the front, you watch the flanks.'

With the butt of his rifle locked against his shoulder, the muzzle at a forty-five degree angle to the ground, Urwin stealthily advanced. A low moan froze him in mid-stride, the rifle barrel automatically swinging towards the sound. Taking slow silent steps, the source of this was found at the foot of the bank. A youth of about seventeen lay face down in the grassy turfs, bleeding from a wound in his buttocks. With Forbes covering, the sergeant, laying his rifle to one side, stooped to search the wounded man, heedless of the cries of pain as he rolled him onto his back.

'What's your name chum?' questioned Urwin, pulling open the man's jacket to feel inside.

'Am I die'n? Oh Jaysus, am I die'n?' babbled the youth, disregarding the question.

'Do I look like a fucking doctor?' retorted Urwin. 'Now what's your pissing name?'

'Kevin. Kevin Drum', he finally admitted.

'Who were the others involved? What are their names?' the sergeant pressed.

'What others? Don't know what you mean.'

'He's lying, Sarg', contradicted Forbes, taking a step forward. 'I heard at least two legging it through the brush towards Connaught Park.'

'Lying English bastard', denied the gun shot victim. 'I was on my way to get a loaf of bread for my ma. Don't know what you're on about.'

'At a quarter to midnight?' asked Urwin, looking at his watch. 'Keep an eye on him. I'm going back to let the Company know what's happened', he directed the young soldier before picking up his rifle.

On passing Haydon and Ottoway he told them to get a shell dressing on the wounded youth.

Approaching, they found him pleading with Forbes.

'Get me a doctor. You shot me, now it's up to you to get me a doctor.'

'Okay mate, we'll look after you', assured Ottoway.

'Are you a doctor?' asked the Irishman hopefully.

'Sure! Sure I am', smiled the Paratrooper reassuringly, reaching for his shell dressing.

'Thank fuck you're back, Sergeant', said Buckley with relief as Urwin reached to take the radio head set and speaker from him. 'The O.C.'s on the other end going spare.'

'Yah, I bet', agreed Urwin. But before he could transmit, Corporal Jones arrived at his shoulder to ask 'What's the score?'

'It looks like Forbes shot the fucker who set off that bomb. Hit him low though, the bastard will probably live', answered Urwin quickly.

'Where is he now?' asked Jones, wishing to be kept in the picture.

'Back off the road about twenty metres. Your lads, ah . . . Ottoway and . . . . Haydon are there keeping an eye on him', replied the sergeant adjusting the head phones over his ears.

'What!' exclaimed the tall blond corporal. 'Those two looking after a wounded Mick!'

Turning at a run, he hurried off in the direction his sergeant had pointed.

His unheralded arrival proved his concern not to be unfounded. As Forbes stood watching, Ottoway, who had applied his shell dressing to the wounded youth's mouth, was holding his struggling body down while Haydon, with a pencil pushed three or four inches into the wound, was trying to enlarge it.

'You two! Get ta fuck out of it', ordered the corporal angrily.

'Come on Jonesy, we're only trying to dig the bullet out of the poor geezer', defended Haydon.

'Bollocks', retorted the disbelieving corporal, pushing Ottoway off the wide-eyed, terrified youth with his boot.

When 9 Platoon, the standby Platoon, arrived to cordon the ambush site off, prior to it being fully examined by A.T.O., Army Intelligence and Special Branch, Urwin and his men were ordered to bring the wounded victim back to the Company location. This was a painful journey for our young, would-be terrorist. Dragged more than carried out to the road, he was bundled into the back of the Humber. Sprawled unattended on the floor he was first trampled on by the men boarding their vehicle then forced to endure a bumpy journey made even more unacceptable by Buckley driving into every pot hole he could find. At the Colinglen he was dragged again, this time up to the school to be dropped beside the cook's hot plate. As agonising as the journey was he did not really have cause for complaint. For considering this mindless slug had just attempted to turn every man of the Section into stew meat, he had been handled in surprisingly good humour.

The duty cook absent-mindedly tried to bring him a mug of tea but was stopped by Len Hatton's firm command.

'These cunts don't get my rations.'

The first to attend our young Irishman was Corporal Vic Seaten, the Company Medic, an over-weight, red face Geordie piss artist.

'Right', he said bending to pull the wounded man's trousers down to examine the injury.

'Let's see what the fooks oop with you.'

'Get away! Get away!' howled the youth, expecting more of the Haydon-Ottoway treatment.

'Suit yourself', complied Seaten, moving off, leaving him to bleed.

With everyone in the location not asleep or on duty crowding into the assembly hall to gawp, the atmosphere turned Vaudeville. This was ended by Sam Kyle ordering out everyone who was not needed.

Jim Sinclair, who was temporarily in charge of the location's Intelligence Cell while his boss, a Colour Sergeant, was away on his four day's rest and recuperation leave, made a request to Major Bates, pointing out that Drum, wounded and in pain, could, if handled properly, be persuaded to talk. The O.C., considering it worth a try, called an orders group to put together an acceptable plan of approach.

The first member of their hastily assembled repertoire to appear on stage was again Corporal Seaten. He returned this time totally out of character. With pillows and blankets and kind soothing words, he comforted the patient. This was followed by the arrival of the M.O., rushing in to emotionally examine every inch of the poor youth. Black bag, stick on tongue, made to say 'ah', light shone in each eye, heart beat listened to with stethoscope, pulse taken, made to cough, all good drama!

Finally, the captain, standing up with a wink, gave Seaten his cue.

'Shall we get him aboard the ambulance now, Sir?'

The officer, doing his best Doctor Kildare impersonation, shook his head solemnly.

'You don't mean . . .', responded the corporal, projecting shock, dismay and sadness all in one.

Without answering, the M.O. knelt on one knee beside his patient.

'I want you to be brave, son', he said, removing the stethoscope from around his neck.

'What? What are ya mean'en?' came Drum's worried voice as he tried to rise onto both elbows.

'Steady Kevin, steady', cautioned the Medical officer, placing both hands on the younger man's shoulers. 'There's nothing we can do.'

'Jaysus flaming bloody Jaysus', Drum raged, tossing his head from side to side.

'You've lost far too much blood', continued the captain, his voice oozing compassion and sorrow, 'and the bullet has damaged vital organs.'

'Oh, be Jaysus, be Jaysus! Holy Mother of God', cried Drum in anguish, dropping back onto the pillow, his eyes and head rolling.

Clutching his stethoscope to his chest, the M.O. looked down to fix the young attempted-murderer with what he hoped were pitiful, watery eyes.

'It won't be long. Your time is very near', then looking away asked, 'do you wish for a priest?'

'Yes', came a cry of despair. 'Holy Mother of God. Yes! Yes!'

Looking up to the far entrance of the hall, Captain Ravenscroft raised his eyebrows and cocked his head at a man who had been awaiting the call to take centre stage.

The Battalion's Roman Catholic Padre, Father Buchanan, could not have been better cast. A short, sandy haired Scotsman in his late thirties, he had taken up the calling after spending two years National Service as a private in the Royal Scots. This was probably why he became a priest. For living that length of time among sinners such as those, his ability to remain sane could only have been by turning to either God or alcohol.

After first skipping across the room, he arrived at the doctor's side with slow measured steps and an appropriately reverent expression.

'Ah, Padre', introduced Ravenscroft in a solemn tone. 'This is Mr. Kevin Drum, who has been fatally wounded in an unfortunate shooting incident. Tragically, there is nothing that can be done. May I leave him in your kind care?'

'Yes, of course, Doctor', replied the Scotsman, his voice clear but low.

'You can trust Father Buchanan, Kevin. You're in safe hands now', assured the M.O., resting a hand on Drum's arm before standing to withdraw.

'Come Corporal Seaten, we will leave the good Padre to his sad task.'

With the two medical staff exiting stage left, Buchanan knelt to ask Drum 'Do you believe in God, my son?'

The Irishman, his face torn with despair, unable to speak, bobbed his head vigorously.

'I will pray for you', said the Padre, coming down on both knees to lean forward, resting a hand on Drum's forehead. Then Buchanan, bareheaded, dressed in a dark civilian suit with a white dog collar and an embroidered clergyman's stole around his neck, bent over the whimpering terrorist to pray.

'Don't want to die, Father. Oh why? Why?' burst out Drum, finding his voice.

'Courage, my son, courage', comforted the Padre, interrupting his recital.

'Mother! I want to see my mother', pleaded the Irishman, gripping the older man's arm.

'They've been called for. Both your mother and father are on their way', lied the Scotsman, again interrupting his prayer.

Consoled for the moment, Drum laid back in a disturbed sweat as the holy words tumbled about him.

Finishing with a brief spell of silence, the padre again leaned forward to say 'I will hear your confession now.'

'Confession', replied the youth, suspicious of the request. 'I confessed to my own priest a few days ago, Father, it's not needed.'

'Yes, but Kevin, tonight you joined with others in an attempt to kill. Although in your eyes, as a soldier of the Republican movement, this was for a just cause, it is still an unchristian act in the eyes of God which must be forgiven.'

Unsure, Drum worriedly pondered over this while Buchanan, keeping up the pressure, continued, 'You must decide, my son; we may not have much time.'

'Are you hot and flushed? Can you feel your heart pounding?'

Well of course he was and could, gearing the young man up to even greater heights of panic.

'Alright Father, hear my confession', pleaded Drum finally.

Over the next few minutes the padre, crouching forward, listened as Drum, obtaining final absolution from his sins, admitted among other things nicking two quid from his mother's purse and groping Sarah McGory behind Duncan's Garage. When he got around to his involvement in the attempted ambush, the confession was a simple admittance of guilt, but the good father required more detail than that, and with guarded reverent tones asked questions like; 'Those who accompanied you on this night's work, who were they?' and 'The explosive, Kevin, where was that collected?' Thus he was able to extract much useful information regarding names, addresses and operational planning.

At a point where the padre was beginning to find it difficult in being subtle about his questioning, Jim Sinclair, who had been concealed behind the hot plate, stood up. With a thumbs up to Buchanan he folded his note book and left the room.

Climbing to his feet, the padre fumbled in the side pocket of his jacket.

'Want a fag?' he asked of the death bed bomber.

'No, Father, I don't smoke', came Drum's puzzled reply.

'Well, you don't mind if I do? I'm bloody gaspin',' said the padre, putting a cigarette to his lips. Then, before lighting up, he removed it to shout towards the far doorway, 'Tom, he's all yours now.'

The M.O., stepping into the room, signalled corporal Seaten and another man carrying a stretcher.

'Thank you, Reverand. Okay Corporal seaten, get that cunt into the ambulance and down to the Royal Victoria.'

Laying the stretcher beside Drum, the two men, grabbing an end each, pulled him into the air.

'Leave me, yah bastard. Leave me, I'm dy'n', he protested.

'Dying fook', disagreed the corporal, as he and his mate dropped Drum onto the stretcher from half a yard. 'All you got is another hole in your ass!'

'Tell ya what though, old son', continued the coarse Tynesider, ignoring the patient's screams as his wound crashed onto the floor below the canvas cover. 'You were fookin' lucky. That was a canny boo'let, just missed your brains by inches.'

Switching on to what had been done, Drum began to turn the location blue with his foul oaths and threatening curses directed at everyone and everything British. This raving, as he was carried out to be dumped in the converted Humber that was the Battalion ambulance, went almost unnoticed, for Charlie Company had other things to do. With the information from Drum's confession that Jim Sinclair had jotted down, Major Bates put the whole Company on standby.

Gathering selected patrol Commanders into the intelligence cell briefing room, he tasked each off with a name and address. Then, with a member of D Company attached to each lifting party for identification purposes, they were dispatched to bring the suspects in. Needless to say, knocking on people's doors and dragging them out of bed at two a.m. made the Paratroopers very, very happy.

That afternoon at the Royal Victoria Hospital, Drum, who was recovering from an operation on his wound, was rescued. Three gunmen entered his ward, shot dead the Police Constable who was on duty there, and then fled with him by car across the border into the sanctuary of the Irish Republic.

Kevin Drum and 5 Para were to meet again.

*　　　　　*　　　　　*

Despite these odd occasional attacks on the members of the Company, for most the tour had turned out to be a crushing bore. Locked away in their location for days at a time, released only to patrol through a limited and familiar area, tedium lay heavily. No doubt if there was a disco operating as there had been in the first tour it would have taken the edge off. But for security reasons this could not be allowed. Also considering the local hostility this would probably have been a non-event anyway. So it was with some relief that a good old, full-blooded riot was produced for everyone to sink their teeth into.

In the early hours of the morning, B Company had lifted a known baddie who had come into their area to hide. This sparked off first small demonstrations followed by organised protests. Then, as the day progressed, mob rioting, taking over entire streets securing them with improvised barracades.

The Commanding Officer, recognising that the situation was beyond B Company's control, withdrew them to a role of watch and monitor, whilst calling up reinforcements from the rest of the Battalion. These he held back until dark, not wishing to send his men in as easy targets for concealed gunmen. His plan of battle was a simple one; attack all barricades simultaneously, reducing the chance of having to deal with a single large mob.

The district was one of the city's oldest, mainly red brick terraced houses with shops on most corners. The locality had only one main street, off which, pointing outwards in straight lines, branched several others of lesser length. The main street plus these others had to varying degrees been blocked with planks, burnt out cars and assorted large looted objects.

As dusk turned to night 8 Platoon, who had been waiting in the cover of a side street, moved their vehicles into an attacking position. Pulling out into the north end of the main street, Dave Urwin formed his Platoon's three Humbers across it, side by side, facing towards a barricade about two hundred yards to their front. After Lieutenant Taplow had placed his Sections in the protection of doorways and alleys everyone silently waited. When given the word, the object of their attack was to be the barricade. This was built of cars, metal drums, beer barrels, timber and household junk, just heaped together in a hasty pile. About fifty yards in front of this was a secondary obstruction, a rough line of large concrete pipes. These, about six feet long and four feet in diameter, had been rolled out of a nearby council yard.

From a side street the two Landrovers of the Commanding Officer's Rover Group pulled up a short distance behind the Platoon's Humbers.

'Your people all set, Peter?' the C.O. asked the lieutenant as he moved to greet his colonel.

'Yes, Sir. Just waiting for the word', confirmed the younger officer.

'Right! Well, when you go in, go in hard; I want skulls cracked down there', ordered the C.O. in a resolute tone, his face firmly set.

The man who stood beside Taplow, surveying the fires, the damage and the hostile behaviour of the figures silhouetted in the flickering light, was a changed one. Some weeks before his policy towards the ghetto population had been one of benevolence and tolerance, but not now. The previous Sunday night, on his way back to the Battalion H.Q. at the Summerhill Police Station, his Rover Group had come under attack. While passing a side street, an automatic weapon opened fire, dotting a wobbly line of bullet holes in the lower half of his vehicle just below where he was sitting. Since that incident his attitude had, to say the least, hardened.

'Get your men aboard, Peter. The moment you start to move I'll release the rest of the Battalion', ordered the C.O., turning to retrace his steps back to his mobile command vehicle.

'Right, Sir', replied Taplow crisply, passing this on. 'Sergeant Urwin,' he cried softly 'get the men on. We're going in.'

As the word to mount up was passed around the men, there was a scramble to get aboard the A.P.C.s, for no one intended to miss the fun. Discarding riot

114

shields, the Platoon, wearing steel helmets and flak jackets and looking more like pirates than soldiers because of the amount of anti-personnel weapons they carried, trampled each other to gain a place.

With all doors secured and their lights off, the engines were brought to life. Taplow took command of the centre vehicle, while his sergeant had the front seat of the left hand one and Corporal Jones the right.

Looking through the heavy mesh wire covering the windscreen, the lieutenant gave and got a thumbs up from each of his flanking vehicles. Then with a command to the driver, he initiated the attack, 'Let her rip, Buckley.'

With the engine revving at full throttle, Buckley engaged the clutch.

As if as one, the three hollow blocks of metal strained forward in eagerness, racing with each other. As the drivers worked their way up the gears, first one nosing in front and then another, their speed increased. Corporal Jones, brushing a lamp post, snapped it off at its base. With the drivers in top gear, standing on their accelerators, fifteen tons of armoured vehicles ploughed through the first barrier of concrete piping, brushing them aside or smashing them into unobstructing pieces; all that is except one. This, more solid than the others, caused the centre Humber to mount it, but because of the momentum it continued on below the vehicle as a central fifth wheel. Balanced like a circus elephant on a large ball, the vehicle charged on keeping abreast of the others.

'Jonesy' Jones, a few feet to the right, looked up at Buckley as the shock of what was happening registered on the driver's face. Spinning his wheel in desperation hoping to gain some sort of control and finding none, he locked his grip and waited. Jones, spellbound by the presence of this metal monster hanging above him, did not see his arrival at the second barricade. Like three express trains the Paras struck the barrier. Well, two did. Mr. Taplow's vehicle, leaving its concrete scooter behind, vaulted a Ford Cortina to crash onto the street beyond. The flanking Humbers, charging through the barricade, scattered its material like an exploding bean bag. With drums, beer barrels and chunks of wood flying in all directions, the three vehicles careered to a halt.

From the back of Urwin's and Jones' Humbers the men hurriedly spilled out, eager to seek and destroy. The third A.P.C. reacted slightly differently. For many long seconds it remained still and silent; then finally the back door opened a crack. This was widened by a kicking leg that hung for a short time before again moving. It took some minutes for everyone, bruised and disorientated, to disembark themselves. Luckily their steel helmets, and being tightly packed had saved them from any serious injury.

Stunned, Lieutenant Taplow recovered to ask, 'Buckley, you okay?'

Seeing the soldier's head nod, he clawed at the door handle to make his exit. Throwing it open he stumbled out to collide with Dave Urwin who, concerned for his Platoon Commander, had come to see how he was.

'You alright . . .?' he began to ask but was interrupted by Taplow, anxious that there be no let-up in their task.

'Never mind me. Keep the men at them. Don't let the bastards form up.'

'No need, Sir, they're gone', replied the sergeant smiling.

'What? What?' exclaimed the officer, looking around. Except for the voices and clatter of his own men the vicinity was deserted. When his vehicles had crashed through the first barrier of concrete piping, everyone in sight had fled, leaving their end of the street empty, and for the men unentertaining.

The only person found was a reporter from the Daily Telegraph who, bareheaded in an overcoat, stood holding up his press card.

'I'll say this about you Paras', he commented, 'there may not be many of you, but by God you certainly are spectacular.'

*   *   *

'Let's knock it on the head, Jim.'

Jim Sinclir, checking his watch, agreed with Mick Pridmore's suggestion. 'Ya, you're right. I can't see anyone turning up tonight.'

Both men had been looking across a factory yard to the back entrance of a house that had been unoccupied for several weeks. An informant had led them to believe the house was now used from time to time for I.R.A. meetings.

Returning to rejoin the rest of their Patrol who were waiting with their Humber tucked into a side alley, the two corporals found a message waiting.

'On the way back Three wants us to check out a disturbance in the Tartan Club', informed Reg Berrill, doing radio watch in the front seat.

'Oh, bollocks', retorted Sinclair. 'That's the Vehicle Patrol's job. What are they on?'

'Tied up just now', shrugged Berrill.

'It's past midnight', pointed out Pridmore. 'What's that place doing still open?'

'Come on, we'll have a look see', complied Sinclair, ordering everyone into the Humber.

The Tartan Club was situated in a small Protestant peninsular that jutted into Charlie Company's area of responsibility, just off the Summerhill Road. Turning into its street, Jim had the driver halt some distance away.

A man waiting at the entrance began to wave his arms on seeing them arrive. De-busing his men, Jim brought the Patrol forward on foot.

'Jesus, I'm glad you come', began the man in a worried voice, now recognisable as the owner of the club.

'That bastard Billy McDonald's upstairs with some of his boys. I've been trying to talk him out of the place but he's not budgin'.'

'McDonald, eh' pondered Sinclair. 'What's he doing now?'

'Drinking my stock and not paying', replied the owner, more as a statement than a complaint.

'Has he made any threats, or given the idea you're going to be seeing a lot more of him?' asked the corporal, suspicious of the reason for McDonald's presence.

'Just him being here is threat enough. I don't want nothin' to do with him and his bunch', stated the owner simply.

Jim did not press him; he had a good idea what was going on. McDonald was a throw up of these troubled times, a Protestant bully boy who found, because of the lack of police presence, he was now being given the opportunity to carry out lucrative criminal acts. His base of operation had been a bar next door in Support Company's area, but recently they, having had enough of him, had thrown him out with the gypsies warning not to return. Without asking the owner directly, Jim could see that McDonald had made it clear to him that his bar was about to become the new H.Q.

'Who's up there just now?'

'McDonald, three of his boys and my barman.'

'Right, we'll get them out, you go around the back to your office. After we've gone you can lock the place up', ordered the Scotsman. Then turning to the members of his Patrol he explained how he wanted the coming minutes to be

116

handled. 'It's late and I want some kip tonight, so let's make this short and sharp. Mick, I'll shut the bar, you and the others get McDonald and his gang frisked and down the stairs into the 'Pig'. We're not going to fuck about, if these cunts come hard we get nasty.'

The Club itself was a large room, one floor up above several smaller street level shops. Entering, Sinclair turned to rest one hand on the bar. The barman putting a cigarette between his lips looked at the corporal.

'Shut this up Sandy, and get off home.'

'Thank fuck', murmured the barman in gratitude, reaching up to pull a side shutter down.

'Hey, what'cha doing?' came a voice from across the room, where four men in their mid-twenties sat at a corner table drinking.

The Paratroopers recognised the one who spoke as McDonald's right-hand henchman.

'The man says shut it up', pleaded the barman with a shrug, extending his open hands towards Sinclair.

'Well, leave it open, we ain't finished drinkin' at the minute', ordered the henchman.

As he spoke Mick Pridmore followed by Paddy Kieron, Reg Berrill and 'Yorky' Rush arrived at their table.

'Get up Wilson', commanded Pridmore in a quiet voice.

Wilson, solidly built with thick black, wavy hair and a rough, heavily-lined face, sat slouched in a chair, one arm resting on the table fingering his glass.

'Eh', he replied contemptuously, pretending not to understand.

Mick, taking a pace forward, drove his right boot into one of Wilson's shins causing him with a curse to leap to his feet.

'You're a pretty tough man with that gun in your hand', taunted the dark Irishman.

Pridmore, reaching behind to lay his rifle on a near-by table with his right hand, brought it back as a fist straight into Wilson's face. Crashing through several chairs, he arrived sprawled and bleeding from the mouth at Reg Berrill's feet.

'Get up cunt', he commanded, kicking him to his feet.

'Right, all of you against the wall', ordered Jim Sinclair, arriving at the table.

Paddy Kieron pulled McDonald up out of his chair with one hand.

'That means you, hard man.'

'What is this? We're just havin' a quiet drink in the place', protested McDonald, a thin, sallow-faced man with eyes that darted like a cat's.

'It means you've over-stayed your welcome; now spread yourselves on the wall. Let's see what you're carrying', informed Sinclair angrily.

Each was slammed against the wall, then with kicks and punches made to lean on it, legs and arms spread. Yorky Rush, frisking each man, produced two knives, a sharpened screw driver and a hatchet.

'Right, now we're all going to take a little moonlight ride', announced the Scotsman. 'Mick! Yorky! Lead the way and find these gentlemen a comfortable seat in the Pig.'

Without a word the Irishmen followed Rush and Pridmore to the stairs.

Starting down, one of the thugs thought he could get a subtle dig in by pretending to stumble, clipping big Mick on the ear as he did so. Pridmore, without looking around, grabbed the arm and in one clean movement pulled the man over his shoulder, tumbling him down the stairs into Rush. Yorky, in a reflex action, took hold of a loose limb and continued the man's journey over his own shoulder to crash face down and bleeding on the street pavement. The trip from top to bottom took him about three seconds.

Inside the Humber the four villains were made to lie face down on the floor.

'Wilson, you're bleeding all over my Pig, now clean it up', instructed Reg Berrill throwing a rag down at him, ensuring the job was done right with jabs from the butt of his rifle.

Twenty minutes later Sinclair told his driver to halt.

'Get them out', he ordered, pulling the rear doors open.

'Where the fuck is this?' asked McDonald, looking up and down a street of old, red-brick terraced houses, their front doors flush with the pavement.

Jim, taking the Irishman by his shirt front, pulled him forward to shine his torch on a street sign above their heads; Leeson Street it read.

'Jesus, are you people crazy bringing us here?' whispered McDonald, fear showing from every corner of his face. This was understandable for Leeson Street was a centre of hardcore I.R.A. support.

'Let's get something straight McDonald; you will never come into our area again', ordered the corporal, biting each word. 'If you or any of your goons do, we'll bring you back and tie you to that fucking lamp post over there, understood?'

'Billy, come on', called one of his ashen-faced gang as the other three edged their way towards one of the exits.

'I said 'understood?',' repeated Sinclair, pulling McDonald's shirt front even tighter.

'Sure! Sure!' promised the Irishman. 'We only came in for a drink anyway. You won't be seeing us again.'

'That's good for your sake. Now piss off', advised Jim, pushing McDonald away.

As the four hoodlums hurried away, Paddy Kieron began banging the confiscated hatchet on the side of the Humber.

'What's your rush McDonald?' he called, 'hang about a bit and make some new friends.'

With the odd house light beginning to come on, the four fugitives broke into a run, not letting up until they had turned off the Falls Road, past the Army location at North Howard Street.

*   *   *

The following evening Sinclair and his men visited another bar, this time Murphy's. Being Charlie Company's intelligence gatherers, they found it helpful to make occasional unannounced appearances at the local bars and social clubs. In doing so they were able to spot and identify strangers and keep tabs on the movements and associations of their own local suspects. After two and a half months, this had become routine, turning up few new faces or surprises. Normally the D Company visits were limited to one each night, every second day or so. Which was probably why in breaking this habit to spring a late second inspection they had the unexpected success they did.

Murphy's had two levels, a bar downstairs and one above. Access to the top bar was by either a staircase leading from the lower bar or a flight of steps that had its own entrance from the street. The simple operational drill adopted for Murphy's was to post two men at the head of the outside stairs to stop anyone up there who might be of interest to them from slipping out. A main group would then enter the lower bar working their way through it and up the inside stairs.

On arriving at the top of these, Sinclair looked across the crowded room to Mick Pridmore and Reg Berrill stationed at the head of the other stairs. Catching the big man's eye, who indicated that he wished to speak, Jim pushed his way across, followed by Kieron and Rush, to find him in a suspicious mood.

'There's a couple of our 'boyos' sat at that far table', he said nodding. 'They got someone with them. I can't make him out with his back to us, but he's not one of ours.'

'Let's check it out then,' replied Sinclair. 'Reg, you stay here. The rest of us will take a look at this bloke.'

As they moved towards the corner table the two men known to the Paratroopers looked up with uneasy glances.

'Alright lads?' asked one of them in faked cheerful greeting as Sinclair and Pridmore arrived either side of the stranger. He, in his early twenties, with loose brown hair and wearing a dark blue suit jacket, sat holding a cigarette to his mouth. Ignoring the greeting, Jim looked down at the new man. In shocked surprise, only half realising he was doing it, Jim pulled the man's hand away from his face. Looking up, both Pridmore and Sinclair's expressions registered recognition to the other. That face had been staring at them from the centre of their wanted person's board since taking over at the Colinglen. Without a word he was yanked from his chair by the two men to be flung against the near wall.

At this point several things happened at once, the first being a dead hush settling throughout the room. As Yorky Rush spun around with his rifle raised to cover the room Reg Berrill on his side of the room did the same, going a step further by cocking his S.M.G. and applying the safety catch. The other two men, under protest, were made to stand up and were then forced away by Paddy Kieron.

'What is this? What the fuck are you playing at?' complained the suspect as Jim Sinclair frisked his body.

'We'll ask the questions, mate', interrupted the Scotsman. 'Let's see some I.D.'

'Don't have any on me', was the negative reply.

'What about a wallet? What d'ya carry your money in?'

'Don't have any; I'm on the brew.'

'What's ya name?'

'Michael Doyle', was the false reply.

'Where do you live?'

An address in the Short Strand District was given.

'Well, Mr. Doyle, we'll take you in to check all this out. Just to satisfy our minds', said Sinclair firmly, taking the suspect's arm to lead him towards the ouside stairs. As they crossed the bar insulting remarks and taunts began to well up from the dimmer areas of the room.

'Reg, get down the stairs and cover us out the door', called the Scots corporal as he approached the landing. Berrill, obeying, leapt down the stairs.

Conscious that a rescue bid might be made, the other three soldiers had turned to fix their attention on the now hostile bar room.

Because of this the only person who saw an overcoat being passed to Doyle was Jim Sinclair, who, concentrating on other things, paid little attention to this simple act, until halfway down the stairs he noticed his charge fumbling in one of the pockets. Realising that if his suspicions were correct he only had a split second to act, he shoved the man head first down the staircase. His push, a forceful one, also caused him to lose his footing, tumbling down to end in a tangled sprawl, his rifle pinned useless under his body.

'Reg, he's got a gun', shouted Sinclair in warning as Doyle scrambled up, a revolver in his hand.

Berrill, standing in the doorway on seeing this could not shoot for fear of hitting Sinclair, so he twisted his body away to collapse on the pavement. Doyle, a moment too late, fired two shots where Berrill had just been standing, then in a crouched run sped out of the door, firing a hurried, unaimed third shot in the general direction the soldier had just fallen. As the bullet ricochetted off the cobble stones beside him, Reg leaped to his feet. Bolting around a parked van that was masking his view, he raised his Sterling, pushing the safety catch forward with his thumb. Doyle was across the street now, about to make the protection of some high bushes.

The snap shot Berrill fired struck home causing his target to falter on one knee, but the second and third shots missed, allowing the wanted man to escape.

The follow up search proved fruitless for Doyle had eluded them, smuggled south to a sympathetic hospital in the Republic where his wound was attended to. Fortunately this medical attention turned out to be inadequate; Doyle, or as his real name was, O'Neil, died on being released some weeks later. Which was only just, for he had been responsible for the murder of two soldiers from the Green Howards.

CHAPTER 8

It was not part of their blood,
It came to them very late
With long arrears to make good,
When the English began to hate.

Rudyard Kipling

Dave Urwin watched from the school doorway as Jim Sinclair and his D Company patrolmen walked up from the police station with wearied steps. Although a bright, sunny, mid-morning summer's day, its uplifting qualities were unnoticed by men who had just worked through the night.

The previous evening Urwin, who had been on duty watchkeeper, received a call over the field telephone from the O.P. sentry above the police station. He reported that a small crowd was attacking the main entrance of Franklin's woodyard with petrol bombs and requested permission to open fire. This was justifiable for recently Northern Ireland Command had issued the order that anyone throwing a petrol bomb was to be treated in the same manner as a gunman. The sergeant, before approving this, first informed Battalion that he was about to do so. As it turned out this was a mistake, for the reply that came back over the radio was an unclarified but defiant refusal to do so.

Even though the legislation for opening fire on petrol bombers was there, some commanders had become prudent in implementing it. This was mainly due to cold feet on their part, reflecting the fact that the first unit to do this, a Battalion of the Queen's Brigade, had sparked off a riot that had taken twenty-four hours to quell.

By the time the mobile patrol and the stand-by section had reached the scene the woodyard's office buildings were ablaze at several points. The arrival of the fire service and the positioning of protection parties for them ate up more vital time, resulting in the loss of the office completely. It was not until the pyjama-clad Protestant manager appeared at the gate to enquire about his night watchman was it realised that loss of life could now be an added factor.

'Got a late breakfast waiting for you,' informed Urwin, as the members of Delta Company reached him.

Sinclair nodded his head wearily in thanks.

'Messy was it?' asked the sergeant.

'The yard's alright but the office isn't much cop,' answered Mick Pridmore.

'The watchman didn't have a chance,' exclaimed Sinclair angrily.

'He got trapped in a hallway.'

121

'The smoke must have got him first,' offered Kieron.

'Go on inside and get your scoff. Then get your heads down for a few hours, but I want you all up before tea,' ordered Sinclair, dismissing his men.

'You had any sleep, Dave?' he asked when the others had disappeared into the building. The sergeant shook his head.

'You want to get yourself some,' suggested the Scotsman.

'Can't,' replied Urwin, 'the Platoon's change over at noon. I got to take a foot patrol out.'

Then after a pause he was unable to hold in his frustration any longer.

'Fuck! Fuck! Fuck!' raged the sergeant. 'I should have let Haydon open up on those bastards.'

'No need to get uptight, Dave,' assured his friend, 'you can't be blamed for that poor fucker getting roasted.'

'I know, I know,' he replied. Then, voicing the thoughts of every member of the security forces serving in the Province, continued, 'but when the hell are we going to stop pussy-footing around with these cunts?'

*   *   *

'Chris, hold up! Hold up, pull in will ya!'

Chris Braithwaite, sitting in the commander's seat of the first of two open Landrovers, looked around to see why Durrant was slapping the shoulder of his flak jacket.

'What are you on about?' he questioned, signalling the driver to pull in.

'It's Seela,' informed the Aberdonian Scot, jumping from the vehicle to run back up the street and halt before two smiling teenage girls standing at the gate of a front garden.

Braithwaite, pushing himself off the front seat, stepped onto the pavement to watch Durrant.

'Who the fuck is Seela?' asked Wally Forbes, still sitting in the back of the rover.

'Oh ya,' said Braithwaite as he recognised one of the girls, 'that's the bird he was knocking off at the disco last time we were out here.'

Then signalling everyone to dismount and take up a fire position either side of the street, he walked to where Durrant was chatting to the girls. Seeing him coming, the Scotsman broke off to walk back a few steps.

'We've been asked in for a cup of tea, Chris. How about it?' he asked.

'Screw the nut jock we're supposed to be on patrol' vetoed Braithwaite sharply.

With Bobby McIntyre away on his sergeant's promotion course he, as the senior soldier had been put in charge of the section.

'Well, how about leaving me here for a wee bit just to have a talk,' suggested the Scot, anxious to spend some time with the girl.

'Fuck off, Willie. If Taplow or Urwin find out I'll drop right in the shit', objected the young commander.

'Have a heart, Chris, we haven't seen each other for almost a year,' pleaded Durrant.

Braithwaite, weakening, pondered this for some seconds before consenting. The estate was one of privately owned homes on which they had never had trouble before.

'Okay, we'll pick you up in about an hour's time. Just after dark.'

A wiser head would have rejected the proposal out of hand but Braithwaite, new to command did not appreciate the danger of what he had just allowed. Not that is until twenty minutes later when he received a radio message for the patrol to return to the location. On asking why, he was told there was a letter that had to be taken to Battalion H.Q. Thinking this would be a simple matter of nipping in, collecting the letter, delivering it and then dashing around to pick up Durrant, he complied.

On pulling into the Colinglen Sergeant Urwin was at the gate waiting for them.

'Park your wagons and get up to the school, the O.C.'s going to brief the company.'

'But I'm supposed to take a letter down to Battalion H.Q.,' protested Braithwaite.

'Forget that, it was just an excuse to get you in. Now shift yourselves, we got an 'OP' on.'

The operation Urwin spoke of was to be a wide ranging one covering the entire Province. This was brought about by the government and the security forces losing patience. For many months there had been a relaxation of the enforcement of law and order, and numerous concessions had been made in the hope that this would lead to a gradual return to normal times. This proved to be a pipe dream. The gangsters were enjoying their power and making too much money to release their hold on the various communities.

The failure of the 'Softly Softly' policy was well evident to Charlie Company. For since their arrival offensive digs against them had increased to the point where blast bombs thrown from the Ballykeady Flats, which bordered their north side into the school yard were more or less ignored.

Throughout the evening and into the early part of the next morning not only C Company, but also the entire Army in Northern Ireland prepared themselves for this historic event. It had been decided that enough was enough and now the security forces were going in to lift all known members of the I.R.A. Within each location the men scurried about, attended briefings, right down to those of individual snatch parties, checking names, photos and addresses of those who were to be arrested and drawing special stores which would be needed in handling them and preparing allocated vehicles.

At the Colinglen extra personnel arrived. These were military and civil police, engineers and Royal Corps of Transport with more vehicles. From H.Q. Company spare officers and N.C.O.s were sent to assist with the arrests.

Finally at 0330 hours in the morning of the 9th of August 1971, with everyone geared up and eager to get on, Charlie Company began to leave the Colinglen. First out of the gate, as silently as possible, were vehicles carrying the snatch parties that had the furthest to go. They were followed by men on foot who were to make their arrest nearby. The last out were the 4-ton lorries carrying barbed wire, pickets and barriers for building temporary holding compounds. Within minutes the location was practically empty. The only ones left were Len Hatton and his cooks who had taken over the guard duties and Captain 'Shush' Austen who with the command post signallers would be monitoring and co-ordinating the Company's operations.

At one minute to 0400 hours all over Northern Ireland arrest groups were poised at the front doors of hundreds of suspects. At 0400 hours they all began to knock. Corporal Jones, not wishing to bruise his knuckles, stepped aside to let Ottoway do the knocking with a fire axe, splintering the door inwards. Internment Day had begun.

The drill was basic; if the knock was answered the individual required would be asked to accompany them. If he refused he would be dragged away. Should there be no answer to the knock the door would be kicked in and the man taken.

Down the street from Corporal Jones's splintered door the pay sergeant was having a spot of difficulty in gaining entrance. His knock was answered by a large fat woman in her late forties with straight greying hair, wearing a dirty dressing gown.

'What do you bastards want?' she asked.

'It's your son Martin, Mrs. Dillan. We'd like a word with him if we may,' he ventured.

'Talk to Martin, you can fuck off,' she replied.

'Is he in Mrs. Dillan?' the sergeant asked politely.

'None of your fucking business.'

'We'll have to come in then, Mrs. Dillan. It's rather important that we speak to him.' This time the sergeant spoke with more authority.

'Kiss my hole,' replied the woman, folding her arms to stand squarely blocking her doorway, daring him to try and enter the house.

'Excuse me Sarge,' broke in Phil Haydon, losing patience with this gentleman of arithmetic and pushing him to one side, 'let me have a word with her.'

Taking a pace forward he lept into the air, flattening the ugly cow onto the hallway floor with a flying head butt. Leaving the pay sergeant standing dumbfounded on the pavement, he trampled her under foot as he went in pursuit of his quarry.

'Where are ya, Dillan? I'm coming to get ya, ya bastard.'

Around the corner Jim Sinclair, Paddy Kieran, and 'Yorky' Rush had been earmarked to pick up a top I.R.A. suspect.

Kicking the door in they rushed up the stairs to burst into the bedroom. In one corner their torch lights found two young children asleep. Switching the room light on a woman in her twenties in another bed was sitting up.

'Where is Keeley?' asked Sinclair abruptly.

'He's living with that bitch next door now,' she answered drily, jerking a thumb to her right.

With neither apology nor reply the three men dashed down stairs to kick the neighbouring door in as well. Upstairs they burst into the bedroom to surprise their man half into a pair of trousers.

Once a man was lifted there was no loitering about, on handing over their charge to the escort teams each group hurried off to another address.

Understandably all this activity did not go unnoticed by those members of the community not directly involved. It brought many out into the darkness of the streets to watch and in some cases protest. As the realisation of what was happening began to sink in a number reacted with anger and hostility.

The last arrest Corporal Jones had to make was at the top end of a particularly pro-I.R.A. street. The man they had to collect did not wish to accompany them, which caused several minutes delay while he was pinned to the floor, his hands bound with D10 telephone wire and then dragged out of the front door. The other lift groups having made their arrests were now gone but the street was not empty.

Clusters of men, women and children, half-dressed or in night clothes, were engaged in heated conversations. Seeing Corporal Jones's men with their captive, they began to converge on the soldiers making angry threats. But "No Way' was having none of this; going to the front he cleared a path by swinging his axe and making threats of his own.

'Get out of the way you unwashed Paddy bastards or I'll cleave ya in half!'

Charlie Company's main assembly point for all those arrested was a roundabout at a main junction on the Summerhill Road. There the centre grassy circle had been turned into a holding enclosure, cordoned with a ring of barbed wire. As the prisoners were handed over to the R.U.C. and military police, their names were ticked off a list, labelled, hands bound, hooded with a sandbag, and made to sit down and wait within the compound.

When Sam Kyle, who was in charge of transportation, could see that an acceptable number were gathered, he would call up a lorry. Still bound and hooded they would be pushed and pulled into the back, an escort detailed to ride with them, and then dispatched to a clearing centre where they would be processed, categorised, interrogated and finally either released or imprisoned. This imprisonment would for most be the newly built and soon to be publicised Long Kesh.

As a military operation it was near enough faultless, meticulously planned and smoothly implemented. This was not surprising for, over past decades in their capacity as an international policeman, the British Army had learned much about countering urban terrorism. However this is not to say mistakes were not made. They were, the most glaring of which was the fault of whoever compiled the lift list.

When C Company's allocation was revealed it did not take much study by the Colour Sergeant in charge of Delta Company's intelligence cell to note a number of discrepancies. Not only were there names of known I.R.A. members not on the list, but there were others on it that to his knowledge had no connection with any militant Republican organisation.

This resulted in a great deal of inconvenience for the innocent whilst the guilty, not believing their luck, fled south across the border, either by road or aboard a very crowded early morning Dublin train.

The authorities were prepared for a back lash due to the mass arresting and internment without substantial evidence, but no one had foreseen the ferocity that was now unleashed. The Irish temper, a hair trigger apparatus at the best of times, went totally beserk.

In theory, with all known members of the I.R.A. either behind barbed wire or on the run, any back lash should have been nothing more than a weak, unco-ordinated affair. What had not been taken into consideration was the anger of the close relatives and neighbours of those arrested. Throughout Northern Ireland and around the Colinglen Police Station in particular spontaneous protesting irrupted and then rioting whelmed and exploded.

Chris Braithwaite and Wally Forbes, returning to the location after completing their duty as escort in the last 4-ton lorry to drop its prisoners off at the Girdwood Park holding centre, were alert and tense. The route coming back, in order to save time, was one that entered several republican areas. From the pre-dawn shadows of some of these bricks and stones were hurled at them. With no canopy on the vehicle all they could do was point their rifles over the sides and keep low.

As daylight began to dim the street lights, their lorry crested a rise on the Summerhill Road about a quarter of a mile from Franklin's woodyard.

'Fucking hell!' exclaimed Forbes, as both men stared at the scene before them.

From scores of points north, west and south of the Colinglen, black oily smoke rose from burning, hi-jacked vehicles. Above the noise of their engine a metallic clatter rolled up towards them as a thousand dustbin lids were rattled on pavements as a rallying call to the masses while punctuated amongst this could be heard the occasional crack of gun fire.

At the junction of the Summerhill and Lisna Carrol Roads a small mob was overturning a van into the roadway. On approaching this the driver accelerated to zig zag around it. Seeing an arm go back Wally Forbes, anticipating a bomb, snapped off a wild shot over the figure's head. That was 5 Para's first bullet of the day, the first of several thousand.

Despite the loss of a night's sleep Major Bates, aware that there would be some disapproval of what had been done, kept every one at full alert.

8 Platoon he positioned at the police station, tasking them to multiple vehicle patrols. 7 and 9 Platoons remained at the school building, 7 Platoon mounting constant foot patrols whilst 9 Platoon, with full riot gear, became an instant reaction force. Len Hatton's cooks continued to do the guard, but still somehow managed to serve everyone hot breakfasts.

With all of the previous night's support units returned to their own bases, it soon became apparent that the forces available to C Company were not going to be able to maintain order throughout their area. Road blocks and blazing obstacles were going up on all major routes. Wherever the soldiers tried to patrol rioters would appear to pelt them with missiles. When charged they would simply disperse to reform elsewhere. Around mid-morning the situation worsened as snipers began to pot shot patrols, resulting in the O.C. pulling everyone back into the location, hoping that with no troops to attack things would cool. Faced with the prospect of losing men or involving innocent civilians in running battles because of these snipers, this was a correct move and in no way could be blamed for the next step in the advancement of the day's violence.

Unable to comprehend that the reason for the early morning operation was to rid the Catholic communities of terrorism by removing the people that committed it, those who should have known better began to take up arms. To many the I.R.A. were their protectors against the jack-boot of British oppression and their only defence should attacks on them by the protestant mobs resume again. They could not judge membership in the I.R.A. by fathers, sons, brothers or neighbours as a criminal act, but one of taking up a just cause. Since the dawn of time misguided patriotism has claimed many lives needlessly; this day was to add to that list.

In the early afternoon with no troops on the ground on which to take out their hatred, the snipers moved up to positions around C Company's location. This forced the Paras indoors, leaving the return of fire to the men in the roof top sangars. This went on for some time, with the O.C. trying to restrict and control the firing of his men. But it was hopeless for more snipers were arriving all the time.

Due to all windows in the police station being blacked out and boarded up, the only point at that moment from which to observe was the sand-bagged sangar on the roof. It was from here that Lieutenant Taplow and Dave Urwin were trying to assess where the most dangerous fire was coming from. They were finding this difficult for every time one of them silhouetted his head in one of the observation slits, shots were directed at the sangar. Taking a breather, both men sat on the floor for a spell, examining range cards trying to plot what limited information they had gained. When the field telephone rang Wally Forbes, one of two soldiers on duty at the time, reached up to answer it.

'It's the O.C. for you, Sir', he stated, passing the receiver across to his

Platoon Commander.

'Hello, Sir.'

'Peter, I find this hard to believe but my number two sangar reports that a body of people are forming up below the banking on the other side of the Summerhill Road, and they look as if they are getting ready to attack you.'

'What?' exclaimed the young officer, finding this hard to believe himself.

'Yes I know, that's what I thought, but the sergeant major has just been up and confirmed that this looks highly likely. Now what can you see from your location?' replied Major Bates in a continuing tone of wonderment.

'Wait one, Sir', said Taplow, scrambling up to take a fleeting look, then dropping down again.

'Can't tell, Sir. That part of the road's in dead ground; besides it's unhealthy up here to stare.'

'Well, what ever is going to happen you'll have to sort it on your own. If these idiots try something we will give you what fire support we can, but I'm not sending anyone across the open ground to you', informed Major Bates in a more businesslike manner.

'Right, Sir. Whatever they're up to I'm sure we can handle it', assured the lieutenant confidently, replacing the receiver before briefing his sergeant.

Downstairs, after borrowing a claw hammer from the duty police constable, the three men, selecting one of several hall windows, pried a piece of boarding away. On taking turns peering out each agreed on the glimpses of activity seen that it just might be possible that some of these mad fools might try to rush the police station. Taplow, taking no chances, ordered a general stand-to.

With hands, bayonets and metal table legs the platoon ripped away the wood covering the boarded ground floor windows. The black painted glass they smashed for vision to engage targets. In no time the south and west sides of the Colinglen bristled rifle barrels like a frontier Fort.

Peter Taplow had done this solely as a military precaution, believing in his heart of hearts that once any would-be attackers saw the station was ready for such a suicide move no one would commit themselves to anything so ludicrous. But what he did not take into consideration was the one overriding factor that counted most. Blinding hot-blooded Irish hatred.

The first attacker to show himself was a reddish-haired man in his forties, wearing a white shirt and dark trousers. Carrying a Thompson machine-gun with a round drum magazine, he scrambled up the banking onto the road, signalling with one arm for others to follow him. As these others appeared swarming up onto the road, one actually waving an Irish tri-colour on a pole, the first man began to spray bullets from the hip at the building in front of him.

Taplow was left no option; his command, loud and clear, vibrated around the inside of the police station.

'OPEN FIRE!'

With that order the station boomed with ear-splitting noise as rifles cracked and ejected cases clattered about the floor, filling the air with the smell of burnt propellant.

The first to fall was the white-shirted leader, struck simultaneously by four or five 7.62mm rounds.

The remainder, between fifty and sixty, armed with an assortment of rifles, pistols, shotguns and machine guns, pressed on firing as they moved. The range being between forty and fifty yards against professional, well-protected riflemen, meant certain death. Dave Urwin, taking aim on a youth firing a semi-automatic rifle as he ran, squeezed his trigger. The youth and rifle dropped to lie still in the roadway. The sergeant had killed before and in most cases, without feeling, but not this time. He was being forced to commit slaughter. But this did not deter him from selecting another target for he knew that with battle joined there could be now no holding back.

The assault lasted only a few minutes for the scathing fire from the South wall butchered the attackers. In an instant the euphoria of the charge had changed to terror, pain and death. What had been moments before defiant screams and curses, could now be heard as screams of pain, moans and pleas to the heavenly Father to remain alive.

From the rough grass fronting the station back across the Summerhill to the rim of the road bank lay bodies and wounded. Others, too frightened or out of ammunition, cowered in the protection of the road ditch. Draped in the concertina-wire that covered the gap between the Colinglen and the school were two men who tried to flank around the staton, shot not by 8 Platoon but by members of the company covering that section from the school.

Realising what a suicide situation they had put themselves in the attackers began to bolt. Most made their way down the ditch to the safety of the lower flats east of the station. Two, in panic, tried to escape across the Summerhill but were brought down by a dozen rifles before reaching the far side. Others pinned down with no avenue of escape remained still, occasionally finding the courage to venture a snap shot.

A woman in her forties wearing a house dress and apron ran wailing out of a side street further up the Summerhill. In a distraught state she entered the killing zone to throw herself down beside the body of a husband or son. With tears streaming down her cheeks she spent several minutes alternately hugging the body, beating her hands in her apron lap and shaking raised fists at the Colinglen. From the rim of the bank another woman cautiously appeared to hurry to the side of the other. She, with words and actions, roused the first out of her grief in order to move the body. With each of them pulling on an arm they dragged the corpse out of sight below the road bank. Considering the Para's blood at that moment was hot and racing, the two women were very lucky not to have been blown away by men prepared to shoot anything that moved. But then it was early days yet.

Dave Urwin, anxious about the justifiable but rapid expenditure of ammunition, hurried around his men giving the same warning to each.

'Conserve your rounds, single aimed shots only.'

His worry was well-founded, for the last thing the Army had expected was an all out attack on one of their locations, resulting in a heavy call for ammunition.

8 Platoon had started the battle with the normal allocation of forty rounds per man. Urwin, in his capacity as the Platoon Sergeant, always kept a small reserve of four hundred and fifty to hand but on present expenditure there would not be a bullet left in the station by dusk.

There was, however, a larger cache of ammunition held by the company in a make-shift bunker up beside the school, under the control of Sam Kyle. Major Bates, on being notified of the ferocity and numbers involved in attacking the police station, ordered some of this to be moved to a more central distribution point.

The key to this bunker was held by the Company Colour Sergeant but he, having left earlier that morning to collect stores from Battalion H.Q., found himself trapped there, unable to penetrate the gauntlet of road blocks and snipers. Therefore the man shouldering his responsibilities was his Lance

Corporal Storeman.

Sam Kyle, too busy to go himself, had sent Corporal Pearson, the Company Clerk, with four men to collect this urgently needed ammunition. However, surprised and angry, the Sergeant Major found that when his clerk returned he was empty-handed.

'Sir, that prick Burbage says we can't have the ammo,' he declared.

'What?' was all Sam said, before storming off.

At the bunker he found a scene being enacted straight out of Hollywood's 'From Here to Eternity.'

A heavy-set, blond lance corporal stood blocking the front of the ammunition store door, whilst in front of him the four soldiers detailed to collect the rounds were swearing and howling for him to open the door.

'What the hell's going on, Corporal Burbage?' raged the C.S.M.

'Sir, I can't let them have it', he began to explain, 'the Colour's been told by the Q.M. that under no circumstances is this ammunition to be issued. It would throw his accounting all to fuck. Besides the Colour's got the key.'

Kyle, struck speechless for a second, found his voice to take on the roll of Burt Lancaster, uttering his lines almost word for word.

'Get him out of the way and smash that fucking door down.'

Despite the initial attack turning the Summerhill Road into an abattoir, the assault was not given up. From the police station people with guns spread left and right until the entire location was surrounded and under seige.

Although brave and prepared to have a go, most were naive when it came to adopting basic battle drills. Many on taking up fire positions silhouetted themselves in windows and were soon punished for it. Others ran about from cover to cover as if playing harmless cowboys and Indians and were also soon killed. The classic crime was committed by a man firing from one of the Ballykeady flats north of the school. Bursting through a set of balcony doors he stood in full view firing a sten gun on automatic bursts until his magazine ran out. Then he dropped down behind a plastic dustbin to reload. For a moment there was no reply, the Paras stunned in awe at his stupidity. Then as one, twenty odd rifles were raised and fired.

The dustbin disintegrated; the gunman behind in a similar state leaked his blood over the balcony for hours. The distance from him to the school had been less than forty yards.

*   *   *

The Company Colour Sergeant was not the only one to be cut off when Irish tempers erupted. Jim Sinclair, Mick Pridmore, Paddy Kieran and 'Yorky' Rush had spent most of the morning at one of the holding areas identifying those arrested for photo purposes. Their vehicle, an open Landrover, was not suitable for forcing barricades and road blocks, which meant they had to pick a long roundabout route through safe areas. This got them as far as Support Company's locaton, which was another school situated in the protestant estates on the high ground to the east of the Colinglen.

When word of the attack on Charlie Company reached their O.C., he dispatched the Anti-tank Platoon to the nearest street which overlooked the police station. Given permission to accompany them, Sinclair's party, boarding their Landrover, followed behind.

On debusing the Platoon Commander tried to find a position that overlooked C Company's location and which also gave his men cover to fire from. This proved difficult for the only ground suitable was that at the back of the houses on the edge of the estate near the brow of the hill to the east of C Company. However, the ground itself was not acceptable, for the hill, being a grassy convex slope, allowed no cover and obscured their vision of the stream bed and the open ground beyond. It was the local householders who solved their dilemma by inviting them in, giving them free access to the upstairs rear windows.

The house Jim Sinclair and his men were let into was occupied by an elderly couple.

'Is that all right for you, son?' asked the woman of 'Yorky' Rush, who was standing on her toilet seat, his rifle barrel half out the bathroom window. 'Can you shoot them from there?'

'Aye love, this is champion,' confirmed the Yorkshireman.

'And you boys,' she continued, moving on to the bedroom, 'is this satisfactory?'

'Ya, this is just fine,' replied Kieran by the window, in a satisfied tone, keeping his head low as he took stock of the unrestricted view and fields of fire presented to them.

'Look, Mrs. Walters, we'll probably have to break some glass here,' apologised Jim Sinclair, eyeing the framework of the window.

'Oh don't bother. Don't bother,' she assured the Scotsman, 'you lads just get on with whatever you have to do.'

'Now then,' she continued, 'will you all have tea or would you prefer coffee?'

'Tea will be fine, love,' replied Pridmore, turning with a set, unemotional expression from the side window, 'just one sugar for me.'

'What have you got, Johnny?' asked Sinclair of Paddy Kieran, after the woman had gone.

'Well, on the left I count six clear targets,' he answered, crouched at one side of the window adjusting the range of his rear rifle sight.

'What about you, Mick?'

'I see about three or four plus a group of them behind a bank the other side of the stream,' assessed the big man in a flat voice.

'Right. Let's get to work before Support Company scare them all off. Johnny, you and me will work on the left. Mick you and 'Yorky' take the right. Our boundary is Woodlake Drive where it bends away from the school, okay.'

On agreeing, Pridmore raised his voice to shout through the wall.

'Yorky.'

'Yah,' replied Rush.

'We got everyone to the right of Woodlake Drive. You got any preference with who you want to start?' asked the big man.

'Yah,' came back the Yorkshireman's reply, 'those two fuckers at the far end of the middle landing in Allison Flats.'

Shattering the window glass to give themselves flexability in taking on several targets, the view they overlooked was nothing less than a nineteenth century frontier action. With the back drop of a dozen pillars of oily smoke dulling the late afternoon sun, the Army location had become a mini Alamo. Without let up, from without and within shots were being exchanged, while bodies, some in the open, others crumpled on roof tops and in doorways, lay as a testimonial to the stupidity of the assault. Refuges families caught up in the firing were trying to make their escape. Women carrying babies and men dragging young children were all running away from the killing. Groups from the flats below the police station could be seen crawling along the landings and down the stairs to follow the stream bed across to the safety of the Broughshane. Old men and women, invalid or too frail to walk, were being carried by those younger to better protected accommodation or away down the route of the stream bed.

Rush, firing a round at his target, took aim again as the first man he selected thrashed about on the concrete landing. Before he could squeeze the trigger for a second time, the other man, who had been lying beside the first, jumped up to crash through a nearby door. Calmly the sights were turned back to the wounded man who was painfully pulling himself onto his hands and knees. The bullet struck his lower right shoulder exiting from the chest to penetrate a thigh and then ricocheted off the landing and away, leaving a dead body behind.

Coming under fire from their rear, the Republican gunmen scurried into bolt holes where they were shielded from both C Company's marksmen and the fire from the Protestant hilltop. But this was not before they had suffered casualties. Jim Sinclair's party and the Anti-tank Platoon had dispatched about a dozen, most of these on an area of waste ground that they were forced to run across to seek shelter in the dead ground on the east bank of the stream.

From the protection of this bank a figure in a black cassock and dark jacket, waving a white handkerchief, ran out to kneel beside one of the fallen.

'What's that cunt on?' exlaimed Jim Sinclair, angry that anyone should risk his life by running into an area under fire.

'Priest, giving last rites,' answered Kieran.

'Fool, bloody fool,' commented the Scotsman heatedly.

The priest, crossing himself, reached out to pick something up and clutch it under his jacket.

'That son of a bitch,' exclaimed Mick Pridmore, who had stepped across to watch. 'Did you see what that cunt did?'

'Eh, whatcha mean?' asked Kieran, looking up from placing a fresh magazine on his rifle.

'Did you see him, Jim?'

'How do you mean, Mick?' replied sinclair, puzzled.

'He's got the weapon under his coat,' explained the big man angrily, 'he's bringing the fucking thing back.'

The others, unable to confirm this, watched as the priest ran, clutching his coat, to disappear below the rim of the hill.

'You sure about that, Mick?' queried Sinclair, finding this blatant flaunting of his neutrality hard to believe.

'Positive,' affirmed Pridmore.

Before more could be said, and not surprisingly, the priest was again seen making a dash towards another of his fallen flock. In silence the men watched as he knelt to carry out the duties of his trade. Then they exploded into curses as he again placed the man's weapon under his coat and hurriedly returned to the near bank of the stream.

Seething with anger the three Paras waited to see if a third journey would be made.

'Bloody cheek,' swore Sinclair as the cassock-clad figure appeared again. Then raising his rifle, he fired several shots into the priest's path in an attempt to force him back. But he paid no attention to these, dropping once more beside one of the stilled gunmen.

Jim, taking aim, voiced his thoughts.

'Don't make me do it, ya bastard, don't make me fucking do it.'

131

'No, not you Jim,' cut in Kieran firmly, lifting his rifle into his shoulder.

Johnny, born and raised in a small County Wicklow Village, took aim and thought of his own priest. Not just found in the church, he would visit every household, walk the lanes to all outlying farms and join in the stories over a glass of Guinness in the local bar during the evenings. He was also the only man who could find Kieran when as a boy he would steal away from school to poach a rabbit or a pheasant in the surrounding fields and dells.

Turning, half bent at the waist, to begin his return journey, Johnny's bullet struck the priest in the chest, tearing a fatal channel through his body, crumpling him onto the rifle he clutched beneath his coat.

'Here you are, boys,' came a voice from the doorway.

Mrs. Walker was entering the room on her hands and knees, pushing a tray with teacups and biscuits before her.

'Here you are young man, just one sugar wasn't it?' she confirmed, passing a cup and saucer across to Pridmore whilst making an apology.

'I'm sorry about the biscuits, they're only digestives; I hope you don't mind.'

*   *   *

'Well, did you get him?' Phil Haydon asked 'No Way' Ottoway as he stooped back from the observation slit having just fired a shot with the Platoon's only sniper rifle. It was a bolt action weapon with a telescopic sight and was left in the police station sangar for the use of those on duty. With the aid of the magnification sighting this gave the firer a wider range of targets than their standard issue Self-Loading Rifle.

'No, missed,' replied Ottoway in a dejected tone.

'Right, my turn,' Haydon claimed, reaching for the rifle.

'Like fuck, I ain't finished yet,' protested the other, pulling the weapon away.

'What do ya mean? You've had it for over an hour. It's my go now,' pointed out Haydon, again reaching for the rifle.

'No,' replied Ottoway, pulling the rifle into his body and turning away to keep it out of his mate's reach.

'Stop being a big kid, Ottoway, and gi'me a crack,' pressed Haydon.

'No, Fuck off! I haven't killed anyone yet,' declared the taller youth in a half-sulk.

'Bollocks ya lying fucker, Ottoway. What about that cunt on the roof of the Merriot Flats?' Haydon pointed out loudly.

'Ah him, he's not dead. I just winged 'im,' assured Ottoway.

'Winged him? Winged him?' repeated Haydon in amazement. 'Well how come he ain't moved for almost an hour?'

'He's playing possum,' dismissed Ottoway with a knowing nod of his head.

'Playing possum my ass,' scoffed Haydon. 'We'll see about that.'

Picking up his own rifle, he took aim and fired several rounds at an arm that was hanging over the roof edge of one of the flats two hundred yards away. Twice it kicked upwards as bullets struck the flesh and bone to repeatedly flop back into its dangling position.

'There, ya still think that geezer's playing possum?' proclaimed Haydon sarcastically, resting his rifle in a corner.

'Could be,' replied Ottoway, unwilling to give up his new toy.

'Oh fuck ya, 'No Way'. Give us the pissin' thing,' demanded Haydon, shooting a hand forward to grab the rifle barrel.

'Sod off, it's mine,' protested Ottoway pulling away.

'Is it fuck? It belongs up here; it's for both of us,' pointed out Haydon angrily. He locked his other hand on the butt, causing the two men to jostle about, tugging the weapon between them.

'Bugger you Haydon, I'm keeping it.'

'Give us it, ya cunt.'

'No. Fuck ya.'

'I'm going to tell Taplow.'

'Go ahead.'

And so it went on into the evening until bad light stopped play.

In the cold, dark early hours of the following morning when the alertness of the besiegers was at its most lax, Major Bates set several minor operations into motion. Len Hatton and two of his cooks, keeping to a shadowy route, arrived at the Colinglen with hot tea and sandwiches. A party from 9 Platoon, stripped of equipment, slipped out beyond the wire to claim a number of the nearer bodies. One of these who had been draped over the concertina-wire since the first charge, turned out to be still alive. The dead, on being searched for identification, were wrapped in polythene sheeting or ponchos and laid in an empty classroom. Over several days they were to be joined by others, their stench ever increasing.

CHAPTER 9

We do not what we ought;
What we ought not, we do;
And learn upon the thought
That chance will bring us through!

Matthew Arnold

Recently promoted, Lance Corporal Reg Berrill woke as the plane carrying him back from his four days R and R leave shook with a jolt as the wheels made their first contact with the Aldergrove runway. Closing tired eyes he attempted to regain sleep but was unable to do so because of the shuffling and chatter of the other restless passengers.

Reg had a good reason for wanting to slip back into slumber; he was sick with a hangover.

He had spent his leave, not with his parents in Swindon, but at Stourbridge outside Birmingham with a girl he had known for the past year. She took the four days off from her work to spend them with him, most of this time in bed. Either Reg was going soft or the girl had caught him out somewhere amidst the earlier periods of lust, for he had suddenly found himself asking her to marry him. Returning to the cold reality of Ulster he could have soon recovered from the embarassment of this passion-induced proposal, except she had accepted.

To seal the bargain she took her fiancé into Birmingham and bought him an off the peg, up-market Burton's suit. He was wearing this suit now, for after spending their last hours together at a late night Midlands Club, she had seen him off on his early morning flight back to Northern Ireland. With her face streaked with tears, he made a number of un-remembered drunken promises about writing, arranging a date for the wedding and not getting killed.

Rocking in a painful stupor, eyes closed, waiting with the rest of the passengers to pass through the airport's security check, he wished he had danced more and drank less. Climbing aboard the Army chartered bus outside the terminal building, which was to return all military personnel to their units in Belfast, Reg, on finding the first empty seat, slumped into it to seek sleep.

Less than an hour later he was woken by the driver shouting.

'Come on, son, this is it, I'm not going any further.'

Peering around through burning eyes he found he was the only passenger left on the bus. Everyone else who had taken the time to watch T.V., listen to a radio or read a paper were well aware that the day before all hell had broken loose in the province. Several minutes earlier they had been given a panoramic view from the escarpment road top before dropping down the steep slope to the city's outskirts, and seeing Belfast apparently burning they had left the bus at earlier, safer stops.

'Where are we?' asked Berrill sluggishly.

'City Bus Station,' replied the driver, impatient to be away.

'Bus Station,' objected Berrill, 'can't ya take us around to the location?'

'Location, which one?' asked the driver out of curiosity.

'Colinglen, up the Summerhill Road,' replied Reg hopefully.

'The Colinglen! Are you crazy? I'm not here to commit suicide!' exclaimed the driver. 'You'll have to get out here, it's as far as I'm taking you.'

'Unhelpful git,' cursed Berrill, under his breath as he picked up his overnight grip to leave the bus. 'What's he flapping about for anyway.'

Stepping onto the pavement to enter the bus station he was unaware of how suppressed his powers of observation were by the dull, alcohol-induced ache that throbbed within his head. If he had drunk less he would probably have wondered, why the bus sped off so quickly or why there was no traffic and so few people in the street. Entering the inner station where several buses stood idle and unattended he made for a bank of telephone kiosks, oblivious to the fact there was no one else about. Stepping into one of the booths he fumbled through his wallet until he found a slip of paper on which he had written C Company's telephone number. After dialling the phone rang only once before being picked up. With the pips making his head hurt, Reg pushed a coin into the slot.

'Yes, who is it? What do you want?' demanded an abrupt voice.

'Oh hello, Sir. It's Corporal Berrill,' he began, recognising the voice to be that of Captain Austen. 'I was just phoning up in the hope of being collected.'

'Collected?' came back the single mystified word.

'Yes, Sir. I just got back from R and R and the bus driver wouldn't take me back to the location, so I was wondering if perhaps a wagon could be laid on to pick me up,' explained the lance corporal in more detail.

'Wagon! Laid on!' replied Austen in stunned amazement.

'Sorry, Sir, we must have a bad line. I've just come back from R and R and the bus driver . . .'

Reg, misunderstanding Austen's lack of comprehension, was cut off by the captain asking 'Who is this?'

'Corporal Berrill, Sir.'

'Where are you, Corporal Berrill?'

'At the bus station, Sir,' answered Reg indignantly, for Austen made his question sound as if it was going to be a secret just between the two of them.

'Belfast Bus Station?' asked the captain in confirmation.

'Yes, Sir,' responded Berrill even more indignantly.

'On your own?'

'Yes, Sir, no one else got off the bus at . . .' the corporal began to explain but was stopped short by an explosion coming from the receiver.

'Fucking hell! Fucking hell! Corporal Berrill, Corporal Berrill, get out of there quick. Put the telephone down, get out onto the street, flag down the first military vehicle you see and get yourself into a location, any location, have you got that?'

'Yes, sir,' replied a very confused lance corporal.

'Right now, hang up! Hang up!' was the captain's final screamed instruction.

Berrill, picking up his grip, stepped out of the kiosk to be blown sideways

135

onto the asphalt as a bomb exploded on one of the buses parked about sixty yards away. Tucking his head under his arms he waited for the deris to settle before regaining his feet. Standing to observe the wreckage in wonderment he became aware of pain in one elbow. Feeling it with a hand he discovered a tear in the jacket.

'Bastard,' he cursed, as once again he was blown off his feet by a second bomb. Not waiting for the rubble to still its clattering Berrill scrambled up to grab his overnight grip and sprinted outside. Up the street a grey painted police Landrover raced towards him. Jumping into the roadway he tried to flag it down. But they were not in any mood to stop for civilians; accelerating, the vehicle charged straight at him. Diving to one side, Reg crashed in a rolling heap against the street curb.

'Flaming Jesus, what the hell is going on around here?' demanded the lance corporal loudly, brushing mud and slime from his brand new Burton suit.

Looking up he spotted an open Army Landrover pulling into the side of the street; whereupon someone from the front passenger seat jumped out to run into a paper shop.

With smoke billowing from the bus station Reg picked up his grip again to hurry towards the Landrover. Approaching, he could see besides the driver there were two men with rifles sitting in the back. All three, by the cap badges on their berets, were from the same county regiment. At the shop doorway a captain stepped out with a bundle of daily papers clutched to his chest. Turning towards him, Berrill reached with one hand into the inside of his jacket to produce an I.D. card. With no more than a few feet between them the officer, seeing this move, his eyes widening, fell backwards against the door frame. In the same instant Berrill froze; for from behind he heard the unmistakable clatter of rifles being cocked. Very slowly he turned his head to see the two soldiers in the back of the Landrover standing up, aiming their rifles straight between his eyes.

'Sir, as slow as I can I'm going to pull an I.D. card out of my coat,' explained Berrill, speaking to the officer but not taking his eyes off the two rifles, the muzzles of which looked as big as cannon barrels.

At their Battalion H.Q. Reg was ushered in to explain himself to the Duty O.P.s officer, who was the Battalion's Regimental Sergeant Major. During the course of this the paratrooper learned how fortunate he had been. For not only was every police station and Army location within Republican areas under siege, but also roving bombers, gunmen and petrol bomb throwing rioters were making movement difficult. In short, for the last twenty-four hours, since mid-internment day, law and order in many parts of Belfast was out of control. The Battalion that Reg had been taken under the wing of was at that moment totally committed on the ground, holding a line that separated large Catholic and Protestant ghetto areas. Just how stretched they were was soon made clear by a subtle question from the R.S.M.

Sitting in a chair, his legs pushed out before him, tapping a pencil on his radio desk, he eyed Berrill up and down.

'What size boots do you take?' he asked.

'Ah! Nine small, Sir. Why?'

'Well,' ventured the warrant officer, 'we're a bit tight here; if I can scare you up some kit, we could use you on the streets with one of . . .'

Before he could finish Reg burst in.

'Fuck off, Sir, I've just been blown up twice, almost shot, scared shitless and had my suit ruined. Besides I'm 5 Para, I ain't going out anywhere without a

Red Beret on my head.'

'Alright! Alright, Corporal Berrill, you've made your point,' calmed the R.S.M., dismissing him to the dining room to get himself a lunch meal.

Filling his plate from the food on the hot plate, he sat to eat his meal with the only other two people in the room; a corporal and a private from a Lancer Regiment. Through general conversation involving the day's who, what, when and how, Reg learned that the two men had a Fox armoured car outside and were about to make a dash up the road to the Summerhill Police Station. Berrill, informing them that this was his Battalion H.Q., asked if he could have a lift.

'Well, we can squeeze you in but it'll be tight, and the trip won't be a picnic. No one's been able to get up to that location all day,' stated the corporal, who was the vehicle commander.

'Oh, I don't mind being uncomfortable for a bit and, what the fuck, inside an armoured car that should be safe enough,' assured Reg confidently.

The two tankies exchanged cold glances but said nothing. In the vehicle yard, after the private had climbed into the driver's seat, the commander told Reg to get in through the top turret. Pulling himself up by the barrel of the armoured car's main armament, a 20 millimetre cannon, he gingerly eased himself in. Not wishing to damage his suit anymore than it already was, he settled, somewhat cramped, as low as he could get to enable the corporal to take up his position above him.

'You'll have to get lower,' warned the commander, dropping his legs through the hatch.

The paratrooper wiggled his body in an attempt to gain depth, but failed.

'Not a hope mate, that's as deep as I can get,' pleaded Berrill.

'Well, without me we don't leave, so you better try harder,' informed the corporal, struggling in to stand on Berrill's back.

'Ugg!' he exclaimed, dropping three inches and feeling as tight as a sardine, 'that's it, that's as far as I can go.'

'Sorry, can't get the turret shut so you're going to have to,' apologised the Lancer, stamping his right boot into the small of Reg's back, pole axing him into a space he did not believe existed.

The lance corporal, wedged so snuggly only fingers could be moved, found himself staring with one eye through a small apperture looking forward of the vehicle. On closing the turret the commander, fitting a set of headphones, ordered the driver to start his engine.

At the entrance barrier, the armoured car turned right towards a junction with a main road. This road was bordered on both sides by Republican houses, the beginning of hostile territory. Approaching the crossing the armoured car idled gently forward to halt twenty yards short, remaining in the cover of two high brick buildings at each corner. Reg, unable to move his head, watched the street in front with his one eye as he listened to the conversation between the two lancers. Although they were in radio communication with each other, Reg, being situated between one above and the other below, could hear them quite clearly.

Commander—'Okay Tim, build the revs up; when we go I want everything it's got.'

Driver—'Right you are.'

The engine built to a vibration of noise.

Commander—'Okay Tim, when I say go lock a right turn on and don't stop for no fucker. Ready, ready, go!'

Reg felt the Fox catapult forward then watched, a prisoner of his vision, as it rounded to the right, unaware he was being taken on a trip through the Valley of Death. As they straightened for their run down the road weapons were fired, petrol bombs, blast bombs and bricks thrown from every side and angle. Berrill watched in horror as showers of missiles landed on, around and in front of them. Explosions and sheets of flame were going up all around whilst the armour plating ringed and pinged as lumps of bricks and bullets glanced off it.

In helpless terror Reg could only watch as his transportation roared through all this, zig-zagging down an obstacle course of burnt out buses, over-turned cars and heaps of rubble.

After quarter of a mile, with no let up in the shooting and bomb throwing, they came to a main cross roads. This was the Summerhill junction. Storming through a narrow gap in the centre of several cars placed to block the road, they brushed aside a red mini resting on its side. Again turning right, the armoured car mounted the pavement to skirt another barrier. Here they came under even heavier attack; a petrol bomb exploded just to their front with the flame washing like a wave over the vehicle in a solid sheet. Reg, blinking, felt the heat on his eyelid. Squirming in petrified fear, he tried desperately, without success, to dislodge his eye from this unwanted hole. At last there was a let up in the firing and explosions, for they were nearing the Summerhill Police Station. Suddenly, they arrived; a sharp left turn and a screeching halt had Berrill staring at a double inward-opening corrugated-iron gate.

Since turning into the Summerhill Road Berrill had listened as the vehicle commander repeatedly warned the station by radio of their arrival, asking for the entrance to be opened. With the Fox poised at the gate, eager to gain the safety of the police yard, the inside of the vehicle vibrated with the curses of both the commander and his driver, understandably impatient to get away from the bombs and bullets. Reg remained silent, crapping blue lightning in speechless fear.

At last the two double gates began to swing inwards. Anticipating their movement the driver, with a roar from his engine, jumped the vehicle forward, only to find himself up against the front of a Landrover that was just as anxious to get out. After several long seconds of shouting at each other it soon became apparent that the Landrover was not prepared to budge.

'Para,' shouted the commander at Berrill, 'I'm not going to sit here like this, we're fucking off, so come on out, you're getting off right here.'

'Okay, okay,' agreed Reg with desperate relief.

Opening his turret, the lancer climbed out and then reached down and took hold of the passenger's collar. Reg, pried loose from his confinement, scrambled out through the hatch like a frightened puppy. At this point a sniper's bullet struck one of the metal gate posts, giving Berrill such a fright that he, dribbled off the armoured hull to crash onto the concrete driveway dragging his grip with him. In a dizzy, painful heap he lay unaware that Burton's best had taken another pounding. Like someone out of the Okay Corral, a dark green uniformed policeman appeared above him, firing a Beretta automatic pistol through the gate, first in one direction then another.

Reg, leaping to his feet, rushed blindly through the first door he saw. Bursting into a hallway he was confronted by R.S.M. 'Nuts' Norris.

'Who are you?' Norris shouted.

'Corporal Berrill, D Company, Sir; just back from leave,' blurted out Reg breathlessly.

'Good, good, come with me,' he ordered.

Through a door Berrill found himself in the Battalion Operation's Room. The adjutant and a signaller sat manning the radios, while the Signals' platoon sergeant stood carrying on a frantic conversation over one of the room's telephones.

'Here, get this on,' ordered the R.S.M., handing him a flak jacket.

'But! But!' stammered the lance corporal, slipping it over his shoulders.

'You'll need this as well,' continued the R.S.M. helping him into a set of webbed equipment.

Bewildered Berrill turned with extended arms to explain that he was still in civvies and could not see the sense in putting this kit on, only to find a rifle being pushed into his hands.

'Sergeant Brumwell,' called the warrant officer to the Signals sergeant, who had put the phone down, 'take this corporal around to the back sangar; it will be his post. Hurry, we've had to leave it unmanned for over an hour now.'

'Right, Sir,' answered the sergeant, jumping up to dash through the door with a quick command to Berrill as he passed. 'Follow me.'

Reg, overcome by confusion, turned again to the R.S.M., only to find this time a helmet being fitted to his head.

'Come on lad, don't dilly dally,' he commanded, pushing Berrill through the door.

Two minutes later he was standing in a darkened, sandbagged cell, staring through an observation slit at a street of depressing brick houses.

Berrill, trying to dust away the grit and grime from the most expensive combat suit in all of Belfast, with his hangover building to a throbbing intensity, was becoming bitterly enraged. Reflecting on the number of times in the last hour that he had narrowly escaped death, it is not surprising that as a gunman sprayed bullets into the outside of the sangar he finally threw a wobbler.

Thrusting his rifle barrel into the slit he began to empty his twenty round magazine at every malicious door, window and chimney pot in sight.

'Come on ya Irish bastards,' he hollared at the top of his voice, 'do your damnedest, nothing can destroy me, I'm fucking invincible.'

*   *   *

On the evening of the second day Dave Urwin took the opportunity of a lull in the sniping that had been almost continuous.

'Yes, I know dad, but I would rather you didn't.'

'Yes, yes, I understand that . . .'

'No, I'm sure that just for a few days until things settle . . .'

'Alright! Alright! But be careful, leave early and take a safe route. I'll phone again tomorrow . . . ya same to you, bye and take care.'

'Bloody stubborn idiot,' swore Urwin, putting the receiver down. He had just spent the last ten minutes trying to convince his father, who lived less than a mile from the Colinglen, not to risk going to work the next morning.

'He can't see the sense of staying indoors until things blow over.'

His comment was made to the shirt-sleeved station's duty police constable who like C Company was also imprisoned by the siege.

'He sounds like a lot of people here, Davey. Just not prepared to let the troubles get the better of them,' he replied, stretching back in his desk chair to clasp both hands behind his head.

'Ya, you must be right; still I'd rest easier if he stayed home. Harland and

Wolfe aren't going to go bust just because he doesn't turn up for a couple of mornings.' said the sergeant, reaching once more for the constable's phone.

'Brian, can I make another call?' he asked.

'Away you go,' he waved, 'I use your razor, you use my phone.'

'Dare I?' pondered Urwin, pausing with a hand on the phone, listening for any upsurge of ballistic noise. 'It's the wife, can't let on what's happening here.'

'Seems quiet enough,' assured the constable.

'Yaahh,' agreed Urwin, not too confidently, picking up the receiver to dial the Aldershot code.

'Hello,' answered his wife's familiar voice.

'Hello honey, just thought I'd give you a quick call to see how you're getting on,' he bluffed.

'Me? Getting on? David Urwin, I've been worried sick for you ever since last night. What's been going on over there?' she scolded in response.

'Why, what do you mean?' asked her husband innocently.

'Good God, Dave, the shooting and bombing; it's all over the papers and on the radio and T.V.,' she replied angrily.

'Oh that,' laughed Urwin, 'yah, we heard there was a bit of a flare up but that's miles away from us.'

'Oh! Oh! I am pleased . . .'

'How are the kids?' interrupted Urwin, hoping to change the subject before more embarassing questons could be asked.

'Oh fine, they're both up in bed at the moment.'

'And Jimmy's school work, how's he getting on?'

'Well, he hasn't mentioned anything about having problems. He seems to be enjoying school. I'll know more next week when they have a parents' night. That will be on either the Tuesday or . . .'

Dave did not hear the rest, having to pull the receiver from his ear to block the speaker with his hand, for a shot had been fired at the location.

From the hallway outside the office voices could be heard seeking the sniper out.

'George, he's in the top window on the corner house on Shepard Street.'

'No, no it's that cunt who's been pissing about in 18.'

Guarding the speaker Urwin placed the phone back to his ear.

'Dave! Dave!'

'Yes pet, sorry what was that?'

'Well, what do you think?'

'Think about what?'

'Haven't you been listening? Jimmy's teacher, should I . .'

Without warning two shots were fired from just outside the office door. Too late, Urwin masked the speaker.

'Davey! Davey! What was that?' demanded his wife.

'Some of the lads are using the shooting range just outside to test their rifles,' came the first answer that jumped into his head. Brian Savage, the police constable, who had been grinning through the whole conversation almost fell off his chair as he began to laugh.

'Are you sure, Dave?' asked Mary. 'It sounds awful close.'

'Well, it would. Here, listen, you can probably hear more of it,' he admitted, deciding to brass it out by holding the receiver towards the doorway as a burst of automatic fire sounded from outside the building. But this move back-fired horribly when a member of his platoon shouted from the hallway, 'George, it's that son-of-a-bitch with the Lewis gun. Get down, get down!'

In that split second, as the outer wall of the building thundered with banging and screams of ricocheting as a burst of .303 rounds struck, the sergeant failed in getting his hand over the speaker in time.

'There see, it's just normal practising. Now, Jimmy's teaching, could I leave that with you? You've always been much better at making decisions than me,' he hurriedly spluttered in desperation.

'Dave, what was all that shouting?' demanded his wife, disregarding everything he had just said.

'Just shouting. It must be some of the platoon horsing around,' he blatantly lied.

'And all that noise?' she pressed.

'Oh, we always get that sort of thing around here, it's a noisy place at times. Now look honey, I'm going to have to hang up; the phone belongs to the police and they've just given me the nod that they need to use it so I'll say bye for now.'

'But Dave.'

'I'll call again as soon as I can.'

From the hallway members of his platoon began to return the enemy machine-gunner's fire.

Bang!

'Dave, what was that?' asked Mary, her voice loud with concern.

Bang! Bang!

'Bye pet, love you.'

Bang!

'Dave! Dave!'

Bang! Bang!

'Well, that was a total disaster,' confessed Urwin, looking up from the quickly replaced telephone receiver.

Constable Savage, rocking back in his chair, could not reply, being too choked with laughter.

With C Company's confinement extending from one day to another, it began to look as if they were to be sealed in for some time. Throughout Belfast the Police and Army were able to do little more than hold lines that were drawn on the first day. The main problem was road blocks and barricades. These, numerous and with few exceptions covered by gunmen and snipers, could not be removed without mounting a major operation involving troops and heavy clearing equipment, neither of which at present was ready to hand.

The bulk of the people manning these barriers and weapons were not hard core I.R.A. Most were either thrill seekers, hot-headed youths, fringe sympathisers of the terrorist groups or just angry, but they were making efforts to kill.

*   *   *

Looking up from the map in his lap through the cold drizzly rain that had been falling all morning, Reg Berrill made another directional suggestion to the Humber driver.

'Turn left Buster, we'll try down there.'

'Reggy, if it's another dead end I'm going to fuck you,' warned Buckley.

He swung his heavy vehicle down a peaceful, flower-gardened residential street.

'Stop bitching, I'll get us there,' returned the lance corporal, watching for the street sign.

'Yes, yes,' he declared triumphantly, 'this is it. Straight on for another half mile, that should bring us back onto the Summerhill.'

The reason Berrill and Buckley were lost in Belfast suburbs was because they were on a mission. C Company, despite the conserving of ammunition, now found themselves critically short. Major Bates made this known to Battalion H.Q. with a request that somehow a re-supply be sent in. The Commanding Officer, as this was a 'Q' problem, passed it on to the Quartermaster. He, a man well drilled in delegating duties could see clearly that the person for this task of blockade running should be none other than Charlie Company's own Colour Sergeant, who had been stranded with them for the last four days. However, getting wind of this and having only eighteen months to go before he was due to start collecting his pension, he declined the offer by hiding in the toilet.

At about the same time that a C.Q.M.S. of the Parachute Regiment was trying to climb under the lid of a cistern, Lance Corporal Reginald Berrill stepped forward to volunteer. This was an act neither of loyalty to C Company nor heroism. Ever since Reg had fallen through the front gate he had been buggered about. At Battalion H.Q., with its high proportion of officers and S.N.C.O.s and scarcity of lower ranks, the drudgery of guards, duties and fatigues were being shouldered by a very few. To escape this Berrill would have volunteered for Devil's Island.

After signing the Q.M.'s 1033 form for almost five thousand rounds, he and Buster Buckley, who had not been asked if he wanted to go, made a dramatic exit through the station gates. Leaving the shower of bullets and bombs behind they turned off the Summerhill Road to race through narrow streets. Eluding the major road blocks they were able to, although lost, reach the safety of the Northern Avenue where sanity seemed to be more prevalent.

Approaching the Summerhill junction the road ahead could be seen to be obstructed by a van and two cars.

Turning his head, Berrill called through the communication window to his passenger in the back.

'We got a road block ahead padre, but it's okay, it's got to be a Prot one.'

'Prots, Corporal Berrill, may be okay for you, but I, as the Pope's lieutenant, will not be greeted with open arms by your bunch of friendly Orangemen up there,' jested Father Buchanan.

'Not to worry padre, it's more than my tape's worth to let you fall into enemy hands,' promised Reg, returning the joke.

Father Buchanan knowing of the number of Catholic dead at the Colinglen, had requested he be allowed to make the journey with the ammunition.

Seeing the armoured personnel carrier approach, those at the road block drove the van to one side allowing them through.

Lowering the side window hatch the lance corporal exchanged a few words as they slowly passed.

'Which way are you trying to get to?' he was asked.

'Up the Colinglen Police Station,' Reg replied.

'You won't make it; the Ravensdale is as far as you'll get. The rest is blocked solid,' was the answering warning.

'Cheers mate,' the paratrooper replied, replacing the metal hatch.

Turning west on the Summerhill Road they shortly came out of the housing area. Here, stretching for half a mile or so, the road on either side was covered only in rough turf grass. In the distance below the Ravensdale Estate sheltered behind a rise, an Army road block of barbed-wire draped wooden cross angles could be seen at one of the main junctions. This turned out to be manned by people they knew.

'Ay'up, look who's finally turned up. It's Lance Corporal Berrill,' called Yorky Rush, stepping out of the shelter of a newly erected sand-bagged post as the Humber pulled up.

'Why aren't you fuckers locked away with the rest of the besieged heroes?' Reg enquired, seeing Jim Sinclair and Paddy Kieran climb from the back of a parked support company Humber.

'Got stranded out here,' replied Sinclair, 'where've you come from?'

'Been with Battalion H.Q. for the last three days.'

'Well, why come down here?' asked Kieran shrugging the shoulders of his rain-soaked smock.

'I'm on an important mission. Got to take ammo into the Colinglen,' Reg informed them in a suitably dramatic tone.

'What! Just you and Buster? You must be around the twist!' exclaimed Sinclair.

'Fuck no, Jim, I ain't that soft. The padre's in the back.'

'Oh, bollocks,' groaned Rush in disbelief, as he and Kieran stepped around to the back of the vehicle and opened the door.

'The padre's not that dumb.'

'Oh yes he is,' assured Father Buchanan, stepping out onto the road, paper cups in one hand and a bottle of whisky in the other.

'Now, how would you boys like some of the Holy Water? Just to keep the damp chill away, mind.'

Before Berrill could be allowed to continue Captain Fletcher, Support Company 2 I/C arrived to organise the departure.

'Are you sure you really want to go?' was the captain's only attempt at persuading Berrill and Co. that the journey would not be all that safe.

'C.O.'s orders, Sir,' stated Reg. 'Besides death is better than having to spend another day in that zoo they call Battalion H.Q.'

As the road barrier was pulled to one side, Paddy Kieran, speaking through the driver's hatch window, gave Buckley sound professional advice.

'Buster, the main road block is about three hundred metres down the slope on the other side of the rise. It's full of cars and junk, but don't try to go through them. On the left they got a white bread van lying on it's side. If you smack it on one end she should shift out of the way.'

'Ta Johnny,' thanked the driver, throwing his vehicle into gear.

Kieran ran back to climb aboard Support Company's Humber for Captain Fletcher was taking men forward in support of Berrill's party. Following them up the rise the second armoured vehicle peeled off to the side of the road, with everyone bailing out to take up fire positions.

Continuing on, the first Humber raced down the sloping three hundred yards of no man's land to the tiny scrap yard that straddled the road. With spray causing a silver wake, for it was raining heavily now, it charged flat out for the left hand side.

'Tally ho, Buster, tally ho! Dive! Dive! Dive!' screamed Berrill, alternating impersonations between that of a Master of the hunt and a submarine commander.

As three figures manning the barrier were seen to scramble away up a bush covered bank, a distant sniper began firing at the metal hull of the A.P.C. Buckley, having set an aim on the rear half of the overturned bread van, braced his arms on the steering wheel.

'Hold onto your rosary, padre, we're going to hit,' shouted Berrill an instant before making contact.

The armoured vehicle skidded only slightly and more or less ploughed straight through, whilst the bread van, cast aside by the impact, almost righted itself before crashing into the verge. Regaining control Buckley steered his steel maverick down into the dip below the Lisna Carrol junction. Thundering out of this they once again came under sniper fire from the eastern flats bordering C Company's location.

'Keep your head down padre, I don't want to lose you now,' shouted Berrill again in warning.

'Bless you my son,' came back the padre's reply.

Cresting the roadway above the stream bed more shots were fired at them, increasing in accuracy as Buckley slowed to turn onto the short drive leading to the Colinglen. Accelerating, with the pinging of bullets sounding on the armoured plating, they crashed through the wooden drop bar that had been left in place at the sentry box since the first attack. Applying his brakes while pulling on a sharp right hand turn, Buckley brought the armoured vehicle sliding to a halt outside the station's back entrance.

Tumbling out of both doors Berrill and Buckley rushed around to pull open the back door.

'Inside, padre, quick,' ordered Reg, pushing him through the entrance doorway, throwing the two men stationed there backwards for all five to end sprawled across the hall floor.

Looking up, Berrill found a smiling Dave Urwin standing above him.

'What's this, Reg?' he asked, 'You seeking shelter from the rain drops?'

'Ya,' replied Berrill breathlessly, 'fucking lead ones, Sarge.'

As it was, Berrill's spectacular arrival proved to be a classic 'in the nick of time', for when the Humber crashed to a halt inside the Colinglen Compound, Charlie Company was down to three rounds per man.

*   *   *

'This is it, padre,' said Sam Kyle, placing a key in the classroom door which was being used to store recovered bodies. 'I keep it locked but there's no real need; the pong is so thick that most people steer clear of this part of the school.'

As he pulled the door open an invisible cloud of stench oozed out to engulf them.

'See what I mean?' confirmed Sam, jerking his head back, a sour expression springing to his face.

'Korea,' uttered Father Buchanan, not flinching.

'Sorry?' queried Kyle, not understanding the one word.

'Korea, haven't smelt that foul odour since Korea.' explained the padre.

'Hope you don't mind Sir, but I'll leave you to it,' apologised Sam, holding out the key.

'Not at all, Sergeant Major,' replied Buchanan, 'I'll be alright without further assistance. You've been very kind.'

Taking the key he entered the room and closed the door behind him. With most of the desks pushed against one wall, a clear area had been made below the front blackboard. There, in one tight row, lay eleven bundled bodies wrapped in either polythene or green army ponchos.

The padre, taking his embroidered stole from a side pocket, draped it around his neck. Then over the next hour he moved from one corpse to another, kneeling in prayer for several minutes beside each. Although dying enveloped in the hot flush of a rage that was driving them on to kill, Father Buchanan forgave this, intent instead on easing their soul's final journey.

*   *   *

It took ten days for the Army's reclaiming operation to reach the Colinglen and only then could C Company get out to patrol and restore their authority. First priority was the recovery of as many of the bodies as possible. Most of those not pulled in by the Paras had already been carried away during the first nights, to be buried in Southern Ireland or disposed of. The Republicans not wishing to make it known who was involved in the fighting, avoided cemetery burials and all the official identification that it would have meant. The lengths they went to were both comical and macabre. Some weeks later three of these corpses were found clogging a sewer running from the Broughshane Estate.

The only bodies left to collect were those that lay in open, exposed areas or on landings and roof tops. Corporal Vic 'Geordie' Seaten, the Company Medic, made a three day career for himself ferreting out and retrieving all these neglected corpses.

One of the first vehicles to leave the location was a Humber detailed to collect rations. During the final stages of the siege Len Hatton had been feeding the company from an emergency stock of tinned compo rations. Now he was being dispatched to Lisburn to fetch fresh food. When this was made known Chris Braithwaite volunteered himself and Wally Forbes to ride shotgun.

Buster Buckley, the driver, was looking forward to the trip. This was his first ride out since steam-rolling into the Colinglen five days earlier and he fancied a journey down safe country lanes. So it was with some surprise that under Braithwaite's directions he found himself doubling back, just skirting some very hard Republican areas.

'Chris, this is not the way to Lisburn,' pointed out Buckley in an annoyed tone.

'I know but it's important; just trust me,' pleaded the stand-in section commander.

Motioning the driver up a street Braithwaite, searching for an address, suddenly shouted a halt. The last time he had been on this street was ten days, fourteen hours and eleven minutes earlier.

Braithwaite was able to quote these figures because he had lived in a perpetual state of worry, each and every second of it.

'Wally, cover the front,' he shouted into the back. Then, before diving out of his side door, he gave Buckley a definite but not very enlightening order.

'Hang on here, I'll be right back.'

Jumping a front garden gate, he sped past a living room window through which he could see a middle aged couple. Racing to the back door he wrenched it open to burst in. Two people sat at the kitchen table eating a meal, both looking up at his unannounced entrance. They were Willie Durrant and Seela Riley.

Braithwaite almost collapsed with relief.

'Oh thank fuck! Thank fuck!'

'Here, you took your time getting back,' commented Durrant with just a trace of a smile.

'Come on Jock, let's go. We got to move quick,' ordered the relieved but nervous paratrooper.

'Wait up, I haven't finished my lunch yet,' protested the Scotsman, pointing with his fork at the half empty plate.

'Screw your scoff!' exploded Braithwaite, pulling Durrant to his feet by the scruff of his shirt, no longer able to suppress the throbbing anxiety that had been with him for the last ten days. 'While you've been shacked up in this cushy little pad, the rest of us have been fighting World War Three. Now where the fuck's your kit?'

'Okay! Okay! Dinna' get violent,' protested Willie, pulling away, 'it's up in the bedroom.'

'Well, go get it, we're getting out of here, fucking now,' shouted Chris. Then as an after thought asked, 'Where's your S.L.R.?'

'Ah,' pondered Durrant, before turning to the girl, 'where'd I put the rifle, hen?'

'Under the bed,' replied Seela, standing up to take his arm, 'I'll show you.'

'Oh, Jesus Christ! Jesus Christ,' groaned Braithwaite in hopeless despair.

A minute later the young couple returned, Durrant with his smock and beret on, equipment hanging on one shoulder, the retrieved rifle under an arm. Seela Riley clung to him with both hands while tears ran from her eyes.

'Come on,' hurried Braithwaite pulling the door open.

'Bye, love. I'll get in touch,' promised the Scotsman.

'Oh, Willie,' she sobbed, taking his head in her hands to kiss him.

Durrant, gripping the rifle behind her back, passionately took the girl in his arms to return the kiss.

Outside Chris met Corporal Hatton coming around the side of the house.

'What the fuck are you poncing around at?' he demanded heatedly. 'I should'a been in Lisburn by now.'

'Yah, I know Ken. We just picked up a passenger. I want you to screw the nut for me. Come on, I'll tell you all about it in the Pig.'

Because of the confusion and hectic situations that were constantly happening during the seige, Durrant's absence had not been detected. Whenever his whereabouts were questioned the privates of 8 Platoon were always able to cover with a convincing reply.

Three months later, in the Aldershot Garrison Catholic Church, Seela Riley and Willie Durrant were married.

*   *   *

'Neil, we got a cup of tea here, do ya want it passed down?'

'No, Bob, leave it there, I'll come up in a minute,' replied Neil Roberts to the offer.

He was working in an excavated hole to one side of a street that the other members of his work team had dug earlier that morning. Now with the telephone cable bared he, as the engineer, was working as speedily as possible to rectify the fault. This was damage caused by a car bomb that had exploded prematurely the day before, killing the two men who were driving.

The street backed on to a notorious Republican area, making the job one best completed quickly. For although they were not in uniform they did represent a functioning service of the British way of life in Northern Ireland. Having peeled back the outer protective casing he was, one by one, checking through the colour coded lines with his detector gauge. Again above him, a figure appeared.

146

'Not long, I'll be up in but a minute,' he called, without looking, thinking it was another of his men to warn him the tea was getting cold.

'You are finished, get out o'dere,' ordered a voice.

Looking up, Neil found a hooded man pointing a revolver at him. Without replying he removed his headphones and climbed out of the hole to find four more gunmen with their faces covered by either scarves or hoods. They were herding the other five members of his crew out of the tented shelter they had erected on first arriving. As all six were being pushed against the side of their own van, Roberts tried to protest.

'Look boys, we've got nothing to do with the troubles; we're just here to repair a telephone cable.'

'Shut your fucking gob,' retorted one of the gunmen, striking a blow to the side of Robert's face with his pistol, causing him to fall against one of his crew, knocking a tea mug from a hand that had been frozen on the handle.

'All Catholics over there,' ordered another of the gunmen, pointing the short barrel of a Sten gun towards a nearby brick wall. This presented each of the crew with a deadly dilemma. Not knowing which side of the community these masked thugs represented, the few steps they took or did not take surely meant life or death.

As two men moved hesitatingly towards the wall, Neil Roberts, blood oozing from his mouth, again spoke up.

'For God's sake, you can't be serious, we're not doing you any harm, just getting on with a job of work.'

After a pause the reply given was a short burst of Sten-gun fire directed at the four men with their backs to the van. The others, joining in with pistols and a sawed-off shotgun, soon silenced all groans and curses of these members of the telephone repair crew now crumpled at their feet. Neil Roberts, with three bullets in his chest and stomach, never felt the final act of a pistol being placed to his forehead, let alone the micro second of the shot, for he was already dead.

CHAPTER 10

But when Night is on the hills, and the
Great Voices Roll in from the Sea,
By starlight and by candlelight and dreamlight
She comes to me.

Herbert Trench

Returning from Northern Ireland, 5 Para settled into the standard routine of training during the day and indulging themselves in pet vices at night.

In the Company Billet after tea one evening Chris Braithwaite, dressing himself to go out, placed one foot on his bedstead to polish his shoe. Looking up he found Phil Haydon and 'No Way' Ottoway entering the room.

'Hi Chrissy,' hailed Haydon, 'me and 'No Way' are going up the smoke for a night out in Soho, ya wanna come?'

'Wrong day Phil; I got a date with a Q.A. nurse tonight,' declined Braithwaite.

'It's on us. You don't have to pay a thing; me and Phil won a packet in a card school last night,' lied Ottoway.

'Not a chance,' replied Braithwaite, pausing in the brushing of his shoe, 'got her own car, she's a dead cert, I can't pass this up. Sorry.'

The two schemers left the room, gnashing their teeth in disappointment.

'What'a we do now then?' asked Ottoway.

'We'll go up anyway and do a recce on the place,' settled Haydon.

Drifting from one seedy pub to another and not finding the contact they wished, our two conspirators lapsed instead into dejected drinking. Leaning on a bar staring into his pint Haydon was being forced to listen to Ottoway trying to chat up two girls next to him.

''Ere, how would you two chicks like to have an evening of dazzling delights with a couple of paratroopers?'

'Ya what?' replied the nearest, a dumpy thing with black hair, a round face and heavily mascaraed eyes.

'Me and my mate,' continued Ottoway, 'we can take you to the pinnacle of erotic desires.'

The other girl, leaning around her friend, asked, just as puzzled, 'what are you on about?'

'No Way', losing patience, laid it on the line to them.

'We wanna take ya down the street to the park and ride the asses off ya in the bushes.'

'You can piss off,' retorted the first girl taking her mate's arm. 'Come on Shel, let's find a table.'

'No Way',' commented Haydon, not looking up from his glass, you're about as subtle as a jock lance corporal.'

'You boys don't want anything to do with those scrubbers, they'll only get you into trouble,' spoke up a short, frail, limp-wristed man in his early forties, standing next to Haydon.

'They're always in here getting free drinks from nice boys like you and giving nothing in return. They're just prick teasers,' he continued.

'Oh ya,' replied Haydon, looking up uninterestedly. 'You in here a lot then?'

'Oh yes, I and my friend like this pub; we meet such nice young men.'

'U'ha,' replied Haydon, returning to his drink, realising the man was as queer as a nine bob note.

'Look,' he pressed, 'why don't you two come over and join us. We can have a few drinks here and then go back to my flat and listen to records. I've a very wide selection and you can choose whichever you wish.'

'Ya ya, maybe, we'll see,' replied Haydon vaguely.

'Well, if you decide, our table's in the corner there. That's Roger in the pale yellow jacket, and I'm Nigel,' he finished, laying a hand on Phil's wrist before picking up two glasses and leaving.

Haydon, glad to be rid of the creep, raised his pint to his lips, then, swallowing, suddenly had a mischievious idea.

'Ah 'No Way',' he began putting his plan to Ottoway. 'Ya see that bloke I was talking to?'

'Yah.'

'Well, him and his mate are a couple of ass bandits and we've just been given an invite up to their flat.'

'So?'

'So we go along with them. When we get up there we do them over and take their cash.'

'Yah okay, but what happens when they call the cops?' pointed out Ottoway.

'No problem,' assured Haydon, 'queers don't call the Old Bill, they don't want the agro. Now come on, tonight ain't gonna be such a financial disaster after all.'

For an hour or so the four men remained in the pub drinking and talking. Well, Nigel and Roger talked, Haydon and Ottoway just gave bland replies.

At last, after downing drinks he had collected from the bar, Nigel stood up to suggest they all leave. Outside the two paratroopers climbed into the back of Roger's car, whereupon, suddenly feeling drowsy, both fell asleep. They awoke the following morning propped against each other on a Thames Embankment bench. Standing up to adjust their crumpled, untidy clothes they found their wallets, socks and underpants missing.

'Let's get a move on or we'll be done for missing first parade,' warned Haydon, bitterly setting off in a westerly direction.

Ottoway, taking a few steps, stopped with a groan.

'What's up with you?' asked his mate.

'My ass,' informed 'No Way', 'it stings like hell.'

They walked for an hour through the empty, early morning London streets until they were able to hitch a ride back to Aldershot down the A3 via Guildford.

A week later their wallets, accompanied by a note, arrived through the post.

"Dear Stanley and Philip,

What a super evening we four had the other night.
So sorry you were not awake to enjoy it all. Perhaps we could get together another time soon.

Love, Nigel and Roger."

*   *   *

Ringing Dave Urwin's doorbell, Jim Sinclair waited in the evening chill for an answer. However, when the door was opened it was by someone he hadn't expected.

'Hello Penny, I just called to see Dave and Mary.'

'Oh, hello Jim. I'm sorry, they're not in. Major Bates has taken his officers and senior N.C.O.s and their wives out to dinner,' explained Penny Roberts.

'Oh that's right, he's leaving soon, isn't he?' said Sinclair. 'It's okay, I only dropped around for a chat and a cup of coffee anyway.'

'Well, come in, coffee's no problem to make,' she invited.

'Look, if you're on your own I don't want to disturb you,' hesitated the Scotsman.

'No, no, come in.'

Accepting, Jim followed her through the door and into the kitchen.

'Where are the kids?' he asked.

'Up in bed,' replied Penny, plugging an electric kettle into a wall socket.

'And little Steven, is he over with you?'

'Yes, I brought him across last week.' Then after another pause, looking at the window curtains, she continued, 'I couldn't stay in the house alone; it was too depressing. Perhaps in a month or so I'll be able to face it but at the . . .'

'Penny, about Neil,' interrupted Sinclair, 'I'm sorry.'

'Thanks, Jim,' she acknowledged, without looking up, preparing two cups with instant coffee.

'I cried Jim,' she confessed, 'I cried for days. I didn't know it was possible to cry so much.'

Sinclair said nothing, just watched in sympathy, unable to think of anything helpful to say.

'It's the pain of knowing he's no longer there,' she confessed.

As the kettle boiled she unplugged it to pour the water into the cups.

'The two men from Niel's crew who weren't murdered came around one evening but they didn't stay long. Not their fault, we just couldn't think of what to say to each other. They're good men, both married, children . . .'

Penny, who had been about to add milk from a small jug, paused to grip the edge of the kitchen sideboard, tears appearing on her cheeks.

Stepping forward, Sinclair took her in his arms, cradling her head on his shoulder.

'Go on love, don't hold it in,' he comforted.

'I'm sorry Jim, I'm sorry,' she sobbed.

Sinclair, holding her against him with one arm, raised his other to stroke her soft, fragrant hair.

'Penny, they didn't kill Neil just to take his life. They did it to spread as much misery and suffering as possible. They're using gun barrel diplomacy to destroy everyone's morals and take over the province after all the good people have had enough and jacked. I know it's no consolation, but Niel wasn't just gunned down on a whim. It was done for a reason.'

Penny, who had never looked at her husband's death in that way before, pulled her head back to look into Jim's eyes, the tears no longer running.

'I'm sorry for being such a cry baby, Jim,' she apologised, wiping her eys with the heels of her hands. 'Here, you take the coffee into the living room; I have to nip upstairs to look in on the children.'

Re-appearing a few minutes later, her eyes no longer red and watery, she asked before sitting down, 'would you like something to eat?'

'No,' declined the Scotsman, holding up a hand, 'I've just arrived back from a course and had a couple of sandwiches whilst waiting for my train connection at Reading. That's why I dropped in here; to ask Dave what the gen is with Battalion before I report back.'

'Fine, I just thought you might be hungry,' she replied, sitting down opposite to reach for her cup and take a sip.

'You know, Jim,' she began, sitting back with a twinkle in her eyes, 'I was in love with you once.'

'What?' exclaimed Sinclair, with a shocked smile.

'Uh ha,' she continued, 'it lasted for about three years.'

'That's pretty good going considering we didn't know each other,' grinned the Scotsman in disbelief.

'Oh, I knew you, you just didn't remember me. It was at Dave's wedding, when you were the best man,' she explained. 'You danced with me just once and I fell in love with you; I was eighteen.'

'Oh, I remember now,' he lied, 'you were wearing a light blue dress.'

'Stop bluffing, Sinclair, you didn't take a blind bit of notice of me,' she accused smilingly, 'the dress was cream.'

Sinclair, saying nothing, cast his eyes to the ceiling in surrender.

'Everytime Dave wrote home after that I would hunt through his letter to see if he had anything to say about you. It was a terrible crush.'

'Good thing you got over it. I would have made a bad catch,' he warned.

Without realising the time, their conversaton took them well past midnight. Just as Jim was about to go Dave and Mary Urwin arrived back.

'Well, if it isn't Sergeant Sinclair,' joked his friend, as he entered the living room.

'What's that?' questioned the Scot.

'Haven't you been in camp yet?' Dave asked.

'No, I dropped in to see you first.'

'Well, it just came out on Part Two Orders today, you've been promoted. Congratulations,' informed his Irish friend.

'Oh good, I can use the money,' half jested Sinclair.

'Yes, that's the good news; now for the bad,' continued Urwin. "Nuts' Norris has left orders with the Guard Commander and B.O.S. that the moment you arrive back you're to move all your kit from your bunk into the Sergeant's Mess.'

'What? You're kidding!' burst out Sinclair.

'You know Nuts, Jim,' chuckled Urwin, 'he gives out ridiculous orders like that and expects them to be obeyed.'

'Bloody hell, Dave,' cursed Sinclair, 'well that's it, I'm not going back into camp now. Can I crash out here for the night?'

'It's all yours, Sarg,' joked his friend, extending one hand towards the couch.

In the early hours of the morning, unable to sleep, Jim reached for and lit a cigarette. He would be thirty in a few months time, unmarried and with no consideration of changing his bachelorhood. During his early years in the Army he had fallen in love and been badly hurt by it, and since then had guarded against any involvement that led beyond sex. But now he found his sleep being robbed from him by the haunting vision of Penny Roberts and the perfumed aroma of her hair that would not leave his nostrils.

*   *   *

'Sir, another detail has just come in. The R.S.M. wants an N.C.O. and six men for a fatigue party to area clean Montgomery Square.' Sam Kyle, having just returned to his office from a tour of inspection of his Company Billet block, took the memo that Lance Corporal Pearson held out to him.

'When did this arrive?' he asked, placing his pace stick on his desk top.

'Few minutes ago, sir,' grinned his clerk.

'Well, for fuck's sake,' protested the C.S.M., 'I know we're Duty Company but we're not a bottomless pit of manpower. Corporal Jones!'

From the adjoining office, 'Jonesy' Jones, the week's Company Orderly Sergeant appeared, to stand in the doorway.

'Have we been able to comply with that last detail for the Q.M.?'

'Not really,' replied the C.O.S., 'they asked for four men, but we could only send Whitely and Higson, and both of them are supposed to be on light duties.'

'So there's no one we can provide the R.S.M. with,' concluded Kyle.

'Not a prayer, Sir,' confirmed Jones. 'If it gets much worse I'll have to prop a figure eleven target up in my chair so I can give a hand washing the dixies in the cookhouse.'

'Okay, Corporal Jones, I get the message. I'll phone and tell him he'll have to find his men somewhere else,' concluded Charlie Company's Sergeant Major.

Picking up the phone he moved around the desk to sit down. After dialling there was a short pause before he began to speak.

'Sergeant Major Kyle, Sir. It's the fatigue party for Montgomery Square; I'm afraid we haven't the men, Sir. Everyone in the Company is totally committed, perhaps you could . . .'

Kyle was interrupted in mid-sentence by the R.S.M. with what sounded to the two corporals like demented raving.

'Sir . . . Sir . . .' cut in Sam, 'as I've just said, I don't have the men.'

The line erupted with more growling and shouting.

'Sir,' Kyle tried to explain, 'you're asking the impossible. I'll come across now and show you our parade state, then you'll see . . .'

More loud shouting exploded from the receiver, followed by a distinct click as the man at the other end terminated the conversation.

'Bastard,' swore Sam through his teeth, jumping up, 'that's it, I've had a gut full of that cunt.'

Rushing around his desk he pushed the two corporals aside to pass into the Company Office.

'Sir, if you're going out you'll need your pace stick,' called Pearson, reminding him of the R.S.M.'s orders that while in barracks all C.S.M.s had to carry one.

'Screw the pace stick,' hollared Kyle, disappearing into the hall.

Once down the stairs it was but a short walk along the front of the Battalion Square to the H.Q. building. Jumping onto the landing outside the Regimental Sergeant Major's office, he stopped one of the Regimental Policemen from entering by taking his arm and pulling him back from the door.

'Hold up, corporal Russell, I'm going in first, but don't go away, he may need you in a minute.'

Stepping through the door he slammed it behind him. The R.S.M., looking up from his desk with some shock, was not given the chance to speak first.

'You get off my fucking back!' demanded Kyle, a finger pointed straight at Norris's face. 'Ever since my company took over as duty company you've been riding me into the deck.'

'Sergeant Major,' roared the R.S.M., jumping to his feet.

'Never mind Sergeant Major,' warned Sam angrily, 'rank doesn't come into this. It's between you and me. Unless you can give me an assurance that from now on you will not bombard my office with any more childish requests that you know can't be dealt with, then by Christ, career or no career, I'm going to punch your fucking head.'

This was a brave threat and Kyle knew it. For Norris, six inches taller and thirty pounds heavier, had in his younger days, boxed for the Army.

'Okay, Sam. That's a fair one. No more hassle,' conceded the R.S.M. without a trace of an expression. 'Is there anything else?'

Surprised and dumbfounded, 'no' was all C Company's Sergeant Major could say.

'Fine then. You may go,' dismissed Norris as he resumed his seat.

On reaching the door Sam was halted by a question from his senior warrant officer, 'what's your drink?'

'Bitter, Sir,' replied Kyle, still somewhat befuddled.

'Next time you're in the Mess tell the barman you're having a pint on me,' offered Norris, not looking up from his desk.

It was not until some days later that Sam was enlightened by the Battalion Drill Sergeant. It seemed that Norris, at the beginning of each week, would pick a name off the senior N.C.O.s list, and then begin making his life hell, just to see how he reacted.

                    *   *   *

Norris did not confine his hair-brained persecution of the members of his mess to that of pre-planned operations. There were times when he sprang his idiotic idiosyncrancies on the spur of the moment. One of these occurred at breakfast shortly after Jim Sinclair had settled into the Sergeants' Mess.

The R.S.M., a divorced man, lived-in, occupying one of the bunks that was normally provided for single members. It was said that his ex-wife, a woman of immense patience and charm, had left him after five years, unable to cope any longer with his daily inspections of her housework and dish-washing.

Entering the dining room, Jim paid his respects to the R.S.M. before greeting the other five men sitting at the long polished dining table.

'Good morning Sir, morning all.'

Norris responded to this while the others just mumbled. Taking a seat to pour himself a cup of tea, he joined the rest in their silent musing. There was a reason for this, for since the R.S.M. had become one of them no one spoke at meal times; whenever it was noted by Norris that someone was doing something or saying something he thought was not right, he would punish the individual by awarding him extra duties.

Hence meals were now taken in sullen silence.

As Sinclair finished his cup of tea Norris looked at his watch and decided it was time for everyone to have breakfast; he signalled the mess waiter to enter the room to begin taking orders. However, before he could start 'Nuts' banged his fist on the table.

'Gentlemen,' he shouted, 'I'm sick and tired of this lack of joyfulness at meal times. From now on, so as to brighten our hearts, all speaking at the table will be done in song.'

Everyone stared at Norris, the silence of before seeming like a construction site compared to what descended now.

'How do you mean, Sir?' ventured a colour sergeant.

'We sing, of course, we sing. Here, I'll go first,' he offered, waving the waiter to him.

'Good morning Private Wiggs,' he sang.

'Morning Sir,' replied the waiter, smiling.

'No, no,' sang back Norris, 'you too must sing Wiggs, now let me have the menu.' Wiggs's smile disappeared.

'Oh yes, oh yes,' began the R.S.M. having studied the menu, then breaking into a Verdi tune, 'bring me orange juice and then a three minute boiled egg a . . n . . d toa . . s . . t.'

On being handed back the menu Wiggs looked around to see who wished to order next.

Most heads, including Sinclair's, went down. The only one up was 'Tutty' McBride, the Anti-Tank Platoon Sergeant. Tight lipped he beckoned the waiter to him.

'Any particular tune, Sir?' he sang, taking the menu.

As the R.S.M. shook his head, McBride, spreading his arm wide, broke into a culinary rendition of 'The Road to the Isles.'

'I want bacon . . . and tomatoes . . . and poached egg on toast with butter and marmalade to sweeten on the side. But you must hurry for I'm late, and the parade, it will not wait and I canna' afford to stay and harmonize.'

The Mess members cut up with laughter at this, and then entered into the spirit of the thing with valid attempts. This innovation to mess etiquette did not catch on though, with Norris having to pack it in after a few days when he found himself taking meals alone.

*   *   *

Someone else who found himself caught in mess peculiarities was Father Buchanan. On accepting an invitation to conduct a midnight mass at a London church, he was obliged to stay overnight, the Battalion chief clerk booking him into the Officials' Mess of one of Britain's most senior regiments.

Arriving for breakfast the following morning he sat down beside the only other person eating, a lieutenant in uniform wearing his peaked cap.

'Good morning,' said the padre, ignoring the dress.

The other officer looked up but continued to eat his cornflakes.

'It's nice to see we have such a bright and sunny morning,' continued Buchanan, attempting to engage in polite conversation.

This time the man did not even bother to look up.

'It should make a pleasant drive back to Aldershot,' tried the padre again. Nothing.

Giving up Buchanan poured himself a cup of coffee.

Looking about he spied the sugar bowl on the far side of his neighbour. 'Could you pass the sugar, please?'

No response.

'Excuse me, could you pass the sugar?'

As if unheard; the cornflakes spoon moved up to the other officer's mouth.

'Hey moosh, sugar,' ordered the padre, pushing the lieutenant in the shoulder, taking a leaf from his barrack room days with the Royal Scots.

This act finally prompted the young officer to break his silence, explaining, 'it is common knowledge, that when an officer of this regiment comes to the dining table in headdress it signifies that he does not wish to be spoken to,' and drew back to fix Buchanan with a facetious, down-the-nose stare.

The good Father, not believing what he had just heard, answered by leaning back in his chair, swinging his feet up and planting his heels in the lieutenant's breakfast bowl.

'Yes,' he replied, 'and when a Roman Catholic padre of the Parachute Brigade sticks his boots in your cornflakes, it means 'please pass the sugar'!'

*   *   *

On the sounding of the final trumpet call, given by an unseen Battalion Bugler, the R.S.M. and the evening's guests, filed from the reception area into the temporary dining room. Following in silence, the rest of the mess members and their ladies found and stood behind chairs in front of which, on the table, were their name cards. This was a formal mess dinner to be conducted in the traditional manner adopted by all Regimental Messes of the British Army.

Because the Sergeants' Mess was too small to take the seating, a room in the education centre was being used. For atmosphere, coloured parachute canopies were draped around the walls, allowing the flickering candle light to play and hide amongst their folds.

To accommodate over a hundred people the dining tables were set out in a large E, with the senior warrant officers and the guests occupying the back of the E, whilst everyone else was stationed according to seniority down the arms. The guests of the evening were the reason for the dinner. The non-commissioned officers of the 5th Battalion The Parachute Regiment, changing commanding officers, were dining the previous one and his wife out.

Dressed formally, the women were in long gowns and the men, being infantry, were in short red mess dress jackets with miniature medals and dark blue trousers. Everyone bowed their heads as R.S.M. Norris said a short grace. Sitting down they began the meal with wine and hors d'oeuvres, the first of six courses, which were to take over two hours. Towards the conclusion of the meal, prior to the coffee being served, the waiters cleared everything from the table top except candelabras and silver mountings. This was in preparation for the Loyal Toasts.

At the extreme lower end of the right hand arm of the E. Sam Kyle sat facing towards the top table. As P.M.C. he was there to guide 'Mr. Vice' through his ordeal.

On his right at the very end of the table's arm sat his wife, Beth, with Mary and Dave Urwin next to her. On his left was Jim Sinclair who as the newest member of the mess, had been appointed Mr. Vice for the evening.

Having to wear his brown khaki number two dress because his mess dress was not yet ready from the tailor, he was being accompanied for the occasion by Penny Roberts. Wearing a gown she had borrowed from Beth Kyle, Jim had asked her to partner him for the dinner as a favour to her brother. Dave, wanting his sister to get out among people who were enjoying themselves, had put the proposal to his friend.

Once everyone's glasses had been filled from the decanters of port, passed by hand down the tables, the R.S.M. caught Sam Kyle's eye. The P.M.C. lifted a wooden gavel from its cradle, and twice banged it down sharply. As the room quietened he called formally. 'Pray be silent for Mr. Vice.'

Jim Sinclair, with a mild case of first night nerves, rose, glass in hand, to recite lines that had been going around in his head all evening.

'Honoured Guests, Ladies, Mess Members, will you please rise for the Loyal Toast.'

With everyone standing he uttered two more words, 'The Queen.'

As this was repeated throughout the room glasses were sipped, then everyone sat down again.

A few minutes later this scene was repeated, toasting The Regiment, but with the ladies remaining seated. The toasts completed, coffee and ashtrays for the smokers were brought out. Whereupon the R.S.M. arose to present the C.O. with a gift from the Mess and allow him to make his departing speech.

On completion of the formalities, the R.S.M., escorting his guests, led everyone the short distance through 5 Para barracks to their mess building, for the evening to be continued to the accompaniment of a hired dance band.

Shortly after midnight Penny excused herself, asking Jim to escort her back to the Urwin's quarter.

Steven had a habit of awakening about this time each night with fits of whimpering so, not wishing to inconvenience the babysitter, she preferred to leave the dance early. Saying goodnight to the R.S.M., Sinclair took Penny's arm to lead her into the hall.

'Enjoy the evening?' he asked, accepting the cup of coffee she made for him after he returned from walking the babysitter home.

'Oh yes,' replied Penny, sitting down in the sofa opposite, 'it was nice to dance again.'

'Sorry about the meal; I had no idea it was to be so straight laced,' apologised the Scot.

'Oh, no I found it so . . . traditional,' she replied, searching for the words, 'I loved it all.'

'Except my cameo act,' smiled the sergeant.

'Yes,' snapped the pretty young woman, also smiling.

'Spoiled the whole evening.'

They both laughed together for a moment before Penny enquired, 'Tell me Jim, was it your idea to ask me?'

'Of course,' he jokingly replied, 'didn't fancy sitting next to an empty chair all evening, had to fill it with somebody.'

'How would you like a punch in the ear Sinclair,' she warned as they both again laughed, each satisfied with the reply; Penny believing Jim had genuinely wanted to take her and the Scot relieved that he had side-stepped giving a direct answer. Jim had wanted to invite her himself but did not wish to give the impression he was making a play for a vulnerable widow or was responding through sympathy, which was frustrating for he did want to spend more time in the woman's company. Therefore he was more than pleased to accept Dave Urwin's request.

'How much longer are you planning to stay?' he asked, changing the subject.

'Another week or two' replied Penny, stretching back in the sofa. 'I've been here over a month now and Mary and Dave have been kind, but it's time I returned. I thought about what you said the other night when I broke down, about Neil and the reason you gave for him being killed. Well, you were probably right. They're trying to drive us out with terror tactics and the blazes if I'll let that happen now. Besides I owe it to Neil and Steven to stay.'

'Where will you be living?' asked Sinclair, having never seen the woman's eyes flash with anger before.

'We have . . .' she began before correcting herself, 'I have a house; Neil's insurance settled the mortgage so it's mine outright now. The street's quiet and the neighbours are very kind with none of the troubles we're getting in other parts of the City.'

'And money, will you be able to live alright?' pressed Jim.

'Should be,' she replied, reaching for her cup, 'there are still some savings but I'll have to get a job again. Before Stevie came I was working in a bank. Hopefully I can go back to that.'

'So you'll manage alright?' confirmed the Scotsman.

'Oh yes,' assured Penny.

'Good, good,' concluded Sinclair, satisfied. Then reaching back to clasp his hands behind his head joked, 'Davy and I will drop around in the New Year when the Battalion returns and pay a call.'

'Oh yes,' she replied, quite serious, 'please do.'

'Not a hope,' smiled Jim, 'if we turned up it would be with a dozen hairy paratroopers riding shotgun.'

'Oh, I see,' smiled back Penny. 'Well, perhaps you could phone instead?'

'Sure, sure,' agreed Sinclair, releasing his hands with a suppressed yawn.

'Here Jim, I'm sorry' apologised Penny seeing this. 'I should have realised you would want to get back.'

'No, no, that's the last thing I want to do. It's pointless going back to the bunk until that band downstairs stops playing.'

'Well, another coffee then?' asked the woman.

'No, just talking to you is fine,' he declined. Then on the spur of the moment made a proposal.

'Pen, I'm buying a car next week, it's second hand so I'll have to take it out for a test spin. If you're still here and Dave and Mary are willing how would you like to come along.'

'Yes,' she accepted, 'that sounds nice.'

'We can head down to the South Coast, and have lunch in a pub on the way.'

Jim, found himself regretting this as soon as he said it for, unable to stop himself, he had broken his pledge not to instigate involvement with Penny Roberts. However, Sinclair could be forgiven of this for the woman opposite was not only enchantingly attractive but herself unaware, was totally bewitching the Scotsman with her natural expressions and near presence.

She had confessed to having once been secretly in love with him but now it was he who was feeling the hollow pangs of longing.

*   *   *

'We'll look in here. If it's not all that brilliant we can try further on,' proposed Jim, pointing ahead of them through the windscreen at a country pub just off the road.

'Yes fine, Jim,' agreed Penny sitting beside him.

These were the first words Sinclair had spoken for several miles for he was still recovering from a mild huff. When he arrived at the Urwin's with his new second-hand car earlier that morning it was to be told that only Penny was free

157

to accept his invitation of a Sunday drive. The excuse given by Mary was that Dave had been called into Camp to go through the Company's weapons registered numbers, as there had been a misplacement of one of the Guards' rifles. Jim said nothing but he did not buy it for one minute, believing his best friend and his wife had hatched a story which insured he and Penny spent the day alone together.

After ordering their meal the couple sat silently at a corner dining table. As Penny examined the contents and ornaments of the low ceilinged oak beamed, seventeenth century room, Jim stared out the window at a surprisingly warm sunny mid-November day.

'Sorry, Jim,'

'Eh?' replied Sinclair, pulling his eyes from the window.

'About being lumbered with me,' explained the lovely, pale brown haired woman with melting blue eyes. 'You're disappointed about having no one to show your car off to except me.'

'Rubbish!' exclaimed the Scotsman in defence, 'I intended to make the drive anyway. I'm pleased to have the company.'

'Is that why you've been so quiet since we left Aldershot?' she smiled.

'Sorry Pen, it's the car, not used to it, been concentrating too hard,' he bluffed.

'Oh yes, never thought of that. I was worried that perhaps you had the idea that a scheme had been concocted for us to spend the day together,' she confessed.

'What you mean, Dave and Mary match making?' asked Sinclair straight faced.

Penny, briefly catching his eye, nodded her head.

'Good God! You've only been a widow for . . . what, ten, eleven weeks? The thought never entered my head,' he said, pretending to be shocked.

'Good,' she replied looking up to smile, then with it fading she continued, 'You know Mary and Dave have been terrific towards Steven and me. Ever since we arrived just by doing the natural things and not overwhelming me with pity, they have allowed me to come to terms with Neil being gone. But because of this I've been wanting to get out more. I'm not bored Jim, it's just that I want the opportunity to breathe a little deeper and look at things I've never seen before. That's why I jumped at your invitation for the drive; hope I'm not taking advantage of you.'

Sinclair listened to this confession and replied in a false cheery manner, 'Not a bit. You want to see new things, well after lunch we'll head down the road and indulge ourselves in a little historical culture.'

Two hours later Jim turned the engine off in the small visitors' car park below Arundel Castle. On reaching the entrance they found the castle closed for the winter months.

'Damn,' swore the Scot, pushing both hands into the pockets of the quilted anorak he wore.

'Never mind,' cheered Penny, shivering slightly from the sun's rays no longer reaching them at a direct angle, as she looped both her hands into one of Jim's arms. 'Let's take a walk around the grounds. Then we can find a pub in the town and have a drink.'

'Okay,' he agreed, 'but it will have to be a cup of tea, the pubs just shut for the afternoon.'

'Alright,' she conceded gripping his arm more tightly, 'tea it will have to be.'

On the return journey Sinclair pulled into a hilltop layby on the outskirts of

Haslemere after a request from Penny to stop and watch the sunset. Stretching away before them was the late autumn multi-coloured greens, browns and golds of the woods and copses surrounding the local farms and estates. In half an hour these were lost as blankets of darkness spreading upwards from the shadowy fields began to shroud the colours. Away on the western horizon, thinly spaced clouds were first stained pink, then deep red, then finally orange as all colour faded below the distant hill line of this rural picturesque Surrey, Sussex and Hampshire border countryside.

With the sunset gone Jim hesitated in continuing, wishing to remain in the woman's company for as long as possible.

'Enjoy the day?' he asked.

'Wonderful,' replied Penny, turning to smile as she tucked both hands between her legs, stretching back into the seat.

'How about the same again next week, only this time we'll drag those two relatives of yours along with us,' suggested Sinclair in a pretend voice of authority.

Penny Roberts, her smile gone, looked at him shaking her head. 'Sorry, Jim I should have mentioned earlier that I'm going back to Belfast the day after tomorrow Steven and I are booked on the afternoon flight from Heathrow.'

'Oh,' was all the Scot could say, unaware he was showing disappointment.

'I couldn't stay here indefinitely,' explained Penny, 'I've got to go back and pick up the threads.'

'Of course,' agreed Sinclair solemnly. 'How are you getting up to the airport?'

'I've booked a taxi,' she replied.

'Good, I'm glad. It's the right step,' assured Sinclair, turning the ignition key to restart the car engine. Then as he pulled out onto the road he began to give blunt but sensible advice.

'Now look, when you arrive back at the house you will probably find it a bad time, for all the happy memories you and Neil had together will begin to flood back. Don't let it overcome you. The last thing you can afford to do is spend the rest of your years wallowing in sorrow and self pity. It's not in the mind or the heart, the pain begins here.' Jim took one hand off the steering wheel to jab a finger just above his stomach. 'So when you feel it coming on you've got to bite back and push it from your thoughts. The nights are the worst so I recommend you have a radio beside the bed that you can turn on to listen to music whenever you wish. What I'm trying to say, Pen, is for God's sake don't let this tragedy ruin your life.' Sinclair was unaware that he had been speaking through clenched teeth.

'Why did you never marry, Jim?' asked his companion softly, making no reference to his outspoken counsel.

'What?' answered Sinclair awkwardly.

'You must have met some girl you liked,' she persisted.

'Paratroopers only marry nice girls. I don't normally get latched onto that type,' he snorted in crude jest.

'Oh' uttered Penny, turning to stare at the headlight-lit road, taking his reply as a warning to mind her own business.

Noticing his foolish response to her question had hurt her, Jim screwed his hands on the steering wheel several times before again answering.

'Got burned once, Pen. Fell in love pretty bad, thought she was too, didn't turn out that way though. I was young, took it harder than I should have. Ever since . . . I've been . . . oh . . . careful.'

'Did it happen before or after Dave and Mary's wedding?' asked Penny.

'Before, why?' queried Sinclair.

'So that's the reason you took no notice of me when we danced together,' she replied with a smile.

Jim, releasing air through his nose, smiled back.

At the Salamanca Quarter he refused her offer of a coffee, pleading instead for a need to return to camp. He could see this disappointed her but would not consent, for his goodbye to her was to be taken in solitude. At the mess he remained in his car for over an hour, one hand resting on the edge of the seat she had been using, whilst breathing in her scented fragrance that lingered long after she had gone.

*   *   *

Filling the boxing stadium building, which bordered on the Farnborough Road, the Battalion fell silent, sitting to attention on the adjutant's command of, 'Battalion, sit up.'

With a nod towards his adjutant the new C.O. of the 5th Battalion climbed up onto the corner stage to give an introductory opening address. This tall, lean Lieutenant Colonel was new in rank only, for as a platoon and company commander he had served many of his earlier years with 5 Para. Jack Chuter, striding to the forward edge of the stage, stood before a rostrum to reverse the adjutant's command.

'Everyone sit easy.'

Facing him was ninety-nine percent of his Battalion for this was a Scale 'A' Parade. Those missing were either in the guard room or manning telephones. The men sitting quietly were in various forms of dress depending on what they were doing or about to do that morning. Some in pullover order, others in smocks and denims holding weapons between their legs. Others in civilian dress had been acting the part of rioters during local training around the barracks.

The reason for the parade was a presentation by a newly formed team. Their job was to inform all units about to begin a tour in Northern Ireland of the latest happenings and bring them up to date on recently introduced procedures. This team consisted of two officers, three N.C.O.s and a constable from the Royal Ulster Constabulary.

Once Lieutenant Colonel Chuter had made the introductions and explained briefly the format of the presentation, he handed over to the team's commander, a Major from the Sherwood Foresters. He spent several minutes giving a broad up-date on all terrorist activities throughout the province. Then he stepped down for a warrant officer of the Intelligence Corps to give a detailed brief on I.R.A. personnel and activity within the area they were to be assigned to.

This was followed by another officer explaining how arrest procedures were to be carried out, and introducing them to something new, the yellow card. On this yellow card were printed a dozen or so paragraphs clarifying when a soldier could open fire. Basically it boiled down to, if a weapon could be seen a soldier could open fire at the holder. Over the next few years this yellow card was to be constantly added to, tying the security forces' hands further and further behind their backs.

The last man to speak was the R.U.C. constable. As he mounted the stage the Paras began to grin and murmur amongst themselves. Before their last tour a member of the R.U.C. had been sent across to give a solo lecture on events in Belfast. He, with typical Ulster humour, had creased the Battalion into fits of laughter with his jokes and funny explanations of all events and situations he related.

This time, however, there was to be no laughter. On approaching the rostrum the policeman in his mid-thirties removed his dark green peaked cap to show neatly trimmed black hair. Placing this on the rostrum, he introduced himself and then in a low key, unemotional voice began to explain their role, the dangers, and how the members of the Royal Ulster Constabulary were facing up to this. He spoke of how limited their powers were, and that because of this many areas of the cities were barred to them. He quoted the number of men who had been murdered and injured by the I.R.A. and told how demoralised the force had become because of this. He then confessed that through worry alcoholism was on the increase and that wives, constantly concerned for the safety of their husbands, were turning more and more towards the excessive use of tranquilisers. He concluded by firmly stating that although their morale was at a low ebb, they, with the aid of the Army were determined to win through. On replacing his hat to leave the stage, the room, which during the entire talk had remained so silent that the light breezes pressing against the window panes could be faintly heard, erupted. To a man the Battalion rose to their feet and cheered and cheered and cheered.

CHAPTER 11

I claim not to have controlled events, but
confess plainly that events have controlled me.

Abraham Lincoln

Staring into a cold, wet, windswept January morning Sergeant Bob MacIntyre watched as once again Belfast came into view through the hazy visibility. 5 Para's journey had begun the morning before by train from Aldershot station. On arrival at Liverpool they found the ferry dock area congested with a Battalion of the Guards disembarking from the ship that they were to board. This was not surprising for since internment the need to provide more troops had increased, causing greater density in troop movements to and from the province.

On docking MacIntyre, now platoon sergeant of 7 Platoon, studied the only visible feature of their new area of operations, namely four large tower blocks less than a mile to the northeast. An hour later C Company's convoy of four ton lorries skirted these and entered the location that was to be their base for the next four months.

Originally Stirling Grove had been a small park behind a community sports hall, but because of the spread of terrorist activity it had been taken over by the Army. Around its perimeter enclosing both the grounds and the sports building, was a high corrugated tin and barbed wire fence. At three key points along this, sandbagged observation towers had been placed. There were two entrances, one leading out to the north which was rarely used because it faced another Battalion's area and the main one exiting south. Recently built Twynem huts provided the base with billets, a cookhouse, dining hall, briefing rooms, a company operations building and a number of accommodation huts for the odds and sods units also stationed within the grounds.

The unruly parish 5 Para had been given to administer was miniature in comparison to their last. From west to east it measured just half a mile whilst the distance north to south was a little over the mile.

Charlie company's district was called the Gate House and lay in the centre of 5 Para's area. To the east B Company took over a locality that, although it was Catholic, acted more as a buffer between the Gate House and Protestant communities further east. To C Company's west was a small box of streets now looked after by A Company. At the heart of this box was A Company's and Battalion H.Q.'s base, the Chiswell Street Police Station. West of this, across

162

the main North Reynolds Road, Support Company had taken over a complex of maze-like concrete flats. These were pro-IRA and a notorious gunman's paradise. Charlie's patch, the Gate House, was also a hard Republican zone and riddled with I.R.A. members and their supporters.

Leaving the location by the South gate, all patrols travelled along a short lane to the junction of Piper Street, that ran straight through their area. Opposite this was the Gate House proper, three hundred yards across and four hundred deep. On the right of this was a broad, four-storey, U-shaped block of flats, whilst on the left were two streets of pre-war, terraced brick houses.

The southern boundary, running parallel to Piper Street, Winter Street was flanked on its north side by blocks of grey unattractive concrete flat-roofed houses. These also ran up Lock Street, which connected in the east with Piper Street and Winter Street, to spread behind the Piper Street terraced houses. In the centre of all this were the four tower blocks that MacIntyre had studied from the ferry deck earlier that morning. Each was eighteen storeys high and named after a species of tree.

South of Winter street lay an expanse of waste ground covering several streets. These had been Catholic homes but were burnt out in the summer riots of '69 by Protestant mobs. Now torn down and the rubble removed, there was nothing but empty ground, criss-crossed by meaningless streets. The only buildings still standing on this featureless landscape were two rows of Protestant-occupied terraced houses which lined the last main street in the Gate House, the Coastway. Across from here C Company's responsibilities ended at the restricted and privately guarded dock area.

The handover, from a Battalion of the Queen's Brigade, was a relatively smooth affair, for both units had been through it all before. Whilst 7 Platoon launched themselves out on foot and vehicle patrols, 8 took over the guard duties and 9 became the standby platoon.

Dave Urwin, not due to take his turn as O.P.s Officer until that evening, toured the observation posts and gate sentries, checking his men's duties and responsibilities. During lunch Jim Sinclair, who had been on the advance party, mentioned that he was taking a landrover patrol out around the Gate House to orientate his recent D Company arrivals. Hearing this, Dave asked his mate if he could come along.

An hour later, with everyone in flak jackets, the two open landrovers, containing Dave Urwin and the D Company Patrol, left through the South Gate. At the head of the lane where it met Piper Street a house on the right-hand side, number 97, had been taken over as an observation post, and was manned twenty-four hours at a time by a section from the standby platoon. Turning left there, they followed Piper to Lock, then down this to make another right turn along Winter Street. Not far up this Jim directed his driver to make across the waste ground towards the Protestant houses on the Coastway. Throughout the journey Sinclair had been periodically twisting in the front seat to point out landmarks to Urwin and others in the back. Suddenly he did this again only to ask a question, 'Dave, did you hear a shot?'

It was not an unusual question for the sound of ballistic firing was constantly being duplicated by everyday city noise.

'Ya,' confirmed Urwin, in a pained voice, 'and he got me.'

Sinclair reared up to see the other sergeant pressing both hands onto the thigh of his left leg that was leaking blood through his denims.

'Christ!' he exclaimed, turning to shout at his driver. 'Danny, back to the location, move it. Get your boot down.'

As the two vehicles raced across Winter Street he snatched up the radio receiver to send a contact report back to Stirling Grove. As they halted in the parking compound the M.O. and Corporal 'Georgie' Seaton were there to take control. Captain Ravenscroft, removing the dressing Paddy Kieran had placed over the wound, made a quick inspection and then told Seaton to get Urwin onto a stretcher and into the Humber ambulance. He was to be taken post-haste to the Musgrove Military Hospital.

Sam Kyle arrived at Sinclair's side as the ambulance pulled away.

'He asked me to phone Mary,' said Jim in not too enthusiastic a voice.

'Come into the O.P.s room,' offered the Company Sergeant Major, 'you can do it from there.'

Picking up the receiver the Scotsman looked at Kyle and shrugged, 'What am I supposed to say?'

'Here, let me,' volunteered Sam taking the phone.

'Hello Mary, it's Sam, Sam Kyle,' he began on the phone being answered. 'Hey, that husband of yours, I always said he was a skiving git, but he certainly showed it today. The jammy swine has just gone and got himself wounded . . .'

He paused for a reaction at the other end.

'Yah, that's right, wounded,' Kyle faked laughter, then paused again.

'No, no, not him, he must have seen it coming. Got in the way to book himself a bed.'

Another pause.

'What, serious? Our Davey, hell no. He's no mug, got himself the proverbial Hollywood flesh wound. He'll be back in the Cambridge next week. Then you'll have him home with you convalescing for a month, getting you and the kids to pour cups of tea down his neck.'

Pause.

'No, no, honest Mary, he's got himself a nothing wound. He'll probably be phoning himself later today.'

Pause.

'Yah, yah, fine, right, thanks Mary that will be a great help to us this end.'

Pause.

'Okay, bye bye, don't worry now.'

'She's going to phone Dave's relatives for us,' mentioned Kyle after replacing the receiver. Then looking up at sinclair he continued, 'Jim, if I ever stop one don't try that stunt with Beth. She'll have your throat out with her bare teeth.'

Urwin's sniper was a local hazard; for several months he had been pot-shooting at the security forces but until now had never been lucky. He was known to be doing this from one of the tower flats but was difficult to pin point.

The previous summer's internment upheavals had taught the I.R.A. many lessons, the most prominent of which was to never engage the Army in shoot out battles. Because of this their attacks on the security forces were centred mainly on sniping, prearranged ambushing and bombing. The number of these incidents was on the increase due to the growth in recruitment, mostly from the very young and by the return of those who had escaped during internment day.

Because the information gained by the Army and police while interrogating I.R.A. suspects was proving helpful, the provisional wing had begun to adopt the cell system. In doing so they were successfully reducing knowledge of each

164

other's identity to a small closely knit group, unable to inform on anyone other than themselves.

Losing Sergeant Urwin, less than a few hours after stepping off the ferry was a set back for 8 Platoon but one quickly overcome. Corporal 'Jonesy' Jones was given his job, while the command of his section was handed to the platoon's trouble shooter, Chris Braithwaite. There had also been changes at the top; Major Bates had moved on to a staff posting in Hong Kong, which now placed the command of the company in the hands of Major 'Shush' Austen. The men, apprehensive of this, were still prepared to follow him anywhere but now keeping at a more respectable distance.

*   *   *

'Hey, come on you two cunts, I thought I told you to sweep this place out,' demanded Braithwaite of Durrant and Fraser.

'Bollocks,' protested Durrant, turning from his observation slit, 'those gungy fuckers from 9 Platoon left it in shit order. I don't see why we should have to clean it up.'

Braithwaite, whose section had just taken over the duties in 97, Piper Street, looked again round the small room which had been modified into an observation post. The room gave a view not only of Piper but also down the street opposite that led onto the Gate House.

'You're a pair of wankers,' he labelled them, taking hold of the broom leaning just inside the door and beginning to sweep.

Turning away, the two men resumed their chore of watching the civilian activity outside.

Forbes' sandbagged six inch high by two foot wide slit gave him a view east up Piper street, while Durrant's looked out into the Gate House and down Piper to the west.

Braithwaite, with a bit of a dog-on, nudged Forbes' boots with the broom head.

'Shift,' he ordered.

The younger soldier obeyed with a half pace to one side. At that moment the slit exploded as bullets struck the bags, casting up spurts of sand. Forbes, catching a cloud of this in his eyes, dropped into a corner holding his face. Braithwaite, spinning away from the observation slit, shouted a warning to Durrant for he had glimpsed the source of the firing.

'Jock, the bus. He's on the bus.'

The gunman was firing a Thompson sub-machine gun from a window of the top deck of a passing empty double decker bus.

'Open up! open up!' shouted Braithwaite again, rushing to Durrant's side.

'He's dropped down out of sight,' shouted back the Scotsman.

'Shoot the driver! Shoot the driver,' ordered Braithwaite loudly, watching as the bus turned side on to make its escape down a Gate House side street.

'I canna', I canna',' pleaded Durrant, 'he might be innocent.'

'Give us the rifle,' screamed the acting section commander snatching it into his shoulder. But it was too late; the bus had stopped out of sight with both the gunman and the driver running away, free to do something similar another day.

Two nights later, perhaps thinking that because no fire was returned the occupants were lackadaisical, a second attack was made on the post. The two sentries this time were Phil Haydon and 'No Way' Ottoway.

A recent addition supplied to the troops in Northern Ireland, to aid their surveillance in the dark hours, was the night image intensifier. This was a large, battery-operated telescopic night sight that gave the user the ability to see in the dark by amplifying available natural light.

Ottoway, with the device attached to his rifle, pushed the rim of his helmet back so as to get the eye-piece against his eye. Pointing this out into the blackness of the surrounding streets he began to traverse in an arc across his front. Because vision was best in total darkness, whenever artificial light was detected it would smudge and blind that particular part of the lens. At the moment this was minimal for it was the early hours of the morning with little road traffic about and most street lights either damaged or shot out. This made it easy for Ottoway to spot the teenage youth pressed against the wall moving towards him down the street opposite.

When no more than twenty-five yards away, thinking he was undetectable, dressed in the night's cloak of invisibility, he raised a pistol to fire at the building across the street. 'No Way', with a deafening crack, beat him to the punch.

The flash from his rifle muzzle burned an image on the lens, rendering it useless for the better part of a minute.

'What the fuck, Ottoway, you trying to get yourself jailed?' demanded Haydon, believing his mate had been playing with the trigger causing a negligent discharge.

'Who's doing the shooting?' asked their section commander urgently, bursting into the room with his rifle but without flak jacket and helmet.

'I did,' admitted Ottoway confidently, 'there was some bloke out there with a gun trying to shoot at me.'

'Where?' asked the corporal, 'show me.'

'Over on the corner; I watched him sneaking up Shaw Street.'

The corporal, looking through the night sight, waited the few extra seconds it took the blindness to clear from the lens, then declared angrily, 'well, he's not there now, are you trying to pull a fast one Ottoway?'

'Here, let me look,' said 'No Way' indignantly, taking back his rifle to hold the sight up to his eye.

'There,' he said smugly, passing the weapon back to his corporal, 'on the right of the pavement near the gutter, he's left his pistol behind.'

At first light a trail of blood was followed around the corner to one of the terraced houses. On entering the search party found in an upstairs bedroom a blood stained mattress. The body, never recovered or reported, was probably smuggled South for burial in the Republic; for the M.O., called to examine the mattress, stated confidently that anyone losing that amount of blood must be dead.

On the first Sunday morning during the handover of the location, Major Austen was taken by the outgoing O.C. to observe a legacy he would be inheriting. Climbing up into the Western perimeter sangar overlooking a side street of uniform brick houses, he was given a brief outline of its function. The sangar was built overhanging the corrugated fencing so as to have unrestricted vision up and down the street.

Below this, in order to counter anyone walking underneath leaving an unseen bomb, a large buttress was built forcing all foot traffic out into the street, or on to the opposite pavement where they could be watched.

Most of the immediate residents accepted this inconvenient structure of tin and light wood as just something else that they would have to tolerate. Most that is, except one.

Timothy Muldoon, who lived in a corner house two blocks down, was not exactly a village idiot but he was the nearest thing the street could boast of. Since the buttress was first constructed Muldoon looked upon it as his own personal house of cards.

The Queens Major looked at his watch.

'About now, Dyke?' he asked the sentry.

'I'm told he was a couple of minutes late last week, Sir.' he replied, 'but it shouldn't be long now, the spectators are beginning to gather.'

Austen, looking out of the observation slit, could see people coming out of houses to stand in the street.

'There he comes, Sir,' warned Dyke, pointing down the street with everyone smiling in anticipation, some giving cheers of greeting. The Major drew Austen's attention to a dark featured, heavy set man in his forties emerging from his corner house two streets away. Waving and returning cheers he climbed into an old, battered, cream-coloured, four-door Vauxhall Zephyr.

'Here we go, Simon,' grinned the Queens Major, folding his arms to rock back on his heels.

Austen, in the dark, as his opposite number wished to keep the event a surprise, watched as the car was started up. Leaping forward, the accelerator flat on the floor, the Vauxhall began to race up the street. With the spectators roaring their approval like a home football crowd, the car at full pelt mounted the pavement to crash through the buttress below the sangar.

Muldoon, waving to his audience, sped on to Piper Street where he collected his Sunday morning paper from a corner shop. This, explained the Major to Austen, began happening every Sunday morning since the buttress was first built. He considered it a source of light relief, giving his men something to laugh about and look forward to. Also it gave him a reason for digging the Battalion Pioneer Sergeant out of bed on a Sunday morning.

Austen, cocking his head to one side, could not see the humour in this at all. In fact he found it most unfunny.

*   *   *

'Johnny! Johnny!'

Sitting in the passenger seat of an open landrover on the West Reynolds Road, waiting for traffic lights to change, Paddy Kieran turned his head to see who was shouting. Leaving a bus queue, an attractive fair haired woman, wrapped in a fawn coloured winter coat to protect her against the morning's cold blustery wind, hurried towards him. Recognising who she was, Kieran jumped from the landrover, ordering the driver to pull into the kerb.

'Hi Penny.'

'Hello, Johnny,' smiled Penny Roberts, 'I hope I'm not holding you up but I saw you halted here and couldn't help giving a shout.'

'Not a bit of it,' replied Kieran. 'It's good to see you, how's the young'n?'

'Oh Steven, he's fine,' she answered, 'he's almost eighteen months now. A neighbour comes in every day to look after him while I'm away at work. That's where I'm off to now.'

'Have you heard from Davey?' asked Johnny, turning his head away as a blast of icy wind swept the street.

'Yes, he phoned the other night,' she replied, pulling the collar of her coat tight against her chin. 'Believes he should be back across in a few weeks.'

'I'll tell the others,' grinned the Irishman, 'we've all been waiting for him to get back.'

'How is everyone? Big Mick and Jim, are they all working hard?' asked Penny with an inquisitive smile.

'Fine,' replied Kieran with slight puzzlement, 'they're all fine. Hasn't Jim been in touch then?'

'Oh no, I suspect you're all far too busy,' she excused.

'Ya, it is pretty chaotic at the minute,' he agreed weakly.

'Here,' he warned, looking up at a bus pulling in, 'is that yours?'

'Oh yes,' she answered, beginning to ease away, 'I'll have to go, it's been good seeing you. Say hello to everyone for me.'

'Yah, sure,' began Kieran, raising a hand to wave goodbye, but then changed his mind.

'Hang on, Penny,' he called, moving after her. Hooking his rifle in the crook of his arm, he pulled a biro from his smock pocket to take her hand, scribbling numbers on the palm.

'If you want to get in touch with us anytime, that's the Int Section's phone number.'

'Thanks, Johnny,' smiled Penny warmly.

'Get a move on you'll miss your bus,' he shouted, parting from her to climb back into his landrover.

*   *   *

'Here, Brian, just tinned milk; if you had caught the bastard who was going to use that rifle we'd give you fresh with your coffee.'

Constable Savage, sitting at a desk, took the cup Bobby MacIntyre handed him with no response except a smile. There was no need, for everyone in the room knew that what he had done that afternoon was unrepayable. Brian Savage, who had spent the whole of the Internment period besieged in the Colinglen Police Station with C Company, was now attached to the Chiswell Station just down the road. At three o'clock an anonymous woman phoned to say a weapon had just been delivered to number 98, Piper Road.

Savage, going off duty when the call came in, realised what this could mean and that if so, not a moment could be wasted, and so ran out to his car.

Screeching to a halt, the two sentries across the road in 97 watched as he flew up the steps of the terraced house opposite. Entering was simple, for everyone in the Gate House was ordered by the I.R.A. to leave their doors open so escape off the streets from approaching Army patrols could easily be made. With the family who lived there conveniently out for the day, he hurried from room to room in a frantic search. Upstairs, leaning against a bedroom door, he found an American .30 calibre Remington sports rifle with telescopic sight.

Pushing the door open, he looked in to see at an angle through the window thirty yards away one of the observation slits across the street. Whoever had planned this intended attack had chosen his time well. Even with a camouflaged net draped in front of the post the early winter afternoon setting sun had the sentry's head and shoulders silhouetted as if by a spot light. This brave act on the constable's part undoubtedly saved the life of a member of the company.

During a pause in the conservation, sipping his coffee, Brian Savage stood up to examine the large boards on the wall of the Intelligence Section's Room that contained the local provisional I.R.A. orbit.

'I see you haven't got McConnell up here.'

'Who's that?' asked Jim Sinclair, sitting up in his chair.

'Coran McConnell; he doesn't live in the Gate House but you'll find him over here a fair bit now,' explained the constable.

'Is he Provo?' pressed Sinclair.

'Oh aye,' confirmed Savage, 'but he won't take an appointment, he's a killer and seems to want to stay a volunteer and do nothing else.'

'What's he wanted for?' asked MacIntyre.

'Nothing; we haven't got a thing on him but he's a killer alright,' answered Savage knowingly, 'one of our boys last year in the Short Strand, a soldier down the Falls before Christmas, and that Captain of yours last spring, bombed in the Summerhill Station.'

MacIntyre and Sinclair exchanged glances.

'And we've got nothing to lift him on?' asked Kieran in confirmation.

'Not a thing, but those three murders were his work, that is definite, and there are others we're not all that sure about.'

The constable, saying this, turned to sit down.

'Why does the fucker come into our area?' asked Berrill, squatting against a far wall.

'He's knocking off a woman in Spencer Flats,' replied Savage. 'He lives over where your Support Company are, with a wife and two kids but for the last two or three months he's been spending a couple of nights each week with Joe Hagan's missus'.

'Joe Hagan, who's he?' questioned MacIntyre.

'Another vermin booked for the Fiery Furness when he goes,' joked Savage bitterly, 'used to be very active, until the Green Jackets caught him in the city centre trying to park a car bomb. He's in the Crumlin Road jail now, doing fifteen years.'

'You couldn't get us a picture of this geezer McConnell, could you Brian?' asked Sinclair.

'See what I can do,' replied the constable draining his coffee cup.

After the policeman had left; Mick Pridmore, who had remained silent throughout the conversation, began to search the address files for a name that began with H for Hagan.

*   *   *

For no explained reason on the second Sunday morning after Charlie pompany took over, the side street containing the sangar buttress filled up with loitering soldiers, two full landrovers and a six man foot patrol also just happened to be nearby.

On time to collect his morning paper, Muldoon appeared saluting the gallery as he climbed into his trusty Vauxhall.

With encouragements of, 'Give 'em a good show,' and 'Go on Tim lad, batter it down,' he charged his car towards the sangar. Hunched on the steering wheel, laughing loudly, the speedometer reading fortythree miles an hour, he plowed into the corrugated tin.

On his way through the windscreen Muldoon may have seen the three foot wide, four foot high concrete bollard he struck but when one has a broken neck one does tend not to notice such things.

Some dirty rotter had found Muldoon's weekly event most unfunny.

*   *   *

Coming around the corner of a spare Twynhem building Haydon and Ottoway found Sergeant Margetts, the newly appointed Sergeant of 9 Platoon, waiting in the doorway for them.

'Where have you two cunts been?' greeted the short, barrel-bellied Senior N.C.O.

'The arms storeman was on sentry stag, Sarge; had to wait for him to get off before we could draw this thing,' answered Ottoway, slapping the heavy 84 millimetre anti-tank gun he balanced on his shoulder.

'Well, get in here now and let's get on with this,' ordered Margetts rudely.

The two privates were about to be taken on refresher drill on this weapon because of the new role they had been given. Corporal Jones, in his capacity as 8 Platoon's acting sergeant, had been told to supply two men for detached duty. Taking the opportunity to get shot of his two problem children, he volunteered Haydon and Ottoway. The duty turned out to be that of working with the A.T.O. Team. When these Ordnance Corps bomb disposal men were called to suspected devices that they thought would be best handled by detonation an 84 anti-tank gunner and loader would be brought in to fire a non-exploding missile into it. Major Austen, believing some time should be spent by the two men in sharpening their drills and handling of this weapon, had told Sergeant Margetts to see that this was done.

Margetts, who had just been posted in after two soft years attached to the Territorial Army in Oldham, enjoying the easy life of only working weekends, was now complying. He, about as interested in weapon training as he was in losing some of the flab around his waist, pulled a pamphlet from his pocket and began to read.

'Yah, well it says here carry out safety precautions.'

With no other assistance as to how it should be done he indicated to his two pupils they were to get on with it by wiggling a hand at them.

'Do that.'

Ottoway with a shrug stepped forward to kneel beside the weapon he had placed on the floor.

The gun, painted drab green and about four feet long, was the shape of a three inch pipe, with a fluted venturi breach at one end which directed the back blast away from the firers. Lifting the venturi end to balance the weapon on its front inverted T-shaped legs, he cocked the mechanism, placed the safety catch at safe and opened the breech. Looking in he closed it again, moved the safety catch to fire, squeezed the trigger, then stood up.

This drill was carried out so quickly Margetts barely had time to find the page of the first lesson.

'Right,' he snorted, 'we'll go on to the Load and Un-load.'

For the following ten minutes, with Ottoway acting as the Number One and Haydon as his loader, the sergeant, reading from the pamphlet, talked them through a number of dry runs, which both men knew off by heart anyway.

'Okay, it looks as if you two wankers have got that alright,' he complimented in a bored tone, 'now we'll try it with bullets. You go get those in the corner.'

Haydon crossed the room to collect two green plastic ammunition containers. Returning, he knelt beside Ottoway who, also kneeling, held the gun balanced on his right shoulder. Pulling one of the large pencil-nosed rounds from its tubular container, he placed it in the crook of his arm then, noticing its colour, asked with some curiosity, 'Hey Sarg, where'd you get these from?'

'Out of the A.T.O. Wagon,' replied Margetts, not looking up from a page of his pamphlet.

'Do you think we should be using them?' asked Phil innocently.

'Why not? Says practice on it, doesn't it?' replied the sergeant sarcastically.

Haydon nodded his head in agreement, trying not to smirk.

'Now on my command,' ordered Margetts, standing to one side of the two men.

'Load,' he cried.

'Load,' shouted Ottoway, cocking the weapon and placing the safety catch on safe.

'Load,' replied Haydon, opening the breech to slide the round in. Closing it he checked the back blast area to ensure the wall was far enough away that none of the rearward blast would deflect back at him.

'Loaded,' he shouted.

Ottoway repeating this, moved the safety catch to fire.

'Take aim at something Number One, then fire,' ordered Margetts, casually turning the page of his pamphlet.

Haydon, crouching as close to his mate as he could get, a finger in each ear, closed his eyes.

With the explosion of the fired weapon bursting several windows, two chairs in the back blast area were bowled to the far wall. Ottoway, jumping up, heaved the anti-tank gun from his shoulder to wobble fingers in his ears.

'Jesus fucking Christ,' he howled, shaking his head.

Sergeant Margett, the colour draining from his face, stood speechless, rooted to the spot in confused panic.

Haydon remained kneeling, his head bowed, choking back the laughter that was struggling to whelm out.

The missile, a non exploding projectile used on ranges to minimise the damage to metal targets, thus the reason for it being labelled practice, sailed through the far tin wall. Its journey continued into the next billet, passing a few feet above the bed of a man lying there holding up a newspaper, who suddenly found himself trying to read a four inch hole.

Luckily it ended its flight soon after by embedding itself in the radiator of a Bedford 4-ton lorry parked on the location's small M.T. compound.

The next day on Commanding Officer's orders Sergeant Margett tried to explain his ignorance involving the word practice, but Colonel Chuter bought none of it. He reduced Margett to the rank of corporal and posted him back to Aldershot.

*   *   *

'Don't fuck around in this traffic, Buckley, my son, get up on the pavement. We've got to get through this lot.'

Captain Ravenscroft, despite his urgency to get around the congeston of vehicles blocking the street ahead, raised his voice but did not shout. The reason the street was so blocked by queues of cars and the doctor's haste was one and the same. Ahead of their lumbering Humber ambulance a bomb had gone off in a city centre café, causing damage, death and many injuries.

Buckley's expert dodging and weaving through the solid, static traffic was finally brought to a halt at a mass blockage clogging a major street crossing.

Turning to give orders in two different directions at once, Ravenscroft kicked his door open.

'Right, Buckley, we'll go forward on foot, you come on when you can. Corporal Seaton, get the medical bergens out, you and I will run it from here.'

Two streets on, having pushed through crowds of emotional, late morning shoppers spilling onto the pavements, the two paratroopers rounded a corner to be met by a scene from Dante's Inferno. The café, which had a large ground floor room, was a popular one, always full to capacity throughout any Saturday. The front of this had been blown completely out with glass and debris scattered over most of the street. This though was incidental; the real tragedy was the people.

Directly outside the café, lying motionless on the pavement, were several bodies. Spreading outwards from these were probably two hundred people, either injured or trying to help. A woman, her face a bloody mass of glass splinters being held against a wall by two men was screaming over and over, 'I can't see! I can't see! I'm blind!'

Another woman, covered in blood, was sat nearby, rocking back and forth with a dead five year old girl in her arms.

Beside a parked car, its windscreen shattered, an elderly woman was attempting to stop the bleeding with a handkerchief on a teenage youth who had lost a hand. Further up the street an R.U.C. policeman and another man were pushing a walking casualty into an already crowded ambulance, and then frantically waved it on with shouts and hand signals. Everywhere dazed, bloodied people sat or stood awaiting attention, while others hysterically reeled about screaming.

Outside a furniture shop Ravenscroft and Seaton set up a hasty first aid post. There, applying bandages and dressings carried in their medical bergens, they tended what wounds they could.

'Got the pig here, Sir, who do you want me to take?'

The M.O., giving a morphine injection to a young girl with a badly slashed face and shoulder wounds, looked up to see 'Buster' Buckley standing over him with a stretcher.

'Take her,' indicated Ravenscroft, pointing at a woman whose legs were soaked in blood.

A sergeant from the Anglian Regiment, who moments before had arrived with a foot patrol, came to Ravenscroft for help.

'Sir, my lads are inside the café trying to help but we have people in there we don't know if we can move or not.'

'Alright, give me a few seconds,' consented the doctor, grabbing the hand of a youth to press it down hard on a dressing applied to his girlfriend's badly bleeding arm.

'Stay with her and keep that pressure on all the way to the hospital, understand,' he ordered, pulling his bergen onto one shoulder to follow the sergeant.

Pushing past one of the young soldiers vomiting at the demolished door entrance to step amongst the bomb rubble, Ravenscroft froze. During his medical career he had witnessed many gory scenes, from multiple gun shot wounds to road accidents, but the carnage within this room was the most horrific he had ever seen.

Everywhere among the wreckage were bodies and bits of bodies. A woman in her thirties, seemingly unhurt, sat propped against a brick pillar weeping.

Elsewhere injured victims were crying or in some cases screaming.

'Here, Sir, this is one,' beckoned the sergeant.

The captain, swallowing hard to control the bile that was freely flowing and threatening to erupt his own stomach, stepped further into the room.

At the sergeant's feet lay a man on his side breathing heavily while his eyes opened and closed uncontrollably.

'Possible fractured skull,' warned the M.O. after a quick examination. 'Don't let anyone move him until on ambulance arrives.'

Soon local hospital doctors and nurses began arriving by ambulance, car or on foot to give experienced aid to the dreadfully injured but innocent bomb victims.

The final casualty Ravenscroft had to deal with was a man who had been harpooned by a tubular metal table leg through the thigh and pinned to an oak-panelled counter. It took the M.O., another doctor, Georgie Seaton and three firemen over half an hour to free the man.

With the last of the injured on their way to hospital the captain and his corporal returned to the cafe to wash their blood stained hands in the partly damaged rear kitchen. In the dining room they found a lone R.U.C. Constable methodically searching through the wreckage, collecting in a plastic bucket fingers, hands and other bits and pieces of human flesh and bone.

*   *   *

Sheltering under a concrete staircase from the sharp March winds that blew down off the ridge of the Black Mountains, Mick Pridmore rocked forward to look once more down the balconied landing. Not seeing who he was waiting for he straightened to work his hands together dissipating the cold numbness that had penetrated his gloves. It was four o'clock in the morning and Mick, along with three others from D Company, had been waiting for over an hour. Checking his watch he knew time was running out for them. Unless their man showed in the next quarter of an hour they would have to pull out to return another morning, for shortly early risers would be on the move and they did not wish to be seen.

Spencer Flats, the U-shaped block on the northwestern edge of the Gate House was a typical 1960s concrete slab structure. Four storeys high, with landings running around the inside of the U, it housed over a hundred families in two and three bedroom flats.

Hearing the click of a door latch locking as the door was gently closed, Pridmore shot his head forward. Seeing a man turning to make his way towards him. On spotting Pridmore approaching the man hesitated in his stride then seeing that the figure before him was a soldier, continued walking.

'Morning there,' he greeted, with a twist of his closely-trimmed bearded head.

'Good morning, sir,' returned Mick, holding up a hand for him to halt. With the same hand he pointed to the wall. Without a word, for everyone in Belfast knew what this meant, the man turned to lean spreadeagled against the wall. With his Sterling sub-machine-gun secured by its sling draped around his neck, the corporal ran a quick, two-handed body search over him.

'Do you have identification on you, sir?' asked Pridmore, finishing and allowing the searched man to turn from the wall.

'Just a brew slip,' replied the Irishman, producing from an inside coat pocket his last week's dole money receipt. This was a common practice for it contained little information but his name, not allowing sectarian gangs who stopped individuals to guess whether they were Catholic or Protestant, which could lead to their death.

'Is this your name? McConnell? Coran McConnell?' asked the paratrooper, handing back the slip of paper.

'Aye, oh aye,' replied the dark haired man, a satisfied look on his face.

'And do you live here?' asked Mick casually.

'Oh no, I was just visiting some . . .'

McConnell's reply was choked off in mid-sentence by Pridmore's gloved left hand shooting forward to lock on his throat like a vice.

The Irishman, caught off guard, instinctively reached with both hands to pry away the grip that was threatening to crush his Adam's apple. Anticipating this, keeping his back straight, Pridmore bent at the knees to shoot his right hand under McConnell's crutch, then straightening again, pitched him head first over the balcony.

The Irishman, disorientated as to what was happening to him because of the speed, found his voice only long enough for a split second scream, before dying, his skull crushed and neck broken.

Pridmore with a snap of his fingers was joined from shadows further up the landing by 'Yorky' Rush. At the foot of the staircase they found Reg Berrill and Johnny Kieran silently inspecting the body. With another snap of his fingers, Mick, having fulfilled a promise to himself, led the way back to Stirling Grove.

His wife Lynda would never be told of it, but the murdering of her son had been avenged.

CHAPTER 12

Religion . . . is the opium of the people.

Karl Marx

As puzzling as it may sound the men of 5 Para did not mind at all being attacked by the I.R.A.. Their engagements were in most cases brief, inaccurate and gave the soldiers something to do. How they missed the fun riots of the earlier tours and the adrenalin inducing shoot outs of the Internment Battles. In short the troops were bored rigid.

During rare off duty periods entertainment was limited to reading, watching TV, playing cards or, if the chance occurred, catching the evening movie shown three times a week by one of the P.R.I. Staff.

Previously the location had allowed a twice weekly disco in the dining room which had local girls streaming in and out of the gate from eight in the evening until midnight. Major Austen arriving on the Advance Party took one look at these mad nights of revelry and with Colonel Chuter's full approval packed it in.

On the first night of the disco closure after Charlie Company had taken over, the South gate was besieged by hordes of females, some in tears, for the soldiers had not restricted their association with girls to that of dancing only. But the decision was a good one as not only was security involved, but there were also the social problems that evolved from all the free nooky being chucked about.

Returning from past tours the Parachute Regiment Battalions found the streets and pubs of Aldershot crawling with Irish girls who, without permission, had followed their boyfriends across to England. Most were told categorically to go away but the situation became quite delicate in some cases when a wife was involved.

One warrant officer, obviously built of pure brass, actually had the cheek to marry a girl whilst in Ireland, which considering the number of times 5 Para were to find themselves back in Ulster, could have proved a satisfactory arrangement for him. However, this ended in harsh words and much hair pulling when she surprised him with a visit to his Aldershot address only to find he was already married.

So, as in the past, time was filled in the only three ways that mattered, eating, sleeping and chasing the I.R.A. One little vice that did turn into an epidemic was the growing of moustaches. The men of Stirling Grove very early began to take on the appearance of a horde of Mexican bandits. The leader of this droopy lipped band was undoubtedly the O.C. himself. Austen sported the bushiest of the lot, earning himself the nickname of 'the Cisco Kid', which was good for morale as it gave the opportunity to poke fun. Around the location wherever 'Shush' went hidden Spanish-accented voices could be heard calling . . . 'Ah . . . Cees . . . coo.'

Humour was important, no matter what the source or at what level, for it kept everyone's mind in the right perspective. When working in the Gate House everything was best regarded as one great big joke.

One section based in Stirling Grove where laughter was at a premium was the A.T.O. Team. These Ordnance Corps Senior N.C.O.s had not joined the Army to become bomb disposal experts. Their trade originally was that of ammunition checkers who, because of the onslaught of the I.R.A. bomb blitz, were now having to step into a different role. One that was proving ever increasingly more technical and dangerous.

Bobby MacIntyre watched with sadness and alarm the decimation of this team in the third month of C Company's tour. Within the space of a week the six men who ate their meals from the same table in the location's miniature Sergeants' Mess were reduced to two.

Haydon and Ottoway had an even closer view of this. When not needed to use their anti-tank gun they would normally provide local cover. This is what they were doing on a Tuesday morning when a suspect car parked on a sales forecourt the night before was being investigated. Unable to get a clear shot at the vehicle they now watched from separate concealed points as one of the team, a staff sergeant, cautiously approached the car. Circling it for several minutes keeping at least one other car between him and the suspect vehicle, he tried to spy a clue which would tell him one way or another what he was dealing with. The telephone call to the police had stated that there was a bomb in the car but like so many this could be just another hoax.

Returning to his command vehicle he told the other members of his team that he intended to blow the boot open with a small charge. As he disappeared out of sight among the vehicles Haydon just caught a glimpse of him crouching to place his charge. In that instant the car exploded, riddling the staff sergeant's helmet, flak jacket, and body with splinters of metal.

On the Friday they answered a call to deal with another suspect car, parked this time outside one of Belfast's larger hotels. With the street cleared, Haydon and Ottoway were given a go with the 84mm. From the protection of a street corner they fired one round into one of the rear doors. Then changing position fired two more into the boot.

If there was a bomb in the car, one of these three shots would have set off the anti-handling device normally fitted. Believing this, one of the bomb disposal sergeants made his way at walking pace in a direct line for the car. Halting, he began to crab in a semi-circle around it at a radius of about forty yards. He continued to do this, reducing the distance each time until he was looking in the side window. Moments later the car exploded blowing a rag doll corpse back across the street.

On the Sunday three men broke into the house of a man who was due to drive a petrol tanker to Londonderry. Holding his wife and children hostage in the house, they gave him a large box to put in his cab and told him to drive the whole rig into the centre of Belfast. Knowing that if he did not comply his wife, and perhaps his children as well would be murdered, he set off.

He only got as far as an Army vehicle checkpoint on a main street with factories and businesses on either side. Leaping from the cab, he warned the sergeant in command of what had happened.

An hour later with the surrounding district cleared of people and cordoned off, the A.T.O. team began their first move towards the petrol tanker. A warrant officer this time made the long lonely walk. Should the package be a bomb it was vital to defuse it as soon as possible for should the petrol go up, the fires it caused would be devastating, as was soon shown when the warrant officer began to climb through the driver's door that had been left open when the driver fled.

The resulting ball of flame caused by the explosion of twenty pounds of gelignite resembled a scaled down Hiroshima, which resulted in half the fire fighting appliances in the city being called out to contain it.

Sifting through the wreckage that had just caused the death of three brave and dedicated men, the authorities discovered something they had been fearing for some months. The I.R.A. were now detonating their bombs with radio controlled devices.

The fourth member of the Bomb Disposal Team to go was not killed; he lost his nerve, if it could be called that. This man, another staff sergeant, was completing his third tour in Ulster and had already received two awards for bravery with a third in the pipe line. He had, as did the others, a wife and children, and felt his responsibility to them far out-weighed his risking his life day in, day out. Coming to this conclusion he requested an immediate posting out of Northern Ireland. A brave decision to make for he would have to live the rest of his life in the knowledge that by stepping aside, others taking his place may well have died.

Still, despite the casualties suffered, whenever the call 'Fetch Felix' went out, A.T.O.'s coded nickname, Felix always came.

*   *   *

'Are you sure, Peter?' asked Austen of Lieutenant Taplow, the Duty Watch Officer, in the Company O.P.s Room.

'Corporal Storey seams pretty definite, Sir,' replied Taplow. 'He had him on binos so he must have got a clear look.'

'Right, so which house had he gone into?' inquired the O.C., leaning forward to study a street map on the wall above the lieutenant's desk.

'28 Lock, just . . . there,' pointed out Taplow with his finger.

'Good! That's good. If we move fast we just might catch him,'declared Austen examining the map. 'Peter, tell the vehicle patrol to seal off each end of Lock Street between Piper and Whitefield. Then get the foot patrol into the alley way at the back of 28, and put the standby section on a moment's notice, I may want them out.'

Turning from the map he then gave directions to Sam Kyle who was standing by the doorway.

'Sergeant Major, get the Rover Group ready to move in five minutes, we have a chance here of lifting Brendan O'Brian.'

Not waiting for an acknowledgement, he crossed the room to push open the door of the Intelligence Section Office.

'Sergeant Sinclair, I've just mounted an O.P. I need your lads for an identification and arrest job; we move in five minutes.'

Jim looked up, trying not to grimace for the last thing he could do with at the moment was getting involved in another of Austen's cowboy stunts.

'Who is it, Sir?' replied the Scotsman, forcing a business-like tone.

'Brendan O'Brian.'

Hearing that name Sinclair sat up, his attitude changed.

'Where, Sir?'

'Lock Street, I want to go in and get him before it gets dark.'

'Corporal Berrill,' ordered the sergeant, jumping up to pull on his smock and flak jacket, 'get the others out to the section pig in two minutes, I'll brief everyone there.'

Reg, grabbing up his own flak jacket and rifle, gave a hurried reply and sped out of the door.

All this activity had been triggered off a few minutes before by a report coming in from an observation post on the top of Oak House. This tower block post was manned all through the daylight hours and overlooked much of the Gate House. Their report had been of a possible sighting of a man getting out of a car and entering a house, who they believed to be the district I.R.A. Battalion Quartermaster. If he could be arrested the information gained from questioning could be invaluable.

Turning into Lock Street past one of 7 Platoon's mobile patrol landrovers sealing that end of the street, D Company's Humber slowed and then stopped. Sinclair's men spilled out of the back to take up positions either side of a red brick terraced house, its front door flush with the pavement. With Jim standing one side and Mick Pridmore the other, the Scotsman rapped loudly with his fist.

'Don't bother with that,' shouted Major Austen, his landrover screeching to a halt, 'kick the fucking thing in.'

Sinclair, stepping back, nodded at the door. Mick, squaring himself, raised one leg and shot it forward. Rushing in, they moved the protesting occupants into their front room and then gave the house a thorough search.

'No luck, Sir, he's not in there,' informed Jim Sinclair, joining his O.C. and Bobby MacIntyre on the pavement.

'Well, that old bastard Daley in there,' began Austen, referring to the middle-aged home owner, 'says no one came into his house. Now we know that's a lie, so he's lying for some reason.'

'My patrol went straight into the back alley when we got the call, Sir, I'm sure he never made it out that way,' assured MacIntyre.

'Damn! Damn!' cursed the O.C., beginning to stamp his foot, 'he's got to be in there. I want him! I want him! I want him!'

Jim looked up at Sam Kyle both men bracing themselves for another of 'Shush's' childish tantrums.

This was forestalled by 'Yorky' Rush coming out of the house to make a much welcomed report.

'We found how he got out, Sir; the brickwork in the loft has had holes punched either side, so anyone wanting to could ferret from house to house up and down the street.'

'We got the bastard then,' whooped Austen, wringing his hands gleefully before escalating the operation.

'No one leaves this block of dwellings,' he began, waving his arm at the terraced houses. 'Sergeant MacIntyre, you and your men sit tight. Sergeant Major, get on the radio, I want 9 Platoon's search team out here. They, starting with number 30, will search every house working left up to Piper Street. Sergeant Sinclair, I'll put Corporal Pearson and one other from the Rover Group up in the loft. You take your men and search every house down to Whitefield. Right,' he ended, 'let's get cracking.'

Two hours later with O'Brian still undiscovered Austen stood beside his landrover hopping from foot to foot, becoming more desperately impatient by the second. So too it seemed was somebody else, bored and cold out on the cordon.

The mush over the radio suddenly cut out as a voice came up.

'I'm pissed off.'

Shush, with lightning reflexes grabbed the radio handset to demand, 'Unknown station, send call sign! Send call sign! Over.'

There was a pause as the voice at the other end pondered his options. Then the mush cut out again.

'I'm not that pissed off.'

With no success as yet Jim Sinclair's men were searching the last of their houses.

'Johnny' called 'Yorky' Rush, from the head of the narrow staircase, 'get the O.C. There's an old cow up here, says she's having a stroke.'

'Where?' called back Kieran, taking the steps two at a time.

'Just here in the bedroom,' replied Rush, puzzled by Kieran's swift response.

Stepping through the door he pushed aside the young couple standing by the bed to kneel down. Seeing this the elderly woman lying on the bed began to wail and cry loudly, 'I'm di'in', Jaysus mother of God, get me a doctor.'

Paying no attention to her, Kieran threw the counterpane back to look under the bed.

Then, making a request between clenched teeth, he reached a hand under to begin pulling something.

'Come on Brendan, ya little rat faced runt, let's have ya out o' there.'

Kieran's grip first produced a leg, then a dark donkey jacket came into view followed by a head with ginger hair and a squint eyed, pointed nosed face.

'English bastards,' he cursed as the two paratroopers jerked him to his feet.

'Guess again,' corrected Kieran, 'this English bastard comes from County Wicklow.'

With O'Brian arrested and pinned to the floor of D Company's Humber by four pairs of boots, Rush asked the burning question, 'Ah, Johnny how come you knew this coont was under the bed?'

'My old dad and uncle used to be in the I.R.A. They told me how lots of times they used that trick to hide people and guns from the Black and Tans.'

Then leaning forward to shout into O'Brian's ear, continued, 'That was the real Irish Republican Army, bollock features. Not you and your bunch of bank robbing, protection racket running, mass murderers.'

Working on past experience that under interrogation most I.R.A. terrorists eventually coughed up names and addresses, Austen kept his Company on permanent standby. Worthwhile foresight, for thirtysix hours after O'Brian's arrest C Company began launching a series of lifts. This went on for another day, not only within the Gate House but throughout the whole of Belfast. Brendan O'Brian had been allowed to meet too many people.

From this Charlie Company had three successes; one of these was the local Robin Hood who had been loose in the Gate House for over a year. This local hero, who among other things had planted bombs killing and maiming a number of people, had a teenage henchman. An underling of much malice, he took it upon himself to bring in gunmen, in an attempt to seek revenge.

Sniping began the following afternoon, increasing notably as the evening turned to night.

Because of the acoustics within the Gate House, which deflected sounds at odd angles off the tower blocks, around the concrete flats and down connecting alley ways, the fire positions were difficult to pinpoint. Major Austen, keeping Battalion H.Q. informed of the build up of shooting incidents against his men, was paid a visit by Colonel Chuter.

The Commanding Officer had come straight from the local television studio, where he had been giving a live interview explaining how successful his command had been in arresting wanted I.R.A. suspects due to the information provided by Brendan O'Brian. He went on to add that this was approved of to a great degree by the majority of the people, especially in the Gate House district, not wishing to have anything to do with the terrorists and criminals who called themselves I.R.A. Listening to Austen's report on the growing number of sniper attacks, the tall C.O. was quick to make a decision.

'Simon, call all your men in off the streets, I want to mount a company attack in one hour's time.'

'A Company attack, sir?' beamed Austen, his moustache rising at the corners.

'Yes,' he confirmed, pointing to the wall map. 'I'll warn B and A Companies on your flanks, and put a platoon of A Company on Winter Street as a stop. If you and your men push down from the North this might well flush them into A Company's arms. Can you see any complications?' he concluded.

'None, Sir,' replied Austen smiling with anticipation.

'Right, I'll expect your first sections to cross Piper street at 1930 hours,' he summed up, striding across the room to leave. Only minutes before he had been praising the good burghers of the Gate House, now he was about to launch upon them the full fire power of a modern British Army Rifle Company.

*   *   *

'Who are you?' asked Dave Urwin of a strange face among the semi-circle of men that stood before him.

'Phillips, Sergeant.'

'Are you in this section?' asked Urwin again.

'Yes,' answered Phillips, 'I arrived from the Depot last week, Sergeant.'

'Okay fine,' replied Urwin, before commencing his briefing.

'This O.P. is going to be a company attack on the Gate House. 7 Platoon have the right, 9 Platoon the middle and we have the left, down Lock Street and into the flats on the right hand side. Mr. Taplow will command 1 Section, I've got you lot and Corporal Jones will have 3 Section.'

Pausing, Dave caught his breath for a second to let this sink in before going into a detailed briefing of how the Platoon was to handle its part in this snap assault. Although he spoke with confidence there were doubts in his mind. He had returned to the company having stepped off the ferry only just that morning, and now here he was being pitched in on a company attack over ground he knew little about.

He was collected from the dock area by Jim Sinclair who, pleased to see his friend, none the less would not have minded if he had not returned at all. His motive was not that of concern for the safety of a mate; it was for a more personal reason.

One evening a month previously he had been surprised to pick up the section telephone and find Penny Roberts on the other end. She said she was just phoning to keep him posted on her brother's recovery. Jim did not care why she called; all that mattered was, although not prepared to make the first move himself, he now had an excuse to speak to her and listen to the velvet lilt of her Belfast accent. On this pretence they found themselves phoning each other two or three times a week. Now with Dave's return any further communication with Penny could only be interpreted as an interest by him in her, something he did not yet think was proper.

Passing through the South gate with 8 Platoon leading, Dave Urwin turned about and, continuing to walk backwards, checked to see that his men were maintaining a correct spacing between each. A figure at the Guardroom door gave him a wave and a thumbs up. It was Len Hatton, whose cooks were once more taking over the security duties of the camp while the riflemen went out to seek and destroy.

On approaching Piper Street the men's posture changed. In helmets and flak jackets, hands and faces darkened with camouflage cream, they bent into a half crouch. The butts of their rifles locked into their shoulders, skirmishing from cover to cover, keeping to shadows and doorways they moved silently until Lock Street was reached; they then paused awaiting the code word which would send them into the Gate House itself.

Urwin, at a disadvantage to the others, looked around trying to pinpoint his position, desperate to remember what the streets ahead looked like. The short tour Jim Sinclair had taken him on before being wounded was all he had to go on.

Had he not been shot, the sergeant would have noticed the significance of the missing sentinels. These were youngsters, who in other days would have been Boy Scouts but were now recruited by the I.R.A. to stand, one on each street corner, to warn of approaching patrols. Wherever the soldiers moved in the Gate House their route was always forewarned by these children. In all weathers they would stand watching and signalling by putting a hand in a pocket, behind the back, or with another normal movement, indicating to similar watchers that troops were near or moving off. With these gone from their posts it could only mean that the Paras were expected.

With the still air smelling of coal fumes from domestic fires, the men pressed themselves into cover to escape the beams of light from the normal evening traffic passing up and down Piper. Tactically speaking, this was probably to be the daftest company attack ever mounted in the history of the British Army.

Urwin, holding a little black oblong police radio to his ear, listened carefully that he might not miss the code word every one was expecting. These radios had just recently been issued for use by Patrol Commanders and were a very light and useful bit of kit. However, the drawback to it was having to hold it against the ear and mouth to listen and speak, an awkward thing when both hands were needed on the rifle.

Hearing the code word the sergeant pushed the radio into his open smock top under his flak jacket. Then, bringing his section up onto their feet with a snap of his fingers he followed Mr. Taplow's men who were already on the move.

Penetrating the Gate House C Company brought reaction upon themselves straight away. 9 Platoon, entering by Shaw Street opposite 97 Piper, were the first to be fired at. A burst of sub-machine-gun bullets skipped down the street towards them followed by a bravado challenge.

'Come on ya English bastards. Come and get it.'

With this firing broke out from several other points, filling the radio net with brief report messages.

'Three Three Bravo, contact automatic weapon, south end Shaw Street, am returning fire, over.'

'Three One alpha, gunman, low velocity weapon, top floor rear of Spencer flats, over.'

'Three One Charlie, have reached Dead Pan, unseen gunman firing from Pine court, over.'

Turning into Lock Street, Dave Urwin heard his platoon commander's voice come up on the air.

'Hello, Three, this is Three Two alpha, being fired at by undetected gunman central Lock Street, am moving forward to engage.'

The platoon sergeant watched for a moment as 1 Section sprinted forward from doorway to doorway either side up the street, the front men aiming and firing. With little cover provided by the doorways themselves, the soldiers were having to kick the doors in to gain cover by stepping into the hallway. With the night air beginning to crackle as the sound of gunfire echoed about the surrounding buildings, Urwin signalled his section to follow him.

In the tracks of 1 Section they moved, heart beats rapid, breathing in unaccustomed raspy gasps, heads turning, eyes searching.

Pressing into a hallway beside his Platoon Sergeant, Chris Braithwaite pointed across the street.

'That's our entrance into the flats there, Sergeant. Once we get into the alley way it forks, we go left down Farndale Walk, running parallel with Lock Street.'

Urwin studied the alley way and the grey two storey maisonette houses either side before answering.

'Who's that across the street?' he asked.

'Durrant,' was the quick reply.

'Right, you two go in first, I'll bring the others in behind you,' directed the sergeant, placing a hand on the younger soldier's arm. 'Off you go.'

Ferndale Walk, about fifty yards long, was narrow and meant for foot traffic only. Stopping his section Urwin signalled them to take cover while he fumbled for his radio to inform the O.P.s room that he had reached their first report line.

'Hello Three, this is Three Two Bravo, Dead Pan, over.'

'Three Two Bravo, Dead Pan, out,' came back the hasty acknowledgement, which was understandable for the net was becoming clogged with messages and contact reports.

'Sergeant! Sergeant!' called Phillips, crouching in an alcove on the opposite side of the walk, 'there's a gunman on the top floor of Beech Court.'

'Where?' asked Urwin, springing across to join him.

'Second window from the right, I seen a flash.'

'Which building for Christ's sake,' barked Urwin impatiently, confessing his ignorance of the locality.

'The one on the left,' clarified Phillips, pointing down the walk at a tower block hanging above them.'

After staring silently together for some seconds the sergeant suddenly raised the radio to speak, for a second flash had appeared.

'Hello Three, this is Three Two Bravo. Contact, gunman, top floor Beech court, facing Piper street, over.'

Not waiting for a reply he shouted a hasty fire order to his men.

'2 Section, gunflash, second window from right, top floor Beech Court, watch and shoot.'

Everyone who was sighted took aim and waited.

When the third flash came there was an explosion of shots that vibrated off the walk's concrete walls.

On the far side of the Gate House 7 Platoon had just been told to cross beyond Dead Pan. Bobby MacIntyre, leading his section through the Spencer Flats complex, halted to peer around a corner. Unaware he was doing so, his left hand was protruding at waist height, holding the radio.

In this position he was actually able to watch a sandy haired youth pop up from behind a low wall and fire a pistol shot that struck his exposed arm.

Drawing back, still clutching the radio, he waved two of his men forward with a warning as to where the gunman was.

'Hello Three, this is Three One Charlie, I've just stopped one, over,' he informed H.Q., using improper voice procedure.

Before control could answer the O.C. came up.

'Hello Three One Charlie, this is Three Niner, what is your location? Over.'

'Three One Charlie, Norris Row, below Spencer flats.'

'Three Niner, can you walk? Over.'

'Three One Charlie, yes, over.'

'Three Niner, hand over your command, then make your way back to Starlight at Piper and Shaw, over.'

'Three One Charlie, Roger, out.'

Bobby, complying, gave his radio to the section lance corporal and then, with a shell dressing wrapped around his bleeding forearm, made his way back.

Firing continued throughout the Gate House for a number of minutes as the company leap-frogged on to its second and final report line, which in theory should have pinned the I.R.A. gunmen against A Company on Winter Street, if not pushed them into their arms. This failed to happen because escape for them was a simple matter of concealing their weapons and then slipping into the first house or flat that took their fancy. With several hundred to choose from detection by the soldiers was very slim.

With everyone closed up to the final report line the section commanders deployed their men into defensive fire positions and waited. On Lock Street Corporal Jones signalled a car, which had somehow gotten through the cordon, to stop. Doing this the driver, a man in his twenties, switched his lights to high beam, illuminating most of Jones's section.

The corporal, screaming at the top of his voice for the headlights to be switched off, was answered by the driver sticking his head out of the car window to say, 'I can't hear ya.'

Realising the man was trying to play the dumb innocent while presenting the soldiers as clear targets, Jones ran to the car, smashing out both headlights with his rifle butt.

Then he moved around the car to do some of the same to the driver, but he, anticipating this, jumped out and fled into the Gate House maisonettes. There he was pursued, caught, given a good kicking and arrested by Haydon and Ottoway.

At about this stage all firing stopped with the I.R.A. gunmen going to ground. Jim Sinclair's section was given the job of trying to trace where some of them could be holed up. This proved to be an impossible task for with all house lights off and most street lights shot out by the Paras as they moved forward, little could be seen.

Shortly before the order came through for everyone to pull back Dave

Urwin heard heavy thudding behind him. Looking over his shoulder he saw Braithwaite and Phillips splintering a door frame as they kicked it open. Seeing this to be the house of an elderly couple who had, without them asking, served the section tea and cakes during the last hour's wait, Urwin became angry.

'What the hell's going on?' he demanded, storming up to the two men.

'They asked us to Sergeant,' explained Braithwaite, 'the neighbours have been watching and it would be safer for them if we make it look as if we made them give us the tea.'

At daylight, patrols began to search through the Gate House following blood trails and collecting spent cases. A pistol and a rifle were found but no bodies. At least not until Urwin took Jim Sinclair and his men to the top floor of Beech Court.

Pushing on the door of the north facing flat they found it blocked. With Urwin and Rush forcing it ajar they discovered the obstruction to be a body lying face down in a large puddle of drying blood. Across the room, below a bullet riddled window, lay an American Springfield rifle from which there was a trail of smeared blood where the body had crawled.

Turning the corpse over Urwin looked at the face with surprise, commenting, 'Well, well!'

'How I bet you wish you stayed in hosptial now pal,' offered Sinclair sarcastically.

'Yorky' Rush was even less sympathetic, stepping forward to kick the body's chest.

'That's for the copper your mates killed, ya little shit.'

The dead youth was Kevin Drum.

*　　　　　*　　　　　*

Looking up after having a late Sunday morning breakfast, Sam Kyle and Jim Sinclair watched as a tall A Company sergeant holding his beret in one hand entered their small dining room.

'Is it alright if I grab a cup of tea here, Sir?' he asked Charlie Company's C.S.M., maintaining correct Mess protocol by addressing himself to the senior member present.

'Sure Brad, drop your kit in the corner,' consented Kyle.

Laying his rifle down to peel off a flak jacket and smock he crossed to the sergeant major's table. Pulling out a chair he slumped tiredly into it.

'You spent too much time on late nights out on the town, Brad. You want to give it up,' advised Sinclair, the humour of what he said showing only in his eyes as he pushed a cup of tea across to 'Brad' Bradley.

'Ya, I know it's a failing of mine, can't resist a good night out with the boys,' countered Bradley, a half smile appearing momentarily on the camouflage creamed face, while spooning sugar from a small bowl.

'What you on?' asked Kyle, folding a morning paper he had been reading.

'Me and half my platoon have been sitting on a suspect car down in the docks ever since midnight. A.T.O. are letting it stew. I just come up with them to fetch some kit, should be going back again in a wee bit,' explained Bradley.

'Docks aren't our patch; why you?' asked Kyle curiously, reaching for a tea pot to pour himself another cup.

'Correct answer,' exploded Bradley, 'the R.U.C. are supposed to deal with anything in the docks. When the message came in to Chiswell those bastards just ignored it. Said they would get around to it in due time. After an hour the

O.C. lost his rag and sent me and my lot down to sort it out. Gutless, they're fucking gutless.'

The tall man's last words were bitten off.

'Perhaps not, Brad,' defended Sinclair, reaching across to offer the angry man a cigarette. 'Perhaps they're just a bit tired of getting ambushed and killed when they answer these call-outs. What chance do they have with pistols and a couple of S.M.G.s when they get opened up on by MI carbines. At least when we get shot at we got the fire power to hit back with.'

'Ya, maybe, but I'm getting jarred off with the whole fucking show. It's time we jacked this place and let them get on with killing each other.'

'You mean let them blitz the place, fire and sword down the Falls Road, burn the Shankhill to the ground,' grinned Kyle, taking a sip from his cup.

'Something like that,' replied Bradley, lighting his cigarette.

'Why should they have all the fun, Brad? Maybe we could hang around and join in on all the rape, pillage and slaughter,' proposed Sinclair, catching his sergeant major's eye, offering a broader avenue of approach in solving the Ulster problem.

'No, I'm serious,' defended Bradley, 'we're not doing a blind bit of good here. We should just fuck off and let them get stuck into each other.'

'What about all the people who look to us for protection. Do we just dump them?' asked Kyle, no longer grinning.

'And then what, Brad?' added Sinclair, 'the same thing as here could start in Glasgow, Liverpool or Kilburn; do we just pull out of there as well?'

'Besides,' continued Kyle, pointing to Dave Urwin sat at a far table with the Company Colour Sergeant, finalising clothing and equipment exchanges for his platoon. 'You see Davey over there. Well, he comes from just up the road here. Now not too long ago in a few out of the way countries we found ourselves standing shoulder to shoulder with bullets coming our way and I don't believe I ever heard him saying anything like, 'fucking Christ, I'm an Ulster Irishman, what the hell am I doing here?'

'Ya ya, I'll buy that, Sir, never in a million years would I think of ditching him. It was that scum in the ghettos I had in mind.'

Bradley was reluctantly back-pedalling now.

'No one likes coming over here; it's a shitty job,' pointed out Jim, 'but there's people even in those areas that look to us for help. Me and my lads were doing a house search the other day. A real grotty place it was, stunk to hell. I had to go outside for air and an elderly dear with tears in her eyes came up, pushed a ten pence coin into my hand and thanked me for just being here. How the hell do you walk away and leave someone like that to the I.R.A.?'

'I still can't see what bloody good we're doing here,' responded Bradley in frustration, draining his cup, 'we're not policemen and we can't get stuck into 'em.'

'We all feel the same, Brad, we're only here to keep the lid on until someone comes along with the answers.' summed up Kyle, taking a drink from his own cup.

*   *   *

Under tragic circumstances Willie Durrant's tour was ended before completion. After their marriage he and Seela set up home in an Aldershot Army quarter. Unfortunately as has happened with many Army wives, when her husband returned with the Battalion to Ulster Seela became lonely and unhappy. Willie did his best to phone most evenings, but this was not enough to prevent her from deciding to return to her parents in Belfast until her husband's return. Durrant desperately advised against this but fruitlessly, for with less than a month of the tour left she returned to her former home.

On the second evening after her arrival, a crowd of howling women, knowing she had married a soldier, broke into the house and dragged her into the street. There her hair was brutally shaven off, hot tar poured over her and then she was tied to a street lamp for two hours as an example to others. With a sign which said 'Soldier's whore' strung across her chest, photos were taken which found their way into some of the more extreme Republican publications.

Eventually released she was taken to the Royal Victoria Hospital where the tar was removed and the burns and razor cuts treated.

The first Durrant heard of this was from Colonel Chuter who arrived in C Company's location to personally take him around to see his wife at the R.V.H. On escorting the Scotsman to Seela's bedside and seeing the frightful state she was in, he immediately did two things. The first was to take Durrant off the streets in case he should, understandably, commit some act of reprisal. The second was to ship them both back to England as soon as Seela could be moved.

Once returned to Aldershot she spent two weeks being cared for, with great sympathy, by the medical staff of the Cambridge Hospital.

*   *   *

To the north of C Company's area, beyond Stirling Grove, was a district very rarely patrolled. This was the responsibility of another Battalion, but because it was a quiet, mainly protestant area military policing was kept to a minimum. Another reason for this was that the Roman Catholic ghetto area to the northeast required the majority of their manpower for high profile patrolling.

Towards the latter end of 5 Para's tour activity against this other Battalion began to increase. For three days Charlie Company listened to firing, both single shots and bursts, sounding from this ghetto area. In fact what was happening was the resident Battalion had gradually lost control, and were forced into sealing the place off by manning street and road blocks.

Realising that this had happened the Protestant mob element from across the West Reynolds Road decided to take revenge against the moderate Catholics living in the quiet zone above Stirling Grove.

The first indication that this was happening was smoke, seen and reported by the top gate sentry, rising from an unsighted street. Not being their domain, the OPs officer asked for permission to investigate. The vehicle patrol sent found themselves driving quite unaware into a full blown riot. Bricks, stones and petrol bombs were hurled at them, keeping the soldiers at bay while they fought a pitched battle with the home owners of a Catholic street in an attempt to burn them out.

Austen, arriving with his Rover Group to assess the report he had received from his patrol commander, needed only one look. Placing his vehicles to block a main street route he radioed back to his H.Q., deploying every man in the location not on duty.

Unbeknown to Charlie Company the occupants of Lyle Street had been fighting in defence of their homes for a number of hours. This, although the main point of violence, was just one of many enjoyed by the leaderless, uncontrolled mob. Whilst undetected they had roamed wherever they fancied, stoning shops beating up those they believed were not one of them, damaging property and burning.

Being in their hundreds or possibly a couple of thousand which moved about in bands, both large and small, Major Austen had to at first position his men at extreme points to check their advancement.

Standing beside his Landrover, a roughly folded map in one hand, radio hand set in the other, he drew them street by street in a loose semi-circle around Lyle Street. The north he left open because of too few men and to provide a way out for those of the rioters who might decide to call it a day.

It was dark when Lieutenant Taplow and two sections of his platoon arrived in Lyle Street. Stopping to de-bus his men from their Humbers at the south end of the street he quickly led them forward.

The sight they closed on could only be described as lawless. The top of the street was illuminated by the fire-light from two end houses on the left which were burning fiercely. Beyond this at the junction, throwing missiles whilst dancing with whoops and curses in and out of the flame light, was a horde of savages. These missiles were aimed at a tight knot of about forty men and youths drawn up behind, but showing no intention of retreating from, a hastily built barrier of cars and household materials. Halfway up the street grim-faced women and girls were gathering and carrying forward pieces of bricks from a demolished garden wall. Of those not involved in the defence of the street, the elderly and mothers with children, watching the Paras pass from their gardens and front doors, few said anything. The expressions were mixed; from deep worry to deeper anger. It was not until they approached the barrier that someone actually spoke to them.

Breaking away a dark, heavy set man in a pale shirt, half torn from his body, ran towards them.

'What's the bloody use of turnin' up now?' he screamed at Taplow. 'They've burned me out, look for Jaysus' sake, bloody look.'

Raging, his face red with frustrated anger, he jabbed his finger in straight armed thrusts towards the fire on the left.

Ignoring the man Taplow turned to wave his first section off the street, indicating that they should take up positions in the gardens and doorways. Seeing this, a small band of men left the barrier to hurry towards him.

'Is this all the men the Army's prepared to send, Lieutenant?' asked a slim man in his mid-fifties, wearing a grime covered cardigan.

'At the moment, yes,' replied Taplow crisply, not prepared to commit himself to decisions out of his control.

'Sergeant Urwin,' he continued, motioning to Dave who had closed up behind him. 'Take Corporal Jones' section forward and clear everyone away from that barrier. And those of the men with baton guns can engage anyone who comes within range.'

'Right, Sir,' responded the sergeant continuing on, the dancing light showing bricks raining down around the barrier.

'I want all your people away from that obstruction,' began Taplow addressing the man in the cardigan.

'As long as they are there it will only antagonise those tribesmen on the other side.'

'Antagonise them! Antagonise them!' repeated the man in dismay, 'I don't think you're quite in the picture, Sir. We were having our Saturday lunch when that herd of animals stormed in here, smashing cars and breaking windows. We've been fighting to protect our families and homes, and now you want us to stand back and hope they'll go away.'

'I realise how you feel but you're under my protection now and I'm responsible should any of you be injured,' replied the officer formally.

'Injured is it?' snorted the Irishman, 'it's a bit late for that now. The ambulance has already taken four of us away; two houses are roaring up in smoke; we've been struggling to hold that pack of bloodthirsty Protestant wolves back for over three hours and you say you're concerned for our safety.'

Pausing, he swept an arm around the street.

'I was almost thirty years in the Army and not ashamed of a minute of it, but how do you think I feel now? I told the people when it first blew up that the Army's been called and on their way. That was over three hours ago. This street had no time for the I.R.A. this morning, but I swear, tomorrow some of these lads will be queuing up to join the Provos now.'

Taplow listened with sympathy but made no comment; messages had been misunderstood or reacted to wrongly before. The work at hand at that moment was to separate those battling in this street.

'Will you speak to the other men and help move them back?' he asked, 'I've a job to do and your people will only get in the way.'

Before an answer could be given, three men ran out from the back of the houses on the right beyond the barrier, opposite those burning.

'They're in the back,' shouted one as they scrambled to get over the barricade. Chris Braithwaite, standing on house steps on the left of the street, raised his rifle to shout a warning.

'Look out!' he hollered, squeezing a single shot at a figure who had appeared behind the three men, a petrol bomb in a drawn back hand, about to throw it. The figure dropped into the pathway, with the released flaming-wicked bottle shattering beside him, engulfing the lower half of his body in fire.

'Sergeant Urwin,' barked Taplow, rushing forward to take control, 'take three or four men, get in the back of those houses, if anyone's there root them out. Leave the one who's shot to me.'

Grabbing the nearest men to them, the officer and senior N.C.O. leapt the barrier. Taking hold of the petrol bomber's jacket collar, Taplow dragged the limp body off the pathway onto a small patch of grass. Tom Phillips, discarding his rifle, attempted to beat out the flames. This proved pointless for Braithwaite's aim was far too good; the bomber's eyes, showing no pain, were beginning to close.

At the back of the house Dave Urwin and his party interrupted a group trying to break in to start a blaze. Flattening one with a baton round fired into his stomach, a melee of pursuit and arrest then ensued across back gardens and over walls. Ottoway apprehended one with kicks and his rifle butt, while Haydon cautioned another with the barrel of a baton gun on the back of his head.

Several minutes later Austen's rover group picked its way up the street. Halting the vehicles to continue on foot with Sam Kyle, he stopped first beside the medical Humber as the body of the petrol bomber was being loaded aboard.

'Dead is he, Tom?' he asked of the M.O.

'Stiff, I'm just shipping it down to the Royal Vic.', replied Ravenscroft. Saying no more the O.C. moved on until he found Taplow.

'What's the picture, Peter?' he asked.

'Well, we had no choice with the shooting, Sir, he was endangering life. But since then the crowd has not depleted; it's increased if anything. It's becoming quite volatile out there; they may have a go at us, but then who knows, they could turn on another street.'

'Yes, I see,' agreed Austen, his eyes darting about the unstable scene, trying to assess where best to begin.

'This fire, Peter, I think it's time we got some appliances up here to deal with it.'

'C.O.'s here, Sir,' interrupted Sam Kyle.

Looking back Colonel Chuter could be seen, without a helmet, wearing instead a beret with a blackened cap badge, picking his way along the pavement.

'Everything in hand, Simon?' he asked with such calmness it could have been a queston regarding the Battalion's sports day.

'At the moment, Sir,' replied the Major, pointing beyond the barrier, 'the rioters are keeping their distance. However, Peter says more have arrived just recently, but I'm more worried about that fire; it may spread.'

'Quite right, I'll get onto the fire authorities,' he agreed lifting one of Austen's problems from him before explaining to his subordinate actions that he wished to be implemented.

'I believe these people are still in some danger here and I would like them out of it. The best thing is to evacuate them back into Stirling Grove. I'll arrange with your colour sergeant to have them put up temporarily in the sports centre building.'

'These are home owners, Sir,' pointed out Taplow, 'they may not want to go.'

'Alright,' consented the colonel, 'the men can stay with their homes but the women and children must go. Now Simon,' continued Chuter, placing a hand on the major's arm to draw him aside. 'Who's looking after the Gate House?'

'An eight man vehicle patrol in constant motion, Sir,' confirmed Austen.

'Good! Now you seem to have this buttoned up so all I want you to do is sit tight. However, I'm giving you a platoon from A Company to keep in reserve just in case. Now have you any spare bodies yourself?'

Austen thought for a moment then remembered Jim Sinclair's crew.

'Yes, they'll do,' replied Chuter nodding his head in sharp jerks. 'I want you to put them on a watch capacity up on Barthorp Street. Some of these goons may try to leak out towards the northeast and I don't want that. The only route I want them to take is back across the West Reynolds Road to their holes around the Shankhill.'

'Right,' smiled the Colonel, rocking back on his heels to hook both thumbs in the belt that held a holstered pistol around his waist. 'That was the good news. Keep this to yourself for the moment, but once you've tidied up around here your company will probably be mounting an Op, in aid of our friends to the north. They've asked for some assistance in going in and dealing with their gunmen. They lost control yesterday but intend to go back and re-establish themselves in the early hours tomorrow morning.'

'Fine Sir, splendid, I and my men will look forward to it,' replied Austen, unable to return his Commanding Officer's happy expression.

'Thought you might,' grinned the colonel.

'Haydon, by the hedgerow, don't let him get any closer, let him have it!'

The officers' conversation was interrupted by a loud shout as Dave Urwin directed Phil Haydon onto a target for his baton gun. The private, firing, broke open the single shot weapon to insert a fresh round whilst the sergeant, looking up, noticed his helmetless C.O.

'You don't want to come much closer, Sir,' he warned, approaching the two officers, 'bricks are still coming our way.'

'I hear you Sergeant Urwin and I will heed your every word,' replied Chuter reverently, 'under no circumstances am I going to allow my meteoric military career be ended by one of your low flying Belfast bricks?'

Urwin's answer to that was a broad smile and a half suppressed chuckle.

'Was that one of your men who shot the petrol bomber?' asked the colonel, losing his comic expression.

'Yes, Sir, Braithwaite,' replied the sergeant, his mouth now a straight line.

'Presented with the same situation do you think he would shoot to kill again?' asked Chuter.

'Yes, Sir,' was the crisp answer.

'Good! Good!' These two words were repeated with deliberate slowness.

'We can expect a lot of flak from the Protestant community on this one,' he continued, speaking mainly to his Company Commander. 'But I don't give a damn. Either we uphold the rule of the law here or we're all on the slippery slope to anarchy.'

The colonel's theorising was interrupted by a voice calling from a gate entrance a few yards behind.

'Sir! Sir! Zero want you, it's a message from brigade.'

This was the C.O.'s signaller, always close but never under foot. He was holding up the handset of the A41 radio, carried on his back.

'Well, here we go, it's bound to be either a reprimand or a well done,' speculated the colonel before taking his leave to reply to the call. 'I'll be off, Simon. Now remember, clear this street, expect those savages to become more hostile before packing it in and hold yourself ready for tomorrow morning.'

Joining his signaller Chuter took the handset, continuing to walk back down the street while commencing a conversation with his operation's officer at Battalion H.Q.

Facing the barricade and the crowd beyond screaming their curses and taunts, Austen took a deep breath. 'Peter,' he called to Lieutenant Taplow, 'get your lads to clear this street, I want that bloody fire out.'

*   *   *

Studying a street map he held in his lap by the light of a torch Jim Sinclair was plotting a route for the driver of his Humber.

'Buckley, what's the name of that street we're coming to?'

'Looks like Herbert, Sarg.'

'Okay, at the next, go right, then left,' ordered Sinclair, not taking his eyes off the map.

'No, no,' he amended sharply, noticing a street name he recognised, 'go right, but don't turn left until I say so.'

Moving slowly without headlights, Jim hunched forward searching for the street names in the moonlight.

'There, Poulter!' he pointed. 'Turn there, Barthorp should be the next corner.'

The street they entered sloped gently upwards with semi-detached houses, fronted by moderate sized gardens, on either side. As the armoured vehicle began picking its way around parked cars Buckley suddenly stopped, leaving the engine idling.

'What's up?' asked Sinclair, looking first through his grilled aperture then at the driver.

'People,' replied Buckley in a cautious tone, staring forward. 'A bunch of blokes just ran out of one of the gardens.

'See,' he confirmed, as two figures ran across the street a hundred yards on, 'there goes some now.'

'Mick,' shouted Sinclair turning his head to warn those in the back, 'it might be bother up ahead. We'll charge in and see what stirs up. When we stop de-bus everyone.'

'Okay, on you go,' replied Pridmore.

'Put your lights on, Buckley, then wind this beast up. Let's see who we dig out up there,' ordered the Scotsman.

'Fucking hell, why is it always me?' groaned the driver. Swaying back and forth, avoiding parked cars, the Humber lumbered forwards, increasing its speed as it progressed. Suddenly in the beams of the headlights a youth bolted from behind a parked car to begin running away, then another and another.

'Stop! Stop!' shouted Sinclair, forcing his door open. On the pavement he was joined by the rest of his men.

'Shake it out; let's clear this street, no shooting except with the baton guns.'

As if in challenge a piece of house brick bounced towards them to rebound off a car.

Advancing in a loose line with the A.P.C., its lights now out and following the five Paras jogged up the street, sweeping the riff-raff ahead of them. At the crest of the slope the twenty or so figures, now swearing and chanting, retreated westward on Barthorp Street. Occupying the junction, Sinclair had Buckley park his vehicle broadside across it, blocking the west entrance.

Jim, showing a concern the others did not understand, first hurriedly reported by radio his location and situation, then leaving Mick Pridmore in charge took Johnny Kieran with him back down the street they had just cleared. Although only eight o'clock there was not a light showing anywhere. Nor the least sign of life. Racing down the even numbered side, picking them out from the street with the aid of a torch, the Scotsman halted at one of these to push open the gate. Hastening up the pathway, at the door he pushed the bell several times then impatiently began to rap on the wooden frame itself.

Kieran, standing guard at the gate, watched mystified as his sergeant bobbed about on the steps trying to peer into the darkened windows. In desperation, still banging on the door, he crouched at the letter box, pushing it open to shout, 'Penny, are you in? It's Jim Sinclair, Penny, Jim Sinclair.'

After a pause of several seconds a hall light came on, bathing the paratrooper with light escaping through the door's large glass panel. This almost instantly was pulled wide open by Penny Roberts who stood, wearing a thick grey pullover and jeans, silhouetted in the hall light.

Her greeting was filled with relieved anxiety.

'Oh, Jim, thank God, thank God it's you.'

'You alright? Has there been any trouble?' asked Jim in reply.

'Trouble! Yes, well I don't know,' she began, confused, 'oh Jim, I'm not sure but we've been terrified. They arrived about an hour ago, shouting and swearing, roaming up and down the street. Everyone's been too frightened to go out. We phoned the police but they just told us to stay indoors and would get to us as soon as they could.'

'I know, everyone's pushed tonight,' apologised Sinclair.

'Oh Jim, I'm so glad you're here I could kiss you,' confessed the attractive young woman, stepping forward to grasp the soldier's arm in both her hands, a relieved smile on her face.

'What about me? Can I get in on that?' called Kieran, walking up the footpath, a broad grin showing through his camouflage cream.

'Oh yes, Johnny, I'll kiss you all,' she beamed. She turned, still holding Jim's arm, to call back down the hall, 'Mrs. Murdock, it's alright they're friends.'

A silver haired woman, holding Steven Roberts asleep in her arms, stepped into the hallway.

'Yes, Penny, I heard and a wonderful sight they are. But you'll have to excuse me, I best take the youngster to his bed.'

'Oh yes please, Mrs. Murdock, if you would,' thanked Penny, releasing Sinclair's arm to take a step back. 'Jim, will you both come in?'

'Not now thanks, Pen, it's still a bit unsettled out here. Now are you sure nothing happened?' replied the sergeant, too aware of what could still happen.

'Well, we did hear some glass breaking over the shouting, just up the street.'

'Where?' asked Jim, turning about.

'That direction, the houses across the street,' replied Penny, stepping onto the front steps to point further up and across the street.

'We had better start knocking on doors, Johnny, they could have broken in somewhere,' proposed the sergeant, stepping onto the footpath.

'Okay, but you better do the talking, no one's going to answer when they hear my accent,' joked Kieran.

'Penny, are there any Catholic families across there?' asked Sinclair, pausing.

'Oh,' she pondered, 'ah yes, an elderly couple, the Doherty's.'

'Which house?' snapped Sinclair, making quickly for the gate.

'I'll show you,' volunteered the woman, reaching back in to the hallway to grab a short leather jacket before hurrying after the two soldiers.

Approaching the house Penny indicated, Kieran was the first to notice the broken front window.

'Look, they've put a window in.'

'Take a quick check in the back, Johnny, I'll try the front,' directed the sergeant in a hushed voice as he climbed the steps.

'Good evening, is anyone in?' he called, knocking on the door.

'Who's that?' came a man's voice from inside.

'It's alright, Mr. Doherty,' shouted Penny Roberts from the pavement, 'it's the Army.'

'Army is it?' challenged a tall but stooped man in his late seventies as he pulled the door open. 'What rank are you, son?'

'Sergeant,' replied the Scotsman, slightly taken aback.

'Well good, so was I, until I lost this in Flanders in 1917 with the Munster Rifles,' he said, tapping one leg with a hurling stick that produced dull wooden thuds. 'But I tell you what my man, if those barbaric thugs had tried to break in, one leg or not, I'd have given them merry hell.'

Well into the small hours of the next morning Jim and his men remained on the junction. Although the street hoodlums had soon withdrawn, their orders were to stay blocking and observing. This turned into a relaxing detail with the local residents, grateful for their presence, constantly plying them with tea and cakes. Around midnight Penny Roberts arrived to invite them down for a hot meal, which at that chilling time of a mid-April night was a welcome offer.

Jim, sending his section two at a time, was the last to eat and remained drinking coffee, watching his hostess wash the dishes.

'You alright now, Pen?' he asked, leaning on the kitchen sideboard. 'From the trouble earlier I mean?'

'Yes, I think so. At the time it was unnerving; Mrs. Murdock came in from next door as soon as they began and for a time we were scared. We've never had any trouble of that kind here before, it frightened us both. I was awful glad to see you, Jim.'

On saying this Penny looked up from the sink to smile at the Scotsman.

With this natural gesture tumbling her light brown hair to one side, framing the angelic beauty of her pale smooth face, she was not to know of the longing it triggered within Sinclair.

'We'll be packing up here next week; have you any plans of visiting Mary and Dave again?' he asked, changing the subject.

'I was hoping to,' she replied, her voice taking a sad tone. 'Things haven't worked out all that well here. After coming in from work, because of the troubles, I hardly go out. People and relatives do visit but, except for Mrs. Murdock, most evenings Steven and I spend alone. It's terribly lonely sometimes.'

'So you'll come across then?' asked Sinclair in confirmation.

'I have a week's holiday due so, yes I will,' she replied.

'Soon,' pressed the sergeant, holding her eyes.

'Well, yes as soon as I can,' she replied. Then taking him to task over the abruptness of his question she continued in a harsher voice, 'look, would you like me and young Steven to come back with the Battalion on the ferry?'

On saying this she turned to face Sinclair, smiling.

'If you could,' he countered, not returning her smile.

'Jim, you lemon head, be serious,' she scolded, picking up a tea towel to begin drying the dishes.

'I am serious; I want to be near you as often as possible. I've fallen in love with you, Penny.'

On hearing this her smile remained for a second but soon faded as she realised the man was not teasing but meant what he had just said.

Bracing one hand on the edge of the sink she gave her approval to this confession with a low utterance of two words.

'Oh Jim.'

Taking a step forward, for all the senses in his body cried out to take her in his arms, he was halted with a sober warning as Penny straightened her back.

'Jim, if you touch me I'll make love to you.'

'No you won't,' he told her, a tender smile appearing as he slowly reached out to take her face in hands. 'I won't let you.'

His lips pressed down on hers, closing their eyes, allowing each to taste and smell. She was fragrance and nectar, while he tasted of camouflage cream, his smock and flak jacket unwashed for weeks giving off a pong. She noticed neither of these, far too engrossed caressing the man she now took in her arms.

'Penny, I love you, I love you,' repeated Sinclair, dropping his arms to circle her body while moving his lips to her ear. 'The nights I've fallen asleep with a broken heart, wishing I was able to hold you like this.'

'Your awful late, Jim,' she murmured softly, 'you were breaking my heart years ago.'

'Penny! Penny!' he whispered, tracing his lips with little kisses back to her own to slip his tongue deep between them. Locked together, both pulling themselves tight against the other, their tongues caressing, neither heard the front door opening.

'Jim,' called Reg Berrill, walking down the hallway.'Jim, ya here?'

'In the kitchen, Reg,' shouted Sinclair, breaking apart to hold Penny's shoulers.

'The company want us back, it looks like they got an Op on,' announced Berrill.

'Okay, coming!' replied the sergeant, kissing Penny quickly once more before whispering 'I'll phone as soon as I can.'

Picking up his rifle and helmet he hurried into the hallway.

'Is everyone with the pig?' he asked, pressing past Berrill.

'Yah, ready to go,' he replied, pushing his head into the kitchen.

'Thanks for the scoff, Penny, it went down a treat,' thanked the lance corporal with a grateful smile.

'Good! Good! Pleased to do it,' responded Penny looking up, unable to hide a guilty blush.

Reg withdrew his head but popped it back in again, this time more to snigger than smile.

'Face cloth with hot soapy water, Pen, that's the best thing to shift it.'

'What?' asked the woman, not understanding.

'Look in the mirror,' he suggested, waving a finger around his face before following Sinclair.

Cocking her head towards a wall mirror, Penny threw her hands up with a cry to clutch a face that had transferred large smudges of camouflage cream from Jim's cheeks to her own.

The operation mounted a few hours later turned out to be a peaceful walk over. After the last few days of free for all gunfire by the Provisional I.R.A. The re-occupation of their area by the resident Battalion, assisted by 5 Para, occured without a shot fired. Either losing their battle or facing up to the fact that perhaps they had bitten off more than they could chew, they allowed the Army to move back unopposed. Recently constructed barriers and road blocks were abandoned, weapons found lying in doorways and on garden paths, with streets totally deserted. To everyone's satisfaction, for it had been a long day. The 5 Para attached elements were released to return to their locations shortly before dawn.

Jim Sinclair took his Humber the long way back, via Poulter Street. With the rest of his men dozing in the back, he stopped Buckley outside Penny Robert's house. Ringing the bell twice he heard her voice asking from the hallway who it was.

'It's Jim, Penny, open the door.'

'What is it, Jim?' she asked anxiously, pulling the door open to stand, dressing gown clad, half behind it.

Sinclair, holding the barrel of his rifle in one hand with the butt resting on the step, spread his arm out to either side.

'Pen, will you marry me?'

CHAPTER 13

I was a child and she was a child,
In this kingdom by the sea;
But we loved with a love which was more than love . . .
I and Annabel Lee.

Edgar Allan Poe

Standing on the 300 yard firing point of a South coast rifle range, holding the receiver of a field telephone, Lance Corporal Chris Braithwaite watched as a line of men moved off the 100 yard point. They were advancing towards the target butts, rifles ready, completing the final stage of a firing classification practice. As they moved, keeping a straight line, a figure following a few paces behind would periodically raise his arm. This was the signal for Braithwaite to notify the butt party that he wished the snap targets to be exposed for five seconds. When the last shots of the serial had been fired the line of men halted, with the rear figure turning about to wave his arms back and forth. This was an indication to Braithwaite that all firing for the day was now completed.

'Hello, Butts,' spoke Chris into the 'phone. 'Take the scores, paste up and pack up. We're finished here so get a shake on and let's all fuck off.'

The message passed, he turned to Durrant, who was manning a radio set.

'Jock, call the lads in, we've finished.'

The range, a naval one, was tucked away in the corner of a pebble beach owned by the forces. Being out of the way it was seldom used, and because of this it lacked proper fencing to exclude the wandering public. A number of points did fly red warning flags, but as most civilians were ignorant of their meaning several men with radios were scattered around the perimeter to warn them off.

'Are we all set to get away from this poxy place?' asked the man who had waved his arms at Braithwaite, as he arrived back at the 300 yard point.

'Not yet, Sir,' replied the young lance corporal, 'one of the vedettes hasn't answered up.'

'Oh, for Christ's sake,' cursed the sergeant major, 'which one of the bastards is it?'

'Three, Sir, he's on that knoll,' pointed Braithwaite.

The warrant officer, raising a pair of binoculars which hung around his neck, watched the knoll for some seconds.

'That cunt's asleep, I can see the radio aerial.'

Without another word he picked up a spare rifle, fitted a full magazine to it

195

and then cocking the weapon took aim at the knoll.

'Hold on, sir, I'll send a man to fetch him,' offered Braithwaite, almost shouting as he tried to intervene in the sergeant major's actions, hardly believing what the man was about to do.

'No, I'll get that cunt moving,' said the WO.2, brushing aside Braithwaite's objections and steadying the rifle.

'Durrant,' ordered Braithwaite in a frantic voice, 'give another buzz, and shout this time.'

'Sir,' he called, now addressing the sergeant major as his first round kicked up a splat of sand at the crown of the knoll, 'you could hit him with a ricochet.'

'Bollocks,' was the reply as a second round struck the same area.

'Sir, shoot over his head then he'll hear the crack and thump as it flies above,' compromised Braithwaite, his skin beginning to tighten.

The warrant officer, heeding this advice, snapped off a series of three more shots high above the knoll.

This seemed to have the desired effect, for Durrant shouted that the soldier had answered. This was confirmed as a skyline silhouette stood up on the knoll, hoisting a radio onto his back.

'Right, Corporal,' commanded Jerry Kettler, unloading his rifle, 'let's get this range cleaned up, then we can all piss off.'

Kettler, after a tour in the Army loony bin at Netley, had been certified sane and fit to return to the 5th Battalion.

Colonel Chuter, knowing the man's history but compelled to accept him back, appointed him as sergeant major of the Battalion Training Wing. There, with luck, he would have limited scope to cause a nuisance of himself.

The next morning Chris Braithwaite, outraged by the incident at the range and seeking justice, knocked on R.S.M. Norris's office door. With no officer or senior N.C.O. at the range to bear witness to Kettler's attempted homicide, he was determined the man be brought to book.

On being told to come in by a loud gruff voice Braithwaite opened the door, stepped inside, reclosed it, and then marched forward to halt smartly at attention before the R.S.M.'s desk.

'Yes, and who are you?' asked Norris looking up from writing.

'Lance Corporal Braithwaite, C Company, sir,' replied the young junior N.C.O. staring directly to the front. 'I've a problem and I don't know how it should be dealt with, Sir.'

'Well of course,' smiled Norris, resting his elbows on the desk to clasp both hands together, flattered that someone actually wanted his advice. 'That is one of my many functions, to guide and assist the junior commanders of the Battalion. Now, what can I help you with? Oh, please stand at ease.'

'I want to know how I go about charging a warrant officer, Sir,' confided Braithwaite, stamping his left leg outwards and clasping both hands behind his back in the at ease position.

'What! Stand to attention when you address me,' roared Nuts, leaping to his feet. 'You, an insignificant lance corporal want to jeopardize the career of someone who has no doubt served the Regiment loyaly and with distinction since you were crawling around the nursery in nappies.'

Norris had charged around his desk and was now screaming into Braithwaite's left lughole.

'Just which member of my mess are you making accusations against?' he snarled.

'Sergeant Major Kettler, Sir,' answered the lance corporal nervously, his mouth suddenly drying. For a moment Norris froze then snapping up a chair from the corner of his office he placed it behind Chris.

'Here son, you sit yourself down. Of course you need my help, we'll deal with this right away' cooed the R.S.M., his voice like a dove's, whilst plucking the thick, red bound Queen's Rules and Regulations from a bookcase.

'Webber,' he screamed through a side door at the orderly room runner, 'bring two teas in here. Sharp now lad, move yourself.'

Sitting at his desk he opened the red bound Army bible to fix Braithwaite with a cheshire cat smile.

'Now what crime has been committed here?'

Unbeknown to the lance corporal, the R.S.M. hated Kettler intensely. Probably through jealousy; for although Norris worked very hard at maintaining his eccentric lunatic image, everyone knew he was only pretending, whereas Kettler was a certified graduate of the Army's number one Bunny Basket.

*   *   *

Digging a finger into the collar of his number two dress uniform shirt, Reg Berrill tried to ease his discomfort by allowing air to reach his sweating body. This misery he was now in had been building up out of his control since early that morning.

Now married, he and his wife had first sat waiting in their Salerno Crescent Army quarter from seven thirty to eight thirty awaiting transport, which was to have been a staff car. However, what turned up was the duty driver in a grubby short wheel base Landrover, explaining that the M.T.O. and his wife had taken the car to Woking, shopping.

An hour late they set out for London with neither Reg nor the driver quite knowing how to get to their destination. Lost on the North Circular, they stopped an ambulance to ask directions. Finally, almost two hours late, they drove through the main gate to park in a rear courtyard among a score of gleaming, black, chauffeur-driven staff cars. Berrill, climbing from the back, brushed Salisbury Plain chalk off his uniform that the vehicle had picked up on its last exercise. Collecting his wife from the front passenger seat, he hurried towards the rear entrance of a large stone masonry building. A uniformed footman directed them up a wide curving flight of stairs picketted at alternate intervals by soldiers from a Horse Guards Regiment in ceremonial dress.

At the head of the stairs Reg's wife was graciously but abruptly separated from him.

'Guests this way, madam,' announced a distinguished, middle-aged gentleman in a black tail coat, ushering her through a doorway.

Berrill was led along the hall into a room to join a group of about thirty people congregated within an enclosure of maroon satin rope. On entering, another man asked him his name and ticked it off from a list he carried on an elaborate mill board. The others were an impressive gathering immaculately uniformed senior officers, including admirals and generals, whilst those in civilian dress were attired in black tie and tails. Five or six women, mostly middle-aged, were there, dressed in appropriate, conventional dresses with elbow length gloves and wide brimmed hats.

Although supposedly late, Reg and the rest of the party waited inside the ropes for two hours until a major-domo appeared to give them a briefing on protocol and how they were to conduct themselves, and then led everyone back into the hall. There they were handed over to the grey-coated Master of Ceremonies, who formed them into a straight line off the hallway, in a corridor leading into a large reception room.

Here Reg now stood for a further hour and a half, sweating, legs and feet numbing, listening to the tension-easing jokes of the two men in front of him, a colonel and a major-general.

Unexpectedly, for Berrill had begun to pass the time by examining and counting the corridor's ceiling pattern, the queue suddenly disappeared, leaving him alone at the head of the line facing the entrance way. Panic now gripped his stomach, throat and mind. As a figure at the door motioned him forward bolts of lightning began to surge through his veins. Automatically his best bulled boots began to pace clumsily along the carpet and into the room. To his right was the main area of the room which was a gallery for guests and spectators. They sat in U-shaped banking, rising ever so gently up three walls or in straight-backed chairs in the centre of the U. On the walls hung huge paintings whose frames spanned fifteen to twenty feet, while above, dominating the whole room, an immense chandalier was suspended.

The paratrooper, his temples and cheeks lined with sweat streaks, halted in the centre of the room to turn to his left. At attention he bowed his head towards an elegantly dressed woman in her middle years, standing on a small platform six to eight inches high. Behind her were large drapes, flags, and waiting silently, a number of aides and attendants.

Stiffly Berrill marched forward to again halt before the woman and bow his head. On looking up a question was asked of him which he answered in a dry voice. From one flank a formally dressed gentleman extended a cushion which held a single medal.

'Lance Corporal Berrill Parachute Regiment, Military Medal,' he murmured.

With a smile, removing it from the cushion, she conveyed her pleasure in being able to bestow this award while reaching forward to pin it on Berrill's chest next his single campaign ribbon.

Other questions were then asked which Reg only vaguely remembered answering, then conscious the presentation was over, he once more bowed his head. Backing up, he again halted to bow for a fourth time before turning left to retrace his steps back down the corridor.

In the hallway Reg rejoined his wife. She, with a pleased smile, tried to kiss his cheek but was held away by Berrill, also smiling.

'Hey, don't get familiar, I've just had an audience with the Queen.'

'Okay, big headed hero,' she replied, settling instead for a nibble on his ear, 'if that's how you feel then you can spend the rest of the week sleeping on the couch.'

When Reg volunteered to take ammunition into the Colinglen to get away from Battalion H.Q., he never once dreamt it would result in a day out at Buckingham Palace.

*   *   *

Striding through the company office into his own, Sam Kyle removed his beret to lay it and his pace stick on the desk top. Pushing Major Austen's door ajar and not finding him in, he returned to the company office.

'Where's the O.C.?' he asked of his clerk.

'Gone to the mess for an early lunch, Sir,' replied Pearson.

'Damn,' cursed Sam looking at his watch, 'the R.S.M. just dropped a bomb shell. 1 Para won't be able to take part in Airborne Forces Day so now we've got to do the parade.'

'Oh fuck,' groaned Chris Braithwaite, the Company Orderly Sergeant.

'Never mind oh fuck' cautioned the C.S.M. putting wheels in motion. 'You get around the lines and find the Platoon Sergeants. I want all three in my office at fourteen hundred hours. We'll have to get to grips with uniforms, best kit and drill as from this afternoon.'

'Does that mean the training programmed for next week has gone for a burton, Sir?' asked Pearson as Braithwaite pulled his beret on and left the room.

'Most definitely; the next two weeks will be nothing but bullshit and drill parades,' replied Kyle, taking a step inside his office, then turning about to continue. 'There's nothing to salvage from the old training programme now. You'll just have to forget about all the hard typing you did and heave the lot into file 13.'

The clerk, his lips puckering together, annoyed at the waste of effort he had put in on the programme, was tapping a pencil on the corner of his desk. Giving one tap too many, it fell from his grip making the corporal stoop in his chair to retrieve it.

As he did so, splinters of glass blew over his head, showering the office as the window behind him shattered. Sam, protected by the door, had the same thing happen to his own window, but was only conscious of wondering what had caused the explosion.

Dave Urwin, leaving the barracks early for lunch, was taking a short cut past the officers' mess on his way up the hill to Salamanca Park. Just as he was about to step off the grass lawn he was crossing, a dark red Austin Mini, parked where it should not have been in front of 5 Para's mess, exploded.

The instantaneous orange flash vanished leaving a cloud of dirty grey, debris-filled smoke. Urwin, blown flat, lay for a time his head covered by one arm, while regaining his senses and awaiting chunks of metal and concrete to land. Looking up he saw that the mess, a prefab concrete and glass three-storey building, was masked by smoke from the blast and from the car's burning shell. Leaping to his feet the sergeant ran towards the explosion. Others were running but these he warned off by shouting at them to stay back. Checking that a second car had not been placed near at hand to cause casualties among the rescuers, he waved everyone in.

Entering the mess through a gap in the prefab wall that had been caved in by the blast, he felt one foot stepping on something spongy. Looking down through the gloom of settling dust he found himself standing on the torso of a legless woman. The room he was in was the restroom of the part-time waitresses who worked in the mess. These women, all six having a cup of tea before the lunch meal began, now lay dead beneath the dust covered rubble. The legless woman he recognised as the wife of the Battalion's signal sergeant.

A figure pushed past him, and he followed behind into the kitchen. It was Vic Seaton who, with others, had rushed up from the M.I. Room.

Two cooks were found sprawled, stunned and bleeding, in the wreckage of their kitchen. Seaton hurried from one to the other passing each as battered but well. Urwin, making his way down a hallway which led to the main entrance, investigated a combination of angry shouts and laughter and found two of the Battalion junior officers gagging with laughter in the toilet. They were attempting to push back a large slab of concrete that had tipped forward against the urinal. Pinned by this, penis in hand, unable to move but squirming from the waist up and filling the room with curses and threats was 'Shush' Austen.

Feeling a hand on his shoulder, Urwin turned to find Captain Ravenscroft asking to accompany him in a search of the upstairs floors.

At the top of a broad spiral staircase they separated to search around in the damage. In the bar, reeking of alcohol fumes from broken stock, Dave found a barman suffering cuts and bruises, unable to regain his feet. Concerned about this the sergeant began to call for the M.O., but receiving no reply went looking for him.

He was found in the lounge, rising to his feet but continuing to look down. The walls of the entire floor consisted of huge glass windows, framed by supporting pillars and girders. These windows, having been blown in, covered the floor and furniture in varying sizes of glass splinters. Many had arrived there harmlessly but with a lethal force, which was shown by the scars on the inner walls and rents in the fabris of the furniture.

If the bomb had exploded twenty minutes later these crystal arrows would have caused many casualties among the officers of the Battalion gathering for their midday meal. But because of this premature detonation only one person was present. Urwin approached to find at the feet of the medical officer the bloody, glass-skewered body of Father Buchanan.

Within a few days, due to the evidence found in the wreckage of the car, an I.R.A. sympathiser was arrested, then eventually tried and sentenced to life imprisonment for the murder of six women and a Roman Catholic priest. Although justice, if it could be called that, was done, it did little to deter others. Murder by bombings throughout mainland Britain by I.R.A. terror gangs had now begun.

*   *   *

'Jim, telephone.'

Jim Sinclair stopped sweeping the glass from the mess dining-room carpet to look around.

'What? Who is it?' he asked.

'Don't know,' was the other man's reply, 'some bird.'

Sinclair, placing his broom against a chair, walked out to the mess foyer and picked up the phone.

'Hello,' he said in an inquisitive voice.

'Hello Jim,' replied Penny Roberts.

'Hello honey! Oh God, look I'm sorry, I was going to call later. We're all running round like ruptured ducks at the moment . . .'

'Yes, I know,' broke in Penny, 'it's been on the news. Now you're alright are you?'

'Oh aye, aye! Should have given you a ring to let you know I was okay. Sorry pet,' he apologised.

'That's alright,' she assured him, 'Dave phoned mum and dad this afternoon to say you were all safe.'

'Oh great, I haven't had a chance to talk to him; I've been on Pirbright ranges all day! Just now everyone's lending a hand with the cleaning up. The bomb went off just across the road so we caught a lot of the blast. Anyway we should have it all sorted before you come over next week.'

There was a brief pause before Penny spoke.

200

'Yes, well, you see Jim, that's why I called. I'm not in Belfast.'

'Eh? What?' he stuttered, unsure as to what she was saying. 'Well, where are you?'

'Heathrow Airport,' she answered.

'Heathrow!' he almost shouted.

'I'm sorry, Jim, I couldn't help it,' she hurriedly cut in. 'When I heard about the explosion I just had to see you, will you come up?'

'Yah, sure I'll be right up,' he replied, still slightly bemused. 'I'll phone Dave and Mary, let them know you're coming down.'

'No! No! Don't do that,' she asked, almost as a plea, 'I'll phone them a little later. You come up and I'll meet you in the Skyways Hotel lounge.'

'Alright, I'll see you in about an hour,' he agreed.

Replacing the phone, Sinclair toyed with the thought of asking the R.S.M. to be excused from the evening's clean up detail, but decided against it in case he was refused, and slipped instead out the front door to his car.

Fingering the car keys he held in one hand, Jim's eyes searched the lounge for Penny. Seeing her sitting alone in a small cluster of easy chairs, he crossed the room returning her smile as their eyes met. She was standing when he reached her, allowing their kiss to be made that much more easily.

'Penny, you're lovely,' whispered Jim, reluctantly pulling away from her intoxicating scent and soft lips, not noticing how deeply her fingers had gripped his arms.

'Do you want another drink?' he asked, pointing to an empty glass on the small table between them as they sat down.

'No,' she shook her head, 'did you?'

'Not really,' he replied looking at his watch; it was almost eight o'clock. 'I thought you would have wanted to get down to the 'Shot' before it gets too late.'

'Jim, I never called Dave and Mary; they don't know I'm here,' she admitted. 'When I heard about the bomb I gave Steven to Mrs. Murdock and caught the first plane I could.'

Jim made no reply as she continued.

'I was afraid. I don't want to lose you. I couldn't stop myself; I had to get across here and be with you.'

Sinclair, reaching out, took her hand with a soothing smile.

'It's not that bad, honey, I don't take chances and I don't go looking for trouble.'

'Jim, you can't bluff me, I know what your job is,' she countered calmly. 'I just wanted us to be together as soon as possible.'

'Do you want to bring the wedding forward?' he asked.

'No, we couldn't change the dates,' she replied, looking down at the hand she held, giving it a light squeeze. 'But we could take the honeymoon early.'

'What do you have in mind?' questioned Sinclair, not knowing whether to smile.

'I've booked a room upstairs, I want us to spend the night together!' Slowly her eyes came up to hold his.

Jim checked his reply for three long seconds. Penny was smartly dressed in a waist length jacket and slacks while he, hardly a hotel guest, was in scruff order of jeans and an old pullover.

'What's the number?'

'I'll show you,' she answered with a pale, but pleased smile, standing to lead him by the hand towards the elevator.

'Alright?' asked Penny, nervously dropping her handbag on a chair as she turned to face Jim, who was closing the door behind them.

'Fine,' replied Sinclair, quietly looking around the room.

'Should we order a meal?' suggested Penny a little timidly.

Jim shook his head.

These circumstances were of Penny's own making. She had hurriedly conceived and implemented this plan to bring her and Jim together for a night alone. But now, here in this bedroom, she was becoming embarrassed with the success of her seduction.

'Jim, I'm sorry about this. You must think I'm an awful tart, but honestly, I've never done this sort of thing before. Neil was the first man I ever slept with. The only reason I brought you here was because that bomb today frightened me. I want to make love to you now, before one of us falls under a bus!'

As Penny finished her confession she turned the palms of her hands upwards in an unconscious request of forgiveness.

The Scotsman, still saying nothing, half turned about to reach back and switch off the light. With the room now dully lit by a crack of light, angling across the floor from an open bathroom door, Jim slowly moved towards the woman he loved so deeply.

'You've done nothing wrong, hen,' he assured her, reaching out to stroke a fold of pale hair that rested against one cheek.

'Like you said, it's just an early honeymoon.'

'Oh, Jim,' she responded with a sigh, throwing both arms around his waist, tucking her head under his chin.

With his hands caressing her back he began to kiss her hair and forehead, working down to her eyes and finally the lips. With his tongue playing about these as they kissed, he eased his hands inside Penny's jacket to slip it off her shoulders and down her arms, letting it fall to the floor. Pulling her close, they kissed while softly whispering their love for each other.

Still holding his lips with hers Penny began to unbutton her blouse, discarding it to join her jacket at their feet. The bra she wore had half cups, exposing the top of her breasts, smooth and milky cream in the restricted light. Jim bent to kiss these and trace them with little strokes of his tongue before working a path of kisses along her shoulders and throat back to her lips. Taking her head in his hands, he ran the silk strands of hair between his fingers as they kissed again.

Despite the warmth of the room Penny began to shiver, a reaction of passion not cold, causing her to fumble as her hands separated the bra strap behind her back, letting it also fall away to the floor. Neither able nor wanting to suppress the sexual desires that surged uncontrolled through her body, she kicked off her shoes and clutched Jim, pressing her bare breasts into the rough wool of his sweater.

Sinclair reacted to this by pulling her even closer for a few seconds then, tearing himself away from the embrace he held her at arm's length. Penny's breasts, showing no slackness from the birth and nursing of her baby son, stood out firm, the nipples aroused and pointing like tiny fingertips, drawing Jim's lips downward. They lingered on the surfaces tasting unseen juices of passion, as he slowly sank to his knees. With hands tracing the curve of her waist he undid the belt of Penny's tight, clinging trousers, sliding them to her feet. Sinclair, now slowly and deliberately transferred his kisses to the flatness of her stomach, her upper legs and peeling her brief panties downwards, the inner V of her legs. As Jim's tongue entered the moistness of Penny's unfolding sensuous lips, he heard a soft cry and an intake of breath. Unconsciously she placed her hands to his head, forcing it closer.

Straightening, Jim found Penny as if drugged, gently swaying, her eyelids half closed, the eyes within slowly revolving unseeing. Triggered by this vision of allurement, stripping his sweater over his head he cast it into the room's darkness and took the woman's hand to lead her across to the bed.

No meal was ordered nor was there sleep for either that night. At six o'clock the following morning they showered together and then parted; Jim returning to Aldershot, Penny on the early flight to Belfast, each taking with them the memory of an interlude that both would cherish to the grave.

*   *   *

The men of Delta Company relaxed in their chairs as Colonel Chuter, entering the briefing room, gave them permission to do so. Removing his beret he placed it on a table, then turning about to face the company he leaned back against it, folding his arms.

'I've called this briefing to pre-empt any out of tune rumours that may start flying about the Battalion,' he began, looking around the men. 'Last week I received a 'phone call from the Commanding Officer of 22 S.A.S. in Hereford. He was requesting assistance very much along the same line as what we did in Borneo: providing back up cover due to over-commitments on their part. This had already been sanctioned by the War Office and Regimental H.Q., so in point of fact I was only being asked if I could provide the men. I told him the company had thinned out of late and was now down to . . .' Chuter pushed himself away from the table to look in a questioning manner into the group of faces, 'twentythree, twentyfour?'

'Twentytwo, counting myself,' obliged Captain Holding, the new O.C. of D Company.

'Well then, low twenties,' emphasised the colonel, holding up a hand in thanks to the other officer. 'This, however, proved not to be a handicap, for the number of men required was only to be about platoon strength anyway,' continued Chuter. 'Being S.A.S. they keep their cards close to their chest so I was told no more on the telephone. But yesterday, having travelled down to Hereford and been given a full briefing, I and Captain Holding are now fully in the picture.' The colonel's eyes began to twinkle. 'But we can tell you very little of it, only what you need to know,' explained Chuter in sly mockery, tapping the side of his nose with a finger.

'What I can do,' he carried on in a raised voice, 'is give you a broad outline as to what will be expected. The location of your activities will be in and with the cooperation of an Arabic country. Your tour is to be six months, of which you will spend all that time within that country or in near proximity to it. The plot is that you will be used only in an instructional capacity, but your patrol company skills will have to be revised and re-adapted just in case.'

The C.O. paused for a moment to let this sink in, then continued in a more serious tone, 'Because of this a training programme, which Captain Holding will go into in more detail in a few moments, has been compiled for the company. This will fully occupy all of you for the next four to six weeks with special emphasis on the medical side and that of your Arabic linguists.

'Well, there you are,' he concluded, informally pushing both hands into his denim pockets. 'There's not much more I can tell you; nevertheless, are there any questions?'

Initially there was silence as everyone mulled over what had just been said.

'Do we have a leaving date, Sir?' asked a voice from the back.

'Yes, but you're not to know it just now,' was the colonel's reply.

'Will we be working with the S.A.S. or on our own, Sir?' asked another.

'Both; they will have overall control of you but I understand it will be on a long leash.'

'I'm due for demob in four months, Sir; does this mean I'm out of it?' asked one of the old sweats of the company.

'No luck, Clarky,' replied Chuter, using the man's nickname, 'all discharges have been frozen until after you return, sorry.'

The colonel showed his sympathy by extending open-palmed hands with a shrug.

However, Clarky did not seem unduly upset at this as he sat back with a smile.

'This place, Sir, is it somewhere we've been before?' asked Johnny Kieran.

'No comment,' was the reply.

'Aden, we're going back into Aden, aren't we, Sir?' spoke up a voice.

Chuter ignored him.

'Is it somewhere in the Gulf, Sir?' piped up another.

At this the colonel brought his phase of the briefing to an end by raising an arm, 'Where is for me to know and you to find out.'

Then picking his beret up to return it to his head, he handed the company over to their O.C., 'Lee, your go now I think.'

'Sit up,' barked Sergeant Major 'Taff' Lewis, standing to attention at the door. With the men sitting bolt upright in their chairs the Commanding Officer, acknowledging Captain Holder's salute, left the room.

Jack Chuter's briefing may have sounded a mite off the cuff but he could be forgiven this for it was not intended to be, but more as an explanation of coming events to a group of men whom he wished to keep fully in the picture. He had initially commanded and trained D Company when it first formed eight years earlier, at which time he had over seventy men, but now through postings, promotion, discharge and casualties they had been depleted to the present number; a hard core clique that refused to die off.

For most of the men he had just addressed, this new assignment was greeted with eager anticipation. With the Battalion increasingly having to allocate more and more of its time to tours in Northern Ireland, the opportunities of serving abroad on exercises and short postings were rapidly diminishing. So this new and adventurous enterprise, shrouded in its secretive introduction, presented an irresistible challenge.

Irresistible for some, but not for all. Pridmore had promised his wife that he would leave the Army when his engagement ran out, which was to have been in a few months time. But now with all discharges cancelled this would have to be postponed. Jim Sinclair took the news with a heavy heart: he and Penny were to be married in a matter of days and he had hoped they would be given the time to settle through the early weeks of their marriage. With her putting up the Belfast house for rent and moving into an Aldershot married quarter, there would be upheaval enough, so with the news that he was about to rush off leaving her very much alone as before, his eagerness to be a part of this coming venture was understandably lukewarm.

Colonel Chuter's withholding of the name of the country or locality that Delta Company would be operating in was justifiably correct, but even he realised its true identity could not be kept secret. The men he had spoken to were not simpletons; they were keen participants of their trade and stayed abreast of all worldwide military events, especially those involving British Forces. Besides from friends and contacts at Hereford, without directly being told, it was not hard to deduce their eventual destination.

*   *   *

The Sultanate of the Oman is a coastal state on the southeast of the Arabian Peninsula, guarding the entrance to the Persian Gulf. Its association with Britain stemmed from a loose alliance that was formed in the days when Napoleonic influence was a threat. The importance since then of this barren stretch of Arabian coast remained nominal until, like its northern neighbours, oil deposits were found which suggested the country was afloat on the stuff.

Another factor even more important was that of geographical location. The northern tip of the Oman jutted out as a blunt peninsula into the straits of Hormuz, narrowing the entrance to the Persian Gulf, the world's supply point for over half its oil, to less than twenty miles. As long as the country was stable and pro-West there was no need for concern over this dominating feature capable of sealing the flow of oil to the free world, but could it remain so?

In the mid-60s, when Britain withdrew from the Aden Protectorate on his Southern border, Siad Bin Taimur, the Sultan of the Oman, governed a society that, with few exceptions was totally biblical. Whereas the Sheikdoms to the north used their oil wealth to benefit their subjects, he disregarded all advice on the expenditure of this revenue, allowing his country and those he ruled to remain gripped in crippling poverty. Nowhere could a visitor look and say that this country was making an attempt to modernise. Agriculture, animal herds, medical facilities, the exploitation of water resources, a liquid even more precious than oil, and schooling were all discouraged or ignored, thus successfully imprisoning the country in a state that was worse than feudal.

Fortunately there was a son, Qaboos, who spent his educative years in Britain, which gave him a broader outlook on the world and attuned him to what his country could achieve with proper use of the oil profits.

However, his dream of this happening was delayed for a number of years, for on returning to the Oman his father, believing him to be tainted by the West, placed him under virtual house arrest. It was not until the summer of 1970 when, through a bloodless coup, his father was deposed, that he succeeded to the throne.

History is logged with uncountable incidents of governmental overthrows that resulted in tyranny and dictatorial injustice but here, at this date and time this was not to be the case.

His Majesty Sultan Qaboos Bin Said proved to be a man of courage, vision and above all a ruler who wished to bring to the subjects of his nation every benefit that the twentieth century could provide. Also from a military standpoint, the young Sultan taking command, like Winston Churchill in 1940, could only be termed as fortuitous.

In the early '60s in the southern province of Dhofar some minor anti-government actions occured involving a number of explosions and harmless sniping. Hardly a rebellion: however, because of hamfisted suppressive retaliations carried out by a Battalion of the Sultan's Army sent to deal with the problem, it did become one.

The Dhofar is unique to the Arabian Peninsula in that it is washed by a monsoon or Khareef for three months of the year. On the coast there are hamlets and towns; the largest Salalah, centred in a rich agricultural garden that once stretched for several miles. However, because of neglect under the old Sultan this was fast becoming a barren waste. Five to seven miles in from the coast rises a plateau that in places, because of the Khareef, is lush with grassy meadows and glens not unlike some found in parts of Britain. These were mostly in the central region but even on the flanks of this narrow one hundred and fifty mile long rib of hills there could be found grass and shrubs for the local tribesmen to graze their heads of cattle and goats. These people were not all of one tribe but several, scattered along the length of the plateau. They did, however, speak the same language, not Arabic but Jebali, which was the name they were known as. This was taken from Jebel, meaning hill, and signified those who lived on the plateau, or hill people. Above the plateau, out of reach of the life-giving rains of the Khareef was a flat, stony, bush and scrub covered terrain known as the Gatn. Sparsely populated, it stretched northward in a downward slope to become the Nego, a burnt out country of sand, boulders and shallow receding wadis, that rolled on until it accepted the embrace of the Empty Quarter, a vast expanse of sand that was the heartland of the Arabian Desert.

When the Sultan's armed forces took reprisals against the Jebalis it was almost certainly members of an innocent tribe, which because, like most hill clansmen—proud men and warriors—the rebellion that never was sparked then burned throughout Dhofar.

It evolved into armed strife between the S.A.F. and a rebel body calling itself the Dhofar Liberation Front. This flared and fired with attacks and ambushes for several years, neither side getting the upper hand. This all changed when Britain left Aden, resulting in the new Marxist state, the People's Democratic Republic of Yemen taking a hand. Training Dhofar tribesmen in Russia and Red China, they formed a communist guerilla force, the People's Front for the Liberation of the Occupied Arabian Gulf. In time, through bribery with money and modern small arms, the D.L.F. joined forces with the P.F.L.O.A.G. but soon regretted it. For the P.F.L.O.A.G., believed that to win the war the Jebalis would first have to be broken of their tribal and religious loyalties. Such a high priority was put on this that if persuasion failed the automatic next step was brutal tortures and executions. These frequently occurred, for to the people of the Dhofar loyalty to tribe and their love of Allah was the bedrock of their society and could never be betrayed. Even so the P.F.L.O.A.G.'s influence became the dominant force on the Jebel, in some instances through armed conflict with the D.L.F. Being simple tribesmen they had seen the danger too late, and by 1970 communist cells and agents were well entrenched in all tribal districts.

For those who did wish to free themselves of the P.F.L.O.A.G. support to do so was becoming harder to gather, for they were winning the war. Under the old Sultan, S.A.F. tactics and manpower had been wholly inadequate, losing control everywhere in the Dhofar except for the province capital town Salalah and few nearby coastal villages. Determined to reverse the situation, Sultan Qaboos, shortly after gaining control of his country, asked Britain for assistance. They, with the pitfalls of Vietnam uppermost in their minds, accepted proposals put forward by the Special Air Service that excluded massive military involvement by the United Kingdom.

Their answer to ending hostilities was a simple one: that of making the tribesmen of the Jebel see that under the new Sultan, life for them would become a more prosperous and healthier one. In peace time this would have been a difficult enough task, but with war raging the hurdles had now increased in number and risen in height.

The S.A.S., although soldiers, were aware that the ending of armed conflict can be achieved in other ways than bludgeoning your enemy to death. This was shown in the sound proposals they had put forward and of their being accepted by the War Office, the sultan, and his advisors.

This called for the development of a formation separate to the S.A.F. but working in cooperation with them. First an intelligence set up had to be established in order to know everything possible about the enemy. Also an information department that could transmit and publish, no matter how hurtful some of this may be, truthful propaganda to the Dhofar tribesmen.

Until now medical cover on the Jebel had been provided by local people with a knowledge of health care that was no better than that of witch doctors. This was also the state of veterinary assistance for livestock, so both fields were highlighted to be dealt with immediately.

Finally, knowing of the brutal methods used by the P.F.L.O.A.G. to convert the Dhofar tribesmen to communism and their clashes with members of D.L.F., a priority was given to recruit Dhofaris who had turned away from the rebellion and persuade them to fight for the Sultan.

The S.A.S., on presenting these proposals which laid out how the winning of the war should be begun, were not surprised when they were themselves told to supply the manpower for making these initial first steps work.

CHAPTER 14

Perplext no more with human or divine,
Tomorrow's tangle to the winds resign.

Omar Khayyam

Releasing their seat belts as the R.A.F. Andover's two whining propeller engines died, D Company picked up their bergens and weapons and filed out onto the runway. Looking around, Jim Sinclair cursed under his breath at the heat as he squinted through the sun's intense glare. Salalah airfield as he had first remembered it from seven years earlier was changed. The first time he had passed through, stopping only to refuel, R.A.F Salalah had been an airstrip controlled from a portable caravan and staffed with only a handful of Airforce personnel. Now everywhere there were accommodation billets and huts, vehicle parks, a control tower, fuel and ammunition bunkers, in fact the complete logistic and administrative facilities necessary to an airfield on a front line war footing.

Parked beside the runway were several types of aircraft. Four Strikemasters, the Sultan's Armed Forces fighter ground attack jets, two chunky Skyvan transports and a number of medium-sized helicopters.

Southward beyond Salalah town the sea could be seen standing out, a deep opal blue, whilst above it stretching away to the four horizons was a sky, also blue, though a paler one, and empty of clouds for the Khareef was some weeks away yet. Inland, the Qara Hills, the Jebel, visible through a rippling, early summer heat haze could be seen rising above the coastal plain. One look at this line of hills that faded away down both coasts was all D Company needed to see why the war was progressing at such a sluggish pace. From its heights not only the movements of aircraft and vehicles could clearly be seen, but also that of individuals travelling on foot over most parts of the coastal low country. No doubt at this very moment their stroll towards a waiting four-tonner on the edge of the airfield's peri track was being noted by someone posted above them on the crown of the escarpment.

Captain Holding and an S.A.S. Major, their reception, exchanged greetings and introductions as the men clambered up into the back of the open truck. With the two officers leading in a Landrover, the Company followed them through the perimeter wire, away from the town and across the plain to a small compound area. Enclosed was a newly erected building and several tents, this was Batt. H.Q.

The British Army Training Team was the title given to the body formed to implement the S.A.S.'s original five point proposal plan. Of those working under this all-embracing name were of course the S.A.S. themselves but in the two years since its formation many others had been incorporated. Doctors and medical staff both civil and military, could be found administering to the population wherever it was safe to do so. Also, engineers working on improving roads and water supplies, and vets tending to the local livestock. Not so evident were the propaganda and intelligence branches, but both had proven successful and were steadily expanding.

In apparent disregard of the fact that the midday temperature was hovering around the 120 Fahrenheit mark, hot tea was the refreshment offered prior to an update briefing.

It was the S.A.S. Major who gave the briefing. Guy McAllister, tall, blond, with a lean but iron frame, was the O.C. of the squadron D Company would be relieving. He, with the aid of a wall map and a great deal of first hand knowledge, explained what had been done, what was being done and what was hoped to be done in the future. At the end of this the Paras sitting in their sweat-stained, olive-green cotton uniforms, knew as much about the way the war was being conducted as security would allow.

Lunch was served to all ranks in the adjoining dining tent, eaten from individual mess tins. Finishing his meal, Jim Sinclair looked up to see Captain Holding approaching his table in the company of a man with dark brown hair, wearing like them, O.G.s, but sun-bleached and well-worn.

'Sergeant Sinclair, this is Corporal Hitchman. He's in charge of the Batt. team you'll be relieving,' announced the captain.

'Oh aye,' greeted the Scot, standing up to extend his hand.

'Hello Sarg, have a good trip out?' enquired Hitchman in a soft easy manner that Sinclair took to straight away.

Having married up the two commanders Captain Holding, promising to get out to his new location within the next few days, left them to deal with other matters.

'Look,' began the sergeant, brushing aside any formal barriers, 'we're not all that keen on rank when out in the field, it tends not to wash when there's a job on. You can call me Jim. What do they call you?'

'Terry,' smiled back the corporal.

'Right Terry, well this is the rest of the patrol,' continued Sinclair, pointing around the table and introducing Mick Pridmore, Reg Berrill, 'Yorky' Rush and Johnny Kieran.

Sitting for the next half hour over a mug of tea the six men got to know each other. The Paras asking questions and the S.A.S. corporal answering them with much additional information.

The post that Terry Hitchman and his three men had been assigned to was a small fishing village called Habahn, about twentyfive miles to the west. Their role was that of training the local militia, providing a medical service and, by their presence, to boost morale. Six months earlier this village had been in P.F.L.O.A.G. control, the villagers having to feed and shelter any bands coming down off the Jebel, who staged their patrols and attacks through them. But with a build up of the S.A.S. in the Salalah area, and their operations extending further and further along both coasts, the scrubland was now proving to be too dangerous for roving enemy units to operate in.

What had been hoped for when Hitchman and his party were first stationed in Habahn was, that like in other parts of the region, their presence would attract enough disheartened Qarra Hill tribesmen to form a Firqat. This was the name given to a body of Dhofaris who had changed sides to fight for the Sultan, normally from thirty to seventy strong. A number of these, although regarded with suspicion by most ranks of the S.A.F. had been operating with great success over the last eighteen months from Batt. locations spread throughout the fringes of the Jebel. But as yet only two men had come into Habahn to pledge their allegiance to the new Government.

Taking their leave of Batt. H.Q., Jim and his men collected their weapons, ammunition and extra gear to follow Terry Hitchman across the compound yard to a pinkish coloured, long wheel base Landrover. Resting with his back against one wheel sheltering from the sun, squatted an Omani. Holding a bolt action .303 Lee Enfield rifle upright before him, he watched as the party of pale, untanned Europeans came towards him. Only when the S.A.S. corporal began to introduce the Paras did he rise to acknowledge their presence with a stony nod of his head. His body was thin, appearing to be constructed solely of bone and muscle, with deep mohogany brown skin that had a natural sheen. Wearing no headdress, he secured his long hair by wrapping a thin rope tightly around his head. He was dressed in a kahki army shirt, sandals and around his waist a dark plaid futa, a thin cotton kilt-like skirt.

Hitchman, in a mixture of Arabic and Jebali, explained who the new arrivals were. Jim Sinclair strained to follow what was being said, for he, along with Rush, had been trained as linguists. But from what he heard of the conversation, he realised he was going to suffer problems of misunderstanding because of slang and awkward dialectical pronunciations.

The Omani's name was Mohammad Kabina, and he was not a true Jebali but came from a plains tribe who lived at the mouths of several of the wadis which scarred the south face of the Qara Hills. Because of the war these tribesmen had been forced to work with and support P.F.L.O.A.G., but for some reason Mohammad had left his home to fight for the other side.

Loading ammunition and spare kit into the back of the rover, they hung their bergens over the sides by the shoulder straps. Then, with Hitchman driving and Jim in the passenger seat, they set off westward along a dusty track.

Ten miles on at Rayzut, a large coastal village, they swung down onto the beach to speed along the packed, damp sand, between the surf and the bleached white dunes.

'Mines,' shouted Hitchman to Sinclair as they raced along the sloping shore. 'The Adoo plant them on all the tracks and likely routes, but down here the tide leaves them exposed.'

Adoo meant enemy and was used to embrace both P.F.L.O.A.G. and D.L.F.

Another ten miles and they had to slow down to weave cautiously between fishermen's nets and small boats, drawn onto the beach, as they passed a second village. When they were once again in top gear, a miniature Beau Geste fort, five miles away on a point of rocky land that blocked the beach, came into view. This fort had been built by the Portuguese some time in the fifteenth century when they were establishing themselves in India, just across the Arabian Sea. To the rear of this, hugging the shore, was a cluster of about fifty houses and huts. The houses were square, brown stone structures with shuttered, glassless windows, most of them two storeys high.

Racing up a small sandy re-entrant, they drove through the village, putting copper-coloured chickens to flight while passing ragged but smiling children at play. Women, dressed in black, loose-fitting, cotton robes from head to toe, watched them silently from behind veils or Birqa leather masks.

210

As they skirted the east wall of the fort, a guard, armed with a Lee Enfield, could be seen sitting on a stool at the closed front gate. In front of him, just off to one side of the stone-surfaced entrance road, was an American 106 millimetre recoiless gun mounted in a sandbagged sangar.

The journey's end was a corrugated tin building, two hundred yards west and in front of the fort. It was a wierd structure, but one plainly erected for defence. The first five feet was sandbagged, with a pillbox guarding the front door. On the roof, which was also sandbagged, was an enclosed observation post with its own layers of sandbags protecting all sides.

Coming to a halt, a sign could be seen nailed above the doorway which read 'Batt. Shack'. Below this appeared a stocky, red-headed man, wearing only kahki shorts and sandals. He walked out to greet them.

'Dinner guests, Terry?' he asked with a smile.

'This is Frank McGibbon, our 'Sparks',' explained Hitchman, climbing from the cab while waving a hand at the Paras.

'If you want to know their names, Frank, you'd better ask them, I've forgotten.'

After removing all the kit from the Landrover into the building, they were offered a powdered lemonade drink by the other two men of Hitchman's team, Gary Teal and a Scotsman, Gordon Hunt.

The interior was spacious, functional and untidy. At one end of the single oblong room was a sleeping area, with camp beds and boxes of ammunition stacked in one corner. In the centre of the room, opposite the entrance, was a six foot folding table with two benches. On the facing wall, make-shift shelves filled with bottles, bandages and other medical stores had been fixed with nails and wire to the inner woodwork.

At the other end of the room were two more tables with three of four chairs. On one of these tables was a battery operated radio for keeping in contact with Batt. H.Q. while the other, with a wall map above it, looked like an operation's desk. With reed matting for a floor, bits of clothing and equipment hanging on the walls and lines of nylon cord stretched across the room it would hardly have passed an Aldershot room inspection. But then that was not the priority. This locaton was stripped for action; not one article of kit nor single sandbag was surplus to requirement.

The next hour was spent by everyone relaxing in the room, exchanging questions and answers. Joining them, after brief introductions, to sit drinking sweet black tea that Frank McGibbon brewed for them, were Mohammad Kabina and his companion Murad Areeb.

Murad, a young man probably not twenty, was a true Jebali whose tribe lived high in the hills. Goat and cattle herds of his tribe grazed the land on the boundary of the Great Gatn watershed.

Although his hair was also long, he kept it in place with a Shamag, a broad wrap-around head cloth. The features of the two men were not significant to the newcomers. Not until they had spent several days in the district would they be able to identify individuals to their race.

Mohammad Kabina, a plains Dhofari was of Arabic stock, which his prominent hooked nose showed, as were the majority of the people of the Oman. Murad, however, was a contrast; his ancestors arriving many centuries earlier from the northwest African coast to settle in the Qara Hills. Remaining in apparent seclusion, free from cross breeding, most still retained their darker ancestral features.

Reg Berrill accepted both men on the simplest of terms, in admiration; to him they were Indian scouts.

After the evening meal, an all-in stew concocted from a number of compo ration tins, the men, aided by a single paraffin lamp, paired off with their opposite number to discuss the grass roots of their jobs.

Mick Pridmore was in command of the patrol, relieving Terry Hitchman. But as this area was due for firmer consolidation by the Sultan's Army, Jim Sinclair was given a new appointment as co-ordinator.

As, one by one, the late evening claimed people in sleep, the lamp was extinguished leaving one man on sentry-cum-radio watch. The first on stag was Terry Hitchman, who was joined by Jim Sinclair to share the warm desert breezes and the brightness of the moonlight as each entered the room through large, bare windows.

'I'll take you up to meet the old Sheikh tomorrow,' said the corporal, offering Jim a cigarette. 'He's the gaffer around here and has the final say in everything.'

'Is he a government man?' asked the Scot.

'Well,' replied Hitchman, making a face, 'he was, under the old Sultan, but when P.F.L.O.A.G. was running loose around here no one bumped him off, and now we're back with the new Sultan in charge he's still up in that little fort of his. I don't think he's a rogue, just foxy. When trouble started brewing he sent his two eldest sons up into the gulf somewhere, Bahrain I think, and he hasn't sent for them yet.'

'What you think of him?' asked Sinclair, wanting to know more about the man he was to meet the following day.

'I like the old buzzard,' replied Hitchman, tapping the ash of his cigarette into a compo tin ashtray. 'There's a section of Omani soldiers stationed in his fort and we use some of his people as village militia, but he hasn't openly declared for the Sultan. We can't blame him for that though; if he did there's a good chance some of his flock in the village would get their throats cut.'

'Even with us here?' ventured the sergeant.

'Oh ya, we're nowhere near beating these cunts yet and we won't, not until S.A.F. can get up on the Jebel and stay there.'

'How do you mean?' asked Sinclair.

'As you know, all our troops are down here on the coast, while the Adoo hold all the hills and until just lately most of the plain as well. Hell, Jim,' he emphasised with a chuckle, 'they were using this place for their R and R. Six months ago it was being run like a Butlins Holiday Camp.'

'No,' continued Hitchman after Sinclair had stopped laughing, 'it's going to be a tough nut to crack. Guns and ammunition are coming up from Aden all the time. They got caves up there chock-full of the stuff and just across the border at Hauf they got a training camp.'

'What about the people?' cut in the Scotsman, 'are they backing this rebellion?'

'Some,' pondered the corporal, 'but a lot would like to jack. The commies have really screwed it up. Mao, in his little red book, says a guerilla army should be the friends of the peasants, but these blokes really got it all ass backwards. They roam around up there like Nazi stormtroopers.'

Hitchman paused, puckering his lips before continuing.

'You see our two lads, Mohammad and Murad Areeb,' he waved a hand in the direction of their tent, 'they used to be Adoo. Mohammad came into us a couple of months ago after his father and uncle died when they were forced to lie on fire-heated rocks for refusing to stop praying each day. Murad came down off the Jebel after killing some commie bastard who raped his thirteen year old sister.'

'Can they be trusted?' asked Jim.

'Yup! Their stories were confirmed by Salalah. All they want to do is get up onto the Plateau and kill Adoo.'

The corporal began to grin.

'Yah know, that was the first question they asked me.'

Sinclair looked puzzled, not knowing what he meant.

'Could they trust you, it's your red berets you see. They know us but you and your lads will have to prove to them you're pukka gen.'

*   *   *

Early the next morning as a bright red sun was just beginning to show itself above the Jebel, Johnny Kieran and Mick Pridmore, the two medically-trained Paras were taken into the village by Gordon Hunt, the S.A.S. medic, to be shown how he ran his daily surgery. Carrying rifles and medical packs, they set off across the sand, skirting the northern side of the fort.

'You'll find this place is minging,' informed Hunt to the other two, warning them what to expect, 'the people are pretty gungy as well. Water is the thing, around here you drink it, not wash with the stuff. You won't find a toilet here either; most shit and piss in the sea, but if they're away from the beach they just squat down and crap in the sand, then leave it for the shit beetles. The shit beetles are the best thing going, they make it into a ball and just roll it away with them.'

In the centre of the village they halted outside several drab shops and stalls. Cloth awnings propped on poles shaded the owners and their goods, but were scant deterrant to the flies that swarmed around the dates, sweet meats and skinned goat carcase that hung in what passed as the local butcher's shop.

'It's not much,' explained Hunt, 'but this is the Souk; means market place.'

In front of these shops was a queue of about twenty men, women and children, sitting in the square of dirty sand that opened out towards the eastern shore. Put out beforehand for the medic's use was a stool and a low, grime-blackened wooden box.

'My office,' declared Hunt. Then, with a smile to the line of villagers, he exchanged greetings in Arabic.

'Salaam.'

'Ahlan Sahib,' chorused the men, the women remaining silent.

Sitting on the stool, he invited the first patient to come forward. Being a Moslem country, the queue was ranged in seniority which meant that men would be seen first. The 'inferior' women and children would have to wait.

The man he beckoned was greeted by Hunt using his first name. Sitting him on the box, his shirt was removed and he turned about so the Scotsman could examine his back. There he had three large bandages secured by elastoplasts. Peeling an edge back from each Hunt tore them sharply from his back, the Arab not batting an eye.

'This fella has bad boils. I lanced them a few days ago and told him to come back today to have the dressings changed,' he informed the other two. He handed the Arab to Pridmore to deal with, saying, 'Mick, take him to one side, clean them up and re-dress them.'

The next man complained of headaches and difficulty in breathing for which Hunt, after looking him over and taking his pulse, prescribed codeine tablets.

'From what he says I think he may be bad, but I wouldn't even begin to know what,' he confessed to the other medics.

'What do you do then?' asked Kieran.

'Sit on it, wait for the Doc up in Salalah to drop around. That's about once a month and that's not slouching. They work bloody hard. There's just not that many of them yet.'

With the men seen to, a boy of about ten limped up to show the three men a deep, sand-filled, blood-weeping gash in the sole of one foot.

'When did you do this, my little fisherman?' asked Hunt in Arabic.

'Yesterday, Sahib,' replied the boy who, obviously in pain, had not once ceased smiling.

'Why didn't you come and see me at Batt.?' asked the Scot, angry but not showing it.

'I did not think it so important to trouble the Sahib.'

'In future everyone with injuries like this will come to Batt. Promise me you'll tell them to do this,' ordered Hunt.

The boy, still smiling, nodded his head.

'Johnny,' he asked the Irishman, 'take this lad to the beach and wash the clag out of that cut with sea water. Then bring him back; we'll have to take him up to the shack, stitch it up and give him a penicillin shot.'

Dealing with women at the tail end of the queue, Gordon explained to Mick that they could only examine the children whom the women brought. To touch them was forbidden. Even just to accidentally glimpse under one of their veils or Birqas would seriously jeopardise the men's acceptance by the villagers.

The last woman to be seen sat on the box balancing an infant on her lap. A young boy explained for her that the child, a girl, was supposed to be having an illness of the tummy.

Hunt, giving her a spoonful of sugared water, began subtly to administer to the real reason for the visit. While holding the child up, the woman had allowed the cloth covering her right arm to drop to the elbow showing a large area of her forearm to be burnt.

Over the next fifteen minutes, explaining to and with the use of the youth's hands, the Scot was able to clean and dress the wound.

'She should be seen to at the clinic in Salalah,' he pointed out to Mick in a frustrated tone, 'but the husband would never let her go. The women are expected to work no matter what state they're in. That's why we have to hold sick parade so early, so we can catch them before they get involved in the day's toil.'

Finished, with the young boy with the cut foot perched piggy back on Johnny Kieran's shoulders, the three soldiers returned to Batt., leaving the village stench behind them.

*   *   *

'Can any of your lads fire that gun?' asked Terry Hitchman, stopping to point to the 106 gun.

'Yah, Mick said he used to fire them when he first joined 5 Para,' replied Jim Sinclair, eyeing the long black barrel sitting on its mount in the sangar.

'Good, that could come in handy,' commented the S.A.S. corporal.

'It was sent down from Salalah as a present from the Sultan, but no one knew how to shoot it. Then an officer on secondment to the Northern Frontier Regiment turned up and told us it won't fire properly until we get ammunition for the spotting rifle, .5, I think he said.'

'Looks good though, doesn't it?' joked Jim, as he followed the other man up the sloping approach to the fort gate.

Exchanging brief greetings with the sentry, they entered the fort. Because the two large, weathered wooden doors were almost always kept closed, this had to be done by bending to step through a small hatchway set in one of the larger doors. An ancient adaptation that always presented any unwanted visitor's neck for instant decapitation.

The interior of the fort was a courtyard with accommodation for servants and a small garrison to the left and right. Above this a parapet ran around the inside of all four walls. Hitchman, without pausing, led the way across the stone surface of the courtyard to the Sheikh's apartments.

Leaving their rifles in the hall, they were shown into a reception room by a grey-bearded retainer, where Sheikh Zayid Bin Al Kamam rose from a European-style desk to greet them. Dressed simply in a plain white robe, he exchanged greetings in Arabic with the S.A.S. corporal. After Jim had been introduced, Sheikh Zayid invited them to sit cross legged around a low, dark teak table.

'You will have coffee, gentlemen?' he asked, which Sinclair understood but before either could reply he tapped the table twice with a ring he wore on his little finger. This summoned the old greybeard who, understanding what was wanted, left again.

For some minutes pleasantries were exchanged regarding health, the heat of the day and speculation on when the Khareef would arrive. It was not until the coffee was being sipped that the conversation came around to the reason for the visit.

'Will you be staying with us long, sergeant?' asked Bin Al Kamam.

'Until Ramadan I believe, Sir,' replied Sinclair, not sure of the date but understanding it to be during their holy fast period just before Christmas.

'And Coporal Hitchman, you will be leaving us shortly?'

'Yes, Sir, shortly,' answered the S.A.S. man, not giving a precise day.

There was silence as the Sheikh raised his glass to his lips and sipped its dark liquid.

Terry Hitchman had referred to him as 'the old buzzard', but Jim would not have placed his age beyond fifty. His hair, although greying, was neatly trimmed very much as a European, as was his beard, which, combined with a long straight nose, gave him a dignified appearance.

'Tell me, Sergeant,' he began, placing his glass on the table and fixing Jim with a warm look, through dark eyes which seemed to probe Jim's very mind. 'You and your men are not from the same regiment as Major McAllister's?'

Terry had been right about this man; he was a fox. D Company had stripped their uniforms of all badges of rank and wings, and on arriving at Salalah had put their berets away to replace them with peeked camouflage caps. In this way they had followed the S.A.S.'s example in making themselves unidentifiable. But somehow their host had learned that the new soldiers would possibly not be of the same high calibre as those who had first been sent to assist in the defence of his district.

'Yes, that's right sir, I and my men are from an Infantry Parachute Battalion,' admitted Sinclair honestly, holding the older man's gaze.

'And this Battalion, have you served with it in this part of the world before?'

inquired Bin Al Kamam, lifting one arm to rotate the wrist in small circles.

'Yes sir, in the mountains of the Radfan and during our withdrawal from Aden.' Jim kept his reply simple and his jaw set.

'I see,' he replied, pondering this for a moment before continuing. 'There is as island some distance from Aden called Muktra. A far removed cousin of mine is the Sultan of this island. Would you possibly have heard of it?'

Terry Hitchman looked at Jim out of the corner of his eye, lost to the reason for the question.

'Yes, sir,' replied the Scotsman without hesitation, 'I have had the pleasure of meeting Sultan Haushabi during a brief visit to the island.'

Except for a few moments discussing the possible conclusion of the war, their conversation for the remainder of this informal audience no longer touched on military matters.

'What the hell was all that island bit about, Jim? The old boy had me lost,' asked Hitchman as they left the fort.

'Five or six years ago that bloke's cousin was about to have his head lopped off when me and the rest of D Company jumped in and saved his bacon,' replied Jim, shifting his rifle to the crook of one arm with a smile.

'Small world this isn't it?'

*   *   *

Their bodies not yet acclimatised, over the next three days the five Paras retreated during the midday hours into the shack to ease their discomfort in the room's cooling shade. There to fill the time they either dozed or got on with any work that could be done indoors. One such job was supervised by Gary Teal, the team's explosives and weapons man.

The S.A.S., expected as a matter of course to be able to deal with any task thrown their way, had more or less an open cheque book when it came to indenting for weapons. One they requested, almost as soon as the Americans had issued it to their own troops, was the M79 grenade launcher. This was similar to the baton gun used in Ulster, but instead of firing rubber bullets or smoke canisters it could send an explosive round larger than a golf ball out beyond 300 metres. As tools of the trade go, this was a welcome addition of fire power by any soldier's standards. However, the S.A.S., exponents of weapon versatility, devised an added characteristic for this weapon.

By removing the explosive projectile from its cartridge case and filling the empty space with wax moulded nuts, nails, bolts, ballbearings or what-have-you, the weapon became a deadly anti-personnel shot gun.

*   *   *

On the morning of the fourth day, the Habahn Batt. Team had visitors.

'Chopper coming, Frank,' called Reg Berrill to McGibbon after acknowledging the radio call that had just come in.

'Right,' replied the S.A.S. man, dropping the jerry can he had just carried from the Landrover after fetching water from the village well, a quarter of a mile away. 'I'll tell Terry and Jim; they're on their way up from the beach now.'

Amid a swirl of sand, dust and twigs, the helicopter settled on the open ground between the Fort and Batt. Before the blades had stopped turning Guy McAllister and Captain Holding were running from it in a crouch, clutching their caps in one hand, rifles in the other. Slowing to an upright walking pace they were met by Jim Sinclair and Terry Hitchman.

'Hello, Corporal Hitchman,' called the major, 'how are your new lodgers settling in?'

'They've complained about the maid service, Sir,' answered Hitchman with a grin.

'And the floor tiles in the bathroom are cold on the feet,' added Sinclair, also grinning.

'Okay, good, good,' replied McAllister smiling, going straight on to explain one of the reasons for their visit. 'I'm just taking Captain Holding up to meet Sheikh Zayid. We'll be back shortly. See the pilot has a cup of tea or something.'

On their return everyone relaxed in the shack with mugs of tea while discussing the location's problems. On being asked his, Jim could only reiterate points that he knew had been raised by the S.A.S. Team before his arrival: that of regular doctor's visits for the villagers, and the provision of a hygienic well head from which water could be pumped, rather than the rope and bucket job that was being used at the moment.

Receiving a hopeful reply, the sergeant sat quiet as Mick Pridmore asked about tracer ammunition for the anti-tank gun.

Once everyone had had their say, McAllister announced to the small gathering the main purpose of the visit.

'Tomorrow night we're all going up onto the Jebel. The Ints. people at Salalah have turned up the information that an arms cache is to be found in an isolated village to the north.'

Letting this sink in, he stood up to move across to the wall map.

'Normally I wouldn't have sanctioned this Op, being so high up in the Jebel, but what makes it tempting is the escarpment route you and Mohammad recced the other week.' The major paused to look at Terry Hitchman. Then with the point of a biro he indicated their positions. 'Here's your route up off the plain and the village is just about there.'

The room's stillness was broken as men stood up for a better view.

'We'll be going up in support of a company of the Musket Regiment. So, as you can see,' he went on, again pointing with the biro 'by using any of the usual tracks up onto the plateau by way of the wadis, there would not be enough time to get there and cordon the village before dawn.'

McAllister stopped to look around the room twirling the pen in his fingers.

'I will brief you all fully here late tomorrow afternoon, when I and Captain Holding arrive with the company of M.R.s. Any questions?'

'How gen is this info, Sir?' asked Gary Teal.

'It's hot from S.A.F. They seem keen to act on it,' was the reply.

'Corporal Hitchman, don't tell either of your two scalp hunters about this just now. I want you to work out a safe route from here to the escarpment, where we can pick up that pathway you recceed. Then, on my arrival tomorrow you, I, Mohammad and Murad will go over the whole journey, there and back, looking at alternative routes as well.'

'This is to be an M.R. show, everything at the village is their responsibility. Our job is to get them up and back again.'

Finishing, McAllister returned the biro to the table.

The next day a normal routine was kept to, in order not to let on to the villagers that anything out of the ordinary was in the offing. Shortly after four o'clock six Beford lorries arrived with the Musket Company and the two Batt. officers. The vehicles hardly let their wheels stop turning, for once the Omani soldiers had de-bused they returned to Salalah by way of the beach, not scheduled to re-collect for thirtysix hours.

As a deception plan to cover this sudden arrival of almost a hundred armed soldiers, tents that had been brought along were erected and fires lit, hoping to give the impression that the troops had come to occupy the town for a period of time. Soon after dark, with the two Batt parties in the lead, the mixed force set out north in single file towards the high Jebel skyline silhouetted in the evening dusk.

For two hours the company group filed silently over the broken ground, crossing shallow gullies and wadis, picking their way around clumps of scrub and camel thorn bushes. A large body of men moving in single file, they had to walk with restraint and patience because of the unexplainable phenomenon that when the front man walks at a brisk pace those at the rear have to run to keep up.

Unexpectedly, for the darkness had shrouded it, after covering five miles or so, they suddenly halted at the foot of the Jebel escarpment. Here they waited for almost half an hour as Terry Hitchman and Mohammad scouted out the approach to the trail which would lead them upwards.

The route was little more than a goat trail, twisting and turning in sharp switch-backs as it steadily crept up the face of the rocky slope. Progress was slow as each man made sure of his footing with every upward step, for being only a few degrees off the designation of cliff, a slip could result in a rather longish tumble.

Despite its ponderous pace the climb was nevertheless a hard one. Time and time again Jim Sinclair had to pull his mind away from the constant gnawing pain in his back and calves to stay alert.

At last a halt was signalled down the column, as once more Hitchman and Mohammad stalked forward to make sure the crest of the escarpment was not picquetted. Continuing through the small hours of the morning, the march, though not that much quicker than the climb, was at least easier on the legs. The ground, now only sloping, was near the lip of the Jebel, patchy with loose stony soil and low bushes. Then, surprisingly, the further they climbed the more un-Arabian the country became. Bushy thickets gave way to, at first, small clearings of grass and clumps of trees, then eventually to wide lush meadows. It did not have to be daylight for the Paras to understand why the Jebalis had settled in, and now jealously defended, this garden of Eden.

Dropping down into a basin between two shoulders of the spur they had been paralleling there was another stop, upon which Major McAllister, Captain Holding and the two Dhofars went into a huddle. Breaking apart, the major, in a whispered voice, called the company commander forward using his hand-portable National radio.

The company commander, like most officers in the Omani Army, was British; this one a Royal Marine Commando major. These officers served under two categories; those like he, seconded from the British Forces, and others on contract to the Sultan. The latter may sound as if they were mercenaries, but this was not the case; they were well vetted and of a high calibre.

Quickly confirming their position and the locaton of the village, the company was led off by Murad and the S.A.S. party to lay a cordon. Platoon by platoon, they filed through on their way to the far shoulder to circle the village at its base with stealth and silence, essential ingredients in making this work. Just the slightest hint of what was happening before the trap was closed could mean the Adoo's escaping with their arms cache, or inflicting casualties on the encircling troops.

Being left as the rear protection party Jim, Mohammad and the other three D Company men (Reg Berrill having been left at Habahn to watch the shop), settled down to wait for dawn.

The high-summer nights they had spent at sea level were warm throughout, but here on the Jebel it was different. At almost three thousand feet the pre-dawn chill was causing the Paras to shiver and one by one they took their smocks from their bergens.

With a dull eastern glow rapidly brightening and expanding to full daylight, a search party was sent into the village, only to find it empty. Gary Teal, with an effortless jog, arrived to inform them of this and to move their position to somewhere where they could not be so overlooked. Jim, the new boy in Jebel tactics, took no chances and asked Mohammad for his advice. Studying the rim of the basin he pointed towards a cluster of boulders in the direction they had entered.

The choice showed Sinclair that his decision to ask someone with local knowledge was the right one. From the protection of the boulders they had an almost unrestricted view in all directions. To the east and west the plateau rolled away into the distance, while above them to the north was a clear view of the stony infertile Gatn. Behind them could be seen the sea, its shore line and the fort standing in a rosy haze from the weakened rays of the morning sun. Below, less than a quarter of a mile away, the village was now visible. Seven or eight huts constructed by erecting a circular stone wall three or four feet high, with a rounded roof of branches and turf.

Pairing up with one man watching while the other brewed tea for both, the next half hour was spent idly enjoying the increasing warmth of the sun.

An interruption to this occurred when Johnny Kieran, ducking his head below the boulder he was behind, called a warning.

'Jim, there's some people moving way out on that hillside to the west.'

'Where?' asked Sinclair, scrambling across to peer over the boulder.

Seeing nothing with the naked eye, he lifted his binoculars to scan the hillside Kieran was pointing at.

'Got them,' he declared, freezing the binos.

Six or seven figures had crossed the skyline two miles away and were walking in a single file, diagonally downhill in their direction.

Sensing Mohammad at his side, the sergeant passed the glasses to him.

His identification of them was brief. 'Adoo,' he said without lowering the binoculars.

For Jim he need say no more; snapping up his National he informed Company H.Q. This brought the Marine O.C., McAllister and Holding doubling up to their O.P. Post.

Explaining what had been seen, a revised plan was hastily worked out for laying an ambush, or as the Marine officer put it, 'can't have the boys going back empty handed; they'd sulk for weeks.'

When the officers left, having told the sergeant and his party to sit tight, Sinclair asked Mohammad, 'Is this a good plan?'

'No, we should leave now,' was the blunt reply, not taking his eyes off the surrounding terrain. Again he was proven right, for an hour later he had everyone clutching their rifles in alarm.

'Adoo! Adoo!'

From a thicket on the brow of a hill, a mile south, several armed men had just raced into the cover of a depression in the ground.

'Christ, they're behind us,' exclaimed Yorky Rush.

As Sinclair informed Company H.Q. of this, another large group of men could be seen stationing themselves on the edge of the thicket itself.

'The next time we come up here I'm bringing a fucking Gimpy,' stated Mick Pridmore dryly, voicing everyone's desire for a weapon that could reach out a bit further than their rifles.

Within minutes of their warning being passed, the Omani soldiers could be seen scurrying from hides and cover to regroup into their sections and platoons. In tactical bounds they gathered together as a company on the side of the basin below the Para's boulders.

On being recalled Captain Holding took them in tow, leading everyone to the head of the company, giving a briefing on the move outlining what was now to take place.

'It looks like we've been rumbled. Can't afford to be pinned down. We're pulling out to the east. Major McAllister says Mohammad can guide us out. It's a long route but should be the safest.' Then addressing the Dhofar plainsman in Arabic he asked 'Can you lead us to flat rock above Wadi Aybat?'

Giving an affirmative reply, he pointed in the direction of a high hill below a sun that was now well above the horizon.

After a hurried request by radio to move, the captain's men set off. Acting as a point section they shook out into a loose arrow head. Behind them the Musket Company followed in file formation, two lines of men in a crocodile.

Major McAllister and his S.A.S. party stationed themselves close up behind, acting as a rear guard. This was not the best deployment to adopt in semi-open country like what they were in, but with the Adoo making steps to surround and cut them off, speed overrode caution.

The journey in distance could not have been all that far. However, the need to conceal their presence made the march, in regards to time, a lengthy one. Villages had to be widely skirted, water holes and grazing pastures avoided, with many pauses sheltering out of sight in scrub thickets and bushes. They had now become fugitives in a hostile land.

Tense but uneventful, they arrived at their destination in the late afternoon. Reaching the lip of a wadi, perhaps two hundred yards across, Mohammad turned south to follow it for another half mile. Sweating from the exertion of increasing his pace, Major McAllister caught them up just as Mohammad brought the Paras to a halt.

'Lee,' he directed Captain Holding, 'we're going down onto the wadi bed; Mohammad will show you where and how. Once we are all down we'll have a rest and something to eat, then push on, and we should reach the mouth of the wadi just after dark.'

Mohammad, moving to the edge of the wadi, across which could be seen a weather-smoothed rock the size of a garden shed with a prominent flat crown, stepped down into thick brush. Jim Sinclair, following, could not make out a path, only a gap in the jungle-tight foliage that suddenly closed around him.

The wadis of the Qara Hills mostly began high in the Gatn watershed. Starting as a gravel ditch, but soon cutting deep into the surface of the plateau landscape, they ran for its full width to end with open mouths gaping into the plain. During the wet Khareef months all the water from the Jebel drained into these wadis to flow away as rivers, streams or mere trickles. This abundance of moisture nurturing the steep wadi sides caused plants, shrubs and bushes to grow with the closeness of a vast hedgerow.

Reaching the boulder-strewn wadi floor, Jim wondered at Mohammad's ability to navigate his way down. As it was most arrived badly scratched, with torn clothes from the sharp branches and thorns that clawed their every step. It took the company longer than Major McAllister would have liked for everyone to assemble in the wadi, and longer still to have a meal. All the men, both Omani and British, were tired and moved sluggishly; it had been a hard night and day.

Again, with the light dimming, for night comes quickly in the wadi depths, the Paras, following in single file behind Mohammad, set off at the head of the Company for Habahn. Picking their way along the uneven surface while remaining vigilant for a possible ambush was a laborious, time-consuming task, which soon caused them to be caught in the wadi's night time tunnel blackness. Progress then became even more ponderous, with feet feeling for balance at every step.

Sinclair, with Mohammad only a few feet in front of him, suddenly noticed the man had frozen in his tracks, looking to the left.

Nearing its entrance the floor of the wadi had broadened with the sides steeper and thinning of vegetation. The point Mohammad was watching twenty yards away had a darker shade to it which Jim, straining his eyes, defined as the mouth of a smaller branch wadi.

Without warning the flash and sound of a burst of automatic rifle-fire exploded from this entrance. Mohammad instinctively threw himself to the ground.

The Paras, like the S.A.S., had brought with them, stowed in their bergens, the M79 Grenade launcher. As soon as it had turned dark the four men, slinging their rifles over their shoulders, armed themselves with the shorter barreled, single-shot weapon.

Now, with bullets pinging off the stony wall behind them, all four weapons were raised into the aim and fired as one. The crashing volley of scrap metal from their home-made rounds resulted for a moment in total silence. Then the sounds of scurrying were heard as the ambushers fled back into the minor wadi.

Picking himself up off the gravel Mohammad was the first to move forward. With rifles now in their hands, the Paras followed him, while Captain Holding sent a contact report back to Company H.Q., strung further up the wadi bed. Covering each other as they moved, Pridmore was the first to come up beside Mohammad, crouched over a body. The upper half badly mutilated from the full blast of the M79s, he lay lifeless, propped sideways against a large rock. The Dhofar plainsman was busy stripping the Adoo of his ammunition, the rifle he already held.

Captain Holding, arriving among them, sent an update report and was in turn told to get the column moving again. With a section of the company detailed to carry the body, he and Mohammad left to continue their task of guiding.

Sinclair and his three men remained behind to guard the smaller wadi entrance against a re-occurrence of the first ambush.

'Yorky,' whispered the sergeant to Rush, 'go back and wait for McAllister and his lads to come up, then nip back and fetch us.'

It takes a long time for a hundred men to file cautiously down a dry river bed at night, and it seems a lot longer when you've just been shot at.

It was midnight before they arrived back at Habahn, tired and body sore from spending practically all of the last thirty hours on the move.

Sitting on the floor of the Batt. shack, resting against his bergen, Johnny Kieran looked up with heavy-lidded eyes as Reg Berrill handed him a mug of tea.

'What are you looking so sorry about?' commented Reg with mock sarcasm, 'all you did was go walkie-poos around the hills for a bit.'

The Irishman in answer held up the M79 he had been balancing on his lap, replying in a sluggish voice.

'Fucking good kit this.'

CHAPTER 15

Speak softly and carry a big stick.

Theodore Roosevelt

Standing to one side of their improvised helicopter pad, Jim Sinclair raised his arm in one final wave of farewell, as the helicopter lifted noisily but gracefully into the air. As it turned towards the fort, gaining speed and altitude, the hands of the four departing S.A.S. men were seen to return his gesture. Jim watched the chopper as it rapidly became smaller and smaller, racing east along the shore towards Salalah, silhouetted with the evening sun setting behind it.

For the sergeant this sight brought on feelings of longing and self pity. The four men he had just said goodbye to would be spending the night at Batt. H.Q., then flying out in the morning for Blighty: something every fibre in his body cried out for him to do. Jim was a regular soldier and had been for almost thirteen years. During most of that time, despite various attachments and girl friends, none were able to get between him and the Army. Not, that is, until he married Penny. From the first day of his arrival in the Oman he desperately missed her. The days were not too bad for he could lose his thoughts in work, but the nights were torture. Lying awake, in the dark heat, naked except for a cut down pair of kahki army trousers, he struggled in despair to rid his mind of memories and emotions. But nothing worked, not a day passed in which Penny was not with him, to touch, to smell, and to taste.

With the helicopter but the size of a pin head, Sinclair, transferring his rifle to another hand, turned towards the shack.

A week now they had been in the Dhofar. A week in which the S.A.S. training team had passed on to them much local knowledge and experience. But in the summer of 1972, after two full years of S.A.S. involvement, the ground work had only begun.

With British support, the Sultan's Armed Forces were just beginning to have success. As Terry Hitchman had pointed out, the P.F.L.O.A.G. still held almost total control of the Jebel and would not be loosened of their grip until sufficient bases and strongholds could be permanently sited throughout the hills. Until that time the heartening results gained through the expanding civil aid programmes were to be capitalized upon and their advantages made known among the tribesmen of the Dhofar.

Fortunately over the following week some of these benefits were channeled Habahn's way. A British medical officer turned up to spend a day with

Pridmore and Kieran, giving the villagers a more thorough medical examination than the patrol medics had been able to. When he left to return to Salalah he took one old man, who had been blind for a number of years, with him, believing a simple operation by the field surgical team could restore his sight. A hygiene party also turned up to assess the elimination of the fly population of the village, the Arabian scourge, and chose a suitable site for the newly planned well.

Major McAllister, not returning to Britain with his squadron but remaining instead as D Company's Liaison Officer, called by one day to drop off .5 calibre tracer ammunition for the 106mm recoiless gun. Mick Pridmore, with one of the Omani soldiers from the fort who keenly wished to fire the gun, spent three afternoons together insuring that it worked and that they had the drills right. Whereupon one morning they took it, dismantled in the back of the location rover, to a point above the beach. There several dozen rounds of .5 calibre tracers were fired with the spotting rifle at a pinnacle of rock on the shore. Then, having got the range right, they blew it into pebbles with three main armament anti-tank Hesh rounds.

On a dawn morning in their third week Jim, setting himself a routine, was scanning the surrounding country from the shack top O.P., as he had done for the last week. Ever since the morning he had looked down on the town from the Jebel heights and seen how nakedly exposed to observation Habahn was, he made a point of looking back. With his binoculars he studied each peak, slope and wadi rim. He had been warned that if not careful the close dominance of the hills could depress and give the jitters or, as it was called, Jebelitis. Sinclair had no intention of letting that happen, he was a Clyde Valley Scot, Highlanders never frightened him.

Lowering the glasses, he watched as an old man leading a child appeared out of the thin bush perimeter that was a natural boundary dividing the beach from the scrub-covered plain. In a straight line they walked directly towards the Batt. location. Coming down from his roof top to meet the pair, Jim was joined by Yorky Rush.

'Salaam,' began the Yorkshireman in greeting.

'Salaam,' replied the old man.

'Do you wish to see us, grandfather, or have you business in the village?' asked Rush, not recognising either him or the boy.

'I have come to see the man of medicine,' he replied, holding up one of the youngster's arms to show a bruised elbow.

'Johnny,' called Sinclair, 'take a look at the lad here, will ya?'

Kieran, like the others naked from the waist up, came out of the building to examine the arm. Tenderly feeling about the bruising, he voiced his diagnosis in English.

'Nothing broken, ruptured vessels under the skin, must be painful but not serious. I'll put the arm in a sling.'

The young boy, aged only five or six, said nothing as the Irishman selected a khaki packet from his medical pack and unwrapped it to secure the arm in a high, tight position across his chest.

Taking water and dates that Rush offered him, the pair withdrew a short distance to sit and wait. There they remained for another half hour until seeing Murad approach both stood as a signal they wished to speak with him.

Several minutes later he walked into the Batt. Room to inform Sinclair that the old man had indicated to him that his son, an Adoo, would like to claim the Sultan's armistice.

'Where is the son?' asked the Scot, sitting back in his work table chair.

'He says the family is hiding in the bushland, but that's a lie,' replied Murad.

'How do you know?' asked Sinclair.

'On their bodies are the bites of ticks and mosquitos. This they would only have because they are concealing themselves in the wadi caves by day and night,' was his knowledgeable answer.

Jim had seen the bites and rashes but had taken no notice of them.

'What tribe are they?' he asked.

'Bair Zakhir, strong Adoo, all mostly P.F.L.O.A.G.,' answered the young Dhofari, puckering his lips.

Jim thought for a moment. If the tribe was so staunchly commie why does this man want to turn traitor?

'Tell the old man to come back tomorrow morning,' decided Jim, 'we'll give him an answer then.'

The next morning at precisely the same time the grey bearded man re-appeared alone. On being told by radio of the proposal, there to question him after driving down the evening before was Guy McAllister, Lee Holding and a sergeant from Batt.'s Intelligence cell.

For almost an hour, sitting facing each other, politely and patiently they discussed the advantages and disadvantages of the son's intention to change sides. On its conclusion, as the old man disappeared into the scrub and camel thorns, the others gathered in the Para's accommodation to mull over what had been agreed upon.

The son and his family would be coming in that afternoon. He, of course, to be taken straight away to Salalah for interrogation, while the family stayed overnight at Habahn to follow the next day.

This event, although unique because of the tribe, was not one that merited the disruption of the location's work routine. At two o'clock when the heat of the day began to mellow, work was resumed. The present job that the occupants of Batt. shack were involved in was the building of a perimeter defence. From both shores it was to enclose the village, the Fort and Batt. in a U-shape. This barrier, nothing more at the moment than a cattle fence of six foot picquet posts with three strands of barbed wire, had so far only been completed on the west side. Now, naked except for shorts and boots, Pridmore, Rush and Berrill were driving in picquets that would divide the bushland from the north side of Habahn.

Johnny Kieran, who had been up in the observation post, climbed down for a drink of water, notifying those below that, on seeing figures moving in the bush, the family must be on their way in.

Placing hats on their heads but without weapons, a reception committee of the three from Salalah, Jim Sinclair and Murad walked out from the building. When a man carrying a rifle came into view the party began to make towards him, but as two others appeared, both armed as well, then a fourth and a fifth, their footsteps faltered. The wire detail, who had paused to watch the arrival, began easing back to where their weapons were leaning on a roll of wire. The five Dhofaris had in the meantime multiplied to about twenty. Most of these were now seen to be women, old men and children, which helped a great deal in calming individual fears. Johnny Kieran, alarmed at the increase of numbers, had sprung quickly behind the location's machine gun, mounted in the sangar at the entrance, but had sensibly refrained from cocking it.

It took some time but at last they stopped emerging from the bush. When the first man halted, about a hundred yards from Major McAllister and his small group, behind him was gathered a crowd of about a hundred people and possibly the same number of goats.

'Sahib,' called Murad in a voice of some urgency but just above a whisper, 'the man in front, the one who came first. It is Salim Mistahayl.'

'What? Are you sure?' asked the intelligence sergeant.

'Yes, yes, when I became an Adoo, he visited our training camp,' confirmed Murad, still in a low voice.

'This doesn't figure, Sir,' offered the sergeant, 'Salim Mistahayl is a protege of the Chinese. He was being groomed for higher things; the last I heard of him he had been sent to China for training and indoctrination.'

'Murad, are you quite sure this man is Salim Mistahayl?' asked McAllister not turning his head.

'Yes, Sahib.'

'Well then, come, let's make him welcome,' decided the major stepping off, head high, back straight, taking set measured paces.

As they closed the distance Jim studied this thin, clean-shaven, medium height leader. His headdress was a dark brown shamag with the traditional futa skirt covering his waist and lower limbs. The shirt was Chinese Army, as was the equipment he wore which held the ammunition magazines for his weapon. This was a Russian AK47 assault rifle he carried with the sling over his shoulder, the rifle under arm, its barrel pointing forward, parallel with the ground.

'Salaam aleikum, Salim Mistahayl,' greeted McAllister, laying the flat of his right hand to his upper chest as he respectfully bowed his head, 'your honoured name comes before you.'

'Aleikum-es-salaam, Major McAllister,' replied Salim, also returning the gesture of greeting. 'Your name too has been spoken of with great respect.'

Sinclair did not know what the others thought of Salim but he took an instant liking to this dark-eyed man from the Jebel who, despite his soiled dress, projected unpretentious sovereign dignity.

Faced with such numbers, transporting everyone did put a sizeable strain on Batt. administration. However, the prize was too good to let slip through lack of logistics. Helicopters were found to lift all but the goat herders up to Salalah. They and the animals were loaded into lorries to make the journey by beach. On the outskirts of the district capital a temporary camp was erected for them which they would occupy whilst under the protection of the Sultan.

Not without justification there were some who treated Mistalayl's supposed defection with suspicion. Until the moment he had walked down from the Western Qara Hills, Salim had been one of P.F.L.O.A.G.'s most staunch junior commanders. It was not until Captain Holding drove into Habahn one morning a few days later, with the intention of informing Sinclair's team what they had learned and how their location was now about to get teeth, that the full story was made known to them.

Salim Mistahayl, born on the Jebel, showed in his youth that he was a bright child. Learning Arabic, he endeavoured to acquire a school education but, under the old Sultan and because of mistrust of Dhofaris by the rest of Arab Oman, this he found near impossible. In frustration he made his way to Kuwait at the head of the Persian Gulf. There for five years he worked and learned. He also saw the wealth and prosperity that was available through oil, and how so long as those in government shared these out, what a flourishing country it could produce.

Returning to the Dhofar in 1968 and finding no change in the primitive life style of his people, nor any sign of an impending change, he quite willingly joined P.F.L.O.A.G. to fight against the Sultan. With them, because of his broader understanding of events thanks to his years in Kuwait, and due to his burning passion for an independent Dhofar, he quickly rose in rank. Completing courses run by Marxist communists and Red Chinese in Hauf and Aden, he soon held the command of over a hundred men, using them in many successful attacks and ambushes. This inevitably led to his selection for advanced political and military training in Red China.

From the very start of this war the communist element had found their efforts to unify and coordinate their battle plans constantly being frustrated by tribal differences and the Jebalis' unflinching dedication to the Muslim religion. The teachings of the Koran especially, were shown to be in total conflict with the principles of communism. To combat these stumbling blocks the P.F.L.O.A.G. hard liners not only used terror and murder but also introduced a brainwashing scheme against the children. These youngsters would be taken from their families and sent to Hauf and possibly Aden for Marxist teaching in schools staffed by communists.

Prior to leaving for Kuwait, Salim's father insisted he marry, which resulted in a son being born to his bride while he was away. Soon after he had departed for Peking, P.F.L.O.A.G. terror squads began to encroach among the villages and glens that Mistahayl had taken under his wing. He did not agree with the methods used by P.F.L.O.A.G. to unite the people of Dhofar, believing it could be done gradually instead, over a period of time. These squads, used to operating with impunity and answerable to no one, began to punish those openly practising their religion and, if need be, to torture and murder. They also began to select and deport children to their schools across the border.

Unwittingly one of these children was Salim's son, now aged eight. His mother, protesting against the child's kidnapping, followed him sixty miles over the hills to Hauf. There she confronted P.F.L.O.A.G. leaders, pleading for her son to be returned. One, a brutish man trained by and working mainly with East German attached advisers, losing patience with the wailing woman, took her son to the edge of a nearby cliff and before her eyes hurled him to his death. The mother attacked the man in a rage but he, large and powerful, grasped her ankles and then, like a rag doll, swung her around until the woman's head, coming into contact with a large rock, cracked open like a melon.

Mistahayl, until his return was told nothing of these deaths and then a lie that the mother and son died as a result of attacks on his village by planes of the Sultan's Air Force. He remained in ignorance until on a visit to his father's village he learned the truth and saw for himself evidence of the terror squads' savage work.

Calling in secret a council of the village elders it was agreed P.F.L.O.A.G.'s cruel dominance could no longer be tolerated. Subsequently, because of favourable reports regarding the fair and honourable treatment of defecting Dhofaris, it was decided that the village would seek the protection of the new Sultan's government. And so, one morning at dawn, killing the village commissar and three of his henchmen, every man, woman and child picked up whatever they could carry and with their goats followed Salim down off the Jebel. Their cattle they slaughtered, an unwished for act, for these were the village's wealth, but one of necessity, for speed and concealment were tactical priorities and cattle were slow and noisy.

In other conflicts their surrender could, because of suspicion, have been rewarded with imprisonment or execution, but this was not the Sultan's policy. He welcomed them as brothers and, because of that, was repaid with their unquestioned loyalty.

This finally brought Holding to the point of his visit; Salim Mistahayl and about twenty of his villagers were to form a Firqat, based at Habahn.

*   *   *

With a Firqat at Habahn, giving it the potential of offence instead of defence, a mood of expectation took hold of Sinclair and his team. But before this force could become fully operational they would first have to learn the drills and battle procedures used by the British and Sultan's Forces. Although most were experienced guerillas, they would all now have to be taught the technique of anti-guerilla warfare as it was to be practised in future.

The first problem this new development threw up was a delicate one; gaining the Sheikh's confidence in having twenty armed ex-Adoos billeted on the doorstep of his fort. Jim Sinclair negotiated acceptance of this during an interview with the Sheikh in which he presented him with the Russian AK47 rifle captured in the wadi ambush. With hindsight it would have been wiser of the Sheikh to reflect on an interpretaton of an old saying from another culture, beware of Scotsmen bearing gifts.

Over the next fortnight Batt.'s routine no longer had blank areas of idleness. With a full training programme drawn up, each member had his share of lessons, classes and practical drills to teach. Weapon training, fieldcraft, ambush and anti-ambush drills, advanced first-aid and much more, all with the intention of attuning the ex-Adoo mind with British procedures and drills. It was important the Jebalis adopt these new ways of operating, for in battle, to be out of step with one's allies could result in disaster.

One point that they, like all Dhofaris changing sides in the past protested about, was that of giving up their AK47s for the Sultan's standard issued F.N. This rifle, a sister to the British S.L.R., was not popular with the Jebalis because of its weight and inability, like the AK47, of firing automatic bursts. But because of the increased range and stopping power of the 7.62mm round it was reluctantly accepted.

These were days of satisfaction and pleasure for the Habahn Batt. The Firqat was a sponge to their instruction, always listening, watching and asking questions, never content to let a drill or weapon period pass only half learned. The Paras put this down to the natural instincts of worrior tribesmen, but they were to learn there was more to it than that.

Salim Mistahayl and his men were motivated by one single emotion: revenge.

*   *   *

The days of an Arabian high-summer are with regard to the weather regimentally similar. The sun rises into a moisture-free, cloudless sky and sets thirteen hours later having spent that whole time neither obstructed by haze nor cloud. The only break given to this unceasing burning, is when the Shamals or hot winds blow from the north to blot the sun with unpleasant curtains of sand and dust.

Having spent the last five weeks looking at this monotonous overhead panorama, it was with some surprise that as Jim Sinclair, lying hidden in a clump of bushes, above him in the dawn sky, puffy white clouds began to appear. The Scotsman was able to watch these form, move about and disappear in detail, for he had just begun a long wait.

At the end of the Firqat's training, it was only natural to blood them as soon as possible. In fact it was Salim himself who suggested the target. Knowing the schedules and habits of the P.F.L.O.A.G. in regards to moving on the Jebel, he put it to Major McAllister that they should ambush a small monthly column that came up from Hauf on or about the same date. This party was a mixed bag of messengers, ammunition and supply carriers, men returning from leave and courses and occasionally foreign advisers on inspection visits. The S.A.S. major at first vetoed the idea, putting forward instead a plan to locate and destroy an artillery piece that periodically came into play on the edge of the Jebel, lobbing shells in and around Salalah Airfield. He did this for security reasons to keep the plan off everyone's tongues until the last moment. For the proposal was a sound one that incorporated all the qualities in which a Firqat could best apply its skills, operating over ground they knew and against an enemy whose routine they were familiar with.

Arriving before dawn Salim himself guided everyone around, siting each ambush group and indicating their arcs of fire. The main killer group was the men of the Firqat concealed in an extensive clump of bushes a quarter of a mile from a waterhole. The route of the Adoo column always ran to this waterhole, then eastwards past the bushes.

Salim, applying the joint skills he had learned on the Jebel, in China and now from the British, placed his ambush as a broad trap. A short distance north beyond the killing ground was a bare grass ridge on the crest of which, but out of sight, was a four-man Batt. team brought in as reinforcements for the operation. To the east, concealed in a fold in the ground, was a second Batt. cut-off group, blocking the Adoo's path. Habahn Batt. shared the same clump of bushes as the Firqat, but two hundred yards apart, at the extreme western edge, facing the waterhole.

Major McAllister as overall commander had positioned himself with Salim's killer group. Beside him lay Mick Pridmore who, true to his promise, had before him a General Purpose Machine-Gun, G.P.M.G. or Gimpy as it was nicknamed. This sat with its barrel propped on its front two legs, the pistol grip resting on the ground, the working parts cocked and the safety catch applied.

The Habahn Batt. had brought a second Gimpy with them, which, manned by Yorky Rush, was pointing towrds the waterhole. The rest of Sinclair's cut-off group were Reg Berrill and Mohammad Kabina; Johnny Kieran, his turn to step down, was back at Habahn.

Mohammad had become more or less an attached member of their Batt. team. On the formation of the Firqat, Murad Areeb, although of a different tribe, was a Jebali and being accepted, readily joined. Mohammad though, a lowland Dhofar preferred not to but had no compunction in swapping his Lee Enfield for a brand new F.N.

It was he who became aware of the waterhole's first visitors.

Hearing the tap of a finger on a stone Jim, looking across, saw him point to his ear then nod towards the waterhole. With a frown the Scotsman looked and listened but it was some minutes before he too began to hear the lowing of cattle. Very soon these, with short horns, level backs and black, brown and white multi-coloured hides, climbed out of the sloping ground to the west of the waterhole. The herdsman, yodelling to his sixteen animals, followed to take up a standing watch beside the water in the shade of a massive-trunked tamarind tree. There in the shadows of its spacious branches, stick in hand, he remained, periodically yodelling a recall to an individual cow that appeared to be wandering off. Few did, for it was the twilight of the dry season. The best grass grew around the edges of the water, while the rest, dry and bent, would soon have to make way for fresh green shoots that the Khareef rains would nourish.

These were not far off, for the puffy, white infant clouds above their heads were but advance guards. Before the week was out this scattered reconnaissance force would be replaced with shrouding masses of dripping grey fog that stayed almost without let up for over two months. Although bringing the Jebels' life-blood of water, it was not a good time on the Qara Hills. The chill and constant damp the Khareef brought made the high plateau unhealthy and uninhabitable. Soon the Jebali tribes would be leaving the round houses of their villages to seek, at a lower altitude, the drier but less comfortable shelter of the wadi caves.

At midday, with the cattle sluggish and mostly lying down, the herdsman retired to sit on his haunches with his back resting against the tree's wide trunk. There he unwrapped from a cloth and began to eat his lunch. Four hundred yards away the members of the Habahn Batt. joined him.

Opening a packet of hard-tack biscuits, Rush passed them to his left and right. For a few moments the men, each chewing, watched the waterhole with abject gazes but then simultaneously, in mid-action, their jaws froze.

From the western dead ground, steadily growing above the dark form of a resting bullock, was the head and shoulders of a man. Behind him another came into view, then another. Slowly with deliberate steps they approached the waterhole. The herdsman watched the three men in peaked caps, carrying rifles at the ready, with a stare that was less than interested.

On pausing at the water's edge to exchange greetings, other men came into sight behind them. Jim Sinclair, reporting the Adoo's arrival by his National radio, began to count the men as they approached in single file. Fourteen joined the herdsman one by one under the shading canopy of the tamarind tree for their noon halt. The Paras, tense and silent, face veils tied about their foreheads for extra camouflage, furtively raised their eyes above the cover of the clumps of dead grass which lay thickly at the edge of the shrubbery, noted every movement. The scene at the watering point was painfully tranquil. These men, in the centre of territory they controlled, lounged at their ease, believing danger to be far away. Across the surface of the muddy water dragonflies hovered, then sped, then hovered once again. On the receding shore, as it dried in the drought-creating sun, several species of butterflies darted about the mud seeking moisture.

It was a full hour before movement indicated that the journey was to be resumed. Standing, packs were seen being lifted onto backs, and rifles slung or balanced over shoulders. Just as they had arrived, their departing order of march was with three men in advance. The direction they took showed those watching that they would pass to the front of the main ambush killing party at a distance of about a hundred yards.

Reporting that the Adoo were on the move, Sinclair, keeping his head as low as possible, scanned the column of men for signs of danger. The three point men, if not alert, were looking about but gave the bushes only scant glances. On the ambush being sprung these left-hand four men should not be able to see any of the enemy. In theory only those lucky enough to escape back out of the killing ground would present a target. Unintentionally, however, a target was provided for them. Two men, lingering to fill water containers, had caused a large gap to separate them from the main party.

Extending an arm across Rush's vision Sinclair first held up two fingers then pointed towards the pair who had dropped behind. Yorky, without taking his eyes off the two men, lifted the gun butt to gently ease it sideways so the barrel was kept ahead of this pre-selected target.

On the north side of the bushes, pressing themselves tight to the ground, Guy McAllister and the Firqat remained motionless as the three point scouts passed. Fortunately, and again most likely because Salim knew it would happen, the day's warm breezes blew from the waterhole up the vale, eliminating any chance of discovery by the Adoo detecting any tell-tale body scent. In the centre of the killer group the S.A.S. major counted each man of the main column as they came level with him. When he reached six his right hand, which had been poised above Mick Pridmore's back, dropped.

The big corporal, in the aim, the butt of his G.P.M.G. clamped tight to his shoulder, squeezed the trigger, sending a burst of fire towards the sixth man. He, in khaki shirt and trousers, shrugged without a cry as a bullet struck him, then turning sideways he crumpled to the ground.

In an instant the quiet little glade erupted with ragged volleys of mind-numbing gun fire. The Firqat, who had been waiting for the machine gun to open up, now engaged with their own fire.

Reaction among the Adoo was mixed, some with no choice dropped dead or wounded. Others, battle-wise, flattened themselves to the ground. One, possibly his first time under fire, stood bewilderedly clutching his rifle for a brief second until cut down. Another, realising the grass provided little cover and knowing the only way to escape this ambush was to take flight, dropped his rifle and ran. Gaining fifty yards because all shots were being aimed at near targets, he one by one began receiving the attention of a dozen rifles and Pridmore's Gimpy. Discarding his pack and zig-zagging in a desperate manner, he ran north, scrambling up the slope of the ridge. All around him turfs of grass shuddered showing small patches of bare earth as bullets thumped into the ground. His bid for life deserved that award but it was not to be. In a crouching run he topped the ridge to be knocked backwards by half a dozen rifle shots, from the Batt. cut-off group lying in wait there.

The three point scouts turned about as the ambush was sprung and, going to ground, began to fire automatic bursts into the bushes. However, the leader, seeing it was pointless remaining, shouted for the others to follow him. His escape route was a logical one, east out of the vale and away from the ambush.

Tragically for them, blocking their path was the third Batt. Lee Holding, watching them come, waited for the range to decrease to about eighty yards then, taking aim through his rifle sights, killed the leader with a bullet through the chest. The other members of his party also fired bringing a second down. But before the third man could be put away, he cried out in Jebali, and released his rifle to raise waving arms above his head in surrender.

On the first shot from Pridmore's G.P.M.G., Yorky Rush twisted his body behind the pre-positioned machine-gun and lifted it by the pistol grip into his shoulder at the same time as pushing the safety catch to fire with his thumb. As one of the two tall men, who had a moment before been laughing at a joke, dropped into his sight picture, he fired. In the act of unslinging his rifle the man was pitched backwards by the force of the rounds. His companion also went down, felled by rifle fire from the other three men beside the gunner.

Seeing no return fire coming from the men lying in the killing ground, Mistahayl shouted for his men to cease firing. With silence returning to the glade after eighty seconds of noise and death, the leader of the Firqat called to his fellow Jebalis to surrender. At first there was no response, the only sound being the moans and cries from the wounded, and the distant hysterical hollering of the herdsman as he, stick flailing, drove his cattle away to the west.

'Brothers,' called Salim again, 'we wish to kill no more; surrender and you will live. This I promise.'

Cautiously, from among the dead, a man rose to hold his arms in the air, then a second stood up, clutching a bloody wound on one forearm. Using his radio McAllister now ordered all sub-units to check the dead and wounded.

Moving in pairs, one covering the other, teams of men scurried from their concealment to disarm, search and separate the living from the dead.

Moving out to the two stragglers they had shot, both teenagers in futa skirts, Jim Sinclair and Murad found one dead and the other so badly wounded in the hip that there was little chance of him surviving. Regardless of this Jim took the time to bandage the bloody, torn flesh. Then taking his morphine capsule from where he had it taped to his I.D. discs hanging on a cord around his neck, he injected the Jebali to dull the torturing pain. Hopefully by the time it wore off he would be dead, for even if found alive by other Adoo there was nothing they could do to aid him. The P.F.L.O.A.G. went to a great deal of trouble supplying the Dhofar tribes with arms, but the need for a doctor or medical orderly was completely beyond their comprehension.

An ambush when properly planned and executed should produce maximum results, and this one had done just that. But it was not totally one-sided. When the three point scouts had returned fire one of the Firqat took a bullet in the cheek, shattering several upper teeth. Mick Pridmore, padding this with bandage gauze, taped his jaw tightly shut to stop the flow of blood.

With less than fifteen minutes of the ambush showing on Guy McAllister's watch he ordered a withdrawal. Taking the prisoners and walking wounded with them, and carrying the enemy's weapons, they set off south for the escarpment and the security of the plain below.

The dead and badly wounded were left. This was not done callously but as a necessary act of war. The bodies, in fact, had been treated with reverance and respect for, like themselves they were also Jebalis and as such, of the same blood. A fact which only highlighted for the British that, whoever was to triumph in this wretched conflict, it was painfully obvious that the only losers at present were the tribesmen of the Qarra Hills.

*   *   *

Stepping through the hall door into the corridor, Johnny Kieran took off his rain-soaked peak cap to beat it against his trouser leg. Over the last few days the Khareef had at last arrived filling the sky with dark grey clouds that drizzled thin rain throughout the coastal plain and hills of the Dhofar. Replacing his headgear, the Irishman continued down the corridor until he came to a side door marked 'Dispensary'. Pushing it open, he banged the counter that blocked his entry to the room beyond.

'Shop,' he shouted, banging his fist twice more.

'Who da fuck's that,' came a Merseyside voice, the owner hidden from view by ceiling high metal shelves filled with medical stores that lined most of the room.

'Doctor Schweitzer, ya scouse cunt! Who da ya tink? Nobody else would bother visiting this dump of yours,' responded Kieran.

'Cheeky git,' replied the voice as the scraping of a chair was heard.

'Should have known it was you, ya Irish pillock,' joked a deeply tanned corporal in soiled medical corps white shirt and trousers, as he poked his head around a shelf. 'Come through and have a coffee.'

'Take a chair,' he offered after introducing Kieran to two off-duty cooks who had joined him for a late morning N.A.A.F.I. break. 'What can I do ya for?'

'Need a re-sup. of medical stuff,' explained Kieran, dropping his empty bergen on the floor beside him. 'Would 'a' been down earlier but had to wait for the pissin' tide to go out.'

'Got a list?' asked the medic handing Johnny a full coffee cup.

As Kieran reached into a breast pocket, runnng footsteps could be heard in the corridor.

'Kenny! Kenny! Casevac chopper coming in,' shouted a voice from the doorway.

'Right, comin',' shouted back the medic, almost spilling coffee into Kieran's lap as he diverted it to a table. 'Johnny, give us a hand: we got wounded.'

'Ya, sure,' replied the Irishman following the other three outside.

The Salalah Airfield casualty helicopter pad was sited between the runway and the field surgical hospital, about seventy yards from the building. As they arrived at the edge of the pad a doctor in a white coat and two orderlies with stretchers joined them. Faintly, in the distance, the distinctive rapid pulse beat of an American Huey helicopter could be heard.

'The battalion up on 'Crossbow' has had a mortar attack on it. We don't know how bad, but there are casualties on this chopper,' informed the doctor.

'Crossbow' was the code name for an operation to hold a defensive location on the Jebel throughout the Khareef period. With the inhabitants gone a foothold was hoped to be gained in this vacuum, but was also the beacon for Adoo retaliation.

The helicopter now in view was skimming just below the rain clouds at little more than two hundred feet. Its landing approach was in the form of an assault, at full throttle it dropped in a shallow glide towards the pad. Only at the last moment did the pilot pull in the reins, lifting its nose for the skids to drop back gently onto the concrete surface.

Rushing forward to the open rear passenger compartment, the doctor hurriedly ran an examining eye over the four wounded men inside. Three were Omani, two of which lay on the floor whilst the other with a bandaged head wound sat on the rear bench seat beside a British soldier in his mid-thirties. With the rotor blades slowing and the noise decreasing the doctor beckoned for assistance. A cook and an orderly with a stretcher were told to take one of the Omani's on the floor into the operating theatre. The dispensary corporal led the man with the head wound after the stretcher as the other medic and cook carted the third Omani away to the adjacent morgue.

'Bring him and follow me,' ordered the doctor of Kieran, pointing to the British casualty on the far side of the compartment.

The Irishman, his eyes watering from receiving a blast of turbulent air as the aircraft landed, blinked and leant in to reach a hand across.

'Here ya are mate, let's have ya out.'

Then, seeing who it was, automatically broke into a joke. 'Oh hello Sir, what's this? Your piles acting up again?'

Taff Lewis, his face ashen, his forehead marked with the word morphine and the time he had been injected, heaved himself unaided from the helicopter.

'Take care of this for me will you, Kieran? There's a good lad,' he asked, handing Johnny an arm severed above the elbow.

Kieran stunned, stood transfixed by what he held in his hands. Then looking up at his Company Sergeant Major whose left limb was but a bloody bandaged stump, watched as the big Welshman followed the doctor through the dripping rain towards the surgical theatre.

Johnny, in a voice hardly above a whisper, uttered his thoughts.

'Jesus Taff. Jesus fucking God.'

CHAPTER 16

Huntsman, rest! Thy chase is done.
Sir Walter Scott

'Dave, is Sam giving you a lift back into camp?' called Mary Urwin to her husband from their kitchen.

'Not that I know of,' answered Urwin, sitting at the dining table in the next room eating his lunch.

'He just pulled up outside,' she replied, wiping her wet hands before answering the ringing doorbell.

'I hope you're enjoying that home cooking, Davy, because it's about to be your last for some time,' announced the sergeant major as he entered the quarter's combined living and dining room.

'What?' replied the Irishman, lowering his knife and fork.

'Sorry, Mary,' apologised Kyle to the woman who had followed him into the room, 'Dave's being sent out to join D Company in the Oman.'

'What?' repeated Urwin, only louder this time.

'Oh God no, when?' asked Mary.

'Tonight,' replied Sam with an embarrassed expression.

'What?' choked out Urwin for the third time, exploding to his feet. 'Whose bloody idea is that?'

'The C.O.'s,' answered Kyle.

'Well, for Christ's sake,' wailed the sergeant in frustration.

'Dave, stop swearing in the house,' ordered his wife.

'Stop swearing! Honey, I got a right to swear. We got block leave coming up next month and you and me and the kids are booked for two weeks in Spain, remember,' pointed out Urwin in helpless anger.

'Well, maybe you'll be back by then,' suggested his wife, hopefully, turning to Kyle for confirmation.

'Don't think so, Mary. Dave's going out as a replacement. Could be promotion in it though,' replied the sergeant major trying his best to cushion the shock.

'Replacement? Whose replacement?' asked Urwin, his tone serious.

'Oh, it seems Taff Lewis picked up a bug. Malaria I think the signal said. Anyway he's been sent back to B.M.H. Cyprus to recover,' informed Sam, ignorant of the truth.

Urwin, saying nothing, sat down again to clasp both hands together resting his elbows on the table. He felt sorry for himself and looked it.

'Don't come in to the company this afternoon,' instructed Kyle, 'stay here and pack your kit; you're flying out of Brize late tonight, I got a rover laid on to take you up.'

Dave, looking up, nodded his head.

'Got a set of jungle greens?' asked the sergeant major.

'Ya, out in the lock up somewhere; I'll dig 'em out later,' replied Urwin, resigning himself to his fate.

'The C.O. wants to speak to you at four o'clock so nip in and report to the Adjutant, then drop around the office after. I'll see you before ya go, okay,' were Kyle's final directions.

'Oh aye Sam, I'll do that,' promised the Irishman, now deep in thought about where to start in tidying his affairs with the short time left to him.

In the interview with the Commanding Officer, Colonel Chuter was apologetic for the upheaval but adamant that he should go. His explanation for sending him was the need to fill Sergeant Major Lewis's post as the operations officer. This was an appointment best handled by someone with patrol company experience, and Urwin, unfortunately, was found to be the only man in the Battalion qualified and available to do the job.

Before leaving the orderly room the chief clerk gave him his travelling instructions. He was booked on a midnigt VC10 from R.A.F. Brize Norton to Masirah Island, then on the next day by Andover.

He would be stepping off the aircraft at Salalah airfield in just over twentyfour hours.

*   *   *

Giving a shiver, Mick Pridmore, on the location's morning radio watch, stood up to pull on his smock. The Khareef's pre-dawn chill entering the room had caused the big man to seek added warmth and to exercise his limbs. Leaning forward into the open space that was the north window, he looked down the building's right side searching the eastern skyline for signs of sunrise. Seeing a dull smudge through the low hanging drizzle that had been persistent for the last few days, he turned away to light a small blue gas stove to brew water for a cup of tea.

The monsoon period was showing the newcomers what an uncomfortable time the Dhofar wet season could be. Gone were the blue skies and the sunshine, replaced instead by banks of grey, moisture-laden foggy clouds.

As foul as the weather was, it did attribute to everyone taking a short stand down. After the concentrated training of the Firqat and their successful ambush it was decided as a reward, to give them a week's leave with their families at Salalah. This made the Habahn Batt. more or less redundant, occupying their days with local routine and administration points.

Preparing a cup with sugar and dried milk, Mick Pridmore's back suddenly went rigid. A familiar sound had come to him through the damp morning air; the hollow thump of a mortar being fired. Remaining still, spoon poised in hand, he waited, giving himself the benefit of the doubt. Perhaps it had been a similar noise from the village or fort. But no, unmistakably it came again.

'Jim! Jim!' he shouted towards the sleeping accommodation, 'we got trouble.'

'Ah, what is it?' came the Scotsman's sleepy voice.

'Mortar, Jim! we're gonna get stonked,' announced Mick with unwanted confidence.

'Where? Where?' stuttered Sinclair, bolting from his camp bed, his mind still gripped by sleep.

'Up. Up,' responded Pridmore in a short tempered burst, jabbing a finger towards the sky while lifting a G.P.M.G. into his arms. 'Christ, I don't know Jim, but the bombs are on their way.'

As if to confirm this another dull thump was heard from somewhere out on the plain followed by an explosion from the beach.

'Stand to! Stand to!' shouted Sinclair, pulling on his boots.

The other three men jack-knifed off their beds to thrash about for clothes, equipment and weapons.

'What is it, Jim?' asked Berrill.

'Mortar; get up on the roof with the spare Gimpy.'

The second bomb exploded somewhere in the village.

'Yorky, give Mick a hand with the sangar gun. Johnny, lay out the M79s with ammo handy.'

While shouting orders to his men Sinclair's mind was racing, trying to cover all immediate actions for defence.

As he reached for the radio handset a third mortar bomb landed on the far side of the fort.

'Hello Zero, this is Four Two, Bravo. Contact. Contact. Over.'

Switching off the reading light and Mick's primus stove, Jim sent a full contact report. Whilst holding the handset he hopped about, peering first out one window and then out of another, trying to pierce the grey gloom.

'Can anyone see anything?' he called, desperate to know what was happening.

With everyone calling back negative answers a sixth figure came into the room to begin draping belts of ammunition around his shoulders. It was Mohammad, who Jim had forgotten about. Hearing the mortars he had hurried from his tented accommodation to the Batt. building. Pointing to the roof, indicating his intention of joining Reg, he left as silently as he had arrived.

'Four Two Bravo, six all wide spread, over,' replied Jim to the radio's question of how many bombs had landed on the location.

Looking towards the fort, he could see no movement and was seriously concerned about what support he could expect from there. The Sheikh, his village militia and the Omani soldiers just might find it prudent to sit quietly behind their walls should any real shooting begin.

With the mortar bombs arriving on the average of one a minute, from the scrub line to the far right a machine-gun began to stutter in sharp, rapid bursts.

'Reg,' shouted the Scotsman, 'Can you see that fucker?'

'No,' replied Berrill, 'he's in dead ground, but he seems to be aiming for the fort.'

'Shit. Shit,' cursed Jim, raising the handset to his mouth, 'hello Zero, Four Two Bravo. Enemy machine-gun about five hundred metres to the northeast has now opened fire on the fort. Due to location I am unable to engage, over.'

'No, over,' was his reply when asked if the fort had returned fire.

'Mick, do you think you can get that cunt with the 106?' called the Scot out to the sangar.

'Ya sure, Jim, should be able to see him from the gun pit,' confirmed Pridmore.

'Right, you and Johnny get across and see if you can snuff that bastard out. With luck it might spark those dozey pricks in the fort into doing something. Okay Johnny?' he asked the Irishman in confirmation.

'No prob, no prob a' tall,' replied Kieran, fastening on his belt order and picking up a rifle.

With Pridmore relinquishing the G.P.M.G. to Rush's care he too collected a rifle and set off at a crouched run, followed by Kieran.

Leaning over the radio set to watch his two comrades making their dash for the fort, Jim was surprised to find visibility had improved to the point where he was able to follow them most of the way. Distracted by a radio message from Batt. H.Q. he pulled the handset up to his ear.

'Unable to confirm, over,' he replied to a question about strength and nature of the attack.

Vaulting the gun pit's low sandbag wall, Pridmore leant his rifle against it as he pulled the dust covers from the breech and spotting rifle.

'Johnny, fetch a round out o' the ammo bay,' he shouted to the Irishman as he opened the lid of a brown metal ammunition box. Picking out a magazine of twenty tracers, he fitted it to the .5 calibre Springfield, then cocked a round into the chamber.

'How do ya open dis fuckin' ting,' demanded Kieran, holding a 106mm shell cradled in the crook of his arm while struggling to open the breech.

Pridmore, with a deft, one-handed movement, reached over, pushed the breech level down and back. Supervising the insertion of the round, he then squatted, facing the L-shaped telescopic sight.

'Johnny, come forward or the main armament back blast will roast ya,' he warned, searching through the sight with the elevation wheel for the machine-gun. With bullets striking the fort wall behind them, Mick laid the sight pattern on the flickering flashes and, pulling the trigger mechanism, fired a spotter round. The .5 tracer went left and high; adjusting he fired again. This time it was low. Once more he re-aimed and fired. It seemed to strike where the now silent gun was, so pushing the dual mechanism he fired the main armament. With an ear-splitting roar the heavy anti-tank shell arced out over the perimeter fence to explode with a thunder clap. The Hesh round was not an anti-personnel weapon but the shrapnel could kill and its detonation was devastating.

'Pick da bones out o' that ya bastards,' howled Kieran, ejecting the empty casing before collecting a second round. Bending to push it into the breech, a burst of machine-gun fire from another gun struck in and around the pit. One of these, skidding off a sandbag, sliced the outside flesh of his left arm from elbow to shoulder.

'Son of a bitch,' he cried, falling backwards.

Pridmore quickly left the gun to crawl across to him.

'Let's have a look, Johnny.'

'Fuck it Mick, it's just a nick,' dismissed the Irishman believing it to be nothing more, his right hand clapped over the torn flesh.

'Bollocks, give us a look,' demanded Pridmore.

While he lashed a shell dressing over this to stop the bleeding a figure appeared over them driving the unloaded round home.

'Taaman, Ahmed, taaman,' thanked Mick of the Omani he had trained and who now joined them, having dropped down from the fort wall.

'Reg, can you see that second gun?' shouted Sinclair, anxious to start retaliating in support of the fort and gun team.

'No, no, that fucker's hidden in the . . .' Berrill, halting in mid-sentence, began shouting at the top of his voice.

'Jim, the scrub line, they're coming out o' the scrub line.'

With the machine-gun above him cracking short bursts, Sinclair jerked his eyes to where the tracer rounds were landing.

In the bleak, but no longer concealing, dawn light men along a quarter- mile front in a loose line of separate but inter-supporting formations were advancing out of the bush.

'Fucking hell, it's a company attack,' gasped Sinclair under his breath.

Snapping the handset to his lips, his frantic radio report was almost drowned by Rush's Gimpy joining the clatter of Berrill's.

'Four Two Bravo, under frontal attack. One hundred plus assaulting from north. Must have air support immediately, I say again, immediately, immediately, over.'

Jim did not wait for a reply; pitching his intelligence table onto its side out of his way he grabbed up an M79. Aiming it on a high trajectory through the window slit he jerked the trigger. Not taking his eyes off where he had judged the rough alignment aim, he broke the weapon open and reloaded it. Seeing the exploding flash of his launched grenade go off short of a badly spaced section, he re-aimed and fired again. With the barrel at a shallower angle for more range, the explosion this time was near enough to force them to go to ground, by which time Jim had the gun pointed in another direction.

On the roof, ejected empty cases and black metal connector links from Berrill's machine-gun belts were tumbling into every corner of the O.P. floor. Wildly he engaged first one target, then another, constantly swinging the gun from danger point to danger point. Seeing that his belt of ammunition was running out he slapped Mohammad on the arm indicating he wanted it replenished. The Dhofari, releasing his rifle, picked up one of the belts from a shelf but, because he did not know how to clip it, was unable to connect it onto the one already on the gun.

'Bloody shit!' exlaimed Reg, balancing the gun butt on his chest to rectify the problem himself. As he did so the lance corporal received the first of his wounds. A bullet entering through the firing slit to embed its metal case in the sandbag roof, neatly carved his right ear in half.

Unaware that this had happened he resumed firing at the attacking figures that were now nearing the perimeter cattle fence. His fire was doing its damage; men he aimed at were going down and not rising but the force as a whole was still coming on.

In the sangar below, Rush, now joined by Sinclair after running out of M79 rounds, was experiencing the same dilemma. Wherever he fired the attackers either became victims or faded from view, but they always re-emerged, pressing forward.

Sinclair at his side, keeping the ammunition supplied and pointing out targets, instinctively ducked his head as the air was filled with a rush and roar. Skimming over their battle area below the clouds, which were stationed at about fifty feet, raced a jet Strikemaster. Jim, hurrying back into the building, snapped up a Sarbe portable radio, which would give him communication with the pilot, then quickly returned to the open sangar.

'Hello, Sierra Mike, this is Habahn Four Two Bravo,' began the Scot, before cutting himself short realising he was on the wrong channel. 'Fuck! Fuck!'

'Hello, Sierra Mike,' he began again, 'this is Habahn Four Two Bravo, Four Two Bravo, over.'

'Sierra Mike, do you have a target for me? Over,' replied the pilot keeping his request basic.

'Yes, yes, the perimeter fence; zap the fence and anything north of it,' screamed the sergeant, his voice procedure disintegrating in understandable desperation.

The pilot acknowledging, banked blind in the clouds to make a return west-east run. Easing down until he could see the sea and coast line he turned inland to avoid crashing into the fort. At this dangerous ground level approach, he was forced to make his attack on a target hidden from view. Using the fort and the Batt. shack as a guide, he made two reflex corrections, dropped the aircraft's nose, then pressed the firing button.

On the ground, Sinclair well aware that the low cloud and drizzling rain was presenting the fighter pilot with almost insurmountable problems searched the grey ceiling above him for any sign of the aeroplane. Suddenly from the west a high-pitched engine scream was heard building; then out-running the growing crescendo the fighter, with stunning effect and crushing noise, arrived spitting dual ribbons of 20mm cannon shells that churned the length of the perimeter fence with explosions and sheets of flying sand. It was gone again in the blink of an eye.

'Dead on, Sierra Mike, dead on,' screamed Sinclair into the radio. 'Again, again.'

'Roger, Four Two Bravo, willco. Out,' replied the Sultan of Oman Airforce pilot in a calm and unflustered voice.

A minute later he came in on a reverse run, giving the same spectacular performance.

'Hello, Sierra Mike, excellent service. Can you make your next run on the bush area north of our location, over?' requested Jim, recovering his composure and voice procedure now the immediate pressure was off.

'Sierra Mike, no can do, Four Two Bravo, out of ammo. Will get back as soon as I can, over,' informed the pilot in a mechanical tone.

'Roger, Sierra Mike, thanks for coming, out,' replied the Scot feeling as if he was saying goodbye to an old friend.

An understandable reaction, for this man and his aircraft had undoubtedly broken the attack and, for the moment at least, saved their lives.

Peering over the sandbag parapet Jim could see a number of survivors from the attack dashing in short sprints back to the scrub. For several minutes the Paras were given a brief reprieve of incoming fire, but gradually as the enemy recovered and reorganised, shooting directed at Sinclair's men and the fort began to increase again.

Throughout the engagement, almost as background activity, the men on the 106 gun had been providing fire support on the right of the attack. With the fighter gone it was judged by the Adoo commanders that this gun was the key to Habahn's defence. Making that decision, all their mortars and machine-guns were turned to concentrate on the gun pit and the fort behind. Their casualties from the Strikemaster's strafing runs were heavy, but this P.F.L.O.A.G. attacking force had no intention of calling it a day. In past months the Sultan's Forces had chalked up a string of minor successes which had resulted in an increasing trickle of defections. This, combined with the Crossbow operation sitting smack in the middle of what they claimed as their territory, compelled them to take action. A blow had to be dealt against the Sultan that would show the doubters on the Jebel that P.F.L.O.A.G. was still a powerful military organisation capable of attacking hard and fast, anywhere they wished. Habahn was the target they chose for this show of force, and as such it was a battle they could not afford to lose.

*   *   *

Checking the luminous hands of his wrist watch, Dave Urwin swung his legs over the edge of the bed and stood up. Sleeping in only fits and starts because of the strangeness of his surroundings, he decided to rise early. Returning to his tent from the ablutions building where he washed and shaved, a jet fighter coming in to land on Salalah airfield down the road, streaked low over his head, towards a dawn that was yet to give full daylight.

'Jesus,' he thought to himself, 'the R.A.F. never get up this early.' Knowing it to be too soon in the morning for breakfast, Urwin made his way to the Batt. H.Q. building hoping to scrounge a coffee in the operations room.

On his arrival the night before he had been given a quick guided tour, so he knew there was always a brew on. In the hallway the sergeant noted an unusual bustle of activity for that time of the morning; loud voices and people in the hall hurrying past, apparently without seeing him.

Walking through the open Op's room door he stood for several seconds listening and watching, no one paying the least bit of attention to him.

There were five men in the room, Major McAllister whom he had been introduced to the night before, Lee Holding, an S.A.S. sergeant and two signallers. The two officers were having a heated disagreement.

'For God's sake,' argued Holding, 'they're my men, what the hell do you mean I can't go?'

'Lee, I need you here to coordinate this operation. Now you're staying and that's final,' McAllister concluded by jabbing a finger towards the floor.

Urwin, in the dark over what the conversation was about, nudged one of the D Company signallers.

'Nobby, what's the chances of a coffee?'

'Uh? Ya help yourself, Sarg,' he replied briskly, obviously having been interrupted in his concentration on listening to the radio set.

'Flap on; Habahn's been hit.'

'What do ya mean?' asked Urwin, still ignorant of all the fuss.

'One of our locations up the coast's taken a pasting,' he explained.

'How bad?' enquired the Irishman, his mood changing to instant concern.

'Pretty bad, they just caught a packet, sounded like they almost bought their chips. One of our aircraft got in with a couple of runs . . .' the signaller paused as a voice Urwin knew well came up on the radio net.

'Hello Zero, Four Two Bravo, sitrep. Enemy still engaging, machine-gun fire and mortars mainly directed at the fort. No sign of another attack but I think they're doing a left flanking around the back of the fort. Any chance of speeding up assistance from your end? Over.'

'Wait out Four Two Bravo,' replied Nobby, turning to Major McAllister. 'Habahn are asking about help, Sir,' he called.

'Tell them it's on the way. Thirty minutes, no later,' assured the officer loudly.

Dave's blood had suddenly gone cold.

A helicopter pilot in flying overalls hurried into the room to be instantly given orders by the S.A.S. major.

'Ronny good to see you; this is going to be rushed. I want you and your other lads on the ground on the other side of the road, engines running and ready to take off in fifteen minutes. I'll brief you on the way.'

As the pilot left, Urwin turned back to the signaller.

'Nobby, who's the relieving party?'

'Those S.A.S. blokes you came in with last night. It's a fucking good thing they're here. There's no one else we could call on for miles.'

Dave did not answer, running instead out the door to catch up with the S.A.S. sergeant who had just left.

'Tony, Tony,' he called down the hallway at the stocky, broad-shouldered man he had known while attached to the Special Air Service in Borneo seven years earlier and had travelled out from Brize Norton with the day before.

'Can't stop, Davy,' he shouted back pushing open the entrance door.

Urwin caught him up outside to hurry along beside him.

'Tony, when do you leave?'

'In a couple of minutes, as soon as we get briefed,' was the reply, still moving at a trot.

'I'm going with ya, but I need a weapon,' informed the Irishman.

'What? Who said?' asked the other sergeant, stopping in surprise.

'I did,' admitted Urwin.

'No way, Davy. No way,' refused Tony, beginning to walk again whilst waving both hands crossways in front of himself.

'Tony, for fuck's sake, Tony,' pleaded Urwin, pulling the S.A.S. man to a halt by the shoulder. 'Look, it's Jim Sinclair and big Mick out there; you gotta let me come.'

For some seconds they stood looking into each others' eyes.

'Okay, I can't promise but I'll have a word with the boss and see; we're being briefed in the dining tent, get your equipment and join us there.'

Dave, without another word, sprinted for his tent. Ripping open his bergen flaps he pulled out a set of green webbed belt order. Then, casting its contents of spare socks, washing and shaving kit and waterbottles into the sand he retraced his steps at the run.

The sides of the dining tent being open he could see about twenty men milling among the tables and benches, checking weapons and collecting ammunition. Ducking under the canvas he was relieved to see the S.A.S. sergeant giving him the thumbs up.

A moment later he took him to a corner table where a trooper in his early twenties with tight blond hair was cocking and recocking a G.P.M.G.

'Tim, you've just got a number two for that gun; this is Sergeant Urwin,' introduced the S.A.S. sergeant.

'Oh, ya,' responded Tim in a cold tone, naturally hostile to being lumbered with someone he knew nothing of.

'Ya,' replied his sergeant having to leave them.

'The name's Dave and don't worry I won't get in your way; I'm just here to carry ammo,' reassured Urwin reading his thoughts. 'Got a problem with the gun?' he then asked.

'It's the squadron's spare Gimpy. Never used it before. Seems to be sticking,' he confessed in an annoyed tone.

'Here, let me look,' offered Urwin, taking hold of the weapon to cock it, letting the working parts go forward then stripped the butt from the body. Removing the piston spring and piston group he examined them.

'Here's the problem; some bastard has caked it with graphite grease,' he declared. 'I'll clean this shit off, you get some oil. We'll have to saturate the working parts but then she'll shoot like a dream.'

While the men continued to prepare themselves and their weapons, Guy McAllister gave a hasty but detailed briefing. With the aid of a sketch map he had drawn on a blackboard propped on one of the tables, he explained the layout of Habahn, where friendly forces were and what he knew of the enemy.

*   *   *

Meanwhile the situation at Habahn was becoming more critical by the minute. Not wishing to suffer the casualties of another daylight frontal assault, the Adoo were instead pushing men around their left in an attempt to envelope the defences from the west.

As they skirmished past the northern houses of the village their advance was brought to a temporary halt by rifle fire from the walls of the fort. During the initial attack a mortar bomb had landed in its courtyard killing the Omani corporal. Leaderless, the rest of the section took cover. Only the apprentice gunner, Ahmed, on hearing the 106mm fire, took any action. If it had not been for the Sheikh, possibly no defence would have been mounted at all.

Storming into the courtyard, his AK47 raised above his head, he screamed and cursed at the soldiers and his own militia. With kicks and threats he sent them up the fort's stone steps to firing positions on the inner parapet. There, running from man to man, his old servant following with spare magazines and ammunition, he coaxed, encouraged and directed their fire, taking command in the name of his village.

Sheikd Zayid Bin Al Kamam's loyalty was no longer in doubt; unquestionably he had declared for the Sultan.

Outside the main gate the three men in the gun pit were finding it an unhealthy place to be. Low walled, because of the gun's long barrel and with no overhead cover, they were pinned down by fire coming in from the fringe of the scrub.

'You alright, Johnny?' called Pridmore, crouched beside the gun leg he would normally have sat on to fire.

'Snug, can't see much though,' called back Kieran from his ammunition bunker.

'Look, we can't sit here like this; I'm going to put a round into the bushes and see if we can put them off a bit,' Mick shouted to the Irishman.

Putting his rifle to one side he called to the Omani soldier on the other side of the pit, 'Ahmed! Ahmed!' making signs for him to load the main armament.

The young soldier did this from a lying position, heaving the large round up whilst on his back.

Mick, using the traversing and elevation hand wheels, took a rough alignment not through the sight but by peering above the sandbags. Pulling the trigger mechanism he sent a tracer towards the bush line then, adjusting again, he sent a second and third. Satisfied, he pushed hard with the palm of his hand, delivering his shell like an express train into the bush edge.

Ahmed, forgetting the danger, jumped to his feet to unload. Pridmore, seeing this, shouted a warning as he dived to drag the Omani down.

'Ahmed, for fuck's sake!'

But the big Lancashire man was too late; as bullets screamed and thumped around them Ahmed fell into the sand clutching his stomach. Pridmore, pulling his shoulders against one wall, opened the Arab's shirt. The bullet, entering his back, had torn a hole the size of a shoe heel coming out. Mick, taking the morphine from his I.D. discs, injected him to dull the pain which showed in his anguished face.

Returning to the gun he retaliated as best he could with the spotter rifle, reaching up to change magazines blind. Occupied in this way it was Kieran who first detected a lull in the machine-gun fire and mortar bombs. Cocking his head back, he heard the shooting from the fort walls increasing. Propping himself up he looked to his right; men scurrying through undulating, sandy cover, signalling a second attack was being launched.

'Mick, Mick,' shouted the Irishman in warning, 'there on the right, coming around the fort.'

Pridmore, rifle in hand, crawled to the opposite side of the pit. Pushing a sandbag out of the way he took aim and fired. Kieran, disregarding the burning pain of his wounded arm, turned in the small bunker to bring his own rifle into play.

Their defence lasted only a few minutes. From somewhere out in the dunes a light machine-gun began to pepper the pit with fire, putting a bullet throught Johnny Kieran's shoulder just below the right collar bone. Without a sound from his lips, he fell back crumpled in a corner of the ammunition bunker, both arms now useless.

Pridmore, unaware of his friend's plight, continued to fire. The enemy was close now, moving in well disciplined dashes.

Emptying the magazine of his rifle, he felt through his pouches for a fresh one. Finding none he called out to Kieran, 'Johnny, I'm out of ammo, give us a magazine, quick.'

'Okay, but you'll have to come for it,' replied the Irishman.

Pridmore, responding, rose half-crouched to leap the low wall but instead received a powerful blow on his back, which pitched him forward. Twisting about, the blurred head and shoulders of a figure was seen hurriedly approaching the gun pit. Mick, unable to react, could only watch helplessly, as his vision receded into a blackened void.

Moments later Kieran saw the same figure, an Arab in khaki uniform, standing over him. Pointing his Russian rifle from the hip he fired an automatic burst at the wounded man.

Seeing it coming, pushing with his wounded left arm Johnny half reared up, cursing.

'Fuck ya, ya black bastard,' he screamed, receiving two bullets in his lower leg. Then he watched, still in a powerful rage, as the Jebali rifleman dropped dead, shot twice through the chest and throat.

At the shack Jim Sinclair checked his watch. 'Nine minutes; they'll be here in nine minutes,' he said to himself, forcing his mind to believe the promise he had received on the radio.

'Reg,' he called up to Berrill on the roof, 'are you alright for ammo?'

'Yes, yes, okay,' shouted back Berrill, concentrating on the bush area in front, returning any fire directed at them. This was important, for once pinned down by fire they could easily be taken by a determined rush.

'Adoo! Adoo!' shouted Mohammad behind him, who had been watching their rear.

Reg spun his head as Mohammad fired a rifle shot, then quivering as the back of his head exploded with a shower of particles of blood and bone, dropped dead.

'Jim! Jim! They're behind us,' screamed Reg, struggling to swing his gun around to mount it in the rear firing slit.

Sinclair, rushing back into the building with a rifle, spotted shooting coming from within the empty firqat tent lines and began squeezing half a magazine of single shots into the general area. Above him, Berrill's machine-gun joined in flushing three men carrying rifles who then took cover behind the Batt. Landrover. While Jim fired at the odd arm or leg that showed itself, Berrill with his gun, turned the location transport into a sieve, chopping the three men behind it to pieces.

'Reg,' called Sinclair, returning to the sangar, 'keep an eye out back, we'll watch the front.'

'Fooken'ell,' exclaimed Rush swinging his gun around, 'they're in the gun pit.'

Jim looked up to see men approaching the 106 position at a run.

'Hit 'em, Yorky, hit 'em,' shouted the Scotsman, his fingers digging into the sangar's sandbags.

Spitting burst after burst, the Yorkshireman's gun knocked down one who looked to be about to shoot downwards, while driving the rest back.

'Keep onto them, Yorky,' commanded Sinclair, moving to replenish the gun belt.

Above them Berrill received his second wound. A bullet, ricocheting off the door frame, shattered his upper right arm. Picking himself up off the floor, realising he was no longer any use as a gunner, he called out, 'Jim, I've stopped one.'

'How bad, Reg?' came back the reply.

'Not great, but I can't shoot any more and Mohammad's bought it.'

'Where ya hit?' asked Sinclair.

'It's just the arm,' assured Berrill.

'I'm coming up, Reggy.'

'No! No! Stay there, I'll come down,' countered Berrill, not wanting to put Sinclair's life at risk. Bracing himself in the observation post's doorway, clutching his arm, he bolted the three paces to the edge of the roof to make his leap. In mid-air he received his third wound, a bullet breaking two ribs as it passed in and out of the left side of his chest.

'Bloody hell, Jim,' he moaned to Sinclair as he lay in an agonised heap in the sand beside the sangar, 'this has been my worst fucking day, ever.'

*   *   *

The three Huey helicopters being used to carry the small, twenty-man relief band of S.A.S. soldiers were finding the cloud conditions just as difficult as the Strikemaster had. Skimming the wave tops, they flew one behind the other along the beach. Twice they passed houses on the shore which Urwin was sure he looked up at more than down.

The landing zone Guy McAllister picked was a mile west of Habahn, just above the beach. As the Hueys settled to hover a yard above it the S.A.S. men spilled out, racing a short distance before throwing themselves down. Empty, the helicopters sped out to sea to await any future call for assistance from the major.

Climbing to his feet to begin the advance, Urwin could see in the distance a fort and hear from it small arms fire. Their formation in going forward was an unconventional extended line, but then normal tactical deployment was not wanted here. The important thing was to get on as quickly as possible. Neither was it intended to avoid harm, in fact the object of their advance was to seek out harm and destroy it. For this they had armed well, every second man had a

Gimpy, his partner weighted down with ammunition. Major McAllister was going to the relief of Habahn by punching his way in with overwhelming firepower. Stepping out across the wet dunes at a jogging pace, Dave's jungle green uniform began to turn even darker from the persistent, vapour-thin rain that hung rather than fell. Being on the extreme left of the advance, Urwin and his gunner kept a sharp eye towards the beach as well as the front. But it was not for them to encounter the enemy first. Firing from the right sent everyone to ground, initiating a much more breathless advance.

Working as pairs, the gun teams skirmished forward in short dashes, one covering the other. As they moved, contact with the enemy soon spread south down the line of attackers until even Urwin's gun was firing. Going down at the end of one of their short bounds rifle bullets struck the sand around them.

'There, Tim, that yellow patch of sand,' shouted Urwin, pointing to indicate two men tucked behind a sandy mound.

'Got 'em, got 'em,' replied the gunner, clouding his two targets in veils of sticky sand as his shots bracketed the men and their mound.

Turning on his side the sergeant waved to their partners, signalling that they could now make their next move. Doubling past to one side they continued on for another twenty yards or so, then throwing themselves down, took up their share of the firing while Urwin's gun team rose, zig-zagging to make their dash.

Reaching the sandy mound Dave was not surprised to find one man dead and the other gone. But this was not the end; there was no shortage of targets, and the nearer they came to the fort the more small arms fire they provoked. However, it was not they who were on the receiving end; for every incoming round, the assaulting gun teams sent back ten.

On a three hundred yard front, sweeping all resistance before them, these sweating, breathless but determined men steadily narrowed the ground between them and the fort.

Dropping at the end of a longer bound than normal, Urwin and his gunner found the surface area before them open and unobstructed. For a couple of hundred yards it first dipped into a cultivated basin then rose again for the same distance as sand and gravel to the base of the fort. Across this ground raced men, some veering left to the northern houses of the village but most making for a bush line off to the right.

'Get the ones on the left, Tim, don't let them reach the village,' barked Urwin in breathless gasps.

The blond gunner, without answering, took aim on the running enemy, squeezing off two and three round bursts. Suddenly the gun fired just one shot and stopped. Turning to look, Urwin watched as the gun was cocked, then aimed and fired again. Once more the gun only fired one round.

'Stoppage, Tim,' shouted the sergeant. 'It's either gas or the barrel's too hot. Don't fuck with it, we'll change the barrel. Clear the gun.'

Without replying the gunner cocked the weapon and lifted the top cover to clear the feed tray with a sweep of his right hand.

As this was happening Urwin pulled a flat canvas holdall from his shoulder to take out the spare barrel. snapping one off and the other on, the gun was quickly re-loaded and the gunner again engaging his targets.

With other gun teams coming up to join in, the landscape to their front soon emptied, with several bodies lying still, the only sign of life being two wounded men crawling into a ditch.

Only some of those who ran north escaped; the rest had been caught between the S.A.S. and heavy rifle fire bearing down on them from the fort walls.

'Come on, Dave, let's get across before they recover,' rasped the gunner, his throat dry and hoarse from their constant extertion.

'Done then,' agreed the Irishman, scrambling up to turn and shout to the other gun team that had come up on their left.

'We're moving, cover us across.'

Leading off at a steady lope, accompanied by three other gun groups spread to their right, Dave's legs were beginning to weaken. To skirmish under fire at the pace they had been maintaining required superhuman fitness and, although he had always kept himself in top shape, the belts of ammunition around his waist and draped across his chest were causing him shortness of breath. Still this was not a time to falter and he knew it. Holding his rifle at the ready, he studied the ditch at the point the two wounded men had crawled into it, but on passing they lay motionless, no longer taking part in the battle.

Their approach to the fort was heralded from the wall by red and white-shamaged defenders raising rifles, and cheering. Panting, the two men went to their knees at the fort's northeast corner.

'Ideal! Ideal!' declared Tim, adopting the prone position behind his gun. Urwin, adding approval of their spot, settled beside him, unlooping a belt of ammunition to clip it onto the one already on the gun. From the corner of the wall they were well sited to cover the six gun teams who had remained on the basin edge and who were now moving to join them. The sloping ground running down from the fort to north and west gave clean arcs across a perimeter fence to bushy growth in the near distance. Three hundred yards to his left Urwin could see a bunkered building with a Landrover and a number of army tents to the rear.

The only obstruction masking their vision was a sandbagged gun pit with an anti-tank gun showing above it fifty yards in front of them. With shooting now becoming light and sporadic, Dave, uneasy about the closeness of this gun sangar, decided to investigate.

'Tim, watch my back; I just want to check that gun out.'

'Okay, Dave, come at it from the right and if Adoos pop up, just drop flat,' instructed the gunner, bringing the butt up into his shoulder.

Urwin, discarding the spare barrel holdall, swung to the right in a half circle, rifle at the ready, upper body hunched forward. On his side of the sandbags a kahki clad Arab lay dead, his head cocked against the wall. Reaching the edge of the gun pit Urwin stood for a second staring, then, leaping the sandbags, almost landing on a dead Omani soldier, he dropped his rifle to clutch at a man's shoulders.

'Mick! Mick!' he cried, lying him flat to feel about his body for any wounds. As his hand probed under the big man's back Urwin pulled it away covered in thick, dark blood.

'Oh no, bloody hell no!' he exclaimed in desperation, feeling for a pulse beat at Pridmore's throat just below the jaw.

'Oh God! Damn! Damn! Damn! Damn!' he cried, raising his eyes to curse his grief to the heavens.

'Jim, dat you? How is he? He won't answer me.'

Urwin, standing in surprise, pushed himself over the wall to find Kieran lying in the bottom of a blood-stained ammunition bunker, 'Jesus fucking Christ, Johnny.'

'Well, I'll be screwed! What you doing here, Davy?' asked Kieran, a weak smile fleetingly playing on his lips.

'Where's it hurt?' asked Urwin, crouching over him.

'It did hurt everywhere a bit ago but I jabbed myself with a morphine shot so it's not too bad at the minute,' confessed Kieran, lifting his left hand in a stiff gesture.

'Okay, okay, let me have a look at ya,' ordered Urwin.

'Ever stick a needle in yourself, Davy? Don't half make ya jump,' commented the Wicklow Irishman, the smile returning to his lips. 'How's Mick?'

'He's dead.'

In saying this pain jabbed through Urwin's heart.

Pausing to suck in a deep breath, Kieran spewed out a venomous cry.

'Bastards! Bastards! Ya fuckin' black wog bastards.'

Strapping a shell dressing as best he could around the two leg wounds, Urwin looked up to see a Huey helicopter skimming in low from the sea to land between them and the sandbagged building, rotor blades remaining at full throttle.

'Right, Johnny, I want you up; you're going on that chopper,' commanded the sergeant.

'Don't be daft, Davy, stand? I can't even piss,' protested Kieran.

'Stop fucking whining,' replied Urwin, reaching down to lock his arms around Kieran's back, hauling him out of the bunker to stand one-legged against the lip of the wall.

Dave, dropping his grip, bent to drape him like a sack of potatoes over his shoulder, producing, despite the morphine, a pained groan. Urwin, climbing out of the bunker, set off towards the helicopter.

From the sandbagged building two men, one half dragging, half carrying the other, were seen also making for the helicopter. Major McAllister reacting to a call from Sinclair for Heli Casevac support, disregarding the risk had radioed this Huey in. Narrowing his eyes as he struggled with Kieran's weight into the helicopter's swirling wash, Urwin eased his load onto its rear floor.

Standing back he could see Johnny Kieran, fighting the drugging effect of the morphine, lift his head up briefly for the sergeant to read the words 'Thanks Davy,' on his lips.

On the opposite side Reg Berrill, assisted by Jim Sinclair, climbed in to pull himself along the floor with one good arm until he could cradle Kieran's head with it. Stepping back Sinclair waved frantically for the pilot to take off.

In a rush of stinging wet sand and noise the Huey, banking low around the fort, disappeared towards Salalah.

In silence Sinclair watched until he could see no more of the aircraft then, looking across, caught the other man's eye.

'You look a hell of a state, Jim,' said Urwin.

There was a long pause from the dirty, blood-stained Scot, rifle in one hand, wearing only boots and khaki shorts, before he spoke.

'Where the fuck you spring from?'

'Salalah, flew in last night,' replied the Irishman, neither man showing any form of emotion.

'Penny's pregnant, did you know?' continued Urwin after a moment's hesitation, not knowing what else to say.

'Aye, she wrote,' answered his brother-in-law.

Both men still staring at each other, remained motionless.

'Mick's dead,' announced Urwin, showing just a trace of the bitter sorrow he felt.

Jim Sinclair, torn apart by inner grief, on hearing this could only rock his head gently up and down.

Within the hour Habahn was crawling with reinforcements. Unable to risk the land routes because of mines, they had to wait for the tide to turn but once it did, two Companies of The Sultan's Desert Regiment raced through the lowering surf to their relief. Frustratingly too late to take up hot pursuit, there was little for them to do but provide picquets, gather in the wounded and count the dead.

The attack, well-planned and undoubtedly fought by brave men, should have succeeded. The reason it did not can be attributed to two factors, the P.F.L.O.A.G. Commander had considered and therefore chosen a target which should have eliminated both. He knew that exposing his men under clear skies would only result in certain failure due to ground attacks by the Sultan's strike jets. So he waited for the ground level clouds of the Khareef, when it was impossible for them to operate. The other overriding condition governing his choice was to ensure it was isolated enough to hinder rapid deployment of reinforcements.

But such are the fortunes of war: How was he to know there was a Strikemaster pilot stationed at Salalah who, given ten feet of sky, was prepared to press home his attacks; nor was he to know of the arrival the day before of a small body of S.A.S. soldiers that, with determination and irrepressible firepower, would appear without warning to roll up his left flank and scatter what remained of his men into the barren Dhofar scrublands. Behind them they left over a hundred of their comrades dead.

At noon a helicopter was provided to take the bodies of Mick Pridmore, Mohammad, the Omani soldier, and his corporal back to the mortuary at Salalah. Accompanying them were Urwin and Yorky Rush. Bodies tended to be handled callously at times and they, knowing this, travelled with the four dead men to make sure each was taken into the building's cool interior with gentleness and compassion.

Mick Pridmore did not die without tears. His wife shed many on hearing the tragic news, and so did Dave Urwin that night in the seclusion of his tent. Jim Sinclair had cried openly, unaware he was doing so, while standing on the chopper pad as the helicopter containing the four bodies lifted off to fly westward through the dank, wet midday sky.

In the new year Penny Sinclair gave birth to a baby son, who, some weeks later, was taken to the Church of Scotland church just across Queens Avenue from the Parachute Regiment Depot. There, amid a gathering of relatives, friends and invited members of the Battalion, he was christened Michael Neil Sinclair.

THE END

GLOSSARY

Word/Phrase	Translation
Cadre	Instructional course
Diffy	Deficient
Dulally	Around the bend
Stonked	Mortar bombed

ARABIC or URDU

Khareef	Misty monsoon
Gatn	Barren hill country
Nego	Burnt country bordering desert
Adoo	Enemy
Pukka gen	Proper true
Souk	Market
Ramadam	Holy fast
Taaman	Good

Soon to be published by Galago Publishing Ltd

IN PURSUIT OF HARM
By
Don MacNaughton

The men of 5 Para, involved once more against the I.R.A., in Belfast
and along the border of South Armagh. And on how some, so unwisely
attempted to sell their skills in an African civil war.